RUSALKA

RUSALKA

C. J. CHERRYH

A DEL REY BOOK

BALLANTINE BOOKS • NEW YORK

A Del Rey Book
Published by Ballantine Books

Copyright © 1989 by C.J. Cherryh

All rights reserved under International and Pan-American Copyright
Conventions. Published in the United States by Ballantine Books,
a division of Random House, Inc., New York, and simultaneously
in Canada by Random House of Canada Limited, Toronto.

Library of Congress Cataloging-in-Publication Data
Cherryh. C.J.
    Rusalka / C.J. Cherryh. — 1st ed.
        p.   cm.
    "A Del Rey book."
    ISBN 0-345-35953-4
    I. Title.
    PS3553.H358R8   1989   89-6700
    813'.54—dc20   CIP

Manufactured in the United States of America
Designed by Ann Gold
First Edition: October 1989

10 9 8 7 6 5 4 3 2 1

RUSALKA

1

✠ ✠ ✠ ✠ The winter dwindled in amber evenings and daytime haze: snow melted, puddles multiplied. Icicles dripped and crashed daily into the last snow-banks, with alarming sounds of breakage.

A particularly large one lingered where water ran off The Cockerel's west porch, but it was not ice that shattered, it was aunt Ilenka's butter-churn, when Pyetr Kochevikov rode his horse up onto the porch to reach it.

Sasha Misurov, his hands encumbered with buckets, watched in astonishment as the icicle fell, the horse thundered off the boards, skidded onto the split-log walk and off onto the mud, all four legs miraculously whole—and aunt Ilenka came flying out of the kitchen waving her spoon and calling on the Sun, the tsar, and all his magistrates.

"Pyetr Kochevikov! Look at my porch! Look at my walk! *Oh, god*—" Aunt Ilenka saw the churn with the milk dripping off the porch, and grabbed up her broom from the corner.

"Look out!" one of the young men cried. "Look out, Pyetr! You're in trouble now!"

The broom swung, Pyetr took his horse out of the way, doffed his cap and bowed, and the young ruffians—the second and third sons of rich families in Vojvoda, such were Pyetr Kochevikov's familiars—howled with laughter, pulling their horses back to afford the battle room.

Aunt Ilenka cornered Pyetr between the stable, the court-yard wall, and the bathhouse. Pyetr jumped his horse over the bathhouse bench and thumped back across the split-log walk, throwing up mud that spattered her from head to foot.

Eyes flew wide, aunt Ilenka grasped her broom for a re-

3

newed assault, but the hooligans were fleeing the yard now
with a spatter of mud, a small shower of coin—"For the
churn!" Dmitri cried, to the riders' laughter; and with a second
flourish of the cap: "For the drink!" Pyetr cried, flinging more
coin—and missed riding into The Cockerel's sign by the stableyard gate only by lying back flat in his saddle, whooping
with laughter.

A last spatter of mud hit the fence as the ruffians rode
away.

Sasha set down his buckets, ran and picked the silver out
of the mud of the gateway and took it to aunt Ilenka, who
was no more pleased than one could expect.

"Hooligans!" aunt Ilenka cried. And with a swipe of her
broom at Sasha's legs: "Clean this up!"

As if it was his fault. But most things were. He was unlucky, was Sasha Misurov; and if aunt Ilenka's grandmother's
churn was broken and the butter was gone and Pyetr Kochevikov and his rowdy, well-born friends made a shambles
cf the tavern yard, why, look to Sasha's luck, the more so since
he was standing there like a fool. Thank the god for Dmitri
Venedikov's patching things up or aunt Ilenka would have
taken the broom to him in earnest.

And uncle Fedya . . .

Uncle Fedya might have said, finally, after ten years' patience, "Why do we keep the boy?"

Pyetr himself had no concerns. He had a belly full of drink, a
fine horse he had won yesterday at dice, he had friends with
connections close to tsar Mikula himself, and girls and women
doted on Pyetr Kochevikov for his looks and his wit, all of
which fortune was so accustomed he only scarcely remembered the times he had been hungry, and almost never remembered he had relatives in the town, since none of them
had spoken to him for years except to borrow money.

He had not been, so to say, born to wealth. But he looked
to gain it.

He had not been born to manners, but he had a ready wit
and a rare ability to imitate, and the second sons and the third
and seventh born, who had no prospects and less responsibility

4

in many a noble family of Vojvoda, found Pyetr Kochevikov an antidote, that was what he called himself: an antidote to ennui and a cure for too much seriousness.

As, this evening, riding away from The Cockerel, Vasya said, "Join us at the inn," and Pyetr winked and said, grinning, "I have other business."

Vasya understood, Vasya gave him a wink back, but foolish Ivan said, "What business?" so Vasya and Andrei took off their caps and hit him.

"Only," said 'Mitri, "the rascal won't name the lady. — Who is this, that our Pyetr prefers to dice?"

Pyetr said, archly, "A gentleman doesn't tell," and rode off at a brisk pace through Vojvoda's High Market Street, to stable the newly acquired horse at The Flower, where he lodged, and to buy a handful of sweetmeats—

Since, the weather warming, old Yurishev was off gambling with his elderly cronies, the fair and entirely delightful Irina was, her maid had sworn, entirely unoccupied.

So Pyetr took himself around to the lady's garden gate, and climbed by the bathhouse roof up to the lady's stairs, and so up to the upstairs balcony and the door, which the same maid swore would be, by moonrise, unlocked.

A scant few moments later Pyetr Kochevikov was leaving the front of the house, by a second floor window not till then unshuttered, and old Yurishev himself, sword in hand, was pelting down his garden path and around the side of his house, shouting, "Help, the watch! The watch!"

Pyetr fell as he landed on the muddy street, scrambled up and attempted the stables at The Flower, but old Yurishev's retainers came around the west side of the house and herded him back toward the east.

As their master came panting around the east corner with his sword leveled.

"Oh, damn!" Pyetr cried, slid to a scrabbling halt, writhing aside from the point, and, putting his foot on one of lady Irina's herb pots, Pyetr fell, yelled, and rolled wildly to rescue himself from Yurishev's frenzied thrusts.

"I have you!" Yurishev cried, stabbed again and a third time as Pyetr rolled and scrambled for his feet, and shutters flew wide up and down the street. "Villain!"

5

Pyetr staggered among the remnants of the herb pots, felt something hit his side, looked down at the improbable sight of old Yurishev's sword hilt against his waist, and looked Yurishev in the face, the two of them locked in a dreadful moment of shock. He yelled aloud as Yurishev jerked the blade back through.

Perhaps the shock of the moment lingered on Yurishev. Pyetr staggered and clutched his side, spun about and ran before the retainers could stop him, across the street and into The Flower's stable court—bound for the back gate and the lane.

He caught his breath in the dark, leaning against the other side of The Flower's gate, and heard the search rampaging through the stableyard, a hunt which had the stable and his room in the upstairs of the inn yet to search.

So he started off, no brisker in his walk than any other homeward stroller, his heart thumping from the fright and the running. He felt no pain yet from his wound, felt no great amount of bleeding against his fingers, which encouraged him to hope that the wound had only caught the flesh above his belt and gone straight through—it would hurt in the morning, but it was of no great consequence, and surely would not even hamper him three days hence.

Damn the old man! he thought. Damn Irina, who had not even had the grace to call out a warning of ambush, who had not had the spine to advise him through her maid that her husband was forewarned. Probably Yurishev had confronted her and Irina's resistance had collapsed entirely. Irina might tell her husband everything, Irina might claim the god knew what—

He saw riders pass at the end of the road, the search spread now to the streets and lanes. "He's gone out by the back way!" he heard one rider say to another group. Then the thief-bell started, a pealing that brought other shutters open all along the lane where he was.

He kept to the shadows, then took a shortcut through a garden, which set a dog to barking. He began to run, terror lending him the strength to sprint the three more blocks to The Doe, and finally collected himself to stroll into The Doe's lantern-lit stableyard with a calm face and pay the stableboy there to take a message to 'Mitri in the common room— "Because I have to talk to him," he said, and added, lest the boy fear he meant some harm to 'Mitri: "A message from his sister—" hoping that no word had come there yet, and that the boy would take no alarm at his shortness of breath and his shaking hands. "Hurry, boy!"

The boy went in; 'Mitri came out with him, and as the boy pointed to the shadows where Pyetr waited, Pyetr walked forward, feeling a weakness in his knees now that he was within reach of help, feeling the first pangs from the wound, front and back.

"You're bleeding," 'Mitri exclaimed.

"Old Yurishev's men," Pyetr said. Out of shame, he skirted around saying it had been Yurishev himself. "The lady was under compulsion, I'm sure—"

He came close to fainting then, quite of a sudden. He caught at 'Mitri.

'Mitri shoved his hands off, stepped clear of him, unwilling, perhaps, to be taken in.

"It's not a joke, 'Mitri!"

"Is *that* the commotion in the streets? Yurishev's guards? They *saw* you?"

The thief-bell was still ringing. One could hear it all over Vojvoda.

"They saw me, they've clipped me in the side, for the god's love, 'Mitri, don't be a prig, I need a place to stay till this settles. . . ."

"Not with me! Go find some place, stay *away* from me! I can't afford trouble like this!"

Pyetr stared at 'Mitri in shock. "Then Vasya will—"

"Not Vasya either!" 'Mitri said. "That's the thief-bell, do you hear it? Get out of here!"

"I'll ask him myself," Pyetr said, about to go straight into the inn, but 'Mitri caught his shoulder and pulled him about so hard the pain of his side caught him and almost bent him double.

"No," 'Mitri hissed, his face stark and terrified in the lantern light. "No! We have nothing to do with you in anything like this! Yurishev's *wife*, my god! Dueling with Yurishev's guards, man— His cousin is in the court!"

"Your sister is the tsarevna's—"

"Leave my sister out of this! Mention me, mention her name, mention my *father's* name to the watch and I'll have your heart, Pyetr Kochevikov! Get away from me! Get out of here!"

'Mitri fled back for the light of The Doe's stableyard porch, and Pyetr stood staring after him in the same shocked bewilderment in which he had looked Yurishev in the face. His knees began to shake beneath him. Perhaps it was the diminution of his confidence that began to take his strength, perhaps it was that he had taken blow after blow tonight, and he had measured his strength only to get to the inn and his friends and now he had no idea where to go.

Only he must go somewhere. The stableboy had seen him. The boy knew that he had had business with 'Mitri, and if he brought trouble down on 'Mitri and 'Mitri's father took a hand then he had no hope at all.

He went out the stable gate, ducked down the lane, and heard the thief-bell stop. Good, he thought, breathless and dizzy, good, maybe the furor is dying down.

Or the thieftakers had come, and a wider hunt had begun.

He walked, felt new blood leaking through his fingers, and from time to time heard no sound but the pounding in his ears. The pain in his back and his side made it hard to think at all.

But his eyes made out the street—and knew the doorway and the gate farther on, that it offered at least a hope of refuge.

He walked as far as the public well and then into the gate and inside, down the log walk, reeled off to stand in the mud of The Cockerel's stableyard, hearing laughter behind the light-seamed shutters of the tavern, singing and dancing and the voice of Fedya Misurov himself calling out for another jug from the cellar.

His legs carried him away from that. Fedya Misurov would side with Yurishev, Yurishev would have the magistrates in his pocket; and he thought, seeking the dark of the stable, Only let me sit down a while. . . .

. . . because he was not thinking clearly, and he thought that if he could lie down a while in the dark, on the straw, he could regain his breath and his wits and think what to do or where he could go, or perhaps—

—perhaps make free of the horses stabled here, and absent himself from Vojvoda a while. He had been born in Vojvoda, he had grown up in its streets, and other places were only stories he had heard from 'Mitri and Vasya and his friends; but he was sure there were places to go, he had his winning ways and his cleverness and he was sanguine about his chances—

If only the pain would stop, if only he were not bleeding his life out.

He lay down mostly on his face in the straw, heard the horses moving and snorting their alarm at his presence and the smell of blood in the dark, but the singing in the tavern would drown that, and he lay there resting, kept telling himself that the blood was not coming so hard now that he was lying still, that it hurt a little less.

But he was mortally afraid, because he knew he was lying to himself: blood was still coming and he was close to fainting when the horses moved suddenly and a voice said, "Whoa, Missy, what's the matter?"

He thought there was a light near him. He thought that he heard someone walking in the straw, and that it was Yurishev's men and they would kill him.

But it was a boy who held a lantern over him, it was young Sasha Misurov, who stood there with a shocked, frozen stare, and asked him, foolish question, what he was doing there.

"I'm dying," Pyetr snapped, and tried to move, but that was a mistake. He fell down on his face in the straw, and screamed when the boy tried to pull him over.

"I'll get my uncle," Sasha said.

"No!" Pyetr was able to say, with the straw moving against his face, with his heart beating hard and his breath scant. His whole body was exploring the new limits of the pain and trying to discover whether lying like that was better or worse. "No—just let me rest here a while. Don't call your uncle. I've got some trouble. You don't want him involved. I'll just rest, I'll be on my way in an hour or so. . . ."

"You're bleeding," the boy said.

9

"I know that," Pyetr said between his teeth. "Have you any bandages?"

"For horses."

"Get them!"

The boy went away. Pyetr lay on his face in the straw trying to gather the strength to get up again, perhaps to walk up the street and find a place to sit awhile. Perhaps he could get the boy to collect his horse at The Flower—

No. They were searching the streets. They would have told everyone, searched his room at the inn—

The boy came back to him, the boy knelt down with a rustle of straw and said, "I've brought some water, and some salve—"

Pyetr bit his lip, worked at the knot of his belt as he was lying, face-down and panting in the straw. Finally, when he had the knot loose: "Do what you can, boy. I'll owe you for this."

The boy was careful, pulled the belt free, pushed up Pyetr's shirt and took in his breath.

"Don't gawk!" Pyetr said. "Bandage it!"

The horses snorted and moved, riders thumped into the muddy yard outside with a great blowing of horses and a ringing of the stableyard bell.

"Ho," someone yelled. "Watch!"

"Wait!" Pyetr said. But the boy sprang up and left him, running, and Pyetr got up on his knees and his elbows, lost his breath to the pain, and rested bent over with his head on his arms for two or three deep breaths while he heard the boy and the riders exchange salutations, and heard the riders say,

"Have you seen Pyetr Kochevikov?"

He despaired until the boy said, faintly and distantly, "No, sir."

"Do you know him?"

"Yes, sir, he was here today."

"Has anyone come around here?"

"No, sir, not except they went inside. . . ."

"Check it out."

Pyetr drew deep breaths and told himself he had to take the pain and get up and hide himself in the shadows, that even if Sasha Misurov held to his story, they might well search the stable. He gave a heave of his arms and his back and got himself upright, stood up, reeled sidelong and fell, thinking, Fool!—before he landed on his side.

He held back the outcry. He let his breath go. He could not get another for a moment, or see anything past the haze, except he heard deeper voices in the yard, Fedya Misurov's voice saying, "What did he do?"

"Murder," came the answer. "By sorcery."

"Who?"

"The boyar Yurishev himself. Master Yurishev caught him in his upstairs hall, at his wife's door, and chased the wretch into the street before he fell dead—"

No! Pyetr thought to himself. They're lying!

"If you see him," the man said, "take no chances. There was no mark on the victim."

Men die, Pyetr thought. The fools! He was an old man!

And he waited in bitter anticipation for Sasha Misurov to speak up and say, I know where to find him—because there was no reason Sasha should not. The stakes had risen much too high for a stranger to risk for anyone.

But the riders took their leave and rode away.

God, he thought, is the boy still out there?

Perhaps Sasha was inside the tavern, perhaps it would still happen, the boy would hear and tell Fedya and Fedya would say Run after them—

But he heard the elder Misurov say, "Lock the gate tonight," and young Sasha say, not so far from the stable wall, "Yes, uncle. I will."

Pyetr let go the straw he clenched in his fists and felt his last strength leave him, so that tears leaked from his eyes. Every breath was edged with the pain in his back and his side.

He saw the boy come back into the stable, saw him break into a run to reach him. The boy said it had been the town watch looking for him, asked him to keep still, said he would bandage the wound and take care of him—

Pyetr had no idea why.

2

Pyetr waked with the scent of hay and horses in his nostrils, and felt the pain that came whenever he waked, but the night was past, dusty sunlight shafted through the chinks of logs and the pain, thank the god, was finally bearable. He was afraid to move and start it again. He lay there thinking about moving, he listened to sounds: the horses doing bored, horsely things, the tavern waking up, distant shouts from mistress Ilenka—*Sasha,* she was calling, *take both pails, you lazy lout!* A cock crowed somewhere in the neighborhood.

Then he began to remember why he was lying here on his face in the straw, and remembered that the tsar's law was looking for him, that old Yurishev was irrevocably and truly dead, gone from Vojvoda where he had lived all Pyetr's life, and Yurishev's fool retainers were claiming witchcraft—

It was all too absurd: he remembered Yurishev's shocked face in that moment that they had scared each other, and thought it likely old Yurishev had never used a sword in his life. Probably the shock had frightened the old man into his grave, on the spot—and as for witchcraft, good god, Pyetr Ilitch Kochevikov could hardly afford a two-kopek charm to ill-wish the old miser, let alone hire some foreign sorcerer powerful enough to strike a man dead on the spot—because certainly no wizard who had ever set up shop in Vojvoda could do a thing like that.

Not at least any of the local ilk, who held forth in cramped little shops and collected and dispensed the town's gossip for coin. If there *were* genuine wizards, Pyetr thought, there were certainly none in Vojvoda. What had happened was an old man dying, and Yurishev's guards protecting their reputations. Probably one man had offered that inspired excuse to the inquiring magistrates, and the rest had immediately taken up on it, that was the truth of what had happened last night. Pyetr Kochevikov believed in human weakness far more than he believed in wizards, human weakness being everywhere evident and sorcery being a matter, like the Little Old Man who should ward the stables, of people's absolute will to believe in other people's responsibility.

He had profited from it. Now that same human frailty bid fair to hang him—or give him shorter shrift than that. The watch would run him through without a beg-your-pardon, Pyetr Ilitch, . . . for fear of themselves dropping dead like old Yurishev.

He *had* to get out of Vojvoda, that was the only safety he could count on now, and to do that he had to pass the town gates—

—where, one supposed, the drowsing gate watch occasionally did their jobs and paid attention to who came and went. With a supposed murder in town, they might very well be looking for him to leave, and there was certainly no chance of getting out in broad daylight, as it was beginning to be. So there was nothing for him to do but hide in The Cockerel's stable until dark and take his chances then—providing that he could walk, which, he discovered as he tried to sit up, was by no means certain.

And his wound hurt, god, it hurt, although nothing—*nothing* so bad as it had done last night.

"Are you all right?"

Pyetr grabbed the nearest stall rail to pull himself up. But it was only Sasha Misurov silhouetted in the doorway, buckets in hand, and he let go and sank down against the post.

"I brought you an apple," Sasha said. "And a bit of bread." He lifted one of the buckets he carried. "The water's clean. It only goes into the troughs."

"Thanks," Pyetr said, not cheerfully, regretting the breakfast table at The Flower, and his own bed and his belongings and his horse in the stables—as good as in the moon, all he owned. And none of his friends wanted anything to do with him—which left only The Cockerel's boy, who was, the whole town knew, odd—cursed with ill-luck from his birth, the tongue-clackers said, rumors Pyetr Ilitch had afforded the same credulity as he afforded wizards, wise women, or tea leaves. The boy's parents died in a fire, the culmination of a series of disasters which everyone recalled had begun the day the boy was born—

Look out, people would say in The Cockerel nowadays, bumping each other's elbows, if young Sasha put his nose into the tavern proper, *spill a drop for the House-thing, there's the neighborhood jinx with us*—

He had done it in jest himself, he and his friends.

And if he was tempted on that sudden thought to reflect that his own affairs had certainly gone wrong in young Sasha's presence—

Call him a fool, but if he had had luck anywhere in Vojvoda last night, it had been here, in Sasha Misurov's company.

"How are you this morning?" Sasha asked, squatting in front of him. Sasha fished the bread and the apple from inside his coat and gave them to him.

"Better," Pyetr said, remembering snatches of the night, Sasha bandaging his wound and sitting with him whenever he waked. Or maybe Sasha regularly slept in the stable. It was possible, given the relatives' stinginess with the boy.

"They're saying," Sasha said, "that you broke into the boyar Yurishev's house last night."

He blinked, stopped with the apple on the way to his mouth. "Visiting a friend," he said. "I'm not a thief."

Of course, he thought, the lady and the lady's rich relatives would come out with the charge of burglary. Never let it be said the boyarina Irina was anything but the grieving widow.

"They're saying—you were hired to bring a spell into the house."

"Bring a spell—"

Sasha looked acutely uncomfortable.

"I didn't," Pyetr said with a sinking heart. "—But that's what they're saying, is it?"

"That it had something to do with old Yurishev's business, that somebody hired a wizard and the wizard hired you to bring a spell inside the house, and *that* was why he died."

"Oh, good god," Pyetr said.

"The thieftakers are looking for you. They were here, I don't know if you heard last night. —Dmitri Venedikov is your friend. Or Vasya Yegorov. I could take a message to them."

He remembered 'Mitri shoving him away, and that recollection stung as much as it frightened him.

"No," he said.

"They're rich," Sasha objected. "They could help you."

So, then, *there* was the explanation of why Sasha helped him: the boy said it—rich friends, maybe even a little favor for somebody like Sasha Misurov.

Sasha was, since last night, wrong about the hope of rich friends, more the pity for them both.

"Why?" he asked Sasha, between bites of the winter-withered apple. "Why risk the watch for me?"

Sasha shook his head as if he was still thinking about that.

"Not that I'm not grateful," Pyetr said.

Sasha kept looking at him, till Pyetr wondered if his wits were altogether collected. Finally Sasha said: "What will you do if you don't go to your friends?"

"Oh, of course they'll help," Pyetr said. "They'll know what's going on, don't doubt that. They just don't need to know where I am right now—in case somebody asks, so they can swear they don't know. But they'll settle it. They have influence. All I have to do is stay here, out of reach of the watch."

"How long?"

"I don't know how long, a few days. I can't walk, Sasha Vasilyevitch! If you did go to my friends and anything went wrong, if the watch should get word of it before they can do anything with the magistrates, they'll kill me on sight, no trial, no court, nothing of the sort. You know that's the truth. The safest thing is for me to stay here till my friends can work things out. I can stay hidden, I don't need anything, only a place to sleep, maybe a little to eat, but I don't even ask that—"

Sasha was frowning more and more, and Pyetr found himself suddenly down to pleading with The Cockerel's stableboy, who owed him nothing, and who might, if greed got the better

15

of him, go straight to 'Mitri and tell 'Mitri where he was hiding.

And if 'Mitri rebuffed him, . . . there were other places Sasha Vasilyevitch could go to sell his information.

"I'll get you food," Sasha said with a very worried look. "But people come and go here. How long do you think it will take?"

"Surely," Pyetr said, trying to bargain the most time he dared, "surely no more than four days."

Sasha stared at him, not at all happy.

"All right," Sasha said finally.

After which Sasha moved a horse out of the endmost, darkest stall, and piled up forkfuls of straw in its corner. Then Sasha helped him up and helped him walk that far and sit down, all of which put him out of breath.

"Pull the straw over you," Sasha said.

It itched; but it offered some warmth, better than the drafts in the aisle. Sasha covered the pile with horse blankets, put his bread in his hand and set beside him a grain-measure of water he had saved from the horse pails. That was the comfort he had.

He thought about 'Mitri when Sasha had done his chores and gone, and he grew angry, and angrier; and he thought about the boyarina Irina, who, like Dmitri, had her wealth and her reputation to save—

He thought about Sasha, who probably was out for gain too. Who in this world was not?

But at least one could understand a boy who simply wanted to better himself. Pyetr Ilitch Kochevikov had started life that way, Ilya Kochevikov the gambler's son, Ilya Kochevikov the foreigner to Vojvoda, who had been all too well acquainted with the town watch in his life, and who had died, no one knew by whose hand, for reasons no one precisely knew but everyone in town was willing to speculate.

One would have thought, Pyetr mused bitterly, that after twelve years or so one might have lived down his father's sins. One might have thought that one's friends were one's friends, to rely on in the bad times as well as the good.

'Mitri and the rest of them had their fathers to fear, that was the way the world worked: they would save themselves, god forbid they risk anything for somebody not precisely their own kind—

That was what they would be saying. His friends would sit in the tavern and mutter together how terrible it all was.

Especially they would mutter, once they learned the extent of the charges against him.

How could we have trusted him? they would say. And: Breeding will tell, after all. He was amusing. Now he isn't. Poor fellow. . . .

Perhaps—the thought turned Pyetr cold, and made the bread dry in his mouth—perhaps the lovely, lonely Irina had had a notion how at one stroke to rid herself of a husband and find a scapegoat for it.

No one in Vojvoda would be on Pyetr Ilitch's side against those odds, and there was no town within range of Vojvoda's gossip that would ever be safe for him.

So to comfort himself he thought about the farthest places he knew, about the Southern Sea, fabled Kiev, and the great river, and he made plans about Vojvoda's gates and how he could slip past the watch there. More to the point, he wondered whether the silver in his purse could bribe a stableboy to help him—or how wide and how lavish young Sasha's expectations of reward might grow if the boyar's relatives made public offers.

Irina's relatives, if young Sasha could possibly figure that matter out, were very likely the ones who would bid highest to be sure he died without a trial.

The same ones who had lodged the witchcraft charge— would want no question of his guilt.

Everywhere one looked in spring, there was mud; mud constantly found its way onto the walks when some slightly wandering foot trod off and onto the logs again; and when mud got onto the walks, mud tracked onto aunt Ilenka's wooden floors.

All of which meant buckets of water, and a stiff brush, and a daily thorough washing of the split logs, which made more mud beside the walks.

Sasha had objected that plain fact to aunt Ilenka. Sasha

had said that if the walks were three logs wide instead of two there would be fewer missteps and less mud. But aunt Ilenka was not strong on reasons. Aunt Ilenka wanted the walks and the porch and her floors scrubbed, and he scrubbed, since if there was not that to do, aunt or uncle would find something else for him to do, or maybe—it was always possible—they might *not* find something else for Sasha Vasilyevitch to do, which his aunt and his uncle had begun to wonder about in his hearing.

He was ten years older than the boy his aunt and uncle had taken in, when all the town had said no good could come of him. He was fifteen, tall and still growing, all elbows and knees and feet; and he feared someday, when he had made some inconvenient mistake, uncle Fedya might look carefully at him and see a boy who could, uncle Fedya would say, fend for himself hereafter. Fedya Misurov could certainly say he had gotten ten years of charity from the family, and (as Fedya had once said) the neighborhood trade that came to The Cockerel was an easy-going lot, sorry for a five-year-old boy with no parents and charitably willing to ignore his living there as long as he stayed out of sight, so long as he was on The Cockerel's premises and not their own, so long as the only damage they ever witnessed in or around The Cockerel was spilled drink and the occasional broken mug.

But just let one extraordinary thing happen, uncle Fedya had warned Sasha severely, the very day he had arrived, let there be a fire in the kitchen or let somebody's horse be injured in the stable, and immediately everyone in town would recall there was a particular reason The Cockerel should have luck like that.

So uncle had generally kept him out of sight of the customers, uncle had put him to sweeping after hours or to carrying water or to mucking out the boarding stable, uncle had told him be prudent, and Sasha had been as prudent as he knew how to be. Sasha was careful of the horses, careful of the dishes he washed and the pails he carried, careful of latches and locks and the stall doors, careful of lamps and oil jars and aunt Ilenka's rising bread and the stack of firewood by the ovens. Sasha cleaned and scrubbed and never broke a dish or left a gate unlatched—

But the reputation for luck stayed with him.

Or maybe worse than that.

He knew the gossip, knew what some of his parents' neighbors had said about him when his parents had died. Even uncle Fedya and aunt Ilenka had insisted *that* was not so, that he was not to blame for the fire, else they would not have taken him in: uncle Fedya and aunt Ilenka had taken risks for him, risks to their reputation and risks to their business, which, they had pointed out to him, were not necessarily bound to continue, let him think of *that* any time he thought that they had treated him shabbily.

Most of all he tried not to ill-wish anyone, at any time, because he dreamed about the fire, he dreamed about his parents' voices screaming inside the house, he dreamed about the woman next door saying, The boy's a witch—

His father had beat him once too often, the neighbor woman had said, and the house had burned down. . . .

Sasha put his back into it, as uncle Fedya would say, scrubbed until he could stop thinking about that old woman. He scrubbed and rinsed and scrubbed and rinsed till the walk was clean and the muddy ground beside the logs was standing in puddles.

"Well," someone said from behind him, and he recognized that someone before he ever glanced back over his shoulder at elder cousin Mischa, who had come out in his fancy clothes. Mischa was going up the street to The Doe, where he was courting the tavern keeper's daughter: Sasha had heard Mischa saying as much this morning in the kitchen.

He gathered up his brush and his bucket and moved aside on the walk. There was room enough for two. But Mischa found a way to shoulder him off to stand in the mud.

Mischa thought that was sport. "Clumsy oaf," Mischa said.

Sasha did ill-wish Mischa sometimes, but only in little ways. He dared not think overmuch, now, for instance, of Mischa and his finery landing in the mud, directly after one of Mischa's little pranks: accidents of that kind were dangerous to his reputation and to his welcome with uncle Fedya and aunt Ilenka.

But he furtively hoped for such an accident later, somewhere on the way to The Doe, perhaps involving a very large puddle.

He was afraid when he caught himself at that, afraid to grow angry with Mischa, afraid to think about laying hands on his cousin and flinging him into the mud himself.

Most of all he was afraid that what the neighbors had said about him could be true, and that, without even wanting Mischa to come to lasting harm, he could do what he feared, the same as they said Pyetr Kochevikov had conspired with someone to do to the boyar Yurishev.

Pyetr had asked him forthrightly why he had helped him in the first place. That was easy, Pyetr having done him no harm, and Pyetr seeming in desperate need of help—

Until the watch had come to the gates saying that Pyetr was involved in sorcery—

Then Sasha had wanted to stand very far in the shadows and not have anybody anywhere remember that he existed.

Now—now, he had helped Pyetr Kochevikov, he had brought him food, he had helped him hide from the law, and when he had heard the charge he had known in his heart that Pyetr was not guilty of what they said—not Pyetr the prankster, not Pyetr, who could do such outrageous, wonderful things and get away unscathed—Pyetr never did real harm to anyone. There was never malice in his jokes. Pyetr and murder were unthinkable together.

And Pyetr and *sorcery*—

If they could believe that of Pyetr Ilitch, then they could believe it of anybody; and if the thieftakers found out who had been hiding Pyetr—then people all over town might remember all sorts of things about The Cockerel's stableboy, and nobody was going to ask whether it was true or not.

Sasha wanted Pyetr Ilitch to leave, now, immediately: that was all he could think of for a solution; but Pyetr refused, Pyetr said he had to have more time, and he personally had no idea what to do with a man so weak he could hardly walk. There was no throwing him out, even if he could hope the watch would never discover who had hidden a fugitive from them for a night and a day. He could think about sending Pyetr away, simply telling Pyetr he had to go and making sure that he got out The Cockerel's gate before anyone saw him. He could tell himself that he ought to do it before something terrible happened to the whole household, because they were not responsible for Pyetr Kochevikov, even if he was innocent, and he *was* responsible to uncle Fedya and aunt Ilenka, who had sheltered him when nobody else would—

But he had not the heart to see Pyetr Ilitch caught and killed.

He wished he could think of something.

He wished none of this had happened.

But that kind of wish never worked.

3

✠ ✠ ✠ ✠ The boy came in the evening with a couple
of small boiled turnips and a big piece of
bread, which Pyetr was very glad to see. The Cockerel's
kitchen had been smelling of baking bread all morning and of
stew all evening, with the coming and going of patrons, footsteps on the walk, shouts and banging of The Cockerel's door,
to remind a hungry, hurting man that other people were en-
joying a much happier evening.

At least no one had come in for any of the horses, thank
the god, and Pyetr had felt himself at least the better for a few
hours of uninterrupted sleep—until hunger had set in and he
would have been glad to contemplate yesterday's little saucer
of bread and sour milk on the stall gatepost, which somebody's
black and white cat had gotten after breakfast.

Sasha broke off part of the bread and put it in the saucer
first off; and poured a little of their drink on it—for the Old
Man of the stables, one supposed, and not for the cat—which
probably had its daily round of barns and stables and doorsteps.
It had certainly looked well-fed.

"They're talking in the tavern," Sasha said, between nib-
bles of his own bread. "There's a reward on you. From the
boyarina and her family."

Pyetr felt his stomach upset. "So. How much?"

"They say"— Sasha's voice took on a tone of true respect
—"sixty in silver."

"I can't say I'm insulted."

Sasha looked uncertain then, as if something of the bitterness had gotten through; or as if he thought he should not
have brought that up, here, alone with him.

Why did he say? Pyetr wondered. To find out whether my friends can bid higher?

"Why would they think that about you?" Sasha asked. "About the sorcery—why would they think that?"

Is he *afraid* of me? Pyetr asked himself then, as an entirely new territory opened to him with that idea. Is *that* why you haven't gone to the law, boy?

"Maybe I know a sorcerer," Pyetr said.

"Who?"

This was the boy who put out saucers of milk for the barn-warder, who, even if one pointed out that the cat had gotten them, would say, as the old folk would, that the cat did not get the saucer *every* time.

"I wouldn't be smart to say, would I?"

Sasha bit his lip, frowning, and Pyetr felt no safer considering the deep distress he saw on the boy's face. He had no clue which direction to go, now, or what might gain the boy's help or what might send him running headlong for the watch.

"If you know a sorcerer like that," Sasha said, "why doesn't he help you?"

Perish any thought that Sasha Vasilyevitch was dull-witted.

"I don't believe you did it," Sasha said. "I think the bo-yarina's relatives did. I think they're lying. *His* relatives were saying Yurishev knew you were coming to the house and he set up a trap—but now they're not talking to the magistrates, they're not seeing anybody—and the boyarina's maid hanged herself, they found her this morning. They're saying she helped you—"

God, Pyetr thought, they've killed that poor girl—

"People are scared," Sasha said.

Pyetr raked a hand through his hair.

"If there *is* a sorcerer," Sasha said, "did he do that too?"

"There is no sorcerer!" Pyetr cried. "I was seeing Yurishev's wife. Yurishev set up a trap and caught me and he must have had an attack of some kind; but if Yurishev's family proves adultery, the wife's dowry is forfeit, and her relatives want it back. They've had bad times lately. They need that property. Yurishev built the mill on it! And now they've murdered the poor maid. Do you think they won't murder me—

23

or anyone else they think might testify for the Yurishevs? It's
money involved, Sasha Vasilyevitch, and they're quite willing
to kill you as well as me. Don't mistake it!"

Sasha looked appalled.

"My friends are doing all they can," Pyetr said. "But it
takes time. They have to get appointments. They have to meet
with people. In the meanwhile—what you have to do is find
me some clothes."

"Clothes!"

"I'm all over blood and mud. If I had clean clothes and a
cap or something, someone who walked in here might not
look twice at me. Something bulky, something like your uncle
would wear."

"My uncle!"

"Nothing good. Old clothes. Rags. —Maybe a loaf of bread,
while you're at it. . . ."

Sasha looked as if his supper were sitting uneasy on his
stomach.

"It might be a good thing for everyone," Pyetr said, "if I
could get out of Vojvoda for a fortnight or so—and I need your
help, Sasha Vasilyevitch."

"I—"

The boy went silent. Somebody was walking outside.

"Somebody's coming!" Sasha whispered. "Cover up!"

Pyetr moved for his corner and raked handfuls of straw
over himself. Sasha flung the horse blankets over him and got
up and walked away. Pyetr could hear the gentle breakage of
straw, the soft opening and closing of the stall.

"What are you doing?" somebody said.

"Having my supper," Sasha said. "Resting for a moment."
He was appalled. Mischa stood in the stable aisle, covered head
to foot with mud.

He did not want to ask why. He simply felt sick at his
stomach, the anger of the morning gone and nothing left in
him but a profound horror, his secret misdeed come home to
him—

Thank god I didn't wish worse, he thought.

"Don't stand there with your mouth open," cousin Mischa
said. "Fool! I can't go inside like this! Get me some water and
get me some dry clothes, hear me?"

24

"I'll be right back," Sasha said, and took out running, out the stable door, down the walk, up onto the porch and inside the box of a hallway between the kitchen and the main part of the inn. Straight back, behind the stairs and behind the kitchen led him to Mischa's room, which was latched only when there were strangers in the tavern. He pushed the door open, snatched clothes off the peg and ran out again.

"Where are you going, Sasha?" aunt Ilenka's voice pursued him. "Alexander Vasilyevitch, *what are you doing?*"

He stopped in the outside doorway, bounced on one foot. "Mischa fell in a puddle," he said, and was out the door before aunt Ilenka could say anything.

Steps came closer to the stall. Pyetr refrained from breathing any larger than he had to, for fear of making any motion in the straw and the blankets.

The walker stopped. Someone else was coming at a run. In a moment: "I've got the clothes," Sasha's voice said. "Here."

"I need the water first, fool!"

"I'm getting it," Sasha said. There was the rattle of a bucket. "I'll be right back. You can start getting undressed."

Footsteps left, running. Footsteps walked back up the aisle.

Pyetr held his breath again, heard the advance of the footsteps, heard swearing, heard the rattle of the stall gate as it swung inward. For a moment he could not determine what was going on with the small creaks and grunts, until he realized Mischa Misurov was pulling off his boots, starting to do what Sasha had said.

O my god, Pyetr thought, suddenly putting a cold, wet Mischa Misurov together with the convenience of a pile of horse blankets on the straw in the corner of the stall.

As the footsteps came up to him and his shelter vanished with a snatch of Mischa's hand and an unwelcome flood of lantern light.

Mischa yelled and leaped back, Pyetr gasped and lurched for his feet, grabbing his sword, and Mischa Misurov yelled for help and banged his way past the stall gate, out into the center aisle.

"Help!" he yelled, mostly naked, running and slipping barefoot in the straw. "It's him! It's him!"

Pyetr banged his own way out of the stall, sword in hand, overtook him with a pain that shortened his breath, tried to lay hands on him without running him through, but he missed both chances, bent double with the pain as he lost his grip. Mischa plunged out into the dark of the yard, yelling and howling that he was beset.

"Damn," Pyetr gasped, and ran for the door as Sasha came dashing in, no bucket, nothing in his hands, terror on his face. "Stop the fool!"

"I tried!" Sasha cried.

"I've got to get out of here," Pyetr said, and grabbed him. "Get me a horse!"

"There isn't time!" Sasha cried. "Come, come on!"

Sasha offered conviction and a direction. Pyetr had neither. He yielded to the pull on his arm and ran in the direction Sasha pulled him, out the west door toward the tangled area of the hay-shed and the garden.

"Fool!" he said, pulling back at the sight of the fence, hearing The Cockerel's thief-bell start to ring, hearing doors beyond the stable bang open and a score of men shouting for weapons and the watch. "This is a dead end!"

"No," Sasha said, and he committed himself to the boy and kept going, across the scattered skirt of the haystack, around behind it and up to a corner where The Cockerel's fence failed to meet that of its neighbor.

Sasha squeezed through.

"Easy for you!" Pyetr gasped, and tore his shirt doing it, left skin from his right arm on the boards, but the sounds of pursuit reaching the stable lent him strength. He ignored the pain and ran, half-doubled, the hand that held the sword pressed against the stitch in his side, while Sasha Misurov led him a fox's course through the neighbor's garden, out the neighbor's gate onto the lane that ran behind The Cockerel.

The bell was ringing, the shouts continued, and by now Pyetr was running blind, not knowing whether it was his eyes that were fading or only the shadows where they were.

"Where are we going?" he panted finally, slowing, because

26

his sense of direction told him they were going across the hill, not down it.

Sasha gasped, waving his hands, got out: "Dmitri Venedikov."

"No!"

"*Who*, then? Where?"

Pyetr gulped a mouthful of air. "The gate," he said. "The town gate. That's all there is left. I've got to go away for a while—"

The haste ebbed out of Sasha. He drew two or three breaths before he said, "What are we going to do, then? Where are we going to go?"

"We" was the fact. He realized that suddenly. There was no way, considering how the blankets had been piled, that he could have gotten into that corner with the blankets atop by his own efforts. The thieftakers would know he had had someone at The Cockerel helping him, and Fedya Misurov was only fortunate it was a Misurov who had raised the alarm, or *all* the Misurovs would be involved.

"I don't know," he confessed to the boy. "Let's just get to the gate, do you mind? Then we'll see what to do."

There was a stickiness on his side. He felt his shirt clinging to his skin and hoped that it was sweat that did that. The pain was less. Or the thumping in his ears distracted him from it.

He wandered a bit as they started off. He found his sword sheath and put the weapon away, to make them a little less conspicuous. By now dogs had added their barking to the noise a street away.

"We needed the horses," he muttered. "We could have gotten across town if we'd had time for the horses."

Sasha was doubtless scared out of words. Sasha said nothing, only walked beside him down one twisting lane and the next, downhill, while he tried desperately to think of sources for horses or clothing less conspicuous. Other thoughts kept edging in—thoughts like being caught, thoughts like himself being skewered and the boy who had helped him being run through on the spot or snatched up in the quarrels of the Yurishevs—

That the boy should slip them out of this by blind luck and the eel's course they had run getting this far—was much too much to ask. Pyetr had the most uncomfortable feeling that Sasha expected something extraordinary of him, something like the hairbreadth tricks he was notorious for in the town—

But that was a Pyetr Kochevikov without a terrible pain in his side. There was no joke about this, not in the least.

He felt of his bandaged side, rubbed his fingers and felt a slight dampness. It hurt less now than it had in the night. He thought that might be a bad sign.

And he was quite well out of tricks, out of friends, out of everything but the few coins in his purse—of which Sasha had kindly declined to rob him.

Then the wits began to work again.

"Wait, boy," he said, seized Sasha by the shoulder, set Sasha's back against a fence, and said, "I have an idea."

Then he hit Sasha across the jaw. Sasha bounced off the fence and started to slide to his knees, but Pyetr grabbed his shirt and hauled at him.

"Sorry," he said.

"Help," Sasha Vasilyevitch cried, running breakneck for the gate. "Help me! Murder!"

The gate-guards stood up straight, snatched up their pikes and their lantern, and held up the light as Sasha ran up to them, with the thief-bell still clanging away up the hill.

"God," one said, seeing his face, catching hold of his arms.

"They're killing my uncle!" Sasha cried. "The murderer— his helpers, there's at least three of them! I'm Sasha Misurov, from The Cockerel, and my uncle Fedya— We were trying to catch this man, they found him in our stable— He ran and we ran after him before the watch could come and we caught up with him, but there were more of them— *They're killing my uncle, oh, please*—"

"Calm down, boy, calm! Where is he?"

"Up there!" Sasha pointed a trembling hand toward Ox Street. "My uncle, oh, they're killing him, please, run, *stop* them! There's at least three of them!"

The guards left at a run.

Sasha Vasilyevitch ran up to the tall gates of Vojvoda, lifted the iron latch of the small parley-gate in the shadow of the arch and shoved it open, terrified that Pyetr was not going to show up, that something disastrous could have happened since their courses had parted. Pyetr was bleeding, he had confessed it—Pyetr could have fallen, could be still back on Market Street, and he might be alone here, free of Vojvoda, but with no idea where he should go or what he should do after that. Pyetr was the one who knew, all of it was Pyetr's plan, except to tell the guards at the gate that it was Pyetr and not robbers—and if Pyetr did not come now he had no idea where he should go or how he should live.

But somebody came running up behind him just as he got the gate open, just as the bar swung up with a terrible clang.

"Move," Pyetr said, hoarse and panting.

Sasha slipped through into the dark of the road and it was Pyetr who had the presence of mind to shut the gate after him, after which the bar thumped down.

"It locked itself again!" Pyetr breathed. "That's luck!"

Sasha hoped that it was. He was wishing hard enough, much harder than he had ever wished to make Mischa come to grief. He was shaking at the knees and wishing he had a heavier coat, here in the wind, and suddenly thinking that he wanted to be back in the kitchen of The Cockerel, he wanted to sit down next the oven where it was warm and he could never do that again, never go home, never see his own bed again, never see the horses or the stable or any of those things that made up all his days—and he had trouble thinking to move at all, except that Pyetr took him by the elbow and pulled him along to the left, where the road ran along the wall.

Pyetr was breathing too hard to talk; Sasha was too lost to have any opinion: his lip was cut, his jaw ached, the guard had clearly been appalled at the sight of his face, and he did think that Pyetr might have spared him the second and the third blow.

4

✠ ✠ ✠ ✠ "Where are we going?" Sasha asked when the north road had left Vojvoda well behind, when there was nothing around them but plowed fields and the night sky.

"South," Pyetr said.

"But we're going north!" Sasha said.

"That's the point. If you want to escape the tsar's justice you have to escape the tsar's territory. And you can't go the way they expect."

"But where are we going?"

"There are other tsars," Pyetr said between breaths. "All we have to do is travel far enough . . . Everything will be fine."

Pyetr had to sit down shortly after that. They had reached a point where they had a woods or a ridge or some large darkness in sight eastward: Sasha had no idea what that was, but they were out of sight of any lights at all; and Pyetr sat down on a large rock and held his hand to his side, his head hanging. Sasha squatted down to look at him closely in the dark, more afraid than he had been when he was lying to the gate guards, because Pyetr was bleeding again, he had no doubt of it now, Pyetr was growing weaker, and he had no notion what to do, without medicines, without clean bandages, and no hope of a place to get them. The north road only went to Belovatzd, that he knew of, which was only a village, and nowhere to hide, because it was closer to the tsar than Vojvoda was.

"I'll be all right," Pyetr said, and made an effort to straighten, not entirely successful. "Time we got off this road. They'll be hunting us—if they have the stomach for it. Who knows, maybe a sorcerer helped us get out the town gates."

Sasha felt a chill settle about him when Pyetr said that. Pyetr laughed and said:

"God knows what the guards will tell—or what your fool cousin saw when I came out of that corner! Father Sun, the look on his face! I must have shape-shifted, my sorcerer friend must have turned me into a haystack—"

"Don't joke!" Sasha said. "The Field-thing could be listening."

"It should have a sense of humor."

"It's not funny."

"It ought to be. It's all moonfluff, boy, me 'witching old Yurishev, us shape-shifting our way through the gates. God, I used to play the devil around The Doe's kitchen when I was a kid, used to carry their wood for them, then drop down to the cellar where they hung the sausages . . ."

"You didn't!"

"I did. They kept saying how they had to have done something to set the house-devil off, because he was eating them out of their profits. So they must've figured it was since they hired *me*—and I do bet their profits came up when they let me go."

"You're a thief!"

"I was hungry, boy. I didn't *have* relatives. And in case you've ever wondered, the Little Old Man around The Cockerel's barn is a black and white cat."

Sasha shuddered to hear that kind of talk. "It's not lucky," he said. "Don't say things like that, Pyetr Ilitch."

"Poor Sasha. There *aren't* any House-things. There's nothing in the bathhouse. The bannik won't get you, and it can't tell you any more than the fake wizards on Market Street."

Sasha got up, walked off and squatted down on the other side of the road, where he did not have to be near Pyetr Kochevikov.

The man was wicked. He had no fear. Aunt Ilenka had said it, and he had not believed it; and now he had Pyetr Kochevikov for a guide, if Pyetr was not going to bleed to death on the road before morning and leave him alone with everything that had gone wrong.

No wizards.

He only wished—

But that was the trouble. He could do too much by wishing, and he dragged himself back from that terrible wish he had, that something should bring Pyetr Ilitch to his senses.

"There *aren't* any wizards," Pyetr said from across the road. "The bogeys won't get you."

"Stop it!"

"If the bogles are anything, they'd have come after me long since. It's not stealing to take what people are setting out for the cat—unless you count the cat."

Sasha stood up and faced him. "We're in enough trouble, Pyetr Ilitch. Making jokes isn't going to help it."

"It does help it. It helps not to be fools." Pyetr staggered to his feet. "It helps us that the thieftakers are probably suspecting the haystack or the horses, and the gate guards who let us out aren't going to admit they were tricked off their post, they're going to say they were 'witched, and *they* aren't going to come out here in the dark looking for wizards and shape-changers who walked right through a locked parley-gate. So be grateful that *they're* fools."

"Where are you going?" Sasha asked, for Pyetr was leaving the roadside, heading off through the meadow, eastward.

"To blazes," Pyetr said. "Come with me or go back and explain to the thieftakers how you were 'witched, too."

"I can't!" Sasha cried.

But Pyetr kept walking, slowly, and there was nothing to do but run after him.

They came on a road in the dark, or at least a memory of one, so overgrown and weedy it was almost more trouble than the open field, but better, Pyetr thought, to be on it, since a road, however old, promised a sure way through. The god knew he was in no way for climbing or rough ground, and from time to time he would come back to himself with the feeling that he might have been wandering—except for the road, which at least kept them on a course for somewhere, at least guided them away from Vojvoda, and steered them clear of dead ends and drops over banks—one hoped.

"Talk," he said to the boy finally, because he knew that his wits were drifting.

"About what?" Sasha asked.

"Anything. I don't care."

"I don't know anything to talk about."

"God. —What do you want to do, where do you want to go in the world, what have you always wanted to see?"

"I don't know. I never thought. —I thought we were just going to hide a while, till your friends—"

"Don't be naive. —Did you plan to work for old Fedya for the rest of your life?"

Silence.

"Did he pay you?"

"No," Sasha said in a small voice.

"That old skinflint. —Mischa spends him blind and you're jack-of-all-work, is that it?"

"Mischa's his own son."

"And you call *me* a thief." He had no wish to argue, he had not the strength, but the boy's docile gullibility infuriated him. "He took you for a fool, boy, he worked you like a tinker's donkey, so his son could squander his money in every inn in Vojvoda, and you make excuses for him."

"He didn't have to take me in."

"Oh, he took you *in*, boy." He felt the pain come back, riding every step, and he wanted to drop the whole conversation, but the argument called up old, disturbing resentments, and he wondered if he had ever understood the boy. "You should have beaten Mischa's head in—years ago. It might have done both of you some good."

"I couldn't."

"Mischa's soft—soft, and you aren't, if you ever added it up. You let people push you, they get used to it and they don't even think about it. Same with Mischa, same with your uncle, not mentioning your aunt. You want a witch, boy—"

"That's the trouble!" Sasha said. "That's the trouble. You don't believe in witches. But I might *be* one."

"You might—*be*—one."

Perhaps Sasha comprehended that that was sarcasm. Several moments went by in silence.

"Boy, everybody makes-believe. Everybody has terrible hidden powers, everybody is going to get back at the fools around him. And then you grow *up*, boy!"

"Everybody says I'm just unlucky," Sasha cried. "But I *wanted* Mischa to fall in a puddle, you understand? I *wanted* us to get through the gates and them not to follow and the bar fell down—"

"So did I *want* it, boy, luck's got nothing to do with it."

"It does with me! My parents' house *burned*, Pyetr Ilitch. Mischa fell in a puddle and we got through the gates and they haven't found us. Sometimes it's good and sometimes it's bad, but you can't always tell whether a thing's going to be good or bad when you wish for it, you can say I don't want my father to hit me anymore and your house can burn down—"

The boy was crying.

"That's nonsense," Pyetr said.

Sasha sniffed, turned his face away and rubbed his eyes as they walked.

"Did your uncle tell you that?"

"Our neighbor did. Our house burned down. People say I'm a jinx, uncle Fedya wouldn't let me come near the customers, he said if things ever did go wrong, people would believe it was my fault."

"Kind of him."

"But it's not just bad luck! Things happen that I *want*."

"So why don't you want to be tsar?"

Sasha sniffed again, and said nothing to that.

"So don't say things happen that you want," Pyetr said.

"You can't say how it could happen. If you wish for things like that, the tsar might die, there might be a war. I don't wish for things like that. I don't even want to think about things like that!"

"Large thoughts. What *do* you wish for, boy?"

"I don't."

"Don't make wishes? Wish we were out of this, if you believe it'll work."

"You don't understand. You can't wish for things like that. If we were dead we'd be out of this. It can come true that way. You have to think of something that hasn't got any harm in it, and even then you don't know if you've thought of everything—"

"So you try not to wish for anything, you try not to want

34

anything. That's really hell, Sasha Vasilyevitch. That's *hell* you live in."

Sasha wiped his nose.

Pyetr was amazed at his own stupidity, to be betrayed by everyone he knew, and find himself doing it all over again, believing the boy with a conviction and a trust he had never placed in anyone so much as now—seeing he had lately had his own delusions, chased his own moonbeams—which had, whatever else, at least been pleasant while they lasted.

Not Sasha's.

Poor crazed lad, he thought. The boy's not altogether sane. At least they've not encouraged him to be.

"You don't go at things the right way, boy. You've been wishing for things *likely* to happen. What you do, you wish for the tsar himself to ride along and recognize us both for the honest, upstanding sort we are, and make us rich and happy. Wish for us both to marry tsarevnas and die at a hundred and twenty, rich as lords and surrounded by great-grandchildren—"

"It doesn't work that way."

"You're too honest, Sasha Vasilyevitch. You should learn to laugh. That's your trouble. You're too serious." He clapped Sasha on the shoulder as they walked—which was a very good thing, because he turned his ankle on a rock and depended on that hold quite suddenly.

"Pyetr!"

He got his feet under him again, with Sasha's help. "Joke," he said.

But it had hurt. He walked a few more steps, Sasha never letting him go.

"I think I'd better sit down for a while," he said, short of breath. "I've come a long way for a man in my condition. Have pity."

Sasha snatched up standing weeds, gathering dry ones that way, the same way a good stableboy never took hay or straw from the damp ground. He gathered another armload and piled it over Pyetr's arms, Pyetr lying on a mat of more such weeds, against a thorn-bush with tightly-laced branches, the best shelter Sasha could find in this season before leaves were out.

No blankets, Pyetr in a shirt, himself in only the lightest of coats—Sasha kept reproaching himself for the horse blankets and the extra clothes they might have brought, if he had had his wits about him and not thought only of running—

Or there was the food he might have had in his pockets, if Pyetr had only said, plainly, Let's run away, once and for all. . . .

Pyetr was chilling now that they had stopped walking. The night cold came on the edge of a wind, and the wild grass was the only blanket he could think of.

"Good boy," Pyetr said between chattering teeth. "Good lad. —More sense than 'Mitri and that lot ever will have. . . ."

Sasha pulled weeds until he was sweating, until his hands felt raw, and built up a bank beside Pyetr, higher and higher, until he could lie down and rake the weeds over them both.

He was warm, at least. He burrowed under the weeds, opened his coat and put himself up against Pyetr's chilled body.

"Wish us a warm day tomorrow," Pyetr muttered. "Wish us a horse or two while you're about it. And the tsar's own carriage."

"I'm wishing you to *live*," Sasha said, and did, as hard as he had ever wished for anything. He was trying not to shiver, up against Pyetr's chill side as he was, but it was not the cold, it was fear.

"Good," Pyetr said. The shivers were down to little ones now. "I'm glad you're minding the details."

A moment later, Pyetr said, with a small shudder, "But do spare a wish for a horse, two of them—fast ones, if you find the time. I've always fancied black, myself."

5

✳ ✳ ✳ ✳ "No horse," Pyetr complained, in the morning—a frosty morning, Sasha found, in which it might be a great deal warmer to stay where they were, but fear of the thieftakers and the sting of Pyetr's ridicule made it unlikely he would rest.

"No horse, no coat, no carriage," Pyetr said. "I expected the tsar for breakfast. For supper tonight, do you think?"

Sasha got up, picked weeds out of his hair and felt bits of them go down his collar.

"No sense of humor," Pyetr said.

One could be very angry at Pyetr, except he tried to move and sit up, and it hurt him, so that he caught after the branches of the bush and stabbed his hand on the thorns. Sasha winced, himself, while Pyetr just drew back the bleeding hand, shook it and sucked the blood with a weary, aggrieved frown—and held it up then, still bleeding, with: "Do you do *small* cures, perchance?"

"No," Sasha said sorrowfully, and came to help him up. "I truly wish I did."

It took a bit to get moving, cold as it was, but it was the only help for a stitch like that, just to work it out by walking, the boy trying to help him the while.

"It's better," Pyetr said, finally, when moving and the warmth of the sun on his back had helped what it could. And, his wits being a little clearer, he thought that the boy was very quiet and very unhappy this morning. "Cheer up," he said. "We're away, we're not on the main road, we'll come

37

across it again, eventually, beyond any distance they'd search for us. . . ."

"But what town are we going to? Where does this road go? Don't they say—don't they say east is the way to the Old River, don't they say—people don't go that way any more? Only outlaws—"

"What do you suppose we are?"

"But—" Sasha said with a distressed look, and seemed to be thinking about it.

"But?" Pyetr said, and when Sasha said nothing to that: "We'll follow the river south," Pyetr said. "There has to be a road. Or the river itself. We can build a boat of sorts. It goes all the way to the sea. It'll carry us to Kiev. People are rich in Kiev."

Sasha trudged beside him, arms wrapped around his ribs, hardly looking confident.

"So serious," Pyetr said.

Sasha said nothing. Pyetr clapped him on the shoulder.

"It'll be all right, boy."

Still there was nothing. Pyetr shook at him. "No wishes?"

"No," Sasha said in a dull voice.

"No horse?"

"No."

"You let me devil you too much."

No answer.

"Boy—" Pyetr flexed his grip on Sasha's shoulder, and held his temper. "You go where you want. If you want to go back, go back. If you want to go ahead, go ahead. Make up your own mind. If you don't want to hear about horses, say, Shut your mouth, Pyetr Ilitch. Try it. It's good for your stomach."

Sasha twisted away from him. Pyetr held on.

"Say it, boy!"

"I don't want to hear about horses!"

Pyetr let him go. "Then I beg your pardon." With a bow as they walked, the doffing of an imaginary cap—a mistake: it did hurt.

They walked a while more in silence.

"Your uncle is a bully," Pyetr said. "I am a profligate, a gambler, a liar and occasionally a person of bad character, but

I do swear to you, I have never been a bully, and you insist to make me one. *Look me in the face, boy!*"

Sasha looked up, stopped, startled as a rabbit.

"Good," Pyetr said. "Say it again, about the horses."

"I don't want to *talk* about the horses, Pyetr Ilitch!"

"Then accept my deep apology, young sir."

Sasha looked as if he feared he had gone mad, and kept looking at him.

"You've got it right," Pyetr said, and slowly, slowly, the boy's face lost its frown. "Go on. You've almost got it. Don't be so glum."

"Why shouldn't I be? We've no blankets, no food, the law wants to kill us—and probably the outlaws will."

"Then what worse can happen to us? Only better. If you could only wish us up a supper—"

"Shut up about the supper, Pyetr Ilitch!"

He laughed. The boy glowered, and he laughed until he hurt, holding his side.

"Stop it!" Sasha cried.

So he shrugged and started walking again, shaking his head.

Sasha overtook him. "I'm sorry," Sasha said.

"Of course you are," he said, not kindly.

"I'm not mad," Sasha said.

"Of course you aren't. That's the problem, lad."

"I *can't* be," Sasha said, "don't you see, I *can't* be! I can't—"

"Because your wishes come true," Pyetr said in disgust. "God, boy—*forget* that nonsense. —Or conjure us the horses."

There was an intake of breath, a moment of silence.

"If you're afraid to lose your temper, boy, . . . then laugh. Can it hurt?"

Another deep sigh from the boy. A miserable little try at a laugh.

"More practice," Pyetr said.

It should be absolutely the worst time of year to be out and living off the land, Sasha thought, the winter berries spent, the new growth merely swelling in the bud, the tubers all dug, the insects still in the egg—all of which meant a mouse could not have found a living in The Cockerel's in-town garden in this season, let alone two shivering travelers turned out in the wilderness. But grain had seeded here, gone wild and sparse from a time, perhaps, when this all had been cultivated fields, or it was simply the drift from fields closer to Vojvoda, Sasha had no idea. They could pick remaining heads caught in thickets, up against stones, where the heavy winter snows had not altogether flattened and spoiled it. There were a withered few berries in the center of bushes, food that the birds must have missed, but perhaps they were poison, Sasha had no idea, and Pyetr said he had none, and they were small anyway.

Pyetr did not say, Wish us well-fed. Sasha did it on his own, hoping for food and safety they could find without being found, but he was not sure where that wish might lead, here, in the wilderness. He was sure of nothing that The Cockerel's walls did not contain, he had no experience else, and he kept thinking of bandits and trying most desperately *not* to wish for his own bed and aunt Ilenka's kitchen, or anything else that might bring them more than they wanted.

But there was no food more than the heads of wild grain he could gather; and as they walked, the forest shadow that had been on their left since last night began to spread across the horizon, making clearer and clearer where the road was going.

He was sure there were bandits and worse things beyond: travelers who came to The Cockerel told of forest-devils and things that snatched and clutched, evil spirits which misled a man, and left him to ghosts and wild beasts. He mentioned these to Pyetr, but Pyetr said they were granny-tales, and scoffed, as Pyetr would.

Sasha kept his fears to himself thereafter. He had never *seen* a forest, but he knew the worst of it, and this one looked less and less savory, winter-barren across a winter-ravaged meadow.

There would be snow remaining in that shade, he was sure. There would be all too much of shade in a place like that, there would probably be drifts still standing, and there would be cold. Their thin clothes were scarcely enough to keep warmth in their bones while the sun was shining on their backs and the wind was still.

"I think we should stop," he said to Pyetr, while there was still daylight, "and rest, and not go in there until morning. I can find us grain, still. I think we ought to go in with some in our pockets. And I can make us a bed of straw tonight."

They were at the top of a brushy slope, where the road was completely overgrown, and below was the last of the meadow and the first of the forest. Pyetr stopped there, and gave a great sigh and leaned on the sword he had begun to use as a walking stick. "Good lad," he said, hard-breathing. "Yes. I think that's only prudent."

There was a fair good stand of wild grain about the scattered thickets and rocks, there was the standing brush, and they might at least, Sasha thought, pulling heads of grain for their supper, sleep relatively secure tonight.

Except by twilight, as he was cutting straw with Pyetr's sword, he heard a distant sound that might be horses coming, and he looked up in alarm.

It came again, with a flash of light on the northwestern horizon, above the rolling hills.

The straw was the best hope, Sasha had said, any they could gather, however wet and half-rotten, and Pyetr sat with Sasha's coat around him, clenching his teeth against the cold, binding handfuls with straw twists to tie it around stalks of brushwood, the way Sasha had shown him—very much like thatch, Pyetr saw, once they laid the brushwood sticks down on a rough frame, a roof, poor though it was and full of gaps, on a frame laid up against a boulder and a leafless clump of brush. The thunder muttered and they built, handful by handful, row by row, Sasha hacking handfuls of straw and bringing it back, building up a bed of brush and a layer of straw, in a nook he had hacked out between the large gray boulder and a berry thicket.

"You're very resourceful," Pyetr was moved to say, teeth chattering, when Sasha joined him in the roof-making. "Sasha my lad, I don't know a gentleman in Vojvoda I'd have in your stead."

"I should have brought the clothes," Sasha said, and flinched as the thunder boomed. His hands were white while

41

they tied knots of twisted grass. Came a second terrible crack, lightning throwing everything into unnatural clarity in the growing dark. "I'm *sorry*, Pyetr Ilitch."

"We were rather hurried at the time, both of us. And if we had them they'd only get wet tonight."

Another peal of thunder.

"I'm a jinx!"

"Yesternight it was 'wizard.' "

Sasha scowled and looked hurt at that gibe. "Maybe my wishes only work when it's going to go wrong. Maybe that's the curse on me. Maybe that's why the wizards wouldn't take me."

"Wouldn't take you."

"My uncle brought me to them. After my parents died. There was talk. He asked them might I be a wizard, and they said no, I wasn't. They didn't find anything in me. But they said I was born on a bad day."

"Garbage."

"I'd think they'd know."

Crack and boom. Sasha flinched again.

"They're fakes. Every one of them."

"I don't know about that."

"I do. Jinxes and wizards are a hoodwink. You tell a wizard your troubles and ask him what to do, and he tells you; and he sells everything you tell him to the next customer—probably your rival."

"Don't you believe in anything?"

"I believe in myself. Tell me this. If those wizards are so powerful, why aren't they richer than they are?"

That stopped the boy for a moment. He gathered up another bunch of straw. "There's wizards," he said. "There's real ones."

"Because you know there are."

"I know there are."

"And the cat gets the saucers. I believe in the cat, boy."

"Don't talk like that." The boy made a sign, a fist and thumb. "The Field-thing left us grain, we shouldn't talk like that."

"Field-thing," Pyetr said.

"There *is*. We should leave him something. We should be polite. We have enough troubles."

"Because the straw-man will get us." A man could begin to worry, listening to this sort of thing, in the dark, in the chill of the rising wind. "Hah."

"Don't."

"Maybe you're just afraid, boy."

Sasha's jaw set. He tied off his knot, while the thunder muttered threats.

"It's only reasonable," Pyetr said. "That's a big cloud. We're not so big. I don't think you raised it. I don't think you can send it back. —That's the really terrible thought, isn't it? That that cloud doesn't care we're already cold and we haven't had a proper meal since yesterday and you really wish it would miss us. Go on and try."

"Don't joke! It has lightning!"

A man could believe in anything with the thunder rolling. A second shiver went down Pyetr's neck.

Which often made him a fool, especially when there was someone watching him.

"So maybe we should wish the lightning away. Petition old Father Sky."

"Don't talk that way."

"Well, hey, old graybeard," Pyetr called out to the sky in general, squinting in the icy wind and the blowing bits of grass. "Hear that? Do your worst! Strike me dead! You might have better luck than old Yurishev! But do spare the boy! He's very polite!"

"Pyetr—shut up!"

It was thin amusement, anyway. His side hurt too much, the wind had turned to ice, and his hands were shaking. But he said, "I'll wager you breakfast lightning won't strike us."

Thunder cracked, right overhead. Sasha jumped.

So did he.

And when the rain was coming down and the thunder was racketing and cracking over them, the both of them tucked into a shelter rapidly leaking despite their efforts, Pyetr Kochevikov began to think that he might indeed die before morning, by slow freezing; and after an hour or so under a shared coat, thoroughly soaked from the dripping water, he began to wish that he could speed the matter, because he was so cold and because the shivering hurt his side, and he could not sleep, he could not straighten his legs or move his arms in the little shelter.

Sasha slept, at least, a still warm lump against his body— and a barrier which kept him from shifting his knees that small amount he was sure would relieve the pain in his side. He tried two and three times to wake the boy—and gave up, finally, figuring that there was no place for the boy to move in the shelter, and that there was a chance of the cold finally making the wound numb if he could just think about that hard enough and long enough.

It was very, very long before the sun came back.

"Wake up," he said, shoving the boy hard. "Wake up, dammit."

And when he finally had signs of consciousness from the boy: "You see. We're alive. The old man missed us."

"Stop that!" Sasha said.

"Move," he said, his eyes watering with the pain and the immediate prospect of relieving it. "Move. You owe me breakfast."

Sasha got up and lifted their soggy roof off with a thump of small rocks and a cascade of water droplets. But Pyetr lay there trying to make his legs work again, and it was several painful tries before he could figure out a way to get up, using his sword, and the rock at his left, and finally Sasha's well-intended help, which hurt so he yelped.

"I'm sorry," Sasha said.

He nodded. It was all he had the breath to do.

And it was, inevitably, a breakfast of raw grain, his hands shaking so he could hardly eat and his teeth chattering so he could hardly chew it. He simply tucked it in his cheek to work on over the hours, not sure whether living was worth this.

"You shouldn't have said that to the god," Sasha said as they started out. "You should beg his pardon. Please."

"Of what?" Pyetr said. "He didn't hit us, did he?"

"That's a forest we have to go through. There's leshys and the god knows what. Don't offend things! Please!"

"Nonsense," Pyetr said, in less than good humor. "I've a wizard to help me. Why should I worry?"

"Don't *do* that, Pyetr Ilitch!"

"So go back to Vojvoda. Tell them I was an impious fool. Tell them I kidnapped you and forest-devils carried me off, and you ran home. I don't care. I don't need your nattering, boy!"

He was not, admittedly, in the best of humors. He tried the muddy downslope, with his sword for a cane, his knees shaking with the cold, and Sasha fluttering along by him. Every misstep and every jolt hurt him this morning, now that cold had set into the wound, and he swore when he hurt himself and swore when Sasha got in his way.

"Please," Sasha said to him. "Please."

He tried to hurry. He skidded on the mud and Sasha caught him. Thank the god.

Thank the boy, too, who was so stubbornly, seriously good-natured, no matter his other failings. Pyetr stood there braced against the lad and finally patted his shoulder and gave a breath of a laugh and said, panting, "Steady, lad. Steady."

"Yes," Sasha said. "Lean on me."

He did that, took his balance from the boy, down to level ground where he could catch his breath, a little warmer now, despite the chill of their soaked clothing.

"Nasty place," he said, looking at the thicket which closed off everything ahead, a dead-gray and lifeless wall across their path.

Sasha said nothing.

"There's Vojvoda," Pyetr said. "You could still go back, boy. Nothing you've done's so serious. You could lie to them. You don't have to tell them about helping me—"

Sasha shook his head no.

"Well," Pyetr said, nerving himself, "it can't be far to the river. One hopes."

But bending down then, Sasha took a little of their precious grain and poured it on a rock.

"Field-thing," Sasha said. "We're leaving. Thank you."

And he stood and flung a little more, into the forest. "Forest, we're only walking through. We won't do any harm."

Pyetr shook his head. Probably, he thought, the only thing it made well-disposed to them was starving squirrels. But he added to Sasha's little offering a couple of precious grains from his own pocket, to please the boy, then flung another two or three at the thicket ahead of them and called aloud, feeling altogether like a fool:

"Forest, here come two desperate outlaws! We'll do you no harm, so do us none, and get us safely to the river!"

The wind shifted. What breathed out of the woods was colder than the meadow air.

"Small good that did," Pyetr muttered, caught his breath of that cold air, and limped ahead, saying: "Look out, devils."

"Don't joke," Sasha said. "Please don't joke, Pyetr Ilitch. Don't you *know* what they say? Forests are the worst to meddle with."

"I don't know. I don't bother with such tales. They're not healthy."

"There's leshys, for one, that have their feet on backwards. We mustn't follow tracks. There's Forest-things that sing to you and you have to follow. . . ."

"We follow the road," Pyetr said, setting his jaw. "We take nothing. We talk very politely to the devils and the Forest-things, and we keep walking and we pay no attention to singers in the trees, who are likely to be birds, if any live here."

"Deer should have eaten all the grain," Sasha said.

"Deer didn't. I'm very grateful."

"Maybe wolves got them all."

"Boy—" Pyetr began, and found breath for argument too short and too hard come by. "Then they're well-fed wolves, and we'll be safe. Be cheerful. Stop wishing up trouble."

"I'm *not*," Sasha exclaimed, indignant. "I'm *not*, Pyetr Ilitch, *you* are."

"Well, I'm not the wizard in the company, so it doesn't matter, does it?"

Sasha gave him a very worried look, as if he was not sure of that reasoning.

"There's no such thing as luck," Pyetr followed up his

46

advantage, "with certain dice. And I doubt Father Sky needs your help with his."

Sasha's mouth was open. He shut it and walked without saying anything for a long while.

A man could feel ashamed of himself, the boy was so good at heart . . . precisely the sort of person who offered himself to persons like himself, Pyetr thought, and usually, at dice or in some prank, he was only too glad to find someone of Sasha's gullible sort; but Sasha had tallied up favor after favor until a body stopped looking for the turnaround. The boy simply was more persistent in giving things away than anyone Pyetr had ever encountered in his life, that was the addition and subtraction of the matter; and Pyetr had long since passed from reckoning Sasha Vasilyevitch as clever and apt to sell him to the highest bidder, to realizing him as gullibly useful (in which realization, being a moral sort of scoundrel, Pyetr had set himself certain strict limits of that use) and finally as a person who needed a keeper and a protector, which Pyetr was nobly resolved to be, at least as far as keeping the boy from hanging.

But this morning he revised all those calculations. The boy had some wit; the boy *knew* a scoundrel when he met one: one hardly, Pyetr reasoned now, worked at The Cockerel for ten years without knowing the breed. Certainly Sasha must have realized by now that his dear aunt and uncle were scoundrels, else he would be running back to The Cockerel; but Sasha, taking all that aside, had suddenly taken advantage of his pain-muddled wits to appoint himself the protector and Pyetr Ilitch Kochevikov the fool who needed looking after.

Pyetr could hardly understand how this had happened to him; and he had the most uneasy thought that perhaps he should come full circle, and conclude that the boy had in mind some nefarious scheme of his own—

Except the boy had every mark of the gullible.

It was all bewildering, and entirely seductive—considering Pyetr Ilitch remembered his father explaining there were two sorts of people in the world, those who lived by wit and those who lived on luck; and followed that by showing him what luck was worth with loaded dice. . . .

A boy had sat on a Vojvoda street corner once upon a time,

47

and watching a mother coddle a child, had suffered a certain pang of curiosity, which of them was gullible and whether either of them was a fool—

A boy had watched a father showing his son woodworking once, had seen the skill change hands and wondered if the father would deliberately hold back some things to stay better than his son—but perhaps, too, he had thought, the son was clever enough to spy out the things the father would not willingly pass on—

A young man had thought once that the right friends would make him rich and happy, and as far as fools went, that one was the worst, young Sasha was quite right to pity him.

Besides, his side hurt and his head ached, because this particular fool had also thought himself so handsome no lady could ever think of anything beyond him.

All in all, Sasha Vasilyevitch seemed to have very little need of him, and still kept on being kind to him, and this absolute persistence, while it looked altogether like stupidity or villainy, did not agree on the one hand with Sasha's competency in certain things; and on the other with Sasha's tenderheartedness.

All in all, it was too much to think about with his head throbbing and his side aching with every step. Perhaps he had fallen in with a precocious lad who sincerely knew he needed a scoundrel and a gambler to protect him (which he was not doing outstandingly well, but leave that aside)—or, most incredible, with a poor boy so taken in by his manners that the lad cultivated him as a gentleman of potential help to him.

I think you mistake me, Pyetr would say if Pyetr were totally a fool. —You must have mistaken me for an honest man, Sasha Vasilyevitch.

—Except he can surely see what I am. We hardly met under the best of circumstances.

—So why, then, be a fool? Pyetr thought as they walked beneath the dry, laced branches. Mind your manners, Pyetr Kochevikov! The lad's half-mad, so give him his fairyfolk and don't torment him with the truth. He's over all kinder than sane folk know how to be.

—And somewhere, when we're through this—when we

reach Kiev, and civilized men, I should teach him to protect himself.

At least . . . from other, less scrupulous scoundrels.

The sun lent them some comfort in the morning, but the road descended by afternoon into the very depths of the winter-barren forest, where branches raked and closed about the road, where the trees eventually locked their branches overhead and turned day to dusk.

"Eat," Sasha insisted, while they were resting on a fallen log in a little spot of sun, and while they had water from a little ghost of a brook to wash down the grain they had. He gave Pyetr the most of what he had gathered; and after a little selfish consideration on the matter, and knowing how cold the wind was: "Here. Put on my coat again. . . ."

Because he grew more and more worried about Pyetr, about the tremor in Pyetr's hands and the paleness of Pyetr's skin and the listlessness which took him from time to time. Aunt Ilenka would say that a healing man needed proper food and a warm bed to rest in; and there was nothing of the sort in his power to produce, nor looked to be, and Sasha felt—he could not help it—that if aunt Ilenka was in the habit of blaming him for everything that happened in The Cockerel, Pyetr should surely have a heavy claim to lodge against him—counting that, if not for bad luck, Mischa and a mud puddle, Pyetr might have left The Cockerel more rested, warmly dressed, and better-provisioned. But Pyetr insisted not to blame him for his misfortunes, and gave him a grateful clench-jawed nod for the loan of the coat.

Which touched Sasha in a strange way—the more so because Pyetr himself seemed to realize his danger from the cold, but had never asked him for the coat; and because he might truly *be* responsible for Pyetr's condition, if only for failing to snatch up the blankets, and Pyetr had never once cursed him or blamed him for it. Pyetr's only word on it was a gibe or two about his luck when he rallied, foolhardy jokes that worried him more than they stung—and worried him most for Pyetr, who, weak as he was, challenged far more than the sweep of aunt Ilenka's broom or the sturdiness of uncle Fedya's porch, and dared far less patient things than the lazy Old Man of The Cockerel's stable.

Certainly, Sasha thought, if he might be responsible for Pyetr's bad luck, he also must be responsible for things nature had not equipped Pyetr Ilitch to feel or see—since perhaps the Field-thing heard Pyetr Ilitch no better than Pyetr Ilitch heard the Field-thing; and no better than Pyetr Ilitch felt the chill in these woods which had nothing to do with the remaining snowbanks; and no more than Pyetr Ilitch understood that, by all the talk that drifted around The Cockerel's kitchen hearthside—eastward was not a good direction to travel.

"I've heard," Sasha said while they rested on that fallen log, at that stream side, "—I've heard there used to be farms this way. I've heard there used to be travelers and towns and all, but things stopped coming from the east, and the bandits set in, and the tsar built the south road because it was just too hard to do anything about the bandits."

"You've heard," Pyetr said hoarsely, and dipped a hand in the icy water and washed his face with it before he worked himself, grimacing and biting his lip, into the coat. "Let me tell you about Kiev, boy. There's towers tall as mountains, with gold on the roof ridges. Have you heard that? The river goes down to the warm sea, where there are crocodiles."

"What's a crocodile?"

"A kind of dragon," Pyetr said. "A dragon with teeth like spears and armor on his sides. He weeps tears of pearls."

"Pearls!"

"So they say."

"You don't even believe in banniks! How can a dragon cry pearls?"

He should not have asked. Pyetr thought about that a moment, and his cheerfulness faded and he looked harrowed and wan. "Truthfully," he said, hard-breathing from his struggle with the coat, "I doubt the dragons. But the Great Tsar lives there. That much I know is true. The Tsar of Kiev is rich, his boyars are rich, and rich folk shed gold coins like birds in moult, never miss it, never care. That's what I've heard. All the gold there is comes sooner or later to Kiev. So there has to be a little of it for you and me."

Pyetr's eyes brightened when he talked about the gold. And

he had said *you and me,* which nobody had ever said in Sasha's memory—*you and me* was much rarer and much more desirable, in Sasha's reckoning, than pearl-weeping crocodiles. Pyetr doubted the Field-thing; Sasha doubted Kiev and the gold-capped towers; but *you and me* was precious here and now.

For the rest, Sasha knew his luck, and hourly watched it fade—

Yes, he said to make Pyetr happy. Yes, I want to see that, yes, of course I believe in Kiev.

Mostly he believed that they were lost, and that if they went back to Vojvoda the tsar's men would hang Pyetr and perhaps hang both of them; but if they went on there was no food in this woods and there was no hope either.

When we get to Kiev, Pyetr would say as they walked that afternoon; and told him about elephants with snakes for hands, and the great roc that laid eggs for the king of the Indee.

Truer than the bannik, Pyetr said with a wink, and shortly after that, hurt himself with a catch of his toe in a root and took a terrible stitch in his side.

"I'm all right," he said after that, white and shaking; and would not let Sasha open the coat to see his bandages. "Let be," he said, waving him off. "Let be."

But the pallor did not go away and Pyetr did not joke after that, or tell him stories while they walked.

The bed they had this night was a pile of rotten leaves next an old log, on an evening so chill breath frosted in the twilight, and Sasha tried, with rubbing sticks over tinder and with the most earnest attempt at a spell he had ever tried in his life, to wish a fire into life; but he only overheated himself and blistered his hands and got not so much as a curl of smoke.

Perhaps, he thought, the wood was too damp, even the driest he could find; or perhaps it was because in his heart of hearts he knew that fire was the one spell he most feared, fire had killed his parents, fire was his curse and his worst luck, and he was direly afraid of it, even as desperate as they were.

"I'm sorry," he said, panting, and Pyetr said:

"Boy, stop, your hands are bleeding. You'll get nowhere."

At least he was warm. He had that to lend. They shared the coat. Pyetr avowed he was not in so much misery this night, and that he would be better in the morning; perhaps, Pyetr said, they would get up early, and walk in the last of the night, when it was coldest, and sleep during the day, hereafter, when it was warmest.

But the last of the night seemed the only sleep Pyetr had gotten, and the road was tangled, and it seemed to Sasha the height of folly to go walking by dark, when they might lose the road and with it, whatever hope they had.

So he said nothing; and Pyetr said nothing the next morning about their being late on their way. Pyetr took a long time getting on his feet, sweated when he had done so and remarked that the morning was warmer than the last, when in fact Sasha felt no such thing and saw their breath frosting in the dawn.

Increasingly Sasha had a feeling of doom and disaster in their circumstances, while Pyetr once again began to talk disjointedly about Kiev, about the Great Tsar's court, about elephants and rocs, and golden roofs and how his father had seen the tsar once, and how his father had been a trader's son, and his grandfather had come out of the great east with a caravan; but of a mother Pyetr never spoke and Sasha finally asked:

"Had you no aunt or anything?"

"No," Pyetr said lightly, lying, Sasha was sure. "I didn't need one. My father got me in a dice-game."

"That can't be so."

"Ah," Pyetr laughed, but thinly, hard-breathing as they walked along the way. "The lad knows something, at least. Had you ever a lover, boy?"

"No."

"Not even a stray thought, yet?"

"No." It was embarrassing. It made him sound the fool. "There just weren't so many people." That was hardly right either. The Cockerel was full of neighbors. "At least—not my age."

"No girls."

"No girls."

"There's the tanner's daughter—Masha. . . ."

He felt his face burn, and supposed that Pyetr and his friends had scouted all the town.

"Or the brewer's girl," Pyetr said. "—Katya, isn't it? With the freckles?"

"No," he said miserably.

"Not one."

"No, Pyetr Ilitch."

"No wizardess, eh?"

"No," Sasha said, shortly this time. "What girl would have my luck?"

"Ah," Pyetr said, with a sudden little frown, as if the whole matter were news to him. And Pyetr nudged him suddenly with his elbow. "But if you had money, you could have a curse and warts and you'd have every father in Vojvoda pushing his daughter at you. And one sees no sign of warts."

The warmth stayed in Sasha's face. He knew it was red and he was glad of the forest shadow.

"The girls in Kiev," Pyetr said, and stopped, and put his hand on a tree trunk, saying nothing for a while, while Sasha stood there helplessly. "Damn!" Pyetr breathed finally.

"Pyetr, let me look at it. Let me see if I can do anything."

"No!" Pyetr said; and more quietly, on a second breath: "No. I'll be better—it's just a stitch. They come and they go."

Sasha had a terrible cold feeling of a sudden, not in the night this time, when things were always unreasonable, but by plain daylight, and all Pyetr's jokes had no power to dispel it.

"Let me see the bandages," he said. "Pyetr, please."

"No."

"Don't be a fool. Please let me help you."

"It's all right, dammit, let me alone!" Pyetr shoved away from the tree, walked again with his sword for a cane, not the Pyetr who had defied aunt Ilenka with a flaunt of his cap, but a tired, hurting man with his shoulders hunched and his steps short and unsteady.

Please the god, Sasha thought, and wished Pyetr Ilitch well with all the strength he had, for once completely sure of what he wanted and with no doubt in him that it was right to wish.

And perhaps Pyetr was right and he was only a silly fool, because it did not seem Pyetr was any the better for it, not immediately and not for hours afterward. The only thing that could be said was that Pyetr stayed on his feet, walking slowly, and that Pyetr seemed to have no more such pangs, but Sasha had not the least idea whether that was a good sign or bad.

He could not make fire, he could not find so much as a minnow in the ice-filmed brooks they met, he found few berries and not a fluff of fur or a feather of any game in these woods.

Everything was dead. It was that time when the winter died, and much else did, and spring was not yet alive; it was the month for ghosts to walk and the sick and the old to die, and for ill luck and unseasonable storms and for fevers to set in and aches to find old wounds: that was what the townsfolk always said; and the last night before the turn toward spring, the townswomen would go out and unbraid their hair and shake out the knots from their belts and their laces and plow a trench about the walls of Vojvoda, beating on drums and calling on the Lady, at which time every male creature took cover and stayed there till dawn; excepting wizards, who were exempt, and who also beat on drums and spoke to the gods and the friendly spirits to guard the sick in this terrible season.

But Pyetr had only a borrowed coat and a boy with notoriously bad luck, and if there was a place in the land unblessed it was this forest, which, far from having the outlaws and the wild beasts they had feared, had only dead trees and dying bushes, barren ground and lifeless brooks.

If there was even a Forest-thing here, Sasha could not feel it; and secretly that night he took a few berries and a few grains and put them on a dead leaf and said, beneath his breath, while Pyetr was washing, "Please don't let us be misled. Please don't let Pyetr stumble, it hurts him. Please get us to some friendly place."

It seemed too little an offering to appease a remote and unhearing spirit, which might well be hostile or itself as unhealthy as its forest. So Sasha took a thorn and pricked his finger and squeezed out the blood until it fell in heavy drops. He had heard of sorcerers doing the like. He had heard of terrible things that could go wrong, once blood was in an offering, how there were things that liked it all too well.

"What in the god's name are you doing?" Pyetr asked him, from the stream side where they had stopped to rest, and he was afraid Pyetr would say something to offend the spirits of the place, so he said, desperately,

"Looking for roots."

"You're not likely to find any," Pyetr said cheerlessly, in the same moment that Sasha realized that he had just lied at the very worst of times; and that if he had called the wrong thing to hear him there was all too much blood in their company.

Jinx, he thought, accusing himself. —Oh, Father Sky, keep wrong things away from us. Pyetr never meant to hurt anybody. Pyetr doesn't deserve this trouble.

But Father Sky was not a god to trouble himself often, especially not for scoundrels and fugitives in trouble, and it was too much to expect that Father Sky would save a fool from his folly, for whatever it was worth.

6

✠ ✠ ✠ ✠ Pyetr slept, at least, laid his aching head down on his arm and waked in the morning in somewhat less pain than he had been feeling. That encouraged him for a moment, until he heard the crack of thunder and saw the forbidding gray of the sky.

"Damn," he said, and shut his eyes again, not wanting to move, not believing any longer in anything. Kiev was a dream. Like dreams, it was for people more fortunate. What Pyetr Kochevikov got was a cold bed on cold ground in an endless forest and both he and the boy he was with starving to death in a very stupid series of mistakes.

Mistake to have come this way. Mistake to have hoped, mistake to have expected, mistake to have left the fields at all. Hanging was better than this. Surely it was better than this.

A raindrop hit him in the face. Another did.

"Father Sky," Sasha said, on his knees, desperate. "Don't do this."

"Father Sky isn't listening," Pyetr said in a voice more ragged than he had thought. "Father Sky was drinking late last night and he's in a rotten mood."

"Please don't do that!"

The boy was scared as he was. The boy believed in banniks and Forest-things and they had proved as treacherous as the thunder-rolling heavens.

The boy came and helped him to his feet and found his sword for his hand while the chill rain came spatting down through the branches and pattering against the leaves.

The boy found a berrybush while they were walking in the

56

drizzle and the thorns raked him cruelly while he gathered the winter-old black fruit. Blood ran in the rain spatters on the backs of his hands.

"Breakfast," Sasha said, and Pyetr took a handful and tried to eat, but his throat hurt when the tart flavor ran down, and he had no appetite for it. He felt warm this morning despite the drizzle that slicked the branches and turned the leaf mold treacherous. "Take the coat a while," he said. "I'm warm from walking."

But the boy would not. "So am I," he said; but Pyetr knew he was lying.

He slipped once. It should have hurt. He caught himself, pain-free, giddy with relief. He made a flourish of his hand past Sasha's white, frightened face, laughed at the heavens and said,

"Let it rain. Father Sky missed us with his lightnings. He's having a tantrum. Rich men are like that."

"Be careful," Sasha begged him; and tried to take his arm, but he flung off Sasha's hand and walked down the slope, slid to a stop in a clear space and looked up into the rain, blinking stupidly at the drops.

"Pyetr!"

"Old Father," Pyetr called out, holding up his hand. "One more chance! Best shot!"

"Pyetr!" Sasha came running down and slipped, himself, to one knee.

Pyetr shrugged and spread his arms. "No thunder, even. The old fellow's shot his bolts. He's an old householder. He's thrown all his pots and his brickbats. Now he's just down to complaining." He shook his head and watched Sasha get to his feet again, then turned and walked on the way the forest gave them, perhaps the road, or not the road, one could lose it now and never know. It was a ghost, a dream, like distant Kiev.

False, like the promise of gold.

Dangerous, like the warmth that protected him against the rain, that made him think he had no need of the coat. He walked with white daylight coming through the branches and once found himself on his knees, with the boy shaking his wrist and telling him he had to get up, he had to walk. The

57

day passed in memories of branches, of leaf-strewn slopes, of bleak dead trees and the boy, always the boy with him, saying, "Pyetr, Pyetr, come on, you've got to keep going—"

And himself saying finally, in the hoarse voice remaining to him, "I'm too tired. I'm too tired, boy," because suddenly he was, and his head was hurting, and the whole world seemed one never-ending muddle of branches. All the places in this forest had become cruelly the same, one tree and another, one leafy bank and another, one dimly lit stream and another, and the pain was threatening again, less from his side than from his skull. That was what the fall had jolted, and he found himself near blinded.

"Listen," he said, "this is foolish. It's near dark."

"Get up," Sasha said. "Please, Pyetr Ilitch—it's smoke, don't you smell it?"

He could smell nothing, with his nose running and his throat so raw. The boy was lying: he was sure that Sasha was lying, only to make him walk.

But he walked, with Sasha holding him up on one side, guiding his wandering steps. They were on clear road again, more leaf-strewn ground among dead trees the bark of which was peeling as if they had died years ago.

And so desperate he was that he could imagine the smell of smoke, and that he could imagine among the dry trees a clear, wind-swept road ahead, and then a gray board shed, a fence, and a gray, ramshackle house, spotted with lichen and bearded with moss like the trees that concealed it.

He stopped, winced with the boy pulling at him, and gripped Sasha's shoulder. "Speak of bandits—"

"What else can we do? Where else can we go for help?"

Pyetr leaned on his sword and tried to take his arm from Sasha's shoulder—truth to tell, he had no idea why he was a fool. It only seemed sensible which of them should walk up to that door. But he wobbled badly, and Sasha held on to him and half-carried him down the road, the two of them weaving in their steps. The gray boards and the gray trees blurred together in the twilight as if the barren limbs had grown to the house or the house had grown and died and weathered with the trees.

The closed shutters showed no light. The porch posts

leaned, mere gray wood spotted with lichen; the yard was grown up in weeds, slanting down toward more of the forest.

But beyond those trees, they could see from the front gate, was the river, a landing, a bell post, and a boat as decrepit as the house.

"God," Pyetr said in a painful whisper, "it's a ferryman's house. It's an old ferry. We've come back to the road again."

Pyetr thought about bandits as they passed the gate and walked a bare dirt path that showed usage, headed for the long wooden walk-up to the porch. He thought of the chance of them being murdered, he thought of the terrible things that could happen to both of them, while he leaned against the wall by the door and listened to the boy batter away with his knocking.

"No one's home," Sasha said in a voice which had begun to be as hoarse and as desperate as his own.

Pyetr passed a glance up where the latchstring came down. "Evidently they don't mind visitors," he said, "and it's no time for niceties. Probably the ferryman's in back somewhere. Just pull the string. We'll invite ourselves. Country manners."

Sasha pulled the string. The bar came up inside, and the door swung in when he pushed it.

"Hello?" Sasha called out, for fear of startling someone sleeping and perhaps a little deaf. He stood there in the doorway, looking about him at the firelit shelves and the bed and the table and the general clutter of small pots and herb bunches and bits of rope and tackle, all casting shadows from the small fire in the hearth. Warmth and the smell of food gusted out at them. "Hello, anyone? We're looking for hospitality."

"Or whatever we can get," Pyetr muttered at his shoulder, and pushed him across the threshold, himself in no good way to stand. Sasha flung an arm about his left and helped him across to the warmest place in the cottage, the hearthside, where someone's supper simmered in an iron pot.

It smelled like fish stew. It smelled wonderful. Pyetr was intent only on sitting down there on the warm stones, but Sasha swung the pothook out a little to put his finger in and taste a little. It was indeed fish stew, with turnips.

Pyetr rested back against the fireside with a groan and leaned his head back, saying, "All I own for a drink, boy. Do you find any?"

Sasha felt a pang of doubt about that—kitchen-nipping being a sin of one magnitude and searching the house like a burglar being quite another.

But Pyetr's condition was excuse enough for pilferage, he was sure. He filled the washing bowl from the water barrel by the door and washed the dirt off his own hands, spattering little pockmarks into the old dirt on the board floor. There was no cloth to dry his hands, and he wiped them finally on his muddy shirt, hearing in his imagination aunt Ilenka's stinging complaint of this cottage, its debris, its dust—

But it was wonderful. It was with its rustic clutter rich as a tsar's palace in terms of things they needed; and he laid eyes on a bowl and took it back to the fireside, dipping up a little of the stew for Pyetr, and kneeling to put it into his hands.

"I'm looking for the drink," he said. "Eat what you can."

He thought then that if he was borrowing stew for two people, he ought to add a bit to it, so he pulled down a couple more large turnips from the strings, found a knife on the table and diced them up fine, added a bit more water, a little bit of salt—a touch of dillweed and savory were what it wanted, he decided, after one and the next tastings that amounted to several mouthfuls.

He found the dill hanging in a bunch from a rafter, crushed it in his hands and tossed it in and stirred it; and took a bowl for himself before he swung the hook back full over the fire to boil.

Pyetr had finished his, down to scouring the bowl and licking his finger; and Pyetr said, wistfully, "Can you find that drink at all?"

"I don't know." Sasha set his stew down on the hearth and investigated jugs one after the other, staggering, he was so tired, and afraid he might crack one, his hands were so unsteady. He found mostly oils of various sort, and once something that made him sneeze; he was anxious about meddling with things that smelled more like poisons than cooking oil. Untidy housekeeping, he reasoned to himself; simples; poisons to kill vermin: The Cockerel's shed held such things.

Aunt would never approve them in the house; but, then, The Cockerel had too many hands in the kitchen to be proof against mistakes.

He found the trap in the floor, a cellar as dark and cellar-smelling as he feared it would be as he got down on his knees and gingerly peered inside. He could see nothing but the wooden steps, the wooden floor below, the hint of jars along the wall, hanging bits of rope and such. . . .

It was plainly thievery he was contemplating; and there were warders in a house, no matter what Pyetr believed. The hair prickled on his nape as he eased his way down the narrow steps into the damp, cool air, only five or so steps down into the musty dark, a short search of the shelves down below. He found jugs of likely shape, took one into his arms, unstopped and sniffed it.

Indeed. No doubt about this one. No poison and no noxious oil.

He *heard* something then on the far side of the cellar, a small scratching that might be vermin.

He did not fly up the steps; he was calm and brave and quietly whispered, reasoning with himself that no House-thing was going to object to a jug of vodka if it had not objected to the door opening:

"Please excuse me. My friend really does need it. We're not thieves."

He poured a little on the floor for the House-thing, if it was listening. Then he scrambled up the steps and let the trap down gently, his heart thumping with fright.

He felt the fool, then. Talking to rats, Pyetr would say— he wished Pyetr would say, and show some liveliness; but Pyetr looked much beyond jokes at the moment, his dirty, stubbled face lined with pain and patience.

"I'm hurrying," Sasha said. He found a bowl on the kitchen table and poured, and brought it to Pyetr; he spied a pile of quilts in the corner by the bed and brought them to Pyetr too, heaping them around him against the warm stones while Pyetr drank, cupping the bowl in dirty, bloody hands and looking so weak and so miserable—as if Pyetr was suddenly beginning to sink, the way sick people would when their strength ran out and fever set in.

Someone had to do something soon, he thought. He had doctored horses enough to know that, but the thought of dealing with a wound going bad all but turned his stomach. He hoped for the ferryman returning, hoped he would know better what to do; but at least he could have hot water ready for compresses, and if there was only wormwood and sweet oil somewhere in the house that was a start on things.

So he put water to heat on a second pothook, and sat down a moment with his bowl of cooling stew—not even his sore throat and the prospect in front of him could discourage him from that. Pyetr at least seemed happier and more comfortable, placidly watching him.

But Pyetr looked to be in pain for a moment. Sasha watched him, the spoon in midair. Pyetr said, "It's all right." And extraneously, a line between his brows: "What's in the cellar?"

"I don't know, stuff. Jars. Turnips." He almost said, rats; he wanted something to distract Pyetr from his misery, which was what he thought Pyetr wanted. He was afraid, making light of things: it went against his nature. He made the effort, nonetheless. "Something went bump. I came up."

"I thought you did," Pyetr said muzzily, and the line left his brow, as if he had been worrying about his quick run up the steps, but, then, he was a little drunk. "Not the owner, then."

"No," Sasha assured him, waiting for Pyetr to make some gibe about bogles, but the line came back to Pyetr's brow and Pyetr's lips made a white line.

That finished Sasha's appetite. "I've got some water warming," he said. "Want to wash?"

Pyetr seemed to agree with that. Sasha got up and got a cloth and soaked it for Pyetr to wash his face and hands. And carefully then, delicately, Pyetr not objecting, he worked Pyetr's coat loose.

Blood soaked the shirt beneath it, repeated old stains and a large, bright new one.

"Wounds do that," Pyetr said confidently. But Pyetr looked both sick and worried at the sight of it.

"Another drink?" Sasha asked.

Pyetr nodded. Sasha fetched him one, and Pyetr sipped at

it slowly, resting his head back against the stones while Sasha untied his belt, pulled up his shirt beneath his arms, and tried to work the bandaging loose.

"Ow!" Pyetr gasped suddenly, and drink slopped from the bowl onto his stomach and rolled down; some had spilled on the bandaging. "Oh, god," Pyetr moaned, while it soaked in, "oh, god—" He went white then and all but fainted against the fireside stones. He could not hold the bowl any longer. Sasha took it from his hand and Pyetr sank back against the wad of quilts, broken out in sweat.

Sasha's own hands were shaking. It was a worse wound than anything the horses had ever done to themselves. It was far worse than he knew how to deal with, and he knew absolutely nothing other to do than to soak the bandage free.

"A little tender," Pyetr gasped, between breaths. "Just let it alone tonight. Morning's soon enough."

"It's going bad," Sasha said, shivering despite the fire beside him.

"Wounds always get a little fever. It means it's healing."

"Not with the horses," Sasha said. "I'd soak it in warm water and pack it with herbs."

Pyetr shook his head. "We don't know who owns that pot of stew. If you go at that again I won't be fit for anything, and I don't think that's—"

Someone was walking outside. Someone slowly stumped up the log walk and Sasha's heart began to beat with a heavy thump-thump-thump as Pyetr groped after his sword. "Get me on my feet," Pyetr said, and Sasha, finding no other protection for them, put his shoulder under Pyetr's good side and heaved, desperately, while Pyetr flailed out after the stonework and got a grip on the mantle.

The bar lifted, the door swung back, and a skinny, thin-bearded old man in a ragged cloak stopped still in the open doorway, firelit against the dark.

"Bandits!" the old man said, indignant. "Thieves!" He had a scowl like a carved devil's, and he had a stout staff in his hand which he showed every disposition and capability of using.

"No!" Sasha cried, holding Pyetr by the arm half for fear of Pyetr using that sword and half because he was all that was holding Pyetr on his feet. "Please, sir! We're not thieves. My friend is hurt."

The old man shifted his grip on his staff and glared at them—one eye seeming better than the other, those hands on the staff gnarled with age but strong enough, with two sharp butt-end blows, to do for a boy and do terrible damage to a man in Pyetr's condition.

"Drop the sword!" the old man ordered, staff poised. "Drop it!"

"I think we'd better," Sasha pleaded with Pyetr, whose weight was heavy on his shoulder. "Pyetr, it's his house, we've nowhere to go, do what he says!"

"Drop it!" the old man said again, and angled the butt of the staff perilously toward two unprotected skulls, while Pyetr ebbed slowly, helplessly toward the floor, banging his head on the stones of the fireplace as he sank.

Quite, quite unconscious.

Sasha let him to the quilts and looked up at the old man, past the butt of a staff that trembled a scant arm's length from his face. "Sir," he said, trying not to let his teeth chatter, "my name is Alexander Vasilyevitch Misurov. This is Pyetr Ilitch Kochevikov, from Vojvoda. We're not thieves. Pyetr's hurt. We were coming through the forest—"

"No one honest comes through the forest."

"We ran away!"

"At his age." The staff made a threatening jab. "Tell the truth."

"He was in love with a lady and the lady told lies about him and her husband stabbed him; and I helped him get away."

"And steal my food and my blankets and make free of my house!"

"Money," Pyetr murmured, with a weak move of his hand. "I've money. Give it to him."

"Money! What's to buy here? Do you see anybody? I fish the river and I break my back in my garden and you offer me money!" He poked Sasha's shoulder with the staff, poked it twice with an attitude that reminded Sasha most uncomfortably of a wife at the town market. "On the other hand—" The staff lowered, thumped against the floor, and Sasha glanced from that point of impact up to the old man's face, thinking he had never seen a grin like that except on a carved wolf, or eyes like that except on painted devils.

"On the other hand—you don't have the look of thieves."

"No, sir. I promise you."

"Do you know how to work, boy?"

"Yes, sir," Sasha said on a breath. It sounded like a bargain, it sounded like food and shelter and of a sudden he had at least a small hope for them both.

Except he did not like the old man taking hold of his arm and pulling him up to his feet, or staring him in the eyes until he had the feeling he could not look away. The old man's fingers were strong. His eyes were watery and dark and they let nothing go that they examined.

"Do you follow instructions, boy?"

"Yes, sir."

Pyetr tried to sit up, and the staff came down, clang! on the sword Pyetr reached for at their feet.

Sasha dropped to his knees between that stick and Pyetr's skull; and stayed there, his heart pounding.

But of a sudden the fire hissed, stew boiling over apace.

"Get that!" the old man said. "Fool!" And Sasha jumped for it, wrapped his sleeve over his palm and pulled the pothook around to rescue the stew from the heat, as the old man collected Pyetr's sword from under the heel of his staff, took it across the room and swept the scraps of the turnips from the table with the sword edge.

"I see. You eat my supper, you steal my stores—"

"I only added more turnips, sir, it seemed with two more of us—"

"I'll have my supper," the old man said, kicked the bench up to the table, set his staff and Pyetr's sword against the wall, and thumped the table between them with his bony knuckles. "Boy!"

"He's crazy," Pyetr whispered, trying without success to push himself up against the stones. "Be careful."

"Boy!"

Sasha grabbed a bowl from the untidy stack, grabbed up the ladle and filled it full from the pot, brought it and a spoon to the old man, and while he ate, poured him a little drink into a second bowl.

"Knew where *that* was, did you?" the old man snarled. "Thief!"

"I beg your pardon, sir." Sasha made a nervous little bow, and stood with his hands behind him while the old man took a sip.

The old man's wispy eyebrows lifted a little and came down again. "What did you do to this?"

"Salt, sir. Just salt. A little dill. It—" But it seemed presumptuous to say it had needed it. Sasha shut his mouth and bit his lips.

The eyebrows moved again, not in so profound a frown this time. The old man took another and a third spoonful and seemed quite pleased with it. He had a drink, a fourth spoonful, and finally he picked up the bowl and drank it dry, leaving pale drops on his wispy beard.

"Another," he said, thrusting the bowl toward Sasha's hands.

Sasha filled it again; and the old man took his spoon to it.

"Walked clear from Vojvoda," the old man said without looking up.

"Yes, sir."

"Him too."

"Yes, sir."

"Stabbed in Vojvoda."

"Yes, sir."

"Stubborn fellow."

"Yes, sir."

The old man let his fist fall onto the table. "My name is Uulamets. Ilya Uulamets. This is my house. This is my land. Only my word counts here."

"Yes, sir."

"I take it you want your friend taken care of."

"Yes, sir."

"Food, doctoring, that kind of thing."

"Yes, sir— If you can, sir." Sasha was at once hopeful and very uneasy. It was much too fortunate. "Do you know doctoring? I'm good with horses, I—"

The old man rapped on the table, and took another spoonful. "Doctoring, herbs, what you like, boy, trust me I know what I'm doing. But there's a fee for my services. There's a fee for what you eat and what your friend eats, supposing he survives. There's a fee for my blankets and my fire and the nuisance he poses me. *You* I have use for. Shut up," he said, the instant Sasha opened his mouth. "Do as you're told and don't be a bother to me or I'll turn you both out in the cold and the drizzle, and how will your friend fare *then*, hmmm?— How do you think he'd fare? —Die, wouldn't he? —Would you like that?"

"No, sir," he said, and swallowed at a lump in his throat.

"Keep that crazy man away from me," Pyetr called out from the fireside behind him. "Let me alone. I don't need his help."

"Please don't listen to him," Sasha said. "He's fevered. He's been fevered for days."

"I don't need his help!" Pyetr shouted, and made to get up.

"Excuse me," Sasha said with a hurried bow and ran and laid hands on Pyetr only in time to keep him from hurting himself. "Please," he whispered, "please, Pyetr, don't—"

"That old man's crazy," Pyetr whispered furiously. "Keep him away from me, that's all, I'm all right—"

"I'll watch him," he said, but Pyetr just leaned the shoulder of his bad side against the stonework and said,

"He's not touching me."

While the old man, Uulamets, slopped more vodka into his bowl and got up from his bench and rummaged on a nearby shelf, found a bottle and poured a blackish liquid into the same bowl—medicine, as Sasha supposed, watching the old man bring it toward them.

"I'm not drinking that," Pyetr said.

"This is for the pain," Uulamets said. "There *will* be pain." He made then as if to pour it on the floor, and Sasha sprang up with a cry and righted the bowl, which Uulamets let him have.

"Please," Sasha said to Pyetr, kneeling down again, offering it. "Please drink it." —Because there was nothing else to do and no one else to ask and no other hope but the old man's medicines, with the fever starting to set into the wound. "You'll die, else."

Pyetr frowned, reached after the cup of black stuff. He

tossed it off in a single mouthful and gave a sudden shudder, as if it tasted as bad as it looked, then glanced around where Uulamets was clattering about in a cupboard, with a rattle of knives.

"What's he doing?" Pyetr asked. "Boy—what's he after?"

Sasha did not want to answer. He saw what Uulamets was taking from the cupboard, the array of knives and bowls and pots and boxes, and he felt Pyetr sinking against his arm and heard him saying, "Stop him, boy, for god's sake, don't let him cut on me—"

But one had to, sometimes, horse-doctoring, Sasha understood that. He held on to Pyetr as carefully as he could until Pyetr's head dropped and Pyetr went half-dazed, he laid him out and helped Uulamets cut away the bandages.

"They're stuck, sir," he said, wiping his nose quickly on his sleeve. "Please, be careful."

"Do you tell me my business? Boil water. Hot! Make yourself useful."

"Yes, sir," he said, shoved the hook with the water pot back over the fire and was quickly back to be sure Uulamets was doing nothing crazy.

"Front and back?" Uulamets asked. "It went entirely through?"

"Yes, sir?"

"Sword?"

"I think so, sir."

The old man muttered to himself, and pressed, and Pyetr screamed.

"Not good," the old man said, but Sasha could have told that for himself. Uulamets soaked a bit of moss with oil and set it on the remaining square of bandages, got up and poured more vodka into a bowl.

And drank it, sip by sip, while he selected this and that from the cupboards.

Sasha dared not a word, only folded Pyetr's limp hand in his and sniffed and mopped his running nose and shivered, despite the fire, despite the old man's promises.

It was bad, he knew that it would be when Uulamets came back to lift the bandage off; he wanted to shut his eyes, but he had told Pyetr he would not.

7

✠ ✠ ✠ ✠ There was terrible pain. Somehow Pyetr
had lost his way in the forest and fallen in
with devils and leshys, most of whom had old friends' faces
and one of whom looked like a horse and another a black and
white cat.

Finally he was in a dark hovel by a fireside, and a terrible
old man was singing at him, not singing *to* him, but *at* him,
and leaning forward to blow smoke into his face from a bone
pipe.

He coughed. He stared in horror at this painted apparition,
lit in fire, and in the way of all nightmares saw Sasha Misurov's face hanging in the smoke, firelit and malevolent in its
presence, while the song buzzed in his ears and the smoke
stung his throat.

He coughed again. The singing stopped. "Keep him warm,"
the old man said; and gathered up his pipe and his foul smoke
and loomed up as a shadow against the cluttered rafters.

Sasha leaned forward, strangely distorted, strangely ominous, and he could scarcely move or breathe as Sasha dragged
a quilt up to his chin and weighed him down under it. Whatever Sasha or the old man would have done there was nothing
he could do to prevent it. "Lie still," Sasha said in a voice that
buzzed in his ears. "Lie still. Everything's all right. It's all over.
You can sleep now."

He could not remember what should be over. It sounded
frightening. He saw the shadows move on the ceiling, like
scampering cats in the rafters, strange shapes like creatures
lurking and slithering and pausing again.

"I'll be here," Sasha said.

"Good," he said thickly, finding speech difficult. He was not sure whether he could trust Sasha, or at least this dream of Sasha. It looked highly unreliable, and friends had played wicked games on him too often in his life—he did not remember when or why, but it seemed to him that one had attempted his life lately, and that this place was the result of it.

"The old man is a wizard," Sasha whispered, tucking the blanket under his chin. "I know you don't believe in wizards, but he truly is. He says you would have died if you hadn't come here. He says you have to stay very quiet and not try to get up even if you feel better."

He was not sure he felt better. His head was throbbing from the smoke or from the singing, and his side was bound so tightly it felt numb. But Sasha said, "I'm going to sleep right beside you. I won't leave." It seemed that that had been the condition for some time now, and that they had wandered a very long journey under those terms.

Daylight streamed into the clutter, light in which dust danced, and Sasha lay warm and dry, a condition which argued he should be in his own room in The Cockerel. Instead he was here, in this strange, object-crowded ferryman's house, watching Uulamets fling the shutters open one after another, bang and rattle. Sasha's nose had stopped running. His throat was only a little sore, despite the days of cold.

And Pyetr was by him, stirring a little, pulling his quilts over his head—which Sasha was glad to see. He had wakened from time to time through the night to assure himself that Pyetr was alive and well; he had seen the terrible sights all over again every time he had shut his eyes and fought his way back to sleep, and now that Pyetr seemed awake enough to defend himself from the daylight, more sleep was what he would only too gladly have had—pull the covers up between himself and the light and truly rest now.

But if it were aunt Ilenka opening up the shutters, she would take a broom to a boy lying abed, no matter how hard it was for that boy to move this morning, and he had no wish to start off badly with the old man; so he got up and ran his

hands through his hair and made a respectful bow to Uulamets.

"Can I help, sir?"

"Take the bucket," Uulamets said, "go down to the river.
Fill the water-barrel. Mind you don't get sand."

"Yes, sir," he said, pulled his bloodstained, dirty coat off
the peg by the door, took the bucket and went out to do that.

It was several trips up and down the narrow track to the ferry
landing, under the arch of dead trees—a clear sunny morning
with bright edges to everything—a nip in the air, but a promise
of warmth by noon: sunlight on the broad, tree-rimmed river
that went—by everything Pyetr had sworn was true—down
to great, golden-roofed Kiev.

Once their debt to Uulamets was satisfied, Sasha thought
on his first trip downhill. Then Kiev. He tried not to think
about the debt part of it, because he knew Pyetr would be
angry with him when he knew he had bargained himself into
an agreement with the old man—a very unlimited and vague
kind of agreement, namely that he should help the old man,
and the old man had not said how long this should be or what
form this help should take—

Yes, he had said, and spoken for Pyetr, too; and Pyetr was
surely going to take exception to that. —Even if it was to pay
for Pyetr's life, Pyetr would insist there had been nothing
wrong and Uulamets was a faker like the wizards in Vojvoda—

Pyetr might be angry enough to go off to Kiev and leave
him; and *that* prospect, being left alone with the old man—

Sasha recollected smoke and fire and the terror the old man
had put into him whenever he had flinched from the old man's
orders. He opened his eyes wider to the daylight and tried to
drive that vision out of his eyes and the feeling out of his bones
that there was something terribly dangerous and sinister about
Uulamets beyond the obvious fact that he was a wizard.

The ferryman's house he was sure had never been Uulamets' proper post; no more than that boat, that very large,
age-grayed boat which rode at its moorings in the river—had
ever belonged to Uulamets . . . who therefore had *taken* this
place. The god only knew what had become of the ferryman,

or how long ago, or what the old man did here, in these woods
so dead there was not even the sign of a rabbit—

Uulamets was at work in the root cellar when Sasha came
back with the first bucket. He poured it in the barrel and went
out again, not without looking to be sure Pyetr was still safely
asleep and that nothing had happened, because he had a sudden, horrible imagination of Uulamets as a Forest-thing of
particularly malevolent sort, who might for some reason
known only to magical creatures be powerless so long as it
was the both of them; but singly, and against a sleeping man—

It was a childish kind of fear. Duck the head under the
covers and be safe from goblins. As if there was anything, he
told himself, that Uulamets could not have done last night,
when he had worked with knives—

He could not put it out of his mind, how Uulamets had
started to pour the pain-draught on the floor, with that look
of hateful satisfaction in the act—

No, not hateful. Malevolent. Hating. *Wishing* Pyetr to suffer—

Sasha hastened his steps, filled the bucket and soaked his
knee slogging uphill and up the sloping walk to the porch.

But there was nothing, when he opened the door, but old
Uulamets poring over a book at the table, in the yellow light
from the parchment windowpanes, and Pyetr still sleeping
with the covers over his head, peaceful and unmolested.

He told himself he was a fool and trekked after the third
bucketful, banishing thoughts of long-nailed demons and
Forest-things. Uulamets was a wizard, absolutely: he had
watched the color come back to Pyetr's face last night, he had
watched Uulamets hold his hands over the injury and seen
Pyetr's sweating, pain-twisted face settle slowly to ease.

No wizard in Vojvoda could do that . . . or there would be
no people hurting who could afford the cure. Everyone in town
would know it: people would flock to that wizard and make
him richer than any boyar could dream—he would be the
tsar's own physician.

Uulamets could surely go down the river to Kiev and make
his fortune with such skill—

Could he not?

Then why did he sit in this hovel, beside a ferry crossing

where no one came anymore, in a woods that had not a rabbit or a squirrel to populate it?

Bandits, he had called them.

But where were the bandits that everyone believed lived in this forest? And if they were off in some secret camp deep in the woods—how did they feed themselves with no travelers to rob and no game to hunt, except they lived as old Uulamets claimed he lived, by fishing and by gardening? That hardly seemed the life brigands would practice.

There was a rightness about the morning and a wrongness about the place which counseled Sasha he might be in greater danger than the bright sun could warn him of, and he might well, if he were wise, wish himself back in Vojvoda, carrying buckets to his ponies that he very much missed this morning, or expecting the cat to walk the rail and wish him good morning—

—all the homely, ordinary things that just were not here, in this musty, dusty place on the edge of a river that saw no boats.

He had Pyetr, without whom he did not know what he would do. The thought of being alone with the old man appalled him for reasons he could not precisely lay a name to, and he was not so naive as Pyetr accused him of being: he knew which of uncle Fedya's customers to avoid and how to give the slip to trouble.

But Uulamets, he thought, lugging the bucket the third time up the hill—but the way Uulamets looked at him with those eyes that did not let him look away, eyes that once fixing on him had made him fool enough to mumble yes when the old man asked would he pay the price he asked, not asking first what it was—

Because otherwise Pyetr would die and he would be alone here.

Pyetr could not leave without him, Pyetr could not be so cruel as that, Pyetr surely would owe him some gratitude—

—that because he was not wizard enough to heal him, he had made such a fool's bargain with one who was.

By afternoon Uulamets had put him variously to scrubbing the log walk-up and the porch (more water to carry) and mending a loose plank and a broken shutter. By afternoon Pyetr was awake, sore and very weak, but avowing himself free of pain. He took a little tea, which Uulamets prescribed, and then got up, wrapped up in his ghastly rag of a shirt, and tottered outside for necessities, with Sasha's help, scarcely steady enough to walk.

Pyetr had very little to say, except that the tea was good and that he felt better—and finally, before they reached the porch again, he said that they had best stay a couple of days before they were on their way again.

"We can't," Sasha said miserably. "—The 'be on our way again,' that is. The old man holds us to account for your doctoring."

"Well, we'll *pay* him."

"We tried that," Sasha said, realizing that Pyetr might have dropped many more things than that from his recollection of last night, and he stopped while they were still alone. "He's a wizard. He says he doesn't want money."

Pyetr laughed, a weak, desperate sound. "All wizards want money, it's what they do best."

"Not this one."

"The old man's a good herb doctor. His stuff works. We pay him a couple in silver—I've got it—and we pay for our lodging and our board and *maybe* for a passage, if we can persuade the old goat to take that boat out—"

"He's not the ferryman. I don't think there's been a ferryman here for ages. Not since the East shut down. And he won't take money, Pyetr, he's not interested."

"Well, what *does* he want?"

It was not the question Sasha wanted at the moment nor the one he knew how to answer, and he shrugged. "I think he likes my cooking. I think maybe he just wants company for a few days—" That sounded entirely lame. "Maybe just some things cleaned and fixed. I told him I would. You need to rest, and I can scrub his floors and carry his water for him, that's all he's asked so far. That surely keeps us even for room and board."

"That crazy old goat's been working you all morning, I've been awake now and again." Pyetr was white with the effort it cost him to stand, and he leaned trembling against the rail of the walk-up. "You've got yourself another uncle Fedya, he's so anxious to do you favors and have his floors scrubbed. I'd *watch* this old fellow! I don't trust him."

There was real fear in Pyetr's eyes. Sasha wondered how much of last night he *did* recall, or how much of the singing still ran through his brain.

"There *are* wizards," Sasha said. "This old man is one, I don't have any doubt about it, and it's not safe to cheat him. There's no telling what he could do."

"Damned right there's no telling what he could do! Drug our tea and carve us up for bacon is what he could do! *Listen* to me!" Pyetr seized his hand where it rested on the rail. "I don't like his look. I don't like dealing with crazy men and I don't like eating and drinking with a crazy man brewing the tea and for all we know doctoring the soup. You've never been out on your own. You don't imagine the kind of world this is and you don't imagine what kind of things people will do to each other. For the god's *sake,* boy . . . don't trust this man and don't consider yourself obligated to him for anything."

"I promised him—"

"Listen, *I'd* patch a man up if he was bleeding on my floor, boy, and *I'm* not an honest man. What did it cost him? No more work than you've given. We're even. That's all. We're quit."

"He's a wizard!" Sasha said. "Pyetr, you were dying, and he pulled you back—"

"Horsefeathers! I was tired, I was cold, I needed a bed and a meal—"

"You don't remember! I watched him do it! Look at you. You're sweating, you're white as a ghost, you couldn't have gone on another day."

"You *watched* a good show, boy, it was already scabbed over, I wasn't dying, I'm not dying this morning and I have no plans to be staying here any longer than takes me to get my wind back."

He said that. He was hardly able to go on standing.

"Get out of the wind," Sasha said. It sounded too much like an order, but he was not dealing with a sane man this morning. He tried to soften it. "Please, Pyetr Ilitch. Please be patient, please just get well and do what he asks for a few days and *don't* go off and leave me here. . . ."

Pyetr was shivering now, his teeth chattering. The cold was getting too much for him, and the shirt was hardly more than a rag. "I won't leave you here," he said. "Damn if I will. Don't promise the old goat anything. Don't let him bully you. If he makes threats, tell me."

"I promise," Sasha said. He would have said anything to silence argument and get Pyetr inside and get another cup of hot tea into him.

There were things Pyetr would understand and there were things Pyetr would refuse to understand—or to believe in, until it was too late.

Maybe he was a fool, Sasha thought; and maybe Pyetr was entirely right; but if he had ever had a danger-feeling about a thing it was this place and this man.

Pyetr's reasoning seemed sound to him, except in one thing—that it reckoned on simply walking away down the river shore; and he did not think Uulamets would allow that right now.

When he would allow it—or *if* he would allow it: that was the problem.

Uulamets put him to tidying up the cabinets and dusting before supper; and to cooking after that, which was not so bad— one could filch a little while one worked, and Sasha did learn, in dusting off the lids of the smallest pots and rearranging things, where more of the spices were—and where other things were, some of which had clay seals, and some of which had scratches in those seals he thought might be magic signs; or perhaps—because aunt Ilenka had had her marks, too, although she had no reading or writing—they might simply say what they were: things like mushrooms and moss and lichens, wormwood and what he thought was belladonna, and other things he had no idea at all.

Uulamets spent all the rest of his time reading and writing, by window light and by candle, except when he went out to the river and came back with a pair of good-sized fish, which he gave Sasha to clean; Pyetr offered his help at turnip peeling while Sasha cleaned the fish at the edge of the yard.

Of a sudden wings fluttered and cracked, and Sasha looked up in alarm as a raven settled to the ground and strutted solemnly over to pick at the offal.

It was the first bird, the first living creature he had seen in all this place except the fish they had for dinner, and by the way it looked at him, with a single black liquid eye—the other was put out—he was quite glad to feed it the offal, only so it let the fish alone.

"Be welcome," Sasha said to the creature, and it dipped its head in the way of its kind, which might have been a bow, or only an inspection of its dinner. "I don't suppose there's a flock about? A rabbit or two? A deer?"

The raven looked coldly up at him with a fish liver in its beak, and after due consideration, bolted it whole.

"Quite," Sasha said. "Too many questions. Excuse me, brother Raven."

It gulped another mouthful and regarded him again with not quite disinterest.

One did not take such a creature for ordinary, not in this forest. He was glad enough to leave it the offal and take the fish up to the house, not without a backward glance.

But it was only a fish-loving raven.

"There's a black bird down by the river," he said to Uulamets, who was still at his studies.

"He comes and he goes," Uulamets said, without looking up, so he took the fish to the boiling pot and threw it in, washed the fish-smell off his hands and took to the spice-bottles.

While Pyetr drowsed in the corner, or wisely pretended to, to evade quarrels.

The boy was a good cook, Pyetr decided, give or take the fact it was fish stew again. And he was not in a mood to complain. He had made up his mind to keep his head down and take Sasha's very sensible advice, in fact, since he was weak as a day-old kitten, and since the old man and his stick were not inconsiderable.

But he kept score, and reckoned up the tab at this irregular inn, and assessed whether there was anything valuable to be had, beyond a clean shirt and maybe a coat or a blanket or two—reckoning that Uulamets would have worked at least that out of the boy in the time it took him to heal.

In particular he kept his eye on Uulamets and the old man's access to the stewpot and the tea, this evening, in the case their kindly host decided to add to the recipe.

Uulamets sat all day long hunched over a book, following the lines with his finger—only rousing himself to give Sasha more orders.

Maybe that was all he ever did in this desolation—sit at that table all day and read that book, and set his fishing lines and cook and read that book again.

God knew what he was reading, or what could occupy him hours on end, just the occasional whisper of a turned page, about every candlemark or so.

Old man in a dead woods, reading his book till the words ate up his mind.

Except he enjoyed Sasha's cooking.

"Good," Uulamets said, tapping his spoon on the bowl. "More."

And when Sasha had filled his bowl again:

"Set one outside," the old man said.

Sasha bowed politely and went and did that—with the night and the dark out there which had once seemed halfway safe so long as they were in it; but which now, with light inside the cottage, seemed blacker than it had ever been. Pyetr watched that dark carefully, not able to figure just why the hairs were rising on his nape, but he was anxious until Sasha had (quite hastily) shut that door.

Foolish, Pyetr told himself. There was nothing different about the night than any other night.

But he spilled a little of his tea when a flurry of wings battered at the shutters.

Sasha spun around and looked at it, as if doubting the security of that window.

"What in the god's name is that?" Pyetr muttered.

"Only a bird," Uulamets said. "Just a bird."

It was surely just exactly that, Pyetr thought; and thought

that he would be just a little more confident of the honest, solid world if this damned old man had not said that: he was set to believe nothing Ilya Uulamets said, and Uulamets stole the truth and left him with this most foolish half-heartbeat of doubt what ground he was standing on.

Pigeon, perhaps. Perhaps the old man fed them and strangled them for his dinners.

"Tonight," Uulamets said, gesturing at one and the other of them with his spoon, "tonight is the full moon. I have business tonight. Roots, you understand. Digging roots." The white eyebrows lifted, and he took another spoonful of stew, smacking his lips. "I'd finish the pot. Wouldn't waste this." He set his bowl aside and rose. "Then I'd get to bed. —Would you care to come along, boy?"

"No, sir," Sasha said; and Pyetr took a quick, measuring glance toward his sword, over against the wall with Uulamets' staff.

Uulamets shrugged and took down his coat from the peg by the door.

Pyetr got up from the table, and walked over to pick up his sword and the old man's staff.

The old man held out his hand. Pyetr thrust the staff into it.

"It's boring work," Uulamets said, "—digging herbs." He lifted the latch. "Young people. They never like the working part. Just the results. My daughter was like that."

This withered old man had had a daughter? Pyetr thought to himself. Incredible. Probably with the look and disposition of a shrike.

Uulamets went out into the dark and pulled the door to. The latch fell.

Pyetr let his breath go.

"We're getting out of here," he said. "Tonight."

Sasha gave him a frightened look but he said nothing. Pyetr went over to the pegs by the door and took down the shirt that was hanging there and pulled it over his head. Sasha was still standing there as if he had no notion what to do or what to say.

"Get the quilts and some rope," Pyetr said, and when Sasha

hesitated: "Do I have to do it myself? Take down a string of turnips. The smoked fish there. It's a long way to Kiev."

"Pyetr, he's not just any old man. And he helped us!"

Pyetr glared at him.

"—At least," Sasha said faintly, "at least we don't have to take a lot. One quilt. One string of turnips. We can get by."

The boy's disapproval stung, foolhardy as it was. Pyetr stalked over to the hearth and gathered up both quilts, cursed under his breath and threw one down, pulled down a coil of light rope from one rafter, while Sasha took down a string of withered turnips from the other.

"Can you walk that far?" Sasha said, jumping down off the bench, looking his direction with concern. "Pyetr, there'll be other chances. Let's not do this. We don't know what the old man may do. . . ."

"There's nothing the matter with me. There never was. The old faker puts on a good show. He drugged me. You drank the tea. God knows what he put in it. He could make you see anything." He took the turnips and rolled them up in the quilt on the table, doubled the ends toward the center. "Take a knife. We could always use a knife."

"I won't steal!"

"It's not stealing. It's fair pay for the work you've put in. Take the knife over there. And take the fish, while you're at it. He gets them for free."

"No," Sasha said.

"Fool," Pyetr muttered, and tied the quilt at either end, with the rope for a handle. He slung it over his shoulder, took his sword from beside the table and picked up the knife himself, and took his belt and Sasha's coat from the peg. "Listen, boy, if you want to stay with him, you just do that. But if you have any sense—"

"I'm coming," Sasha said breathlessly, and Pyetr tossed the coat at him, tied his belt, lifted the latch and opened the door.

Something doglike the other side growled and snapped at them.

"God!" he cried, as it lunged.

He slammed the door so fast it hit it with a thump, barking and snarling and spitting, shoving it inward as he shoved out.

Sasha threw himself against the door and both of them pushed, while it scrabbled and snarled and hissed.

"What is that thing?" Pyetr yelled, fighting to get the bar thrown, while it jolted them and scrabbled at the wood. "What in hell is it?"

The bar went down. They leaned there panting, and heard the click of nails as it walked the porch.

It hit the window next, and scratched at the shutter. The shutter bar jumped and rattled under a sudden assault.

"My god," Pyetr said. His knees were shaking. He tried not to make that evident. He stood away from the door, drew his sword and listened while the thing abandoned its attack on that window and padded, click, click, snuffle, whuffle, back along the porch.

It tried the door again, scratching like a dog at the corner and growling.

"It's the Little Old Man," Sasha whispered.

"Man, hell! It's a damned black dog!"

"It isn't a dog. It isn't a dog, Pyetr, it knows we're stealing—"

He heard the scratching, the click of claws. Perhaps it was only a trick of haste and bad light, the way it had looked, all black hair and teeth. He tried to make a dog's shape out of his memory of those jaws, or to reconcile it with that spitting sound it made.

It did it again, and hit the door hard, so it rattled the bar.

Then more pacing. His hand sweated on the sword grip.

Something else moved, underneath the flooring.

"We should put things back," Sasha whispered.

"It's just a dog, for the god's sake!"

"It's not a dog—" Sasha unfastened his coat and hung it back on the peg by the door. He held out his hand. "Please."

A man felt like a fool. If he were not recovering from a wound—if he were not still weak, he should fling the door open and behead the ill-tempered creature.

If there was only one.

It hissed at the door crack. And gave a cat's ear-piercing shriek.

He winced.

"Pyetr!"

81

He shed the bedroll and Sasha moved quickly to untie it and to put everything back in its place, rope, turnips, quilt and all.

Another battering and scratching at the door.

"It hasn't improved its disposition," Pyetr said. "Dammit, boy, it doesn't listen to your granny-tales."

"Don't make fun, Pyetr, please! It's not to make fun of—"

"I swear to you I liked the Old Man at The Cockerel better. Pleasant cat. Scratch its ears and it behaves. This one—*God!*"

It hit the door with a force that brought him around on his guard, shaking in the knees. Its claws had to be ripping wood from the door-frame.

And something thumped under the boards beneath his feet.

He stood there with his breath coming hard and this terrible feeling that he was locked in a nightmare, that things had not made sense since they came to this house and that they might not make sense ever again.

He had no wish to be killed by a bogle in which he resolutely did not believe.

"How's your luck tonight?" he asked Sasha. "Wish that one away. It's rather well your line of work, isn't it?"

"Put the sword up," Sasha cried. "It doesn't like it. Put it up. Please put it up."

The boy was serious. So was the thing on the porch. And Pyetr had a most dreadful suspicion that tonight, this moment, nothing he knew for certain was certain at all.

"Put it up!" Sasha said.

He sheathed the sword. He walked back to the center of the room with a shrug, a swagger, and a misgiving glance at the door.

There was quiet outside.

He liked the conclusions that offered almost as little as he liked the slithering under the floor.

Sasha took the jug of vodka from the table and uncorked it, which Pyetr thought an excellent impulse.

But Sasha poured a little onto the floor, where it ran down between the cracks.

"Don't make it drunk," Pyetr said. "Haven't we got enough trouble?"

Sasha glared at him. Sasha took all this appeasing of spirits with disturbing seriousness, and the stableboy was for a moment the one of them with no doubt what he was doing.

Pyetr lifted his hands. "I apologize," he said. "I most earnestly beg its pardon."

There was quiet then, just a little creaking of the boards. He and Sasha looked at each other a long, quiet moment. There was no sound but the wind.

"I'll make tea," Sasha said. "I think we can use some tea right now."

Pyetr wanted the vodka. But he was ashamed to say that, so he sat down at the table, telling himself the wobble in his knees was only his recent injury and the tremor in his arms was surely natural after all the days they had gone cold and hungry.

He was glad to have the boy fussing about something as ordinary as making tea, which let him think about that instead of what might be on the other side of that door. The tea gave him, finally, something to do with his hands and something warm to hold.

"I think it's settled down," Sasha said, sitting down opposite him at the table.

"What 'it'?" he retorted. "I don't know what kind of livestock the old man keeps, but as cats go—"

Sasha looked at him from under his brows and bit his lip unhappily.

Like an accusation for a fool, Pyetr thought, denying the foolishness his eyes had seen, while he was shaking from having seen it—or not having seen it clearly enough or quickly enough to see it for what it was.

If things came out of granny-tales and attacked a man going out a door, then other things could be true, which he had no wish to think about.

He dropped his head against his hands and wished they had gone some other road but this.

There was the boat. He had no idea how to manage a boat, large or small, but he supposed that if one cut the ropes and set it loose even a big boat would drift; and the river had to be a safer route to Kiev than any shore with creatures like that roaming the woods. It might come to shipwreck. . . .

He could not swim. Probably the boy could not.

So it was back to wandering the shore, and, he told himself, if they had made it here without accident, they could just as well go south with as great a confidence.

"We'll try again," he said; and Sasha whispered, anxiously:

"The old man's a wizard, I tell you. He's terribly dangerous."

"Well, so are you," he retorted. "Isn't that what I heard all the way from Vojvoda?"

"Not like him." Sasha raked a hand through his hair. "He can bring back the dead!"

"I wasn't dead, dammit!"

"You were cold, Pyetr, cold as ice, your color was gone—"

"I was cold from walking three days with no food." He reached after the vodka jug, poured a half a cup and sipped it. He did not want to think about that. Not tonight.

"It happened," Sasha said. "Why can't you see the truth?"

"Because it's not sensible!" he said.

Which was all he could say at this point.

So he drank down the vodka and poured himself another cup.

Pyetr was angry at him, Sasha thought unhappily, while Pyetr drank his way to bed.

His relatives were like that. They said they placed no belief in his curse. But they still looked at him and frowned when things went wrong. Sometimes when she was angry, aunt Ilenka would say, Things happen with you around. I don't know why I put up with you.

Pyetr did not believe in the Thing in the yard, even when it nearly bit him; and he did not believe in wizards, but he looked Sasha's way with a certain frown that said to Sasha that he was certainly under consideration for fault in this— if Pyetr could find one.

And it might be his fault. There was always the chance that it was. In the face of someone as powerful as Uulamets, his I-will and his I-would were a whisper against a gale; but they were there: he knew that they were, with a conviction he had never had until this place—not a happy conclusion to reach.

But worst of all was the fear that Uulamets knew what he was.

That invitation tonight to join him—an invitation to him, but not to Pyetr. . . .

Pyetr's head sank onto his hand. He looked so thoroughly disheartened.

It was a long time before old Uulamets came back. Pyetr had taken to the quilts by the hearth, with his sword tucked in with him, with more than enough vodka in him to account for a sound sleep.

But Sasha waited, drowsing a little, listening for the old man's step on the boards outside; and when at last it came, human footsteps and the tap of Uulamets' staff, and finally the lifting of the latch, he was there to take the old man's cloak.

"Still awake," Uulamets said, a half-whisper as he set his staff against the wall. "I trust nothing disturbed you."

One could not lie to a man like Uulamets. Sasha had made his mind up to that. He went and poured Uulamets a half-cup of vodka.

"My friend wanted to leave. Something objected."

Uulamets took the cup and, with a frown, leaned against the table and sipped it. "I'm not surprised."

"My friend and I—" Sasha made a bow. "We want to go to Kiev, master Uulamets. We want your leave to go."

"After trying to rob the house—"

"Only a quilt and a string of turnips. Of nothing else."

"—without a shred of conscience."

"We understand we're indebted to you, sir. We're not thieves. Only we don't understand what you want from us. We want you to tell us."

"Huh." Uulamets took a drink, wiped his scraggly white mustaches with the back of his hand. "Tell you."

Sasha took a deep breath and ticked off the points on his fingers as he would to a merchant in the market. "We want a string of turnips, we want a quilt, and a string of fish, and if you can sail the boat, we'd like very much for you to take us to Kiev, if you would, sir."

Uulamets stared at him with those wolf's eyes and finally grinned, as pleasantly, Sasha thought, as the Thing in the yard.

"To Kiev."

"Yes, sir, if you can. If not . . ."

"I won't."

"Then the quilt and the turnips and the fish. And a clean shirt and a proper coat for Pyetr. He's a gentleman. He shouldn't go ragged."

"I'm sure. A gentleman with a certain difficulty: light fingers and lighter morals."

"He's not a thief. Neither of us is a thief, sir." His voice began to tremble, and he was afraid it was going to get worse. "We're willing to pay for what we take, but you won't take money. I offered to work and I've done that. It seems as if we should be even. What else do you want?" His voice completely broke and worse, his chin trembled. "If you'll make it clear what will square accounts we're quite ready to do anything reasonable."

Uulamets persisted in that slight wolf-grin. He drank another sip of the cup, set it down and stood up straight. "A bargain, is it?"

"For all the things I said, sir. And that you be fair with us and don't play any tricks."

"A *wary* young man."

"And don't arrange anything to happen to us."

Uulamets turned his back and walked a few steps toward the hearth where Pyetr slept. He scratched the back of his head as if he was thinking, disarranging thin white hair, and slowly turned and looked back.

"A very clever young man," Uulamets said, half-whispering. "Suppose that I did have a task for you."

"What?" Sasha asked.

"I have a need for a clever lad. Tomorrow night, as it happens."

"Doing *what?*"

"Digging roots." Uulamets mouth quirked into a toothy

smile. "And other things. For several nights, perhaps. Until I find what I'm looking for."

He thought that perhaps he was being a fool. He wished he had dared ask Pyetr, but he knew what Pyetr would say to any such thing. He wished he knew whether it was his luck at work again that had made him think of bargaining with Uulamets.

Stronger, much—whatever luck or sorcery Uulamets had.

"That *is* what I want from you," Uulamets said. "And when I have what I want you can take your turnips and your fish and *two* blankets. I'm in a mood to be generous."

8

In the morning it was firewood the old man wanted, another damnable day of sitting about while the poor lad chopped and stacked and sweated.

Pyetr watched, having no wish to admit that he might, perhaps, take his turn. He was healing, with a speed he found alarming—in view of the boy's claims for this place. Yesterday the wound had been scabbed, this morning that scab was peeling to pink new skin, still tender, but he thought he might well be able to run if he had to.

It seemed imprudent to make that clear to the old man.

So he watched the boy sweat and wear his hands to blisters.

And he slept on the porch in the little sun that reached the house, listening to the ring of the axe and the whisper of the river while the sun lasted.

He kept near Sasha at least, telling himself at one moment that now that he was better he might object to the old man's lordly orders, he might simply put his sword to the old man's throat and tell him they were taking the boat, blankets, and whatever in the house they fancied.

But whenever in the circle of his thoughts he was convinced that that was the better course he remembered that his healing was proceeding ungodly fast, and then he would remember that thing the other side of the door last night, and he would think that it might be the prudent course to think it all through one more time.

It was all very unsettling to a man's stomach.

Meanwhile Uulamets took to his book again, inside, where the light could only be worse, and Sasha sweated and chopped until the stack of wood was higher than his head.

After which Sasha had the washing to do, which meant heating water in a kettle and stirring the clothes about with a stick and fishing them out again to dry.

He *could* do something, then, he thought, with a little touch of conscience, so he went over and wrung out the steaming clothes and hung them on a bare-branched tree to dry.

Sasha, poor lad, simply washed the wood chips off his shoulders with handfuls of wash water and sluiced it down his sides until his breeches were mostly soaked, but he had nothing else to put on—

Until old Uulamets came out onto the porch and said he should add their clothes to the pot as well, that he had clothes they might wear until their own dried—no, they might even have them; and they should bathe and wash as well.

"God," Pyetr muttered. "Hospitality. What's into the old man this morning?"

There was no bathhouse—or there was, but the roof had fallen into it, atop the rusty things stored there. Hospitality meant the warm wash water, and clothes meant two musty, wrinkled coats, a cap in the same condition, shirts and breeches that halfway fell off Sasha and which Pyetr found a little short, but it was still a relief. Uulamets even offered a razor and a bronze mirror, and Pyetr sat on the chopping log and scraped stubble while Sasha washed their clothes, in an ever so much more cheerful frame of mind.

Except when he tried to think why the old man was suddenly so pleasant, after last night, or where the dog was that had tried to come in the door, or whether everything was part and parcel of the drink he had had last night.

He did not at all like the answers he kept coming to, as if reason lay in this narrow borderland, and the conclusions he kept reaching were a pit constantly widening its edges, closer and closer to him.

"Did he talk to you last night?" he asked Sasha finally, while they were sitting at the woodpile waiting for the clothes to dry.

"I told him we wanted to go to Kiev," Sasha said. "He wished I'd help him with something before we leave. He said he'd be glad to give us food and blankets after that."

89

Sasha was not looking at him when he said that. Sasha was gazing out across the yard, toward the gray-limbed forest.

Sasha was not telling him all the truth, he thought. There was a difference between the bright, worried lad who had been so resourceful along the way—and this young man who refused to look at him when he answered, and who spoke with that quiet, measured voice that sounded all too rehearsed.

"What does he want you to do?" Pyetr asked.

Sasha hesitated at that. And still did not look at him when he said, "I think it involves magic."

Pyetr snorted—and immediately wished he had not reacted that way, because it at once put a barrier between them.

"You've told him you're a wizard."

"I'm not," Sasha said. "Not—to rank with him at least. No. I haven't said anything. But you have."

"I have?"

"You've said you think it's nonsense. That's not the kind of helper you'd look for in something—if you were a wizard. When you doubt something—I think that could hurt the spell or whatever, even when you're as powerful as he is."

Pyetr kept his mouth firmly shut for a moment and tried to think the way a young and credulous boy might think, who respected wizards and goblins, a boy he firmly intended to get out of this place, even if the boy persisted in being a fool.

Why should I care? he thought. If the boy's content, leave him. Who made me responsible for fools?

And then he thought in less habitual ways, down paths that had no words around the thought at all, only a remembrance of the boy all but carrying him here, and the boy lending him his coat and offering him most of the food, and the comfort it was to have somebody who looked up to him without his having to exert himself, and who had no barb in his wit such as 'Mitri had had, and no selfishness either.

The fact was, the boy was comfortable to be with. The fact was, the boy, without a penny to his name, was his friend in a way 'Mitri and the rest could not in their limited hearts imagine to be; and instead of thinking of ways to avoid work, and of ways to protect himself from practical jokes and from 'Mitri putting jobs off on him, he found himself feeling he really ought to do something while Sasha was working his fingers to the bone.

That was an entirely unaccustomed feeling, one he did not quite understand, any more than he understood why he did not just slip off this morning, forgetting all debts, and go.

"Don't trust him," he said to Sasha in a low voice. "He's no saner than he was. I don't ask where he got these clothes. They're not his size. I don't think they ever were. The god only knows what happened to the owner. What we ought to do, right now—" He thought of going into the house, taking up his sword and taking what they wanted. But Sasha was too honest to countenance that. "—we should go down to the river and cut the boat loose and just sail out of here."

After a moment Sasha said, "I don't think we'd get far."

"You're giving the old man too much credit. It's cups of tea we have to worry about."

Sasha looked at him then, worried. "No," he said. "Please. Give it one more day. We did talk, he said he's willing to help us if we help him. . . ."

"Help him—help him do *what*, for the god's sake? What did he ask you to do?"

"He wasn't entirely specific—"

"God."

"He could be a lot of help."

"For the god's own sake, boy—"

"I think he has to keep his word, that's what they always say about—"

"They. They. The fakes in Vojvoda, who lie three times an hour to every client they have. This man will lie, Sasha Vasilyevitch. He absolutely will lie. Harm he might do us, poisoning us, god knows what. But help—"

"He can't lie in something magical. I don't think so." Sasha's brow furrowed. "You don't know that the wizards in Vojvoda are all fakes. Maybe a lot of them are like me—just a little magic, not enough to really do anything but push things into happening. But I know things, and I know it's dangerous to lie. It's dangerous not to know what you really want. It's dangerous to make wishes without thinking. I *know*, Pyetr. I'm not good, but I know how things work because I *feel* them." He tapped his chest. "Here. I can't explain better than that."

"Good god."

"Things are just like that. Things come back at you and you know better next time."

"All your poor life. Boy—"

"I know. I know. You think I'm a fool. But I'm not, Pyetr!" Sasha got up from the log and walked away.

"Boy—"

Sasha stopped, with his shoulders hunched and his head bowed.

"I never said you were a fool," Pyetr said. "I do apologize. Most sincerely. You're a wise young man, and you don't give yourself enough credit. You're the one who saved my life, not grandfather in there. I don't forget that."

"Then listen to me," Sasha said.

"And do what? Trust this man? I refuse."

"Just don't do anything. Not yet. And don't leave me here."

The boy was scared. That was clear. The boy had not completely lost his senses.

"Don't you go anywhere without telling me," Pyetr said sternly. "If you're going off with the old man anywhere, both of us are going. That's my word on the matter."

"You can't go. If he's going to work anything, you understand, it doesn't help that you don't believe in it. He won't like that."

"This is the man who brought me back from the dead. This is a great master, boy. Have a little respect for his abilities. If he can do what you say he doesn't need my help. I sincerely doubt he needs yours."

Sasha looked extremely upset with him.

"Just don't plan to slip off with him anywhere," Pyetr said. "You're too good-hearted. But if it makes you happy I'll believe anything at least while he's doing his conjurations. I won't do anything to offend him. Except go along."

The clothes dried by evening in a fair wind, the woodpile stood well-stocked, the floor was swept, the fish cleaned, dinner cooked and set and done . . .

Then Sasha expected the old man to get up from table and take up his wrap and his staff and bid him come along. Uulamets did all of that and Sasha said meekly, "Yes, sir," and took his new coat from the peg and put it on with never a look in Pyetr's direction, afraid of the dark outside, afraid of the old man, and equally afraid of what foolish thing Pyetr might do.

Pyetr came and took his coat from its peg, Sasha saw him in the tail of his eye, and Uulamets said, "There's no need of your going."

Pyetr said nothing at all, only pulled tight his sash and pulled down the cap from its peg as well.

"Stay here," Uulamets said plainly.

But Pyetr might not have heard him, for all the attention he paid.

Uulamets was frowning. Uulamets looked in Sasha's direction. Sasha pretended not to notice Uulamets' frown or Pyetr's stubborn insistence, and kept his head down, thinking all the while of the dreadful Thing in the yard and how they had to traverse that ominous dark boundary even to get to the woods.

"Very well," Uulamets said, gathering up his staff. "Very well."

And Uulamets flung open the door and led the way out into the dark of the porch.

A heavy flapping of wings left the roof. Sasha glanced up in alarm and saw nothing but a shadow passing. Pyetr was walking close behind him and Sasha was suddenly, selfishly glad of that—glad of it and guilty at the same time, knowing at the bottom of his heart he had wanted Pyetr's help, and never in his life certain whether wanting counted as a wish. He had a feeling of disasters hovering about them and multiplying, ill-aimed and ready to descend, and most of all he had a sense of something he knew no name for, but it centered about Uulamets like an ill-wish that had no destination and no owner and no one responsible for it. It was danger. It was hazard. And no one was in control of it.

Only he had *wanted* Pyetr by him. And Pyetr came, slogging along the rough path to the old road and beyond, where Uulamets led, down to the riverside and off beside the dock of the ancient boat.

"Where are we going?" Pyetr asked when they had gotten that far, but the old man answered him no more than Pyetr had answered Uulamets; and Pyetr caught Sasha by the arm and stopped him.

"Where are we going?" Pyetr asked again; and Sasha pulled to free himself, knowing better than to try reason with Pyetr, knowing certainly better than to reason with Uulamets. He only wanted to keep the pair of them from arguments and to do whatever Uulamets wanted and to get them safely back again behind solid doors.

Uulamets had stopped. He seemed part of the thickets and the undergrowth, a wisp of something gray and pale in the tangle of bare branches, and he leaned on his staff and grinned in that disquieting way.

"Boy?" he said, a quiet voice, with a deep timbre that cut a guilty soul to the quick—like uncle Fedya's voice and ten times more so: We have a bargain, it said. Remember, boy?

Sasha tugged to be free, and Pyetr held him fast. "Where are we going?" Pyetr asked again, and Uulamets, leaning on his staff with both hands:

"Up the river. Only a little." It was a placid voice, a reasonable voice, that made all fears seem foolish. Uulamets smiled pleasantly—impossible that the same features could have assumed that ghoul's look a moment ago. It must have been a trick of the light, a moment of panic. One was entirely foolish to imagine harm in these woods where they had walked for days unmolested. Uulamets beckoned, still smiling.

One could only move, or feel a fool. Sasha moved. Pyetr failed to stop him this time. Pyetr echoed disgustedly: "A little," and stayed close with him as Uulamets turned and probed their way ahead with his staff. "He's mad," Pyetr muttered under his breath. "Out in the dark, in a place like this. Digging roots at night—"

Branches raked at them. Roots tangled their feet. Sasha reached desperately to catch a branch Uulamets released. It raked his cheek; he winced and kept going, blinking tears of pain, fearing he was going to lose sight of Uulamets in the dark.

"Mad," Pyetr complained. "All of us are, for being out here—"

The river sound obscured the snap of brush even at close range. Water had undercut the bank and their steps splashed now and again into narrow, unexpected puddles. For a fearful moment Sasha lost view of Uulamets altogether and his imagination instantly painted Uulamets laughing at them, abandoning them to the fearsome creatures which might inhabit this dark shore.

He stepped in water to the knee, and stuck ankle-deep in mud. Pyetr pulled him back and held on to him.

"Let's go back," Pyetr said. "He wants to lose us. Let him! Let's go back to the house."

But there was Uulamets ahead of them, like a gray ghost beckoning them.

Sasha walked forward. He had no notion why. It only seemed impossible to run with Uulamets standing there to witness it; and foolish to do anything that would challenge Pyetr's recklessness or the old man's temper. He had no notion now why Pyetr let him go, or why Pyetr followed, except perhaps Pyetr might be thinking the same as he was about the Thing in the yard, and coming to the conclusion that walking back to the house right now was not the safest thing to do: nothing seemed safe at the moment—certainly not the direction that took him close to Uulamets, in a place where the moonlight and the river-sound combined to trick the eyes and the ears.

One hoped it *was* Uulamets.

"Here," the old man said, taking him by the shoulder, "here, there's a good lad . . ." and turned him toward the river shore, down toward the water. "See that thornbush?"

"What are you doing?" Pyetr asked, and caught the old man's arm, but the old man looked at him and Pyetr's expression changed—as if he had laid hands on some stranger by mistake.

In that moment Sasha's heart thumped hard with fright, to see Pyetr Kochevikov daunted and to feel the old man's hand gripping his arm with such painful strength, fingers biting deep even through the coat sleeve. But the old man looked him in the eyes then, lightened his grip, then patted him on the shoulder, and it seemed in the trick of the moonlight that he had never seen such a gentle, fatherly look.

"Good lad," Uulamets said, and took his hand and pressed a knife into it. "There, there, there's a lad, right by riverside— that's where to dig."

"For what?" he had the presence to ask, although it seemed he must be thick-witted not to understand. Everything seemed distant from him, like a dream. He looked back and saw Pyetr standing distressedly behind them, in a clear space the trees left.

"For whatever you can find, lad," Uulamets said, pressing on his shoulder. "Dig here. Mind you don't fall in. . . ."

Sasha edged down to the river margin and knelt there, as the damp of the earth soaked the knee of his breeches. The river-sound was strong in his ears. There was the chance of undermining on this earthen bank: he remembered that in a distant, cool way, only as a fact one must keep in mind—not to lean too close or trust too much to the ground. He began to dig with the point of the knife. He was aware of Pyetr asking: "Has everyone gone mad?" and Uulamets saying: "Hush, be still. Be patient—" as Uulamets withdrew, the river masking all sound but the sharp crack of a thorn branch as it snagged Uulamets' cloak and broke. The incident seemed significant for some reason—perhaps that every incident was significant in this place, on this spell-bound shore, in this moonlight delving after things of magical potency—but he imagined Uulamets speaking to himself, in a soft, soft singsong.

Volkhvoi, Sasha told himself, wizard, magician holding them both with whispers and the hush and the river itself which sang to them in a murmurous voice and wrapped them in dead branches and moonglow—he could not wake: he could not want to wake. The earth and the leaves smelled of moisture and of rot, the silver of the blade caught the moon and sent dirt flying, laying bare a puzzle of roots which ran from the thornbush to the river edge.

But there was no virtue in thorn roots. He had never heard of any. It was something else Uulamets wanted. . . .

What shall I find? he turned to ask of Uulamets. What am I looking for? —But he was amazed into silence, seeing some movement from the tail of his eye. It was gone when he looked. There was only Uulamets and Pyetr standing in the moonlight, both looking toward him—

And Pyetr's sudden alarm telling him there was danger beside him—

"Sasha!" Pyetr cried, and Sasha glanced aside, saw that movement in the tail of his eye again, some white thing floating in the air near Pyetr which vanished as he glanced back, Pyetr standing there with his hands up as if it were visible to *him* and Uulamets leaning on his staff with both hands, his lips moving and no sound coming out—

Sasha hurled himself to his feet at the same moment he saw Pyetr slump bonelessly to the earth. He crossed that space at a run and felt something so cold, so dreadfully cold in the air he breathed, the air seeming dank and rotten.

"Pyetr!" Sasha cried, and cast a look to Uulamets for help. The white thing darted back into the tail of his eye, a wisp that vanished as he glanced toward it. There was only Pyetr— then Pyetr surrounded by that drifting white thing the moment he cast an anguished glance aside to see where the wraith had gone. He realized then he could only see it that way— only from the tail of his eye; and it was not moving: it was hovering continually about Pyetr, whirling and hazing him about. . . .

"Stop it!" he pleaded, seizing Uulamets by the sleeve. "Stop it, do you see it? Help him!"

"*Help* him?" Uulamets cried in outrage, and thumped his staff on the ground between his feet. "Damn him! He's not the one!"

The white thing was still there, flitting about Pyetr—and Pyetr began to follow it as if he could see it in front of him. Uulamets plunged after, dragging Sasha by the coat sleeve, bashing dead limbs aside with his staff, saying, "Do you see her, boy? Do you see her at all?"

Sasha tried, turning his head, making himself victim to thorns and branches as they went. It was a ghost they were chasing . . . he was sure that it was.

"*Do* you see her?"

"Yes," he stammered, breathless, willing to go, trying to see, and giving up that sidelong view for the undeniable sight

of Pyetr, alone, traveling with swiftness Pyetr had never had
on his own in the woods. "Pyetr!" he cried. "Stop!"

But Uulamets shook him like a rat and hit him a dazing
blow across the side of his head with the staff. "Let him follow!" Uulamets snarled. "Let him follow. Only say if you can
see her!"

He could see nothing in any direction for the moment,
being blind with the blow to his head, but he swore that he
could, he gasped a breath and another and swore to whatever
the old man wanted, for fear of losing Pyetr in the woods if
they stopped now—certain that there was no help for Pyetr
or him either except Uulamets' magic, and Uulamets' good
will, however he had to buy it.

"I see her," he lied, and lied again, when his eyes cleared
and he could see Pyetr at least ahead of them, "She's still
there. . . ."

The old man hastened him grimly after, shoving him
through branches that scored his face and hands, Uulamets
panting and swearing as they went, until Sasha stumbled and
lost his footing astride a downed log.

And lost sight of Pyetr in the brush.

"Pyetr!" he called out in fright. *Pyetr!*

"Shut up!" the old man said, wrenching at his collar, and
dragged him up.

Pyetr was nowhere to be seen as he struggled to his feet
with Uulamets' fist holding his collar, as Uulamets pulled him
along a slope of mouldering slick leaves. Sasha fell again, both
of them sliding—

Then he saw something pale lying at the bottom of the
ravine, and scrambled down the slick incline toward it, the
old man panting after him and cursing him, the both of them
scrambling for balance on the slope of dead leaves.

It was Pyetr, lying alone, Pyetr with his face so pale and
his hands so cold—

"Where is she?" Uulamets screamed. *Where is she?*"

Sasha hauled Pyetr up in his arms and tried to find life in
him, Pyetr's hands falling lifeless and limp when he tried to
warm them, his face wet and cold as if he had come from the
river, although his clothes were dry. He had kept the cap somehow. Sasha took it off and called his name, slapping desper-

ately at his face and finally shaking him. "Pyetr Ilitch, wake up—"

Uulamets shoved him aside, knelt down and laid his hand on Pyetr's forehead. Sasha's heart jumped then as if he had touched something burning hot; and there might have been pain, but he was not sure, because Pyetr had moved in the same moment. Pyetr's eyes opened and Uulamets seized Pyetr by the throat and shook him, demanding, wildly, "Where did she go? Fool, *where did she go?*"

Pyetr did not even struggle. Sasha flung his arms about him, turned his shoulder to get him away from Uulamets and cried, looking up and pointing up the ridge: "There!"

Uulamets rose and stared in that direction, and Sasha hugged Pyetr up against him, feeling Pyetr trying to catch his breath.

"Where?" Uulamets asked sharply, and the staff thumped down beside them.

"She's gone," Sasha said, and shielded Pyetr's head with his arm, expecting the old man would strike them.

But Uulamets sank down onto a rotting log close beside them and let his staff fall against his shoulder. "*What* did you see?" he asked wearily. "What did you see, boy?"

"I'm not sure," Sasha said. He was shaking from head to foot. He had to lie and he was never good at it. He held on to Pyetr as the only source of comfort in this place and had this most terrible imagination that whatever he had seen could *be* Pyetr at this moment, shape-shifted, ready to rend them both with claws and fangs. That was what travelers said could happen: Pyetr could be lost somewhere and he could be holding a leshy or worse in his arms.

But Pyetr muttered something half-dazed and vulgar just then, and started shivering, too, which convinced him that it was most probably Pyetr he was holding. Pyetr looked about him of a sudden, tried to get up in his confusion, stumbled free of him and sat down hard, facing Uulamets.

"My daughter prefers *you*," Uulamets said in a harsh, hoarse voice. "I shouldn't have been surprised." Uulamets shoved the staff in their direction, striking Pyetr on the foot. "Where did she go?"

"Your daughter," Pyetr murmured, and shook his head and raked a hand through his hair. "Your *daughter*, old man—"

"Where did she go?" Uulamets shouted. Pyetr drew his knees up into his arms and Sasha scrambled forward, thinking the old man might hit him, thus unprotected. But Pyetr drew a large breath and lifted a hand, pointing toward the woods ahead of him; and Uulamets got up and peered in that direction as if there was something to be seen but moonlight and dead trees.

"Can you see her?" Sasha whispered, and Pyetr shook his head, shook it fiercely this time, and sat there until Uulamets walked back toward them.

"We should go back to the house," Uulamets said, which Sasha thought was a very good idea.

"Yes, sir," he said, and, taking Pyetr by the arm, pulled and helped him to his feet.

Pyetr had nothing to say, not then nor on the trek home, except once to protest that he could walk on his own, although he was limping, and although he faltered at the rougher places and had frequently to catch his breath and his balance.

"Help him," Sasha begged of Uulamets, but Pyetr would have none of that either, shaking him off and continuing on until they were back at the dockside, and then by a steep climb up the hill, in the yard itself.

Something went crashing off into the hedge. "Probably a rabbit," Sasha said, because Pyetr had stopped still at the gate and seemed frozen there. He seized Pyetr by the arm and pulled him along in Uulamets' track, himself afraid to look back or to wonder what might be watching from the hedge.

Everything was real. He knew that it was and he knew that he was a part of it, and that Pyetr was in the most terrible danger, because that creature, that white thing, was dead, and haunting the riverside, and Uulamets had said, speaking to Pyetr, My daughter prefers *you*. . . .

"Just a little further," he said to Pyetr, for Pyetr's strength finally seemed to give out on the walk-up, or the cold seemed to be too much for him.

Then he felt the chill, too, and saw the white visitor from the tail of his eye.

"Master Uulamets!" he said, holding fast to Pyetr.

Uulamets turned quickly about.

"It was here," Sasha said. "It was here, following us—"

"Inside," Uulamets said from the porch, and pulled the latchstring in haste, bringing the door open, bringing a gold flood of firelight out onto them, to make shadows on the porch. "Inside. *Quickly.*"

As if—Sasha thought—as if, daughter or no, the old man was in dire fear of what they had attracted.

9

✠ ✠ ✠ ✠ There was warmth, there were quilts to wrap in when they had shed the dew-damp coats, there was a cup of spirits, and Pyetr finally felt warm again.

He felt foolish, too, and altogether put upon. He stood there in front of the fire sipping vodka while Uulamets went straight to his precious book, by oil light, and Sasha hovered between the fireside and the old man's mutterings, scared and half-soaked from the ground as he was, and both of them like to take their deaths, Pyetr reckoned, from all this foolishness.

"Here," Pyetr said sullenly, offering the cup to Sasha, "have some. Warm up."

Sasha drank a little, made a face as he swallowed, and gave the cup back.

Not a word out of him, not a word out of Uulamets. Only there was something shifting about uncomfortably under the house, like a bear or something that had decided to make a den of the cellar—only it was past that time of year that bears waked, by all he knew, and nothing made sense anyway.

Sasha hovered between the fireside and the table, watching him, watching Uulamets. It annoyed him. He wished most of all that it were morning, when the sun would make sense out of the night made confused, and most of all he wished he would wake up from this bad dream. Probably, he thought, his memory was already confused, probably he had hit his head when he had fallen, and believed the boy's addled nonsense, and imagined the girl who had wafted right through a thorn thicket, the solidity of which his right hand very bloodily attested.

102

He took another sip. Uulamets turned another page and another, opened up an inkpot and wrote, with a black raven quill. Pyetr found himself shivering, his throat pricklish, his stomach upset.

He thought about Uulamets at dinner, about the chance that Uulamets had slipped something into the stew or even— he swallowed a mouthful of vodka too suddenly, and it burned his raw throat all the way down—into the drink. That was too cruel.

He thought, We have to get out of here, tomorrow, first thing, before he does us some violence—

Uulamets rose from his place at the table, closed the ink- pot and closed the book.

Then Uulamets walked over to them at the hearth, frowning. "Did she," Uulamets asked, "did she seem— *unhappy?* . . ."

Pyetr shoved back his hair, lifted the cup, and glared at the old man. "*Who* seem unhappy? Your imaginations? Your con- jurations from mushrooms and whatever you dropped into the tea?"

"My daughter," Uulamets shouted at him. "My daughter. Did she seem unhappy?"

"She's your daughter!" Pyetr cried, flinging off the quilt, ignoring Sasha's reach for his arm. "Can't you tell if she's unhappy?" The whole question was ridiculous. He found him- self answering and disgusted with himself, sat down in front of the fire with his vodka and tugged the quilt up about his shoulders. "She's a damn mushroom. A taint in the tea. How should I know if she's happy or not?"

Except it seemed to him that the girl he had dreamed of had been lost and wrathful, and that she had tried to speak to him—a soundless speaking face all pale and beaded with water—

"Insolent hound!" Uulamets said and snatched the quilt away. "My daughter never had any sense about men. So she's chosen *you!*"

Pyetr stared up at him with the sinking realization that Sasha equally well consented in this insanity. Sasha was kneeling, tugging at his elbow, asking him to answer Uula- mets—

103

"His daughter," Sasha whispered at his side. "He's worried about her. She's *dead*, Pyetr—"

"Well, he has perfectly adequate cause to worry about her, then! This is all crazy, this is all absolutely crazy!" He contemplated his cup in desperation and feared indeed that it was drugged.

"Tell him!"

"She was soaking wet, was how she was," Pyetr snapped, "and I doubt she was happier than I was." His teeth started to chatter and he took a deep drink of the potion that was surely the cause of his visions—but there was no cure for them until dawn, he knew there was not, and he humored the boy, if not the old man. "She tried to talk. She went away—"

"To which tree?" Uulamets demanded of him.

"To which tree? It's a damned forest out there, haven't you noticed? To which damned tree? How should I know?" The grandmothers said that drowned girls haunted trees. Lured lovers to die. He had had to follow, in his dream. The dose of drugs had been too strong and he had fallen, and Uulamets wove lies, encouraging them by his questions to remember, as charlatans would, exactly what he intended they should remember. "I didn't ask her about her *tree*, for the god's sake. It didn't occur to me."

Uulamets walked away in disgust. Sasha shook at his arm and whispered, "Pyetr, I think she's a *rusalka*. And that's a dangerous kind of ghost . . . she's terribly dangerous, even to her own father. She could be responsible for the forest dying. Please. Don't make jokes. Answer him. Tell him everything you saw."

"I didn't see anything," Pyetr said irritably. "He's drugged the damned stew, is what he's done. I told you watch him. Now we're seeing drowned girls and there's a bear under the house." He took another drink, telling himself that if it was drugged, it had proved a dreamless sleep given enough quantity; and that was good enough tonight.

"Pyetr. Did she say anything?"

"I don't want to talk about it."

"Let him be," Uulamets said from across the room. "Let him drink himself into a stupor if that's what he chooses. It's not required he be sober." Uulamets went back to his chair and his book.

"Please," Sasha said, "master Uulamets—"

"Don't be gullible," Pyetr snapped.

"No need of anything tonight," Uulamets said, "except his existence here."

A man could justly feel indignant when the only company he had left sided with a man like Uulamets. Friend, indeed— *boy*, child, ward, charge: he had promoted 'Mitri to *friend*, and most of 'Mitri's faults, he thought, outside 'Mitri's outright villainy and the fact that he was increasingly tending to his father's character—were the faults of a sometimes-man, sometimes-boy. He had his own faults, too, the god knew, among them that he had constantly to look for loyalty in someone younger than himself, because he did not, he admitted it to himself in his most morose broodings, seem to inspire it in more mature folk—

Mature folk who had no sense of humor, damn them all, and who could not laugh, and who plodded about their work and their affairs and their petty concerns as if it was all too grim. Or there were villains, plenty of those, who laughed only at the folk they robbed. That was more than grim, and Pyetr had never wanted to be a villain. His father had been one, the god of thieves knew, and Pyetr did not miss him: he only aspired to pluck the fools a little and make them wiser, and play pranks on the ploddingly sober sort and wake them, and generally to amuse himself and find a handful of well-placed, lively friends and of course a lady or so to admire his wit. It seemed a modest ambition for a lively, easy-going fellow, in a world in which so few people cared to fill that role.

But tonight he decided he must be out of step, he must have mistaken everything, to end up here with no friend in the world, only a boy to take care of, one of the ox-sober ilk who was desperately determined to take the world seriously, and who somehow had taken *him* in hand and bartered and traded him to some lunatic self-named wizard, all for his own good, of course, never mind the wizard was poisoning them with drugs—the god only knew what had happened to his daughter. . . .

He was drunk. Or drugged. Probably the wizard boiled people up in his kettle when he got them to trusting him. Or fed them to whatever he kept in the cellar. Domovoi indeed. Rusalkas. House-things and Things in the yard and things going bump in the cellar under the boards he was sitting on.

He dropped his head against his arm. He listened to the boy talking to Uulamets, who was telling him things about spells and incantations and how he knew that he could bring his daughter back if he could find the right tree.

And the boy stood there and listened to all this.

The boy who thought he was a wizard himself—listened to all this and answered questions like: How did she seem to you?

Sasha said: Just a wispy thing. All white. Like a cloud. Couldn't you see her, sir?

And the old man said, after a moment: No.

Then, the boy asked—how did you know where to look for her?

Liquid gurgled into a cup. The old man said, I didn't. But my daughter wouldn't give up life so easily. Her mother—

The cup banged onto the table.

Her mother's disposition and my ability, Uulamets said harshly. Go to bed, boy . . .

The cup was in danger. Sasha lifted it carefully from Pyetr's fingers and put it on the shelf, and Pyetr never twitched. The old man wanted his book, Pyetr was asleep, and that was just as well, Sasha reckoned: Pyetr just did not deal well with this kind of thing—no discredit to Pyetr: Sasha reckoned that, too, that being deaf and blind to certain things all one's life and then being knocked down and trampled underfoot by one had to disturb a man like Pyetr, who, Sasha figured, might joke and clown about—but certainly, certainly when he had ridden so recklessly under The Cockerel's signboard, and it *looked* as if it was all chance—Pyetr had known better than most folk ever did just precisely where the ground was.

That was what he sensed about Pyetr, and Sasha was greatly put out with the ghost-girl, who after all was cruel—rusalkas were always cruel, it being their nature—but still, *still*, he was the one of the two of them who truly would have wanted a glimpse of her, and the one of the two of them who might have—he hoped—had at least a chance of reasoning with her; and she had gone and played her tricks instead on poor Pyetr, who could have gone all his life quite happily thinking there was a dog in the yard and a bear under the house and that Sasha Misurov's wishes had no power over him.

He *wanted* Pyetr safe. That was all he let himself think about, sitting there beside Pyetr, listening to the slow turn of pages in Uulamets' book; and knowing that the domovoi beneath the house was mightily disturbed and manifesting itself with all the threat it could muster.

He wanted himself safe. He did not forgive Uulamets for tricking them, most of all for not forewarning him, when a forewarning might have helped. He did not forgive himself, for losing his wits in the chase after Pyetr and not remembering that against a magical thing, his wishing *might* have some virtue. So he sat and wanted them safe now with all the strength he had, quite collectedly, and did *not* want to see the rusalka: he dismissed all curiosity toward her, and simply did not want her, as hard as he could.

After which decision the domovoi at least settled down and quit meandering about the basement. He thought that that was a good sign.

He did not let himself think otherwise.

Only, eventually, there came a prickly feeling to his left, and he was aware that there had been a long silence of pages, and that Uulamets was looking at him.

Then he knew by wishing that way he had made a great mistake.

For a long while Uulamets looked at him, and finally crooked a finger. Sasha let go the blanket and got up and came over to the table, with a greater and greater feeling of hazard. Under his feet the domovoi stirred and shook the house beams. He thought of wishing it quiet, directly against master Uulamets, of trying himself against a wizard, but that was only the merest passing thought, and he knew it was foolish, foolish now to do anything but be polite and show respect and not even to attempt to defend himself except as the most extreme last hope.

He bowed. He looked up at master Uulamets and the timbers of the floor creaked softly.

"Who sent you?" Uulamets asked softly.

"Master Uulamets, no one sent us. We haven't lied. Only—"

"Only?"

"When I was very small my relatives thought—" He was going to stammer, he knew that he was, and he locked his hands behind him and got a quick breath. "—I might be a wizard, or unlucky, or something of the like. But the wizards in Vojvoda just said I was born on a bad day."

"Born on a bad day." Master Uulamets snorted and reached after his cup. He took a drink. At the same time Sasha felt his breath stop and his heart lurch and ache and start again, along with his breath. He went very dizzy for a moment, and master Uulamets said, "They're fools."

He had no idea what to answer. He hoped master Uulamets meant fools because they were wrong, and not fools because they failed to drown him at birth. He hoped master Uulamets had no disposition to correct that mistake, if that were the case—and he even hoped, for half a breath, that master Uulamets might tell him something better about himself than any of Vojvoda's wizards.

"How have you gotten this far," Uulamets asked, "without killing someone?"

Uulamets might have stopped his heart a second time. It felt like that. He said, feeling as if he were strangling, "I don't know, sir. I try not to."

"How do you try? Explain to me."

"I try not to wish for things that can go wrong."

"Who told you to do that?"

"Just—when things go wrong. I know better after that."

Uulamets lifted a brow and looked at him a moment before the edge of his mouth drew into a crooked, unpleasant grin. "Know better," he chuckled. "Know better. Indeed." He chuckled to himself for a moment. And a very uncomfortable feeling crawled up and down Sasha's neck. "Know better than to try *me*, for instance."

"Yes, sir."

"Smart," Uulamets said. "Smart lad. Your friend's very lucky."

To be with me? Sasha wondered, and clenched his hands, suddenly beset with a very unreasonable hope in this old man, who was more knowledgeable than anyone who had ever laid eyes on him: but, again, Uulamets might only mean Pyetr was lucky not to be in worse trouble, considering his company.

"Altogether taken," Uulamets said, "you've managed very wisely—concealed yourself quite well, till your inexperience betrayed you. And so impeccably *clean* a warding. Very well done, lad."

"Thank you, sir," Sasha whispered, and wished himself and Pyetr safe against the attack he was sure would come.

"Wary, too. You don't trust flattery."

"No, sir."

Uulamets' brows drew together. He crooked the finger again, beckoning him still closer. No, Sasha thought, and stayed where he was.

Uulamets smiled, and the smile became that unpleasant grin. "An impeccable ward. But an egg is impeccable. And vulnerable. Inexperience and too little strength, young Sasha. I had a student once. He was a fool."

He wished harder that they were safe, wherever they were. He wished so hard he stopped seeing the room around him, or Uulamets in front of him. Only himself and Pyetr, equally, inseparable, indivisible. He was aware of Uulamets getting up, taking up his staff. Walking around him. He let that go. It was Pyetr and their mutual safety he thought about and he did not look at anything.

"Stubborn," he heard Uulamets say. "I've met fools before."

He stayed as he was. Then pain struck his ankle, and the floor came up under his knee.

"Very good, boy. Very good. Magic's so simple for the young." He felt a touch on his hair, and heard Uulamets say: "But much simpler for a creature that *is* magical. Your friend's in danger, you and your friend are in terrible danger, and you can only thank yourself you found this house before my daughter found you. But now she has. I admit I had somewhat to do with that—but I didn't let her have her way, did I? Nor will, if you're reasonable; otherwise—you'll lose, boy. I was strong enough to hit you. I chose not to harm you."

Or the wish worked, Sasha thought, even on Uulamets. So he wished farther, and farther, to forever, and he let go then, and stood up, because that was all he could do.

"The effrontery of you," Uulamets said, standing back, leaning on his staff.

"You said you'd let us go. You said if I did what you asked you'd let us go and give us food and clothes and blankets."

"Oh, that I will," Uulamets said. "But getting out of this woods—that's another matter." Uulamets walked back to the table and leaned his staff against the wall. "The strength of magic depends on age; the ease of magic depends on youth. Simplicity of motives, you understand, makes magic ever so much easier. My daughter is older than you are—but her motives are ever so much simpler. You might say—a rusalka *is* motive. Could you stop her tonight? I think not. Perhaps you'll want advice."

He wanted advice—from someone other than Uulamets. But Pyetr would be for running; and Uulamets was telling the truth in one thing, that they were in very deep trouble, and there was no one else to ask.

"What should we do?" he asked meekly enough. But he was not prepared to believe anything Uulamets said.

Surely Uulamets was wise enough to know that. Uulamets gave him a long, calculating look.

"I want my daughter back," Uulamets said. "It's very simple. She wants your friend. You want your friend alive. Your *wanting* has a certain force that may prove useful—if you can hold on to that singlemindedness of yours and learn a thing or two."

"What, sir?"

Uulamets grinned. "The nature of your enemy. The nature of what you want. The nature of nature itself. I've *wanted* someone like you, boy, for much longer than you've been alive."

10

✠ ✠ ✠ ✠ Pyetr cocked an eye, lifted his head and winced at the pounding ache in his skull.

Much too much vodka last night.

Some muddle of a dream about woods and a drowned girl, a most vivid dream about running through the woods and seeing a face—

That was the pleasant part. The unpleasant part was waking up with a head like this, with the light coming through shutters the old man had been cruel enough to fling wide to the sun.

Uulamets was back at his book, at the table beneath the window. Moreover—Pyetr lifted his head and winced—Sasha was sitting on the end of the bench, in converse with the old lunatic, their heads together as if they were sharing some direly important secret. Most disturbing of all, they stopped whatever they were saying and looked at him, both of them with one solemn expression, as if he had discovered them in conspiracy.

It was all the same thing as the ghost, too much vodka and, he recalled, god knew what in the stew last night. *That* had been the start of the trouble, after which nothing had made sense, and they had gone out in the woods—

Or he had dreamed that they had.

He let his head back and stared at the shadowed, dusty rafters where there was no light to afflict his eyes, and tried to keep his stomach from heaving.

He heard a scrape of wood, heard footsteps. Sasha came and leaned over him, a worried young face against the dark of the rafters.

111

"Are you all right?" Sasha asked.

"I will be," he murmured. Talking hurt.

"Do you want some tea?"

His stomach turned. "No," he said, and shut his eyes. "I'll just lie here."

Sasha patted his shoulder. Pyetr's skin ached. He heard Sasha go and say to master Uulamets, "He's all right."

He recollected, he thought, Sasha and Uulamets talking about him last night. He saw them this morning, cozy and full of whispers, and his stomach felt upset for a reason that had nothing to do with last night's vodka.

He suffered the morning long, until Sasha brought him honeyed tea and some potion Uulamets insisted on. He drank the tea, he refused the nasty concoction Uulamets had made for him: Sasha pleaded with him, assured him there was no harm in it, but he pitched the contents of the cup into the coals.

"Pyetr!" Sasha said.

"Let him suffer," Uulamets said with what Pyetr was sure was satisfaction.

"I'll keep my headache," Pyetr muttered to Sasha. "At least I know it's mine. —Stay away from him!"

"It's all right," Sasha said.

"Fool!" Pyetr whispered. His head all but split from the effort. He sank against the stones of the fireplace with his knees tucked up. Sasha went back to his wizard and Pyetr sat there with his head spinning in a disquieting muddle of last night's dreams and this morning's discomforts.

His sword was leaning against the wall, behind Uulamets. He marked its whereabouts, and that of the blankets, and the clothes on the pegs and the rope over the rafters, and he laid a plan of escape.

Overpower the boy and carry him down to the boat, he thought. The boy would come back to his senses. There was nothing the old man could do against a young man with a sword and an outright intention to escape: Uulamets' apparent skill with the staff and his influence with Sasha were the only things to fear—as long as he avoided the stew.

Pyetr set himself carefully upright finally and went outside, down to the river, for necessities and to reconnoiter.

Sasha tracked him, appeared at the top of the bank and came on down the steep path to the dock where the old boat rode creaking against her buffers.

Pyetr frowned and folded his arms as he came.

"Please," Sasha said, "come on back to the house."

"Of course," Pyetr said. He might have been talking to a dangerous lunatic. He was thoroughly patient. And so doing he measured Sasha's size against his own and decided that indeed, Sasha was tall and strong for his age and possibly more than he could manage in his present condition if Sasha decided to resist being carried.

So he simply turned and walked down the dock toward the boat, and Sasha of course followed him, saying, "Please, Pyetr. We don't belong here."

He paid no attention. He reached the end of the dock and took a jump across to the deck of the aged boat, disturbing the dust and accumulated leaves.

"Pyetr!"

Sasha followed him. He had reckoned so. He walked further, with no intention to alarm the boy or to involve himself in a stationary argument—just to lead him farther toward the shelter of the little deckhouse: no sense starting anything near the edge where the boy could fall in, and no need, either, for the extra work of dragging an unconscious body half the length of the boat, especially considering his headache.

"Pyetr, please!"

"There's no danger," he said, and kept ahead of the boy. "I'm just curious. Aren't you?"

"You're in danger. Please come back."

He walked around the other side of the deckhouse, back to the stern, and heard Sasha coming. Sasha caught up with him; he had the sudden thought that it might be well to be certain first that the boat was truly sailable, so he shrugged and walked back to the tiller, which swayed and moved in the river current, restrained by a mouldering rope.

"Looks as if it could get us a little way toward Kiev," he said to Sasha, rocking at the bar to test whether the bolts were sound. "Doesn't it to you?"

113

"We wouldn't get that far," Sasha said. He had almost come close enough. And stopped. "Pyetr, please, she's dangerous."

"Looks perfectly sound to me," Pyetr said.

A sudden cold wind came up the river, or he had a sudden touch of malaise. He looked up and saw a shimmering in the air in front of him, a pale wispy thing. He blinked.

"Pyetr!" Sasha grabbed him and pulled him back from the rail. He gave backward in shock, seeing something like a veil and a face in empty air where nothing should be, and smelling a waft of water and rotting weed as something wet and cold touched his skin.

"Run!" Sasha cried, and he ran, looking backward, colliding with Sasha in a sudden stop at the side of the boat.

It was gone, then. He stood there with his knees weak, his head pounding, and the wind still icy cold on his wet hand and face. He was not accustomed to run from spots of cold air. He was not accustomed to have them touch him with what felt like fingers.

"Something dripped on my face," he said, looking to the overhanging trees. But no branch overhung the stern. "A fish must have jumped."

"She's looking for you," Sasha said, pulling at his arm. "For the god's sake, she's still here, Pyetr, wake up!"

He wished that he could. Maybe it was still the vodka. Drunk old men saw things in the streets. Maybe they thought watery wisps ran fingers over their faces, too.

"Pyetr! Get back to the house! Please!"

He stepped up on the rim of the boat and jumped for the dock, only scarcely keeping his feet. Sasha landed beside him, seized his arm and hurried him up the hill, but once and twice again he felt that chill.

It went away then with a last swipe of cold fingers, and Pyetr ran all-out this time, came panting and stumbling up the walk-up to the porch before he stopped, leaning against the wall of the house and holding his side.

It was not real. He was ashamed of running, and he looked around again to see only forest and the riverside, but so also was there water running down his neck.

Sasha pushed the door open, and cried, breathlessly, "Master Uulamets, she was here!"

Pyetr stayed where he was, leaning with his back against the wall, as Uulamets hurried out and into the yard, to stand there as if he expected to see the apparition somewhere about.

"Your daughter has cold hands!" Pyetr said, with as much sarcasm as he could muster, taking his part in Uulamets' little play, or Uulamets' madness, or whatever it was. Uulamets came back up the walk in every evidence of anger and disturbance, and said, on his way, "Fool. Stay to the house or there's nothing we can do for you."

Pyetr opened his mouth to protest, but Uulamets brushed past him and inside, and there was nothing to do now but follow or carry out his escape, and what with the tremor in his knees, the throbbing of his head, and the condition of his stomach, it did not seem the moment for it.

"Pyetr." Sasha caught his arm as he started inside. "You saw it this time, in the daylight. You saw it, didn't you?"

He nodded, since that course offered peace. It was not really a capitulation. He did not intend any such thing. He simply went inside and sat down by the hearth and thought about it while Sasha jabbered with Uulamets about how it had come up the river and he could not see it— "But Pyetr did. It touched him. In broad daylight."

"Daylight or dark doesn't truly matter," Uulamets said. "It's only that light distracts us with other details. You can't entirely see her with your eyes."

"You're crazy," Pyetr snapped, from his place by the fire. "How does anybody see without his eyes?"

"Easily," Uulamets said. "We all do it—don't we? You see her in your imagination."

He hated Uulamets turning his arguments back on him and leaving him nowhere to stand.

"That's precisely where she is," he said testily. "That's *all* she is."

"You're wrong. A danger of her kind is most unfortunately not limited to your feeble powers of imagination, Pyetr Kochevikov. Your mischief just now endangered your young friend, which may or may not be a matter of concern to you, and if it weren't for his good sense, you would *have* no further concerns. Lives have gotten very scarce in these woods."

Pyetr looked away across the room, wiped his neck against the persistent sensation of damp and cold, and told himself it had been a branch shedding dew—or some such.

The alternative, of course, was to let go of common, workaday reason once for all, smile at Uulamets and say, I'm sorry, whatever you say has to be true—the way Sasha had; and since Sasha had decided to take Uulamets' side of things, Pyetr found himself their only anchor to things outside this woods. Once he began to assent to Uulamets' personal madness escape became very remote for them.

He sat there all day listening to the boy tell Uulamets what precisely had happened on the river, listening to Sasha, damn it all, *tell* Uulamets about his investigating the dockside, if not the boat; and finally admitting that, too, in Uulamets' persistent questioning. Pyetr stared at the rafters, ground his teeth, and asked the gods why he was saddled with a fool.

But the answer to that, he told himself, was simply that Sasha had found in Uulamets what he had always wanted, a wizard to tell him his fancies were true and his wishes could change things in ways he wanted.

"What about the horses?" he asked Sasha when Sasha came near the fire.

"What horses?"

"Or the tsar's own carriage. Either one would do. Maybe our host could wish them up—you being only a novice."

"Pyetr, listen to him. Please listen to him."

He gave a flourish of his hand. "Of course. All day. Constantly. Inner eyes and all that. God, boy. I did think you had more sense."

"Pyetr—"

"He wants to find a damned tree. Fine. Let's go out in the woods and I'll find him a nice one. And while we're stumbling about in the dark, supposing we don't fall in a bog, he's going to sing his daughter up out of the grave. That should be a sight. I'll pass on the stew tonight. I'll make my own dinner."

Sasha looked hurt. "I never was careless. Master Uulamets—"

"*Master* Uulamets, is it?"

"He's telling us the truth. I swear to you. She's why there aren't any animals. It was my luck got us as far through these woods as it did. It got us to him."

"Bravo. So we can be ghost bait."

"If we can find her tree or if he can put a spell on her—we're safe. We won't be, even here, otherwise. She won't give up on you."

"Persistent young lady. Why don't we just open the door and ask her in?"

"Don't say that. Be careful what you invite her to do. This isn't something to joke about."

He had that cold feeling up his back again.

It was colder, after supper—stew for them and a couple of small turnips for himself, and no drink at all. He had a great deal of trouble falling asleep, with the creaking the house beams made. Unstable ground, he decided.

Until they creaked and the whole floor seemed to shift a little.

But senses could trick a body, especially close to sleep. Sasha was sleeping peacefully beside him on the hearthstones, wrapped in a quilt. Uulamets had finally given up writing in his book and taken to his bed, snoring softly. Pyetr rested his head on his arms in the half-light the dying fire provided and listened to the house creaking and listened to the wind in the dry trees.

Suddenly a single footstep sounded on the walk, and another on the porch.

He took a breath to call out to Uulamets, who doubtless knew his visitors and their habits. But for some reason without reason he held that breath for a moment and made no movement or sound.

Someone knocked on the door.

Sasha stirred. Uulamets sat up in bed.

No one moved for a few heartbeats. Then Uulamets got up and headed for the door.

"Don't open it!" Pyetr cried, saw he was going to do it, and scrambled under the table and past the bench, groping in the near-dark for his sword as the door opened, as a wind swept in and blew at the embers.

He grabbed at his sword and unsheathed it, heart pounding—flung an arm over the bench and hurled himself for his feet.

She was there, white and filmy and wavering in the wind. Dripping with river weed.

Then the wind swept inside, wreaking havoc of falling herb bunches and clanging pots and sparks flying from the fire.

"Shut the door!" Pyetr cried. "For god's sake shut the door!"

For once someone listened to him. Uulamets heaved it shut, Sasha threw his weight at it, and the bar dropped down. The broom thumped down onto the floor. A last cup fell off the shelf and shattered.

"God," Pyetr breathed.

Uulamets looked at him. Sasha looked like a ghost himself, still bracing himself against the door, although the wind had died away.

Pyetr did not even try to sheathe the sword. He laid it on the table, picked up the vodka jug and a cup and managed to get the liquid in it instead of on the table, that was all his hands could manage.

While the house creaked and whatever-it-was in the cellar growled in displeasure.

He truly wished himself in Kiev—or any place else tonight, for that matter.

"Only the wind?" Uulamets gibed at him.

He took the drink and looked up at the old man with a sinking feeling that hereafter Uulamets knew the territory and he did not.

Hereafter *Sasha* knew the territory better than he did. And Pyetr was still far from trusting that Uulamets had any good motives toward Sasha or toward him. The steel sword on the table seemed as formidable as it always had been—except when one dealt with ghosts.

Sasha began picking up the herb bunches and the surviving cups and withered objects that had fallen off the rafters, the god alone knew what some of them were.

"Move, move," Uulamets said, waving Pyetr aside, and Pyetr took his cup, his sword and its sheath and went over to sit on his blankets while Sasha swept up.

He was useless, Pyetr thought glumly, he was absolutely

useless to the old man or to Sasha, if the law of the place favored magic and not honest wit. He had no urge whatsoever to get up and help. It was Sasha's old man. So let him work for him. The old man had wanted Sasha for ghost bait, the old man discovered instead that Sasha had some kind of ability—so the black god take Pyetr Kochevikov, if he was stupid enough to be here, on the peripheries of what Sasha had wished up.

Or what the old man had wished, who knew?

Sasha had no more use for him anyway. Sasha had changed his mind and his loyalties, and who knew? Maybe the old man had 'witched him into it.

But if magic did it, Pyetr thought, and Uulamets was the master in that, then what could Sasha do or what could he himself have done, except to have gotten them away before they ever fell this deep into Uulamets' plans?

And what could he look for in Kiev, but more Dmitri Venedikovs and more betrayals and more of the same as Vojvoda? Sasha was the only friend he had ever had who would endure any inconvenience for him, the only one who would, god knew, have carried him through the woods or defended him from a ghost.

So why go to Kiev, anyway, if the only friend he had was here, at Uulamets' beck and call?

He set the cup down and ran the sword back into its sheath, he cast a jaundiced glance at Uulamets sitting over at the table with his gnarled hands clenched in front of his forehead, his lips moving in some god-knew-what-kind-of-incantation, which might or might not work—he still had his doubts on that score, even if there *were* ghosts. There was no surety spells worked; there was no surety even if some spells worked, that Uulamets' spells did, against—

—whatever she was.

Pyetr said, without moving from where he sat, "Well, what are we going to do about her?"

Uulamets went on talking to himself. Sasha stopped sweeping and leaned on his broom, looking at him with some indefinable expression: worry, maybe.

"So we find her tree," Pyetr said, feeling increasingly foolish with every word that left his mouth. "Then what? Ask her to leave me alone?"

His wits kept trying to rearrange things sensibly. There had not been a wind, Sasha was not sweeping up broken pottery—but this time he deliberately set himself to remember that face that kept fading on him, and the wind, and the fear: he could not believe in it now, but he held on to it, reminding himself that he had made up his mind and that, reason aside, he was going to believe it, if that was what it took to exist here and deal with this woods. And Sasha still had the broom in his hands and a pile of broken pottery at his feet.

"Master Uulamets says he can bring her back to life."

"Isn't that kind of sorcery supposed to be dangerous?"

Sasha had no answer for that.

"How is he going to do it?" Pyetr asked. "What's he need? I'll tell you, I've heard recipes for witches—"

"I don't know," Sasha said. "He says he has to find out where she's staying. He can't see her or hear her. I can, almost, see her, that is. But you can see her plain as plain. Can't you?"

Sasha wanted an admission. He stood there waiting for it. Pyetr nodded with ill grace and frowned.

"A rusalka's very powerful," Sasha said in a half-whisper, while the old man droned on at the other side of the room. Sasha came and hunkered down at the fireside, and leaned his broom against the stones. "Master Uulamets said she was just sixteen; and he doesn't know whether it was an accident or not—if she just drowned, that's one thing, master Uulamets said. That kind of rusalka is bad enough; but if she drowned herself—that's almost the worst."

One had to ask. "What's worst?"

"The ones that were murdered."

Pyetr gnawed his lip and considered the stones between his feet. "So what does she do? Look for men, I've heard that. So what does she do with them?"

Silly question, he thought then, seeing Sasha blush. But Sasha said, "I'm not exactly sure. I'm not sure anybody's ever been able to say. They're—"

"—all dead," he said at the same time as Sasha. "Wonderful."

"That's why we have to keep close to you. We don't know."

He hated that "we." He truly did. He scowled and looked at the sword in his lap.

"Rusalkas sleep a lot," Sasha said, "until they want something. If nothing ever comes along at all, they just fade. But if they wake up, especially the violent ones—they're terribly powerful. And she's not the only haunt hereabouts. That's what master Uulamets says. There's a Water-thing."

He stared at Sasha quite unhappily. "Oh, of course. A Water-thing, a Woods-thing, Things everywhere, and every ghostly one of them with a grudge to pay." He shook his head. "Entirely unreasonable of them, I'd say."

"Don't—"

"—joke. They've got no sense of humor either."

"No, they haven't."

"I don't know why you're so certain. Maybe they've been waiting all these years for a good joke."

"Don't—"

"—talk like that." Pyetr made a little flourish of his wrist. "Absolutely. The whole world abhors levity. I'll apologize to the first leshy I see."

"Pyetr—"

"Earnestly." He held up his cup. "Be a good lad. It's been a hard night."

"You shouldn't have any more."

"No, I shouldn't." He still held up the cup. Sasha took it and brought it back half-full, and Pyetr sat and drank and listened to the snap of the embers and old Uulamets chanting and muttering and mixing things in his pots.

Sasha watched a while, standing by with his arms folded. Maybe since Sasha was in some measure magical, Pyetr thought glumly, he had some special sense for what Uulamets was doing. Certainly Sasha looked neither confident nor happy in what he saw.

Pyetr tucked the blanket around himself and his sword, for all the comfort either was in the situation, and shut his eyes and tried to rest without seeing a wisp of white in his memory—

He could see her face when he shut his eyes now. It was

a girl's face, young and very pale, and desperately unhappy. She had long, fair hair, and a little chin and very large eyes, which looked at him so wistfully and so angrily—

It's not my fault, he thought. I don't know what I ever did. —Though I have my faults, his conscience added with unwanted honesty. He thought of a dozen escapades in Vojvoda. But his conscious self amended hastily, recollecting her nature: But nothing I ever did to you. It's hardly fair of you, you know.

She was indeed hardly more than Sasha's age. He would never introduce Sasha to some of the company he had kept or show Sasha some of the things he had seen—he could not say why, except it would embarrass both of them; and she was so young, she was so like Sasha, he found himself imagining her expression as offended innocence—and her pursuit of him less attraction than vengeful disgust for a scoundrel.

It's still not my fault, he thought. I really don't think I've done badly, considering my father's faults. He really didn't leave me a good example.

She hovered quite close to him—amorously close, he thought, much too close, for a young girl he had no wish to be in bed with.

He tried to wake up, he earnestly tried, in that sense of a dream about to go very wrong indeed. . . .

He felt a grip on his arm and came to himself upright against the fireplace, sputtering and wiping furiously at his face and neck.

But there was no water. He was sitting amid his blankets in a room dark except for the embers, it was Sasha holding his arm, and the cold water running down his neck, real as it felt, was nothing he could touch.

"Are you all right?" Sasha whispered.

He caught his breath, leaned back against the stones of the fireplace and slid a glance toward the old man's bed. He could still feel the cold water around him.

"Damn the luck," he whispered to Sasha, and shuddered, pulling the musty, dry blanket up around his neck. "All the ladies I've courted and the only faithful one's a dead girl."

Sasha's fingers closed on his arm. "Do you want me to wake master Uulamets?"

"It's only a dream." It came out with a shiver. "It's nothing."

Sasha did not move. Pyetr slid down further into his blankets and tucked his arms about him. For a long while he was aware of Sasha sitting there.

He was glad. If he had to believe in the rusalka he reckoned he was morally entitled to believe in Sasha Misurov—in Sasha, he thought, much before Uulamets.

Small good his sword might do, he thought, too, but he kept it close, against the few situations he *did* understand.

11

Sasha came awake with an uneasy feeling, heard the house timbers creak, and heard a small sound from Pyetr—dreaming, he saw by ember light, and in distress.

He wanted to know what had waked him, and his heart all but stopped as he saw a black thing skitter along under the table across the room. It might be a trick of the dim light: that was all that kept him from waking Pyetr on the instant. Then it was the glitter of small dark eyes from under that table, eyes which locked with his so fixedly he was afraid to breathe.

Pyetr stirred, not awake, he thought. And something rattled a shutter. The wind, perhaps.

But the black thing skittered aside and back into the shadows, so that Sasha was left wondering if he had seen it at all. He was still afraid to move.

Then he heard the rattle of the second shutter, that at the end of the house.

Pyetr drew a deep breath and Sasha laid a hand on his shoulder and shook at him, but Pyetr did not wake, and he was yea and nay about wishing it in any concentrated way—totally confused, he thought in some distress, afraid that Pyetr might do something foolish, afraid that noise might bring attack from the Thing under the table or the Thing outside the window, though by what law of the unnatural he had no knowledge. He simply could not reach a decision what to do, even when he heard a board creak on the porch. He sat there like a fool, with Pyetr on one side and Uulamets in his bed both stirring restlessly.

124

Suddenly Uulamets woke and sat up in bed, which in some measure he was very glad to see, and in another way, made his heart turn over for fear the things *were* real. Uulamets put his feet over the side and a warning stuck in Sasha's throat—but the Thing under the bed did Uulamets no harm: instead, it came out and clambered with human hands up onto the bed. Uulamets got to his feet and walked barefoot across the floor, to stand and look about him at a house in utter silence.

"Something's out there," Sasha whispered, and Uulamets looked sharply toward him. "On the porch."

Uulamets walked over to the table and seemed to listen a moment. "This isn't good," Uulamets said. "This isn't at all good." He gathered up a bag and began to stuff it with something dry and brown. Moss, Sasha thought: he recalled a ball of it between the uprights by the table. "Twice in one night. She's getting much too insistent. Or something is."

The Thing skittered across the floor suddenly. "That—" Sasha said, and took in his breath as it reached master Uulamets' feet and climbed up the table-leg.

It reached the table-top and perched there, dark little eyes glittering in the ember light as it watched. It had a flat face, a cat's black nose, its jaw and mouth were very like a man's, and it looked overall, tucked down, like a black ball of dust and tangled hair, the sort of thing a broom might dislodge from under furniture.

Uulamets gave it hardly a look. He was tucking little pots into the bag, and adding more stuffing, while shutters rattled and the Thing turned about on scarcely seen limbs to hiss at it.

Uulamets looked at that window, too. The ember light showed anguish on his face. Or fear. Sasha could not be certain. He got to his feet while Pyetr slept like the dead.

And Uulamets went on with his packing.

"What are we going to do?" Sasha asked.

"We," said Uulamets, "are going to find her."

"Find her . . . —She's *outside*."

Uulamets threw him a scowling glance. "She won't face me."

Sasha had the most uncomfortable feeling then, the same that he had had any number of times, that there were secrets more than the ones Uulamets wrote in his book, and troubles in this place more than a drowning. Uulamets' using them for—as Pyetr called it—ghost bait, he suspected was not entirely the desperation of a grieving father—unfair, perhaps: he had no idea personally how desperate a man could become, but in his own way of thinking, a man who would callously trick his guests into favors of the kind he asked . . . was a man very much like his uncle.

"Wake him," Uulamets bade him.

"Go out there in the dark?" Sasha objected.

"I've told you. Dark or light makes no difference. The danger is the same."

"Then maybe we should wait till daylight," Sasha said, "if nothing else, so we won't fall in the river."

"But there is danger in meeting her on our own ground," Uulamets said harshly. "Never let her in. Never let her into this house. Do what I tell you. Wake him. We have no choice. Are you numb to the danger we're in? Or are you a fool?"

"What about Pyetr's danger?"

Uulamets picked up a metal pan and banged it on the table. The black thing hissed and jumped for the rafters, leaping from one to the other, and Pyetr started awake, his sword in his hands, before he fell back hard against the stone fireside and rested there, the sword half-drawn.

"Pardon," Uulamets said. "Time you should wake, Pyetr Ilitch. We're ready."

"Ready for what?" Pyetr asked, between breaths.

"She's here," Uulamets said. Sasha thought that he should do something, say something—but he had no idea whether he was under Uulamets' spell himself or whether the prickling feeling that said Uulamets was right was from his own senses. "We have to move quickly," Uulamets said, and crossed the room and took his breeches off the bedpost, while in the rafters something thumped, and a mouldering basket fell and bounced.

Pyetr looked up at that, with the sword no further sheathed than it had been. Afraid, Sasha thought, but whether Pyetr sensed anything such as he did or whether it was only the startlement of the movement in the rafters he could not guess.

Uulamets pulled his trousers on under his robe and pulled

on his boots. Sasha stood still, dressed in everything he owned except his coat, and Pyetr moved only to rake his hair out of his eyes.

"Up," Uulamets said fiercely. "Get up."

"And go where?" Pyetr said. The sword clicked home in the sheath. He gathered himself to his feet. His hair was standing up at angles. He looked to Sasha, and ember light and shadow made his face desperate and strange, asking questions Sasha had no idea how to answer.

"He says," Sasha said, "she shouldn't get in here. That we have to go to where *she* is, or we're in worse trouble. That the worst thing is for her to get into the house."

Pyetr ran his hand through his hair a second time. It achieved no better result. He seemed harried and bewildered, as a man might, roused out of a sound sleep, or out of bad dreams. "Find her tree," he muttered to himself, shaking his head. "God. Of course. Fine. In the middle of the night, looking for a ghost and a tree."

He looked toward the door suddenly, with that same harried look, with the sword clutched in his hand.

"Pyetr?" Sasha asked, alarmed, and came and stood by him.

"She's here. Outside. —She's saying—" Pyetr shook his head suddenly and looked at Uulamets.

"What does she say?" Uulamets asked.

"Not to trust you," Pyetr retorted sharply, and Sasha tensed, expecting Uulamets' anger. But Uulamets said only,

"Trust her instead? I wouldn't." Uulamets took his cloak from the peg and slung it about his shoulders. "That would be fatal, for her, ultimately, as well as for us." He began to thread the latchstring through the hole in the door, muttering something singsong as he did so. Then: "Bring my bag, lad. And be extremely careful with it."

Sasha had a last wild thought of refusing, of siding with Pyetr against the old man, but courage or foolishness failed him, even yet he had no notion which. He gathered up the bag Uulamets had packed, while Uulamets took his staff from against the wall and lifted the latch.

There was no wind. There was nothing threatening outside. "Come along," Uulamets said, and they took their coats from the pegs and followed him.

No ghost, no wind, no breath of trouble—until the Thing from the yard scuttled out the door between Pyetr's feet and he stifled an outcry.

"What was that?" Pyetr exclaimed, hand on his sword hilt as the Thing disappeared into the hedge.

"Nothing," Uulamets said, motioned Pyetr to pull the door to, and led the way down the walk-up. He stopped at the bottom and asked, "Do you see anything? Do you feel anything?"

Pyetr slung his sword belt over his coat and pointed ahead into the woods. "I'd say that way," he said. His teeth were chattering, but he started off foremost through the yard, kicked the gate open, muttering something about the cold and the dark and fools. He led them toward the riverside.

Sasha turned his head to bring the side of his eye to bear, and saw nothing of the ghost in any direction. He overtook Pyetr with a sudden downhill rush as they reached the river and the dockside, caught Pyetr's arm and whispered, "Did she really say that? About Uulamets? Pyetr? Do you see her?"

"The old man wants a walk," Pyetr said in a half-voice, "that's what he'll get." He seemed still to be shivering, although of nights they had had, this was one of the warmest. "This is a stupid thing to do, boy."

"Did she say that? About not trusting him?"

Uulamets was almost down the hill, chiding them for breakneck speed. There was no time for any long answer.

"What do you think?" Pyetr said. "Do *you* trust him?" His teeth were chattering still. "Damn, the wind's cold."

"There's no wind here," Sasha said. He felt Pyetr's hand and it was cold and clammy. He clenched it tighter as Uulamets came up by them. He had the strongest feeling that he ought to have doubted Uulamets more, and that he ought not to have encouraged Pyetr to have come out here—that Pyetr had been on the side of common sense all along and that all his caution had done was to bring Pyetr out here tonight.

But Pyetr pulled away and started up the river, the same direction they had gone to find the ghost that first night.

"Does he know where she is?" Uulamets asked, catching Sasha's arm.

"He says so," Sasha said on a breath, not quite a lie, and broke away after Pyetr, quickly, because Pyetr was going faster than was safe in the thicket, along the river edge, through reeds and through a low place that they had to wade. Sasha struggled to overtake him, and Uulamets came close behind him, warning him mind his step, wait, listen to someone who knew the ground.

Pyetr climbed to dry ground and suddenly vanished into the trees and the dark over the ridge.

"Pyetr!" Sasha cried, shoved the sack at master Uulamets and ran after Pyetr in acute fear that with every moment wasted, they risked losing him. He heard master Uulamets far behind him shouting at him to wait, come back, and he paid no attention. He could see the pale gray of Pyetr's coat at the bottom of the wooded hill, and he simply locked his arms in front of his face and charged downhill through the thicket heedless of the thorn branches. "Pyetr, wait, I'm coming!"

Pyetr seemed not to hear him. Pyetr appeared to move with woodcraft he had never had, evading thickets, never choosing a false way. By that alone Sasha guessed Pyetr had a guide who did know the ground all too well, and he tried only to stay close enough to see which way Pyetr chose. Wherever that failed, he simply took the short way, breaking through brush, scoring his hands and face, snagging his coat and tearing through by sheer force.

He wished Pyetr to slow down and use good sense. He wished the rusalka to leave Pyetr in peace. He wished himself to keep Pyetr in sight and he wished that Uulamets would find his track and so find Pyetr's. Common sense said that was too many wishes at once, and that half of them might wish away the others, or do something terrible, but he was too frightened to think things through with any clarity. In a doubtful case, master Uulamets had counseled him, wish only good, and he did that with all the force he could muster, while he was tearing his way through the thickets. He saw Pyetr at the top of a ridge, and dived breakneck down a ravine, clawing his way up the other side in the dark, climbing with the help of roots and branches and coming muddy-handed to the crest in time to gain a little.

"Pyetr!" he cried. "I'm with you! For the god's sake, wait for me!"

Pyetr was already going down the other side, toward the river again—in the gray dim light that Sasha realized was the breaking of the day. Sasha held his aching side and kept going, down the hill of mouldering leaves and down again, by a rill-cut path which ran down to the river.

Something was amiss here. Sasha felt it before he was aware what was so strange in that place to which Pyetr was going: the trees gave way to open ground, a knoll grown over with grass and living moss—or it seemed that way, in what little light they had, in the way the grass gave underfoot: it was some sort of demarcation Pyetr approached, following what sort of illusion Sasha did not know. He only reasoned that if this was the boundary between life and death in this woods things were surely backwards, and that whatever threat there was, was strong here. He ran, vaulted over an upthrust rock and with Pyetr in reach made no attempt at reason: he flung himself at Pyetr's back and knocked him sprawling, caught Pyetr's arm across his forehead as Pyetr rolled and was, the next he knew, flat on his back with Pyetr's hands on his shoulders, both of them gasping for air.

"She'll kill you!" Sasha gasped.

Pyetr leaned on him, catching his breath, looking about him as if he had no least idea where he had gotten to; and said then, between gasps, "Where's the old man?"

"I don't know! You ran off. I followed you."

Pyetr looked the more bewildered. "You were the one who ran off," he said, as if there was no sense in anything. He rolled aside and sat down, leaning on one hand, looking about, while Sasha sat up holding his side, feeling the discomfort of damp ground soaking cold through his breeches. He dared not move. The whole forest seemed too still, no whisper of leaves: those all were dead; no dawn sounds: those were dead, too. There was only the river rushing by the bank.

Then the slow, heavy movement of something dragged by stages over the leafy ground.

"Father Sky, what's that?" Sasha breathed, edging closer

to Pyetr, scanning all the wooded ridges that encircled this smooth-sided knoll.

Pyetr got up to one knee and began to draw his sword as quietly as possible, but at the first whisper of steel the sound stopped, and Pyetr stopped, in a hush so still not even the wind seemed to breathe.

Sasha clenched his hands and shut his eyes a moment, wishing their safety so hard it made him dizzy; and opened his eyes to a woods that looked no different. Pyetr was getting to his feet, sword still a quarter drawn. He pulled it rasping from its sheath and walked a few investigatory steps up to the summit of the knoll—

—and vanished with a yell, straight into the earth.

"Pyetr!" Sasha scrambled forward and flung himself flat as he would on pond ice, crawled to the edge and looked over into the deep, shadowed pit with what might be Pyetr's sprawled body half-buried at the bottom. He could in no wise be certain in the dim light. "Pyetr!" he called.

The gray shape moved, developed an arm and a leg as Pyetr shook himself free of the dirt and the rock, and a flickering length of metal appeared, the sword in Pyetr's other hand, as Pyetr attempted to gain his feet.

"Can you climb up?" Sasha asked.

Pyetr sheathed his sword and tried, climbing up the rocks and the dirt of the slide, only to have more of the pit cave in.

"Look out!" Sasha cried as the ground underneath him dissolved. He yelled and scrambled backward as his hands went out from under him and he slid into a choking flood of dirt and rock.

The next he knew it had stopped, he was head downward, spitting dirt and fighting to get clear, and Pyetr was hauling him to his knees in the spongy earth.

"Sorry," Pyetr said. "Are you all right?"

He blinked dirt from his eyes, stood up and looked despairingly at the circle of sky above the pit, with the irrepressible thought that if he had used half his wit he would not have stood on the edge. He might have found a dead limb or something to put over the rim for a ladder. He might have let down his belt for a rope. He thought of a dozen ways to have done better with the situation, now it was too late.

"Uulamets is following us," he said, the best hope he could think of under the circumstances, and he earnestly wished for Uulamets to find them.

"Small hope in him," Pyetr said glumly, dusted himself off and looked around the pit they were in. Something seemed then to take his interest. Sasha looked, where a darkness marked one face of the pit.

And seeing that darkness he had a very bad feeling, the more so as Pyetr walked over to it, into the shadow of the rim.

"Smells odd," Pyetr said.

"It might cave in," Sasha said. "Master Uulamets will find us. Just be patient. —Please don't go in there! What if it caved in again?"

"It looks solid," Pyetr said, and ducked down. His voice echoed out of closed spaces, like a well. "It might go all the way to the river. Probably floods here in the rains."

"Don't go in!" Sasha cried, with an oppressive feeling like smothering or like drowning. "The whole hill might cave in. Pyetr! Don't!"

"I'm not going in. Just trying to see. Maybe when the sun gets higher—"

There was that sound of movement again, the sound of a weight moving slowly over the earth. A few clods rolled to the bottom of the pit beside them, but the sound came from somewhere behind the earthen wall of the slide.

"Pyetr," Sasha whispered. "Pyetr, please, get back here. Don't touch anything."

More clods fell. Pyetr backed away from that wall and carefully drew his sword.

"I really don't like this place," Sasha said.

Neither of them moved for a moment. The dragging sound started up again and dislodged an earthfall directly over the cave.

"Is it her?" Sasha whispered, taking a grip on Pyetr's sleeve, for fear of him starting forward, into a trap the rusalka had deliberately lured them to—and he fervently wished for the old man to hurry and find them.

Something hissed within the dark.

Something hissed atop the rim, too, and something small

132

and black rolled down the slope, scattering clods as it came. It darted between them and into the dark hole, snarling and spitting, and darted out again, like a small dog away from a larger.

"God!" Pyetr cried, as an undulating black mass came out chasing it.

"Look out!" Sasha yelled and jumped for the sloping dirt as the black mass came after his legs. Pyetr was climbing too, beating it about the head with his sword as he climbed. It tried to follow them, while the small black ball that looked for all the world like the Yard-thing hissed and circled and nipped at its coils below.

"Fools!" Uulamets suddenly called from above them. "Get it, get it, go, you have it!"

"Have *it?*" Pyetr cried, beating at its head. "Get us out of here!"

But it was wilting under the blows, trying to hide its nose with small black forelimbs, writhing aside and dislodging more and more dirt on the slide. Sasha yelled in alarm as a slippage carried him down within reach of the thing. Immediately Pyetr was there, trampling him in the slide, but driving the monstrous thing aside and up and up the bank, where it had no apparent wish to go.

It collapsed on the slope as it reached the light, a black serpent, part scaled, part furred, with helpless naked limbs and a flat head which it attempted to cover. It seemed to shrink, then, sliding down into shadow, into wrinkled skin and fur, into a shape inexplicably like a little old man, while the Yard-thing kept hissing and growling in the shadow of the hole from which the creature had come, keeping it from refuge.

"Ask its name!" Uulamets shouted from above. Sasha looked up and saw Uulamets standing on the rim, then looked toward the cowering creature Pyetr held at sword's point and said, "He wants to know its name."

Pyetr jabbed it. *Hwiuur*, it said. *Hwiuur*, like some strange kind of bird. It edged closer to the hole, but the Thing was there and would not let it in.

"Ask it where my daughter is," Uulamets called down. "Tell it answer or you'll keep it here till the sun rises."

133

"It's a damned snake!" Pyetr cried. "How is it to know where your daughter is?"

But it was not a snake. It seemed more to be a hairy old man, who crouched in the shadow of the earth and shivered, saying, "The sun, the sun!"

"You'll see the sun," Uulamets shouted, "if you don't answer. I want my daughter back."

The creature covered its face, snuffling softly. "I'd do it," Pyetr advised it. "He's a terrible old man."

"Is that all he wants?" the creature whispered between long-nailed fingers. "One thin-boned girl? I can. I can do that. Take the iron away." It peered between the fingers, one pale snake's eye, so it seemed to be. Or at least it was not human. "I know where she sleeps. I can bring her. Bone and all, I can bring her. Tell the wizard let me go."

"Tell me where she is!" Uulamets shouted.

But of a sudden it was a snake again, whipping about at ankle height, bound straight for the cave, as the Yard-thing attempted to head it off.

Dirt poured down. The Yard-thing came backing out spitting and snarling, as the whole bank came down and the hole closed.

"Fools!" Uulamets cried. "You let it get away!"

"Fool, yourself!" Pyetr shouted, turning about, but Sasha quickly caught his arm and perhaps Pyetr thought again, that here were the two of them in this crumbling pit, three, if one counted the ill-tempered Yard-thing, four, if one counted the snake that had just disappeared into the bank, and one had rather not.

"It promised," Sasha said to Uulamets. "It did promise. Master Uulamets, get us out of here."

For a long few moments Uulamets stood there staring down at them, in what had become the first pale light of day. Then he flung down his staff.

"Climb that," he said.

It took Pyetr bracing the staff up the unstable slope with his body length, and Sasha climbing up over him and up the length of the staff, while he showered a great deal of dirt down on Pyetr, who spat and swore and held on.

Sasha reached the top, hauled himself over the rim on his elbows and on his knees to find master Uulamets sitting on the grass arranging his pots in a half circle in front of him.

Sasha turned about and lay flat on his stomach on the rim of the pit, reaching down after the staff Pyetr reached up to him. He grasped it and tried to hold on while Pyetr climbed, but he failed to hold it and flung the staff aside on the grass.

"I'd use a limb," Uulamets said disinterestedly.

"Master Uulamets says get a branch or something," Sasha called down. Pyetr looked up at him distressedly. The Yard-thing was still in the pit with him. Pyetr was resolutely not looking at it. "Then do it," Pyetr said.

Sasha got up and ran down the slope and up again to the edge of the dead woods, where there were rotten limbs in plenty. He picked a likely big one that was already lying on the ground and dragged it back as quickly as he could, past master Uulamets, who was sitting there with several of his little pots in hand, shaking out powders and muttering to himself and singing.

Sasha heaved the dead limb over the edge and Pyetr pulled it to the bottom, breaking off twigs and lesser branches which were in his way. Sasha lay down to hold the topmost branches steady while Pyetr flung himself at the dead limb and climbed, stepping from branch stub to branch. Finally he reached Sasha's arms and hauled himself up and over, while Sasha clenched his teeth and held himself as steady as he could.

"Babi!" the old man called.

The Yard-thing came scrambling up the branches, face on. Sasha yelled and flung himself aside and sat down beside Pyetr as it scuttled over to Uulamets.

But Uulamets simply muttered to himself and scattered powders on the ground, ignoring it crouching there.

"What's he doing?" Pyetr asked. "What does he think he's doing? —What *is* that thing?"

"I don't know," Sasha said. He thought that he ought to feel something if it was true magic master Uulamets was doing. Or if what he was doing was working at all. He felt nothing but a shiver in his bones and a queasiness at the pit of his stomach.

"We ought to get out of here," Pyetr said, Sasha thought quite calmly and reasonably under the circumstances. "We don't know where that thing went. We don't know what it's up to."

"We'll go," Sasha said, wishing that they would, wishing that he understood what Uulamets was up to. "Soon now."

But Uulamets kept scattering pinches of powder and singing, and finally piled up a few handfuls of grass and asked for wood.

"For what?" Pyetr asked. "A fire? Here?"

"I'll get it," Sasha said under his breath, seeing nothing else to do. He got up and ran back to the woods and gathered up twigs and larger pieces, ran panting back to Uulamets and dumped it down, falling to his knees. "Master Uulamets—"

The Thing growled at him. Master Uulamets ignored him and went on with his chanting, which reminded Sasha very unpleasantly of the night Pyetr had almost died. It was the same kind of singsong, under the breath, it was the same off-key tuneless wandering. He saw Uulamets pick up the twigs and break them and put dry grass into the midst. He saw Uulamets take a pungent bit of wool from one little pot and tuck it into the grass. Then he took a cinder from a small fire pot, and Sasha jumped in spite of himself when the pile burst into flame.

"Fool," Uulamets said under his breath, interrupting his singing. And handed him another pot, an empty one. "Water. —And be careful. The vodyanoi's not to trifle with in his element."

"Was *that* what it was?" The question jumped out before Sasha remembered the master was incanting. He ducked his head, murmured a quick Excuse me, and hurried up the ridge and down again where he recollected a stream—terrified at the mere thought of going to the river if *that* was lurking there.

But something came behind him, and he looked back through the dead woods to see Pyetr coming down the slope.

"You don't have to go!" Sasha said, and held up the pot. "I'm just going after water!"

"What are you, his servant?" Pyetr skidded down the slope. "Let him fetch his own."

"Please. Don't fight with him." He reached the little stream, hardly ankle-deep, and dipped up the water, then hurried back again. "He says that thing was a vodyanoi."

"It can be whatever it wants," Pyetr said. "I've nothing more to do with it." Pyetr had, overall, the look of a man who wanted very much to say what he had seen was only a log or a large snake or whatever, but who had gone very much beyond that safe limit. Pyetr stayed with him as he hiked back up the slope and down again to bring the pot to master Uulamets.

The which master Uulamets took, and set in a forked stick he held above the fire.

"Listen, grandfather," Pyetr said, taking a step nearer on the slope, and Sasha winced. "I've a notion to be on to Kiev. Whatever we owe you, we've just paid it. So we're leaving. Hear?"

"Onto the river?" Uulamets asked. "Or through the woods? The vodyanoi or my daughter?"

Pyetr scowled, and beckoned Sasha.

"He's telling the truth," Sasha said. "Pyetr, we won't make it."

"We did well enough. And small help grandfather was, there. 'Bring me wood. Fetch me water.' So he can have his morning tea, I suppose—while we fend off his damn pet and whatever-it-was—"

"A vodyanoi," Uulamets interjected pleasantly, without looking at either of them.

"Vodyanoi. River-thing. Whatever it is, it ran. It didn't like having its nose hit. Your daughter runs cold fingers down a body's neck, but the most she's done is fling a few pots and rattle the shutters. A pretty weak ghost, I'd say."

"Quite," Uulamets said. "I've kept her that way, deliberately. Go on, go running off alone. One of you will feed her. The other will be extremely sorry. You *won't* go, Pyetr Ilitch. You're not a fool. Don't act like one."

For a moment everything Pyetr said seemed reasonable; then everything Uulamets said overpowered it, with such a feeling of danger in the woods around them that Sasha felt impelled to look behind him—but he resisted that impulse, jammed his hands into his belt and thought very hard about Pyetr being right.

A chill ran down his neck. A second one. He was *sure* that something was behind him, even if Pyetr was facing him and showing no sign of anything amiss. For a moment he was not even sure he could rely on Pyetr, or if Uulamets might not have cast some spell on him to keep him blind to danger.

"Stop it!" he said. It was the hardest thing in the world to speak out against the old man. "Master Uulamets, you're doing that, I know you are."

"So I am," Uulamets said, but the feeling did not go away. Uulamets turned his head and looked at Pyetr. "The boy trusts you. He'll fight *me* for you, and for a lad of his sensitivities, that's considerable courage. But he's quite young. He can be persuaded against his better judgment—by a plausible scoundrel. Very much like my daughter. That's why I'm patient with him. But you—having none of his sensitivities, and a rebellious and an entirely selfish attitude, in which the god forbid there should be anything in the entire world outside your personal understanding!—have no hesitation about taking this boy off to your feckless purposes, for what? For Kiev? A place no better than the last that failed to satisfy you, or the next, or the next. Your lacks, sir, are in yourself; and you most unfortunately carry that baggage to whatsoever place you find yourself. Most significantly, you pass for a man, sir, in this boy's eyes, and I suggest you examine the responsibilities of that position."

"And what do you pass for?" Pyetr retorted. "A wizard. A scholar. A man of learning. About *what?* Sitting alone out here in the woods mixing stinking potions and talking to birds and snakes!"

"If you'd had the wit to talk to that one, we'd be better off. Sit down. Stop talking nonsense. What if you'd not had my advice about the sun, what if you'd blithely assumed it was yourself that drove the vodyanoi back, and you'd been fool enough to chase him into his hole? Then you'd have regretted it. So would the boy."

"It did run from the sword," Sasha objected. It upset him that the old man said things so hurtful to Pyetr, even if he knew they verged on true. It upset him the more that Pyetr just stood there, angry, and not doing anything.

"Since the sunlight weakened it," Uulamets said. "Yes. And it's doubtless not feeling well. Hope that's the case. I have a job for you."

"What?"

"There'll be a cave on the riverward side of this hill. There'll be a nest there. I want you to put something in it."

"Don't be ridiculous," Pyetr said.

"Or you can do it," Uulamets said with a particularly unpleasant grin. "Soon, I'd say, since I'm relatively sure the vodyanoi's out of his lair at the moment, and I wouldn't give odds he'll stay away long." Uulamets held up the pot in the forked stick. "This. Just throw it in. You faced down the creature once. You don't really have to go inside. And of course your sword's enough to protect you."

"No," Sasha said.

"It's after all for his own rescue," Uulamets said. "I'll do it myself if I have to. Or you can. But our brave fellow so wants to prove he's right about the sword—"

"I'm not a fool!" Pyetr said.

"Of course not. Nor a coward, are you? Shall I do it? I'm certainly not as agile, or as strong. . . ."

Pyetr walked up and held out his hand for the stick and the pot, scowling.

"No," Sasha said. "Pyetr, don't."

"It's easy," Pyetr said nastily. "Your wizard says it is."

"It should be," Uulamets said, "if one isn't a fool."

"Old man," Pyetr said on a deep breath, and rocking on his feet, "I've a great deal more patience than you and far better breeding. Which, considering I was born in a gutter, I've never been able to say before."

With which Pyetr took the pot in hand, flung the stick down, and walked off while Sasha was still standing there numb.

"Let me go!" he said to Uulamets, and felt the release as sudden as the relaxing of a fist.

He ran, then.

12

✠ ✠ ✠ ✠ Pyetr heard the boy coming behind him as he crossed the ridge, turned around in mid-step and thought with honorable motives the old man had denied he even owned that he ought to order Sasha straight back to Uulamets.

But he thought then, too, that the boy had made a difference against the thing before, that between them, they had been able to handle it, and that if he got himself killed altogether needlessly, Sasha was in a great deal more difficulty being left to Uulamets' keeping.

So he stood there until Sasha caught up, then walked on down the slope to the river, passing the uncomfortably warm little pot from one hand to the other.

"Why don't you let me—" Sasha began.

"No," he said. "Absolutely not."

"He was trying to make you mad."

"I am mad."

"Please be careful."

Decent advice, he thought. He said, "Know how to use a sword?"

"No," Sasha said.

"Take it anyway." He drew the whole sword belt off and passed it to Sasha as they reached the bottom of the hill, on the green, grassy margin of the river. "Point or edge, it doesn't matter. Aim for the eyes. Nothing likes that. Take it! I don't want it banging about my ribs. I've got one hand full."

Sasha took it from him and hung it over his shoulder. "Be careful of—"

"I'm being careful, for the god's sake." The edge of the

140

river was a clean one here, except where a young willow stood, and that—judging where the knoll was situated on the other side of the ridge and where the hole had been on that other side, in the pit—was the likeliest place for a den unless it was entirely underwater.

It was also the likeliest place for the snaky thing to be hiding, and when he came closer and saw there was indeed a dark space among the willow-roots, he had a very queasy feeling in his stomach.

"Well," he said, "if I toss grandfather's potion into the wrong hole, he's not going to be happy. But I don't know how I'm to tell." He set his foot on a willow root and grasped a trailing bunch of willow strands. They were lithe and strong, leafless but budding.

"It's alive," Sasha said in the same instant he realized it. "The tree—"

He looked around into a pale face not Sasha's, and yelled and scrambled back for another foothold as something whipped around his ankle.

He yelled as it jerked: he went down under the water and the yell became bubbles. Muscular flesh wrapped him about. He shoved at it and it threw more coils about him as he suddenly found himself in air again, in the dark, traveling backwards and upwards in the wet soft embrace of a Thing the shape of which seemed to be changing by the instant. He choked, spat, swore at it and kicked it in its soft body with all his might, and when it disliked that enough it spun rapidly about, carrying him upright with it. Breath cold and foul as a swamp's bottom gusted down on his face.

"Damn you!" he cried, terrified, and struggled and kicked for all he was worth. He lost the pot he had in his hand, he hit the soft muddy floor and he skidded down the slick bank into the water.

Huge coils slipped past him like a river in spate and battered him left and right.

He came up choking and spitting, scrambling as far from touching anything as he could—heaved himself up onto the bank and put his hand on something sharp and hard, among a great number of small, sharp objects that rattled with a bony

141

sound—at which he stopped very still, caught a mouthful of air and listened.

He moved from his awkwardly braced position. A bone rattled softly. He braced again, hearing no sound at all but his own breathing, and began to shiver, a slow quiver of one leg and an arm.

It was making no noise. It might be in the water waiting for him. It might have coiled up on the other bank of the cave. The place was full of dark, cold water, and bones; and the longer he delayed the more terrible it seemed to die there. He could see least lightening of the water in the direction he took for the river, and with a great gulp of air he let go, slipped into the water and ducked under the surface, clawing his way toward the light for all he was worth.

His fingers found something soft and oozing at that threshold—only mud, he told himself; and then something hard and odd—more bones on the bottom. The eyeholes of a skull. He shoved it away with a shudder, fighting to escape the hole and the roots.

Then something grappled with him, and he kicked and fought his way to the surface, blind and struggling against what he suddenly realized was a wet and equally frightened boy.

"God!" he yelled, grabbing a willow root and trying to hold on to Sasha at the same time, Sasha gasping and thrashing and trying to hold on to him, flailing with the sword in his other hand.

"I thought you were dead!" Sasha cried.

"Then what were you doing?" he yelled, and choked and dragged the boy as high as he could hold him, so that Sasha could get a grip on the willow.

Sasha climbed, flung the sword onto the bank and hauled himself up where he could be of some help himself, hauling at Pyetr's coat, pulling him up where Pyetr could climb, shivering and coughing, onto the roots and the bank and as far from the water as he could pull both of them.

"Fool!" he shouted at the boy, shaking him, still himself trembling with fright.

Then it dawned on him by the boy's white face and his lack of a coat and his having the sword that Sasha might not have fallen in. That so shocked him he sat there with his fist knotted in the boy's wet shirt and the boy staring at him as if he expected to be murdered, and could not move, except he had to cough, and let Sasha go.

"Don't ever do a thing like that!" he said when he could get his breath. "God, boy."

Sasha just stared at him with his teeth chattering and his lips turning blue. Pyetr gathered his shaking limbs under him and gave Sasha a shove toward the coat that was lying on the bank. "Wrap up," he said, shivering. "Get moving. You'll take your death. . . ."

He picked up his sword. He found the sheath. His coat was running a steady stream of water, water cold as the wizard's daughter favored—

He looked back at the willow, the only living tree in all the woods, and recollected the bones down in the cave.

Sasha pulled at his arm, said, with his teeth chattering, "Come on," and he gathered his wits back and made what speed he could up the hill.

Uulamets still had the fire going. He looked up with a certain surprise—maybe to see *two* of them, Pyetr thought, with thoughts of wringing Uulamets' neck—which perhaps the black fur-ball quite well understood, because it ran forward and growled and hissed as they came stumbling down the hill soaking wet and shivering.

"Get out of my way!" Pyetr snarled at it, and gave it a swipe with his sword. "Get!"

It spat and hissed and kept its distance as they came up to Uulamets.

"I delivered your damn bottle," Pyetr said. "I think we found your tree. It's the other side of the hill. I don't think you'll like the company it keeps."

Uulamets looked alarmed, and got up and went running off up the ridge, abandoning his pots, his bag, everything but his staff. The Thing went running after him. Sasha looked as if he was thinking about it, but Pyetr grabbed him by the arm and shoved him toward the fire. "Keep it going," he ordered the boy, tossed him the sword and went over to the edge of the pit, lay down and dragged the dead limb up the slide.

What he could break off it kept the fire going, at least,

built a fair good fire, at least enough to take the chill off, enough warmth for him to work his coat and his shirt off and to wring out at least the bulk of the water and heat up the shirt before he put it back on. He was doing the same for Sasha's shirt when the old man came back over the ridge, furiously angry, striking at the grass with his staff, the Thing dogging his track down the slope.

Pyetr scowled at Uulamets when he arrived at the fire, ready to give the old man word for word anything he was ready for; but Uulamets said not a word to either of them, only squatted down with a thunderous frown and began to pack up his little jars.

"So what do we do now?" Pyetr asked.

"Stay here and do *nothing!*" Uulamets snarled under his breath, took his bag of pots and left, with the Thing scurrying behind him.

"Good riddance," Pyetr said, gave Sasha's shirt a furious twist and stuck it on a long branch, toasting it over the fire while Sasha stayed bundled up in his coat. "Get the breeches off. And the boots. Hold this."

He went after more wood, squishing as he walked, warming himself with temper and with work. He gathered a good armload up on the ridge, keeping an eye on the boy at the fire, and came back to build the fire three times its size.

"Could you see master Uulamets?" Sasha said, worried. "If it came back—"

"Let it choke on him." Pyetr sat down, pulled his wet boots off, pulled off his own breeches and wrung them out, making a puddle in the grass. He sneezed violently, wiped his nose, and put the breeches back on, wet as they were.

"I don't think I even know where the house is," Sasha said.

It was a grim thought, for a moment. Then Pyetr jutted his chin toward the river. "Good as any road. I know where we are. Use your wits, boy. You don't get everything by wishing."

Sasha's face reddened past its pallor, and Pyetr remembered then calling him a fool and half drowning him.

"You did all right," he said, and pulled his coat off and laid it on the grass, figuring the shirt was the only thing that was going to dry in any reasonable time. He wrung it out a second time, found himself a couple of sticks and spread it on them, to hold over the fire. "Just for the god's sake what did you think you were going to do?"

"Bring you your sword," Sasha said. "Then it came out of the hole. I knew it was out. Before I went in the water." He started shivering again, having trouble with his tongue. "What was in there?"

Pyetr stared at the fire, keeping his shirt out of it, concentratedly keeping it from scorching, keeping his eyes on the bright warmth. "Bones. Lot of bones. I think I know what happened to his daughter."

"You think he knew?"

Pyetr shrugged, recollecting a pretty face. A girl Sasha's age. Not a ghost, a memory of a ghost. "Maybe," he said. "He knew about the Thing in the river. He wasn't surprised, was he?"

"He says he can bring her back."

"Bones are damn hard to bring back. Aren't they?" He remembered Sasha saying, the morning after his own illness—Pyetr, you were dying and he brought you back—

He did not want to remember that. He did not want to guess what the old man was doing over the ridge. He did not want to remember the inside of the cave, or the feel of the vodyanoi's body or that mud in the entrance, with the bones in it.

He said, in Sasha's long silence, "About time we got out of here. We'll get grandfather home, get him settled. He owes us, this time. He can't say we didn't try."

Somehow the prospect of trekking down the riverside was both more and less frightening than it had been. At least, if there was such a thing as a vodyanoi, it could be cut, it—whatever master Uulamets said—hated the sun, it preferred the water, it skulked around in underwater caves and there was a way to avoid it on those terms, simply keeping to the general line of the river for a guide through the forest and never spending the night without fire, which they could get the same way master Uulamets got it, with a clay firepot.

"We walked in," he said to Sasha, "we can certainly walk out again, in a direction we want to go."

"We still need his help," Sasha whispered, as if anything

145

they said could carry across the ridge. "Just please, please don't fight with him, don't make him angry."

He had seen Sasha's face when the wizard was talking. Sasha's deference to the old man infuriated him. But he had thought the Thing was a dog; and sometimes it still looked that way; and he had thought a vodyanoi was a bad dream; and it still felt that way; and he would have said Sasha's wishes were no likelier to come true than anyone's—but he saw at least the chance that an old man twice as stubborn and set on his way could scare a youngster like Sasha, who was convinced his least ill-wish could work terrible, far-reaching harm.

"The old man's damned me often enough," Pyetr said. "If there was anything to *that*, do you think that Thing down there would have gone running?"

"He wanted it to."

"Oh, god," Pyetr said in disgust, and rescued his shirt from scorching. It was hot, and burned his hands. "Damn!"

"Please don't. Not here. Not *now*." Sasha was shivering again, hands clasped between his knees, hardly fit to get the words out.

"Good luck to him, then," Pyetr said, to have peace. "He needs it." And on a more charitable impulse: "He needs somebody to talk him out of this woods, is what he needs. He needs to go downriver, get among sane people. Maybe he is a wizard. —Maybe all this is because he's a wizard, maybe that's all it is, did you ever think of that? Maybe he makes people think they see things."

"You're hopeless!" Sasha cried, as angry as ever Pyetr had seen him. "Do you think all this is for your benefit? It's none of it a joke, Pyetr! His daughter died! Don't make fun of him!"

With which Sasha got up and pulled his coat around him and headed off toward the river, three steps before Pyetr flung his sticks and his shirt down and caught him.

"Don't you be a fool! All right, he's a wizard, he's anything you want, just stay away from there, I believe in it, I believe anything you want, all right?"

Sasha stopped fighting, out of breath. "Something's wrong," he said, trying to twist his hands free, casting anxious looks toward the hill. "Something's wrong with him. You said that—and things just stopped . . ."

"I'm not any wizard," Pyetr said. The wind was cold on his back. The boy's nonsense upset his stomach. "He won't thank you for going over there. If he'd wanted you, he'd have asked. Just stay out of it."

"Just up the hill," Sasha said. "Just up the hill. No more than that."

The boy was set on it. Pyetr tagged after, shivering all the way, as far as the top of the ridge and the view of the willow below.

The old man was lying there, sprawled on the hillside, his pots scattered about him. Sasha started to run. Pyetr did, with a sudden curse remembering he had left his sword back at the fire—slipped and slid down the grassy slope on the boy's track.

The Thing from the yard was lying in the middle of the old man. It snarled at them as they came running up.

The old man was breathing. Pyetr felt an uncharitable regret, seeing that, and the Thing growled the moment the thought crossed his mind.

Sasha spoke softly to it. It sank down then, whining like a dog, and holding to Uulamets' robe with tiny manlike hands.

"Careful!" Pyetr said, when Sasha bent closer.

But it scuttled off Uulamets' chest, seeming smaller still, and hid its face against the old man's sleeve.

Master Uulamets shook his head and stared into the fire, that was all the response he gave to the most careful questions Sasha posed. The pots were scattered and broken, whatever powders master Uulamets had mixed were lost over by the riverside.

And the sun was past noon.

"*I* think we'd better get him home," Pyetr said grimly. "And start now. That Thing likes the dark. How long do we want to sit around here?"

Master Uulamets said nothing to that, either. Sasha looked desperately from one to the other of them, unable to figure why everything came down to him, or why Pyetr was asking him what they ought to do.

Except, when he thought about it, there was no one else to consult. Master Uulamets hardly seemed able to know what had happened to him. And someone had to agree that that was the case.

"I think we'd better," Sasha sighed. "I'd better go back and get what I can salvage—"

"Leave it," Pyetr said sharply. "We're not risking another trip over there. We've had enough accidents, thank you. —Come on, grandfather." He took master Uulamets very gently under the arm and pulled him to his feet. Uulamets did not protest, and Pyetr said, "Get his staff. I suppose he sets some store by it."

Sasha picked it up, and poked the dying fire with it, to spread it out a little in the circle they had made. They had nothing to dig with. He went to the edge of the pit, lay down and took up a double handful of the loose earth, ran back and dumped it on the fire, did it three more times in breathless haste, before he grabbed up the staff and went running down the knoll and up to the ridge where Pyetr and Uulamets had stopped to wait for him.

"Out?" Pyetr asked.

Sasha bobbed his head, winded, expecting Pyetr to find fault with his caution; but he hated fire, he never trusted it, not in the kitchen, not a candle in the stable. When he thought of them arriving back at the house, safe, he thought of a great fire sweeping through the dead woods, taking everything. He wished it dead back there on the knoll—last effort that he could make—with a force that for a moment left him breathless.

"All right, boy?"

He nodded, leaned on the staff and caught his breath. Pyetr clapped him on the shoulder and shook him. "Plenty of time. We're all right. Hear?"

He nodded again, no more able to talk than Uulamets was. It might be fear of leaving a fire. It might be the vodyanoi wanting harm to them. It might be the ghost, it might be all the dead Pyetr said were in this place.

He had only this terrible feeling of leaving something vital undone and unaccounted for, even after he had tried to tie up all the ends. "Master Uulamets," he said, laying his hand on the old man's arm, "is there anything else? is there anything I should do?"

Uulamets did not answer, gave not even the shake of his head or the nod that he had given before. He stood there looking back toward the knoll. Perhaps he had not even heard the question.

Pyetr took Uulamets' arm and pulled it over his shoulders. Sasha took the other side and they started down the ridge.

Thunder muttered beyond the woods.

"Wished the fire out, did you?" Pyetr said.

He threw Pyetr a look past master Uulamets. It was good to know that Pyetr still could make light of their troubles, but he was too frightened and too worried to appreciate it at the moment. He had no desire to have Father Sky vexed with them into the bargain. "Don't—"

"—do that," Pyetr breathed, still mocking him.

"I'm sorry. I'm scared."

"Smart lad," Pyetr said. "Mind your feet."

Master Uulamets took the offered cup in trembling hands, stronger, now, with the fire going strong in the hearth, and the warmth in the house sufficient finally to dispel the chill. Sasha poured another cup and gave it to Pyetr, who likewise sat at the hearth, coughing and worn to exhaustion—master Uulamets' strength not having been enough, after all: Pyetr had had to carry him.

And all master Uulamets had had to say for it was, once, when Pyetr slipped on a leafy bank and fell, "Fool." After which Uulamets had struck Pyetr with his fist. Pyetr had sat there in the rain hardly able to get his breath and said, not joking at all, "Old man, you can crawl home from here for all I care."

But Uulamets had been out of his head with what had happened at the river, and Pyetr half out of his with exhaustion, and when Sasha had tried to carry the old man the way Pyetr had been doing, Pyetr had gotten up, roughly shoved him aside and hauled Uulamets up again. . . .

Sasha poured himself a cup of tea, strong and laced with honey and vodka, and sat down by the fire to sip it.

The Yard-thing had not come back. Babi, whatever its name was, had just gone away at some moment and Sasha had no idea where.

"Have you seen the Yard-thing at all?" Sasha asked Pyetr quietly.

"I've no desire to see it," Pyetr said, wiped his nose and suddenly sneezed. "Damn. If grandfather could just wish this cold away—"

"If you had done as you were told—" Uulamets said with sudden violence, and slopped tea on his quilts. "Damn your interference!"

"What's wrong with him?" Pyetr asked furiously. "What did I say? I nearly drowned with his damned bottle. I carried this whining old man in the rain—"

"Pyetr," Sasha pleaded, and held out an entreating hand. "Just—no. Let be. Let be."

"Leave a simple matter," Uulamets muttered under his breath, "in the hands of your ilk. You *don't believe* in things, do you? Not even simple instructions to stay on your own side of the hill."

"Master Uulamets," Sasha said, "I was the one who crossed the hill. Something had already gone wrong. We saw that. Then we came down after you."

Uulamets wiped his mouth. He looked years older, and full of uncertainties. "It should have worked," he said.

Pyetr shook his head.

"What do you know?" Uulamets asked him sharply. "You're the fault. You're the flaw in this. If you had lent even your most desultory support to this, instead of carping at every turn—I'd have my daughter back. She's gone, do you understand? I don't know what the result was back there. It all went to pieces. And she's gone. What do you say to that? What do you care? What do you care about anything?"

Sasha braced himself for Pyetr's outburst, but Pyetr shook his head a second time.

"What does that mean?" Uulamets said.

"Nothing. It means nothing."

Everything felt dangerous. Sasha wished most earnestly for peace, and master Uulamets turned a scowl his way, at which Sasha froze, paralyzed with the thought that master Uulamets had just felt that wish, and that he *had* made wishes throughout their venture, though he had tried to make them wisely.

"What are you looking at him for?" Pyetr asked. "What did *he* do?"

"One wonders," Uulamets said, and reached out and took Sasha by the shoulder, a terrible look in his eyes. "You've gotten very forward in the last couple of days, boy, altogether forward—"

"Let him be," Pyetr said, but Uulamets did not give up his grip, and Sasha felt colder and colder.

"You do have ability," Uulamets said. "We both know that."

"I never wished anybody harm!"

"You wished your own safety. And his. At what cost? Did you care for that?"

"And yours," Sasha said. "And that you'd find your daughter, and that everything would go right. If one worked, the other should have, shouldn't it? Should it only work halfway?"

Uulamets' mouth made a thin line, and trembled. His fingers bit into Sasha's shoulder.

It is my fault, Sasha thought with a sinking feeling. It seemed entirely, appallingly possible.

Uulamets let him go of a sudden, swung around and flung his teacup into the fireplace. It shattered. Like the pots.

Pyetr flung his cup after it. It smashed, and the fire hissed and flared. But Pyetr said nothing, just got up, hitched his quilt around him and took another cup and the vodka jug off the table. He came back and sat down this time in his usual spot at the side of the fire, looking fury at Uulamets, between unstopping the jug and pouring a cup for himself.

"The boy did you no harm," Pyetr said. "I'd go to bed, old man. Since this is mine, I'm in it. Good night to you."

Uulamets stared at him a moment with an expression Sasha could not see: he only felt threat and desperately wished Pyetr well, because he was very much afraid of what master Uulamets might be wishing him. Uulamets was surely aware of that defiance too, and angry.

"You," Uulamets said to Pyetr, "mistake your place in this house."

Pyetr lifted the cup in salute. "Then fetch another cup and have a drink. Fetch your *own* cup for a change."

Sasha felt the danger, felt it and threw all his effort into stopping it.

The cup in Pyetr's hand—shattered. Pyetr jumped and recoiled, wide-eyed and only then seeming to realize there was nothing accidental in it.

Pyetr began to pick the fragments off his quilt-covered lap with a visibly shaking hand. Sasha got up, quickly, grabbed his blanket about him and said, touching master Uulamets on the shoulder, as carefully as he had ever intervened with a trespassing customer, "Please, sir. It's late. Can I get you anything else? I'd be very happy to."

He was afraid. He felt Uulamets' anger touch him.

And grow quieter then.

"Sir?"

"More cups," Uulamets said, not: cup; cups. Sasha ran that through again, nodded anxiously and went and brought them, one for Uulamets and, as Uulamets seemed to intend, one for Pyetr.

Pyetr poured from the jug, still shaking a little, whether from exhaustion or from having a cup break in his hand that should not have broken. He leaned forward and poured for Uulamets, too, and put a little in Sasha's cup.

Sasha sat down, picked up his cup, and took a sip, only half feeling the burn as it slid down his throat.

Outside, thunder rumbled. A fresh spatter of rain hit the shutters.

"My daughter," Uulamets said quietly. "Did you see her— at any time I was beyond the hill?"

Pyetr shook his head. "No." And looked up as if he had remembered something. "On the river. Before that. At the willow. Just a single glance."

Uulamets rested his elbow on his knee and ran his hand back over his hair.

"But I'm not sure," Pyetr said, "that what I followed there—"

A footstep sounded outside, on wet boards, a little louder sound than the rain.

They all froze in mid-breath. The footsteps hesitated, then came to the door. Someone knocked.

A second knock, then: Pyetr moved to take his sword from its rest beside the fireplace, with the thin hope that if a vodyanoi had no liking for it, other things magical might not— and his first thought for visitors on a night like this was the vodyanoi itself. But Uulamets was already struggling to his feet, with Sasha trying to help him: Uulamets shook him off and headed straight for the door, his blanket tangling and trailing in his tattered robe.

Pyetr caught at his arm. "It might not be your daughter," he said, he thought quite sanely. But Uulamets snarled, "Little you know," and tottered past him.

"Fool," Pyetr muttered, and seized Sasha instead, who was dithering in the way, and put him back to the side as master Uulamets threw up the latch and the wind pushed the door open.

A girl appeared in the lightning flicker, drenched, her blond hair and her white gown alike streaming water.

"Papa?" she said faintly, and flung her arms around Uulamets.

It was *her*, it was the ghost beyond a doubt—but not ghostly white now, only white from cold; and streaming water onto the floor—but it was, after all, raining. . . .

And this girl who had plagued his dreams and eluded everyone else's sight—was most surely visible to all of them.

He ought to have been shocked, perhaps—or glad for the old man, or afraid that she might suddenly transmute herself into weed and old bone . . . with the god knew what sort of deadly intention—

But of all things to feel, as she lifted her head from her father's shoulder and looked dazedly around her, he truly expected—anticipated—that she would be pleased to see him.

She showed nothing of the kind. He and Sasha together might have been a table, an accompanying chair, of passing interest only because they were strange in her house.

Odd, to feel slighted by a ghost.

He watched Uulamets bring the girl to the fire and offer

her the scattered quilts. He let his sword fall, while Sasha alone had the practical good sense to shut the door and latch it against the wind. Sasha also had the absolutely amazing self-possession to ask whether Uulamets' daughter would care for tea.

She would.

Pyetr simply wandered to the far side of the table and sat down on the bench with his sword still in his hands, watching while a doting father wrapped his soaked, rain-chilled daughter in the quilts, while he chafed her hands, helped her dry her hip-long hair, and murmured how cold she was and how he had lost all hope this morning, and how unspeakably happy he was now. Uulamets suddenly seemed to have a heart, for the god's sake, or he was completely out of his head.

While the girl, who was more beautiful than any girl Pyetr had ever seen, soaking wet or otherwise, huddled in the blankets and clutched her father's hands and said how glad she was to be home, and how—here for the first time she truly looked at Pyetr—she had tried so hard to escape her plight, but that she had no wish, considering a rusalka's essential nature, to come anywhere near her father. So she had sought other means to speak to him.

"I'm so sorry," she said, and tears spilled onto her pale cheeks, which blushed with hectic color. "I'm so sorry. Everything's dead—I didn't want it to die. But I didn't want to fade. And I would have. I didn't know anything to do, but to try to stay alive, and they died, everything died, and I'm sorry—"

Upon which she began to cry, while Sasha was attempting, delicately balanced on one foot, to get behind her to take the water kettle from the hearth.

It all should have been ludicrous, the boy teetering on one foot, the recent ghost sobbing away against the old man's shoulder—

But Pyetr watched father and daughter, with the sword lying on the table in front of him, and very much wished that it was his shoulder, and that she would look his direction, and that he could decide whether her eyes were dark or light.

And he wondered if he was only one more of her victims or whether she had had a special, secret reason for choosing him to approach—

It had seemed so to him—it had very much seemed to him, at the willow, that she had been trying to warn him, and last night in the house, after the wind, she had come to him in his dreams, less as a haunt than as a desperately lost girl, speaking to him in words he could almost hear. . . .

She was only a girl, after all. Silly girls threw themselves at him all the time—a distraction, a momentary amusement, a nuisance in some measure: a man with his looks soon learned what it was all worth. Mature *ladies* were his real interest. But every move this girl made as flesh and blood was amazing to him—no longer drifting, but—

—real. . . .

Sasha brought the tea and the girl looked at him and necessarily brushed his hand with her fingers as she took the cup. That touch made his blood run a little faster, which was a feeling he had no notion what to do with—or rather he did, but he had never been within half a step of any girl who made him feel that way, and he backed away, in the same moment stepping on a knot of blankets and having to catch his balance, looking like a fool, if she was paying any attention to him— which he really hoped she was not, just then. But just as he hoped that, the thought occurred to him that a wizard's daughter might know things about people the way he did, being sometimes unnaturally sensitive to the world around her.

That possibility embarrassed him beyond good sense, and of course the harder one tried not to think about a thing, the stronger the feeling got. He reeled away into the shadow and made a wide circuit around Uulamets and his daughter, his face burning. She surely thought he was a complete fool, and she might well resent him, especially since he had what Uulamets called ability, and here he had been sleeping in her house, asking valuable questions of her father—

That was his experience of household situations, at least, in which he always seemed to be the interloper.

He sat down on the bench beside Pyetr and put his elbows on the table, figuring that beside someone as mature and self-possessed as Pyetr he was a good deal less conspicuous.

13

✳ ✳ ✳ ✳ Eveshka . . . that was her name . . . talked
on and on with the old man, much of the
time in words too soft for Pyetr to hear above the patter of
rain on the roof, but Pyetr watched her, all the same, and
caught snatches of Uulamets' answers—how the old man had
feared she had drowned herself, or that she might have met
some accident trying to run away; but no, Eveshka said . . .

"I was walking down along the river," she said, in a soft,
breathless voice, "and the vodyanoi caught me. I should have
known him. I should never have listened. But he looked like
a traveler. . . ."

Odd, Pyetr thought. No one would expect travelers here
. . . not for a hundred years.

But, he suddenly thought, the rusalka had killed the forest.
The forest had been dead—how many years?

How old is she? How old is Uulamets himself? Could
someone like him have a daughter so young?

". . . and I came too close," Eveshka said in her soft, lilting
voice, calmly telling things that would make a grown man
blanch. She was so calm—like a tsarina, he thought: a face
like that, hands like that, feet like that, should be set off with
cloth of gold and jewels; but she wore only a thin white dress
with ragged, dirty sleeves. "He asked my help, I was a fool,
and he suddenly showed his real shape and wrapped me up in
his coils. The next thing I knew I was in the river. I breathed
the water. That was all."

Uulamets hugged his daughter. Liar, Pyetr thought sullenly, hearing the crotchety old man whisper that he loved
her very much, truly he did. If his own dice-loving father had

ever hugged him and said he missed him in that adoring tone of voice, he would have been sure his father was up to no good. The present spate of endearments from Uulamets made his flesh crawl.

But he felt a little gnawing doubt of his own judgment, Ilya Kochevikov having been no good example of a father—and he felt the old resentment for that mixing in all his other feelings about Uulamets, and in his new reckonings about what might have happened to the girl. . . .

How long ago?

Who was her mother, anyway?

"I knew," Eveshka said, her head on Uulamets' shoulder, "that if anyone could help me, you could. I so much wanted to tell you I was sorry. I kept thinking . . . the last thing I'd ever done in this world was quarrel with you, and all through these years, I could see you come and go in the forest and I could watch you working in the yard—oh, I was there! And I couldn't even tell you I was sorry—"

She began to cry again. "Hush, hush, hush," Uulamets said, and stroked her hair and rocked her.

So much tenderness was acutely embarrassing. Pyetr found interest in the wood grain of the table in front of him, and in the firelight on the metal of the sword. He earnestly wished the house afforded somewhere else to go, and likely Sasha wished the same; but there was no such refuge. He would get up himself and rattle around pouring himself a drink and then ask the girl his own morbid questions—except she looked distraught, and where things might go with her then was too uncertain. She might take offense, and that certainly was not what he wanted—although he was far from sure precisely what he wanted from a dead girl whose bones he might well have touched this morning. It was altogether outside his experience.

So he sat still, beside Sasha, who was quite mouselike quiet, until Uulamets proposed his daughter was surely tired and might want to rest.

"I'm sure these young gentlemen won't mind giving up the hearth," Uulamets said. "You'll sleep in your own bed tonight—"

Pyetr inclined his head with some dignity; Sasha attempted to rise and make a bow, inside the limits of the bench as Eveshka looked at them, shyly lowered her eyes and said Thank you in a soft voice that could well get possession of more than a spot by the fire.

Uulamets went to his bed and began dragging another cot from under it. Sasha clambered over the bench and went to help him. Pyetr simply sat still at the table and watched Eveshka watching them, all white and gold, standing there in front of the fireplace, with her hair—dry now—floating around her like the light itself.

He reminded himself sternly then of Kiev, and of the certain fact that Uulamets would in no wise allow a man near the girl, particularly considering Uulamets' estimate of him. Doubtless this dispossession from the hearthside was Uulamets' signal to them both that he was quite ready to see their backs.

So they might set out down the river tomorrow with no thanks and probably cheated of half the provisions they had bargained for—and won!—while the old skinflint kept a girl like her locked away in a dying forest . . .

No matter that the condition of the forest was in some measure her fault. She was certainly no ghost now.

Was she not?

A sane man at least had to think the thought, as he began bedding down in the dark corner beyond the table.

"Do you suppose she's safe?" he whispered to Sasha in the faintest of voices as he lay down to sleep. It seemed to him if Sasha had wizardly talents he might be more sensitive to such things.

"What do you mean?" Sasha whispered back. So much, he thought, for wizardly sensitivity.

"Nothing," he said, and pulled the quilt over his head, exhausted and determined to sleep, entertaining himself with thoughts of Eveshka.

But immediately as he shut his eyes his traitorous mind conjured instead the sudden drop into the pit at the knoll; and when he banished that memory, gave him the cave and the vodyanoi's soft body wrapping around him—none of which promised pleasant dreams or a restful night.

Doggedly he remembered Eveshka by firelight, which chased the dark to the far edges of his mind.

Until his imagination, sly beast that it was, came around to Eveshka's image on the river, and the touch of her cold fingers—and then, by unpleasant surprise, brought back the feeling of the bones in the cavern mud.

So, well, but even as a ghost, Pyetr told himself, putting his unruly imagination to rout again, Eveshka had hardly done him harm, a little cold water on his face, a scowl and a retreat—which he could now attribute to her desperate frustration rather than to any anger directed at him: she had tried so hard to speak, always without a sound. She had tried, there by the willow that was her tree—

The cave came back, perniciously. He heard the vodyanoi saying, "Best three out of five," with his father's voice, which he reckoned was less prophetic than the fact that he had been recollecting his father with unusual clarity this evening.

Back to the fire, then, and Eveshka: his thoughts kept going in circles, and he sincerely wanted to put all of it away and get some sleep—but with darker and darker images beginning to drift through his eyes when they were shut, he decided he had rather stay awake awhile. Unlikely things seemed to have happened to him with such persistence these last few days that nothing seemed quite safe: his mind was all a-boil with sights it refused to reconcile, and he was beginning to have a great difficulty telling the imaginary from the real.

He was not, tonight, with a dead girl dreaming by the hearth and his whole body aching from the battering of the vodyanoi in the cave, entirely certain that he was in control of his life any longer, and he found that a very upsetting idea.

He could go away from here, he and Sasha could just walk away in the morning with no one to stop them (granted they kept an eye to the river), and two or three days after this he would be able to wonder again if he had ever seen a rusalka or a dvorovoi, or wrestled with a River-thing.

But of nights—

For the rest of his life, he feared he was going to dream about things he did not understand. His confidence and his courage were the only assets he had ever had in life, the fact that Pyetr Kochevikov would make a try while everyone else was hesitating. For a man who had a knowledge of the odds for his only inheritance from his father, the existence of unknowables and uncertainties threaded through every situation was a terrible revelation.

One had either blindly to discount them—the action of a fool—or wisely to unravel them, which did not look to be a study of a handful of days.

Of course he could walk out of this woods. He could quite possibly look at the ladies of Kiev in years to come and not compare them too unfavorably with Eveshka's ethereal beauty. And between his light-fingered talent and Sasha's odd ability, he reckoned the two of them could make a tolerably comfortable living in a world of natural men and ordinary risks.

But he would always know there were other rules, and that at some fatal moment they could intervene and tip a balance he thought he had calculated.

It would always be a possibility, even in Kiev, particularly as long as he had Sasha Misurov in his vicinity. There might have been things even in Vojvoda he had been fortunate not to have come afoul of; and one of Vojvoda's wizards might have—

No. Absolutely not. There was no wizardry at all in old Yurishev's death, and nothing but his own stupidity had brought him to that pass.

Unless—

Unless Sasha, the stableboy at The Cockerel, had, in a momentary slip, wished very, very hard to escape his lot, or to find a friend, or to understand what he felt he was—

Or he might once have wished that a real wizard would someday teach him how to handle that deadly gift of his—

Who knew?

God, maybe Uulamets himself had wished—had wished someone like Sasha to help him.

Who was safe anywhere in the world, if wizards could put a thumb on any balance, years and leagues away?

He wanted, damn it all, to understand what he was involved in before he left the place most likely to have the answers, and to know for a certainty whether he had any free will left, even in the choice to go or stay.

—

In the morning Eveshka was up before any of them: Sasha heard the rattle of a spoon, lifted his head and saw that Eveshka was mixing something in a large bowl. Beside him Pyetr was quite soundly sleeping, and Eveshka smiled and waggled her fingers at him to bid him lie down and take a little more sleep himself.

Certainly he had no wish to deal with her alone, Uulamets being still abed. It seemed far safer to take advantage of a little more sleep, so he ducked down in the quilts against the morning chill and shut his eyes.

It seemed only a moment later that he woke with the smell of cakes cooking: he could see past the table legs and the bench a three-legged iron griddle standing in the embers; and Eveshka was turning the cakes, talking to her father, who was up and dressing, and saying she had missed the taste of food.

It somewhat gave one a queasy feeling, thinking about rusalkas, and wondering exactly in what fashion they did sustain themselves, or what exactly her appetites had been.

But he decided he could no longer claim to be asleep, so he gathered himself up and waked Pyetr.

"Our lie-abeds," Uulamets greeted them cheerfully enough, though Pyetr muttered under his breath that he was due a little lying abed after carrying the old man home yesterday.

"We owe our young friends," Uulamets said, and took his daughter by the hand and introduced them each by their proper names, which attention embarrassed Sasha: no one to his recollection had ever introduced him to anyone, since everybody who ever came to The Cockerel had already known him—or had no interest in whether the stableboy had a name. He hardly knew what to do, except to look up at the girl with his face gone burning hot and, he was sure, quite red; while Pyetr in his turn made a bow and said he had never seen anyone so beautiful, not even the finest ladies in Vojvoda.

At which Eveshka looked pleased, and Eveshka was the one who blushed in that exchange, then exclaimed about her cakes and quickly rescued the griddle from the fire and dumped them onto the waiting plate.

161

"They're not burned," she said with a little sigh. "Go, go, everyone wash up. I'll make the tea."

They were wonderful flatcakes, better than aunt Ilenka's, Sasha thought: there were two apiece, with tart dried berries he had not himself discovered in Uulamets' jars, and every crumb disappeared. Uulamets said Eveshka's mother had used to make cakes like that, and Eveshka smiled and laid her hand on her father's as they sat together at the table.

Altogether Uulamets looked very tired, worn to the bone by the last two days, but he looked changed in a better way, too—as if he had let go all the bitterness and the anger he had, and suddenly remembered, with Eveshka in the house, a kinder way of dealing with people. He set his hand over his daughter's and said to them, "I have to explain to you. There was so little I could honestly explain, there was so little I really knew, myself, except that Eveshka—" He pressed her fingers gently. "Eveshka might have run away from me. That wasn't the case. But I feared it might be, and if it had been, it would have been all but impossible to bring her back."

"Papa had a student, Kavi," Eveshka said. "Long ago. I was very young—very foolish. I believed he was innocent of the things papa said. He was very handsome. Very persuasive. But when I did find it out, I was so—" Eveshka looked down, then looked at her father. "I was so embarrassed. You were absolutely right. But I was too ashamed to say so. That was why I left that morning. I only wanted to sit down on the dock and think a while. Then the vodyanoi—"

Tears clouded her eyes and she stopped talking. Sasha sat there beside Pyetr wishing he knew what to do or say to an upset girl who had—he began to realize—been a ghost for perhaps more years than he had been alive, and who was at once a girl of sixteen and much, much older. His stomach felt upset. He remembered the vodyanoi and its malice and felt doubly upset, thinking of Eveshka dragged down into that watery cave.

"I was afraid," Uulamets said quietly, "that she'd killed herself—or that that scoundrel had murdered her. I put nothing past Kavi Chernevog, absolutely nothing." He patted Eveshka's hand. "But you're back. That's all. To the black god with Kavi Chernevog. Do you know, I tried to keep your garden, but I'm afraid all I have luck with is turnips."

Eveshka dried her eyes with her knuckle and suddenly laughed.

"It's all there is to eat around here," Pyetr said, and Uulamets frowned. "But," Pyetr went on irrepressibly, "I can say this place has brightened considerably since yesterday."

The compliment pleased Eveshka. It clearly did not please Uulamets, who immediately stood up and suggested they clear away the dishes and straighten up the house.

Chests in the cellar gave up blankets and clothes—Eveshka's own, one supposed; and more shirts and trousers, fine ones, all of a size. Eveshka ordered a rope strung from the bathhouse to the porch and ordered the laundry tubs rolled out—which activity trampled into submission the weeds around the bathhouse, and meant, Sasha foresaw it, an incredible number of heavy buckets carried up the hill.

But this time—Sasha had not expected it—Pyetr bestirred himself to help, even taking the harder part of the course, carrying the buckets to the top of the muddy, root-laddered path from the river and letting Sasha carry them across the yard to the bathhouse.

Pyetr wore his sword while he was doing this, by which Sasha knew exactly the danger Pyetr was thinking about. Pyetr did not go down to the river with one bucket while he was delivering the other: Pyetr took the harder way, carrying both at a time, then sat on a tree root and waited for him to bring the buckets back, a choice which kept them always in sight of each other, and that, too, said that Pyetr was concerned.

So was he, out under a clear sky, with time enough to get a breath of rain-chilled morning air and to consider that they had had an uncommon amount of good luck in the last couple of days. He was tempted to congratulate himself: perhaps Uulamets' few pieces of advice had helped him manage his gift; or perhaps, as Uulamets had said, it was at least possible to stifle one's ability, to keep a tight grip on it in crises—

"Most people have the instinct for magic," Uulamets had

said to him, that morning that Uulamets had begun to teach him. "Some have a minuscule ability—and don't manage it at all except by smothering it entirely. Or they smother their good sense instead, and make a thorough mess of themselves, wishing this and wishing that to patch what they last wished and never understanding anything: I tell you, good hard work and talent enough to nudge luck a little is a good combination. But everybody wants the one without the other."

"And mine?" he had asked, full of trepidation.

"Might not be small," Uulamets had said. "Let me tell you: it's a law of nature: magicians and magical creatures can be affected by magic more easily than ordinary folk. The very talents which extend them into dimensions impossible for ordinary people likewise mean that wizards can be affected by incantations against which ordinary people would be immune—"

"Can a person—stop these things? Can he—?"

"Turn a spell aside, you mean? Yes. You know how."

He did. He had thought so.

"Let me tell you," Uulamets had said then, at the table that morning: Sasha could still see the old man's cautionary lifting of a finger, feel the danger in the air. "It's always easiest for the young: remember I told you that. Remember this with it: it's very easy for a naïve talent to get quite deep into the spirit world, rather too little resistance to be safe—"

The other clothes they were washing—

Papa had a student, Eveshka had said, *Kavi. . . .*

"—and the deeper you get, the easier it is to bind and to be bound, do you understand, boy? Be careful. Power is very attractive. Aggression is easier than defense. Using is easier than restraining, doing than undoing. Set things in motion only in one direction at a time, or at least remember the sequence of things you wished and know *everything* you're moving, directly or indirectly. That's very important. Most of all beware of ill-wishing anything."

To the black god, Uulamets had said, *with Kavi Chernevog. . . .*

Most particularly . . .

"Where did the flour come from?" Sasha asked, out of

breath, as he handed the two buckets to Pyetr. "Where did the flour come from this morning?"

"Sometimes I have trouble following you," Pyetr said.

"At breakfast." He realized he had started in the middle of his thoughts. "This morning."

Pyetr gave him a very odd look. Or maybe Pyetr was thinking. Pyetr headed down the path to the river and Sasha sat down on the tree root to wait.

He watched Pyetr go down to the riverside and dip the two buckets full. Pyetr came up the trail, hard-breathing, set the two buckets down and said:

"The old man must be trading with somebody. On the river, maybe."

"It wasn't there. Or he had it hidden. Why hide a jar of flour?"

Pyetr gave a large sigh. He looked worried. "I don't know. Maybe it was just left. Maybe she knew where it was."

"Flour won't keep forever. The forest's been dead for ages. Nobody sails the river. . . ."

"So maybe he put a spell on it. Don't wizards do that kind of thing?"

It was a thought. It was better than the thoughts he was thinking, that whatever they had really had for breakfast might be very odd. There was oil. There was flour enough for six cakes, and more, assuming one would hardly use up one's entire store on one breakfast. Oil and flour and berries. It was entirely odd.

Sasha trudged back to the bathhouse with the heavy buckets, up in the yard where Eveshka worked amid clouds of steam. "There," she said; he poured the buckets into the rinse tub and negotiated the boggy ground taking them back to Pyetr at the tree.

"Mostly," Pyetr said when he got there, "I want to know why the spell worked."

"Which spell?"

"The one for her." Pyetr took the buckets. "There were bones in that cave. How do you do anything with bones? How do you bring a body back?"

"I don't know," Sasha said. "That's what that book is, all the things he's ever done or heard, written down."

"Did he tell you that?"

"That's the kind of things wizards have. He told me. You have to keep track of things. You can't forget what you've done or you don't dare do anything. He could have worked years on that spell. Pieces of it. Step by step."

Pyetr looked at him as if he thought he was lying. After a moment he turned and went down the hill.

When he came up again, carrying the buckets full, he said, frowning, "All that book?"

"I don't know. That's just what he said."

"But hasn't he ever tried this before? Why did it work this time?"

That was one worrisome question. He could think of others. "Where's the domovoi? Where's the dvorovoi? Babi, he calls it. We haven't seen him since out there by the knoll."

Pyetr gave a worried grimace, and looked toward the house. "I don't know. I never saw a place that had any. Maybe grandfather just conjured them up to keep him company. Maybe he's forgotten about them now."

Not impossible, Sasha thought. It could be the case. He picked up the heavy buckets and trekked back to the bathhouse, panting by the time he arrived.

"You don't have to go so fast," Eveshka said.

"It's all right," he said.

"Would you tip out the rinse water for me?"

He did. He poured fresh water in. Eveshka's dress was wet and clung embarrassingly and he tried not to stare. He took his buckets back to the tree.

"I haven't seen the raven either," he said to Pyetr. "I'm worried."

"About that damned bird?" Pyetr was being deliberately obtuse, which meant he was annoyed.

"About everything." He was afraid Pyetr was going to propose running off into the woods. But he was far from certain that was not safer than where they were. "I don't think we ought to go running off from here. Master Uulamets may be in trouble, but the kind of trouble I'm afraid of—he's the only one who can handle it. I can't. And a sword can't stop a ghost."

Pyetr frowned more and more darkly. "You think she is."

"I don't know what she is."

"You know better than I do. I never paid any attention to the granny-tales. I never had a grandmother. What's out there? What could be?"

That was a terrible question. All sorts of tales leapt into Sasha's head, things with clutching claws and long, long teeth, things that led you astray and things that pulled you into rivers and things that just took away your mind. "Leshys and such," he said.

"Worse?"

"They could be. I don't know. Sometimes I think Babi's all bluff. But we saw him when he wasn't."

"Damned dog's tucked tail and run," Pyetr muttered, snatching up the empty buckets. "Or something ate *him*."

With which Pyetr flung himself away downslope at some speed. Sasha saw him stop at the bottom and stand, just staring up the river a moment before he filled the buckets and slogged back up the hill.

"She was never malicious," Pyetr said, setting the buckets down.

"Maybe she couldn't be," Sasha said. "Maybe she couldn't do anything. Now—I don't know. He said—he said the more magical a creature is the easier it is to control it."

"That's rot! Cut Uulamets and he bleeds, I'll bet you. That Thing didn't."

"For *magic* to control it," Sasha objected, but it seemed to him that Pyetr had pointed out an essential flaw in Uulamets' reasoning, and he thought about that, and about what a rusalka might do in ghostly form and in a human one.

"What good's magic," Pyetr asked, "if a fool with a sword can cut your throat?"

"I wonder if anything *could* hurt her."

Pyetr looked upset, and threw a glance up the hill, in the general direction of the bathhouse.

"Then what could she want?" he asked. "If she's a ghost, and she's lying, what's she waiting for? Ghost stories never made sense to me. What's all this mincing around, popping up and scaring people, except that they're trying to touch you and they can't. What's to fear, except a guilty conscience? But she can touch things. So if she's a ghost, what's she here for?"

"Because master Uulamets wanted her," Sasha said, in-

167

creasingly disturbed by this line of reasoning. "Because he's a wizard and he wanted her more than she could resist. And he wants her to be what he wants."

Pyetr rubbed the back of his neck. "What if he wants us to stay here? I'm not sure it's safe to go. I'm not sure it's any safer to stay here. I've got two wizards wishing this and wishing that and I'm not sure what I want. I don't like it."

"Three," Sasha said. "There's three."

Pyetr glanced a second time up where Eveshka was working. Slowly his hand fell from his neck. "Four," he said, half a whisper. "There's the vodyanoi: he's not out of the game, is he? How can you ever make up your mind if wishes work? You don't know who's pushing you."

"We don't," Sasha said. "But Uulamets is flesh and blood like us, and I'm not sure anything else is, around here. If something goes wrong, I'd rather be near Uulamets than not. That's all I can think of. I don't want to be out there in the woods or on the river all by ourselves with all this going on, that's what I think."

"You think he made her up?"

From not believing in magic at all, Pyetr had gotten to more precarious thoughts than was good for anyone, Sasha thought, and asked questions he had no idea how to answer, because he had no idea what nature would bear.

Maybe—worse thought—Uulamets himself had no idea: perhaps no wizard who tried the untried could ever know that, and the really powerful ones had no real idea what they were doing. By that reckoning, the more powerful a wizard became, the more foolish it was for him to do anything at all.

He picked up the buckets. "I don't know," he answered Pyetr. "I've no idea." And he added, because a new thought was troubling him: "I wonder what happened to this Kavi Chernevog. I wonder where he is."

"Five wizards?" Pyetr asked.

Sasha looked at him and for a moment could not move, no matter that the weight of the buckets made him short of breath. "I don't know," he said. He thought of asking master Uulamets. But the peace seemed already too precarious. Everything did. Anything might tip it in directions that no one could predict, if there were that many powers with contrary purposes. It was crazy.

No one could predict, if that was the case. If anything master Uulamets had told him was the truth, then no one involved could know the consequences of even the smallest, weakest wish he made.

Wish only good, master Uulamets had advised him, and don't work without knowing what you're doing.

And would a bad man, Sasha wondered, have given him precisely that advice?

One would, perhaps, who was powerful enough to brush aside a boy's efforts and proceed deliberately about his business despite them—but master Uulamets did not seem to be in control of things that were going on. Master Uulamets had ignored his own advice, and worried over that book, and worried over it, and Sasha desperately hoped that master Uulamets was worrying now, much more than showed.

14

✠ ✠ ✠ ✠ The house had smelled of fresh laundry and herbs and baking all day—a curiously disturbing smell, Pyetr decided: not at all like the spirituous odors of the inns in which he had cheerfully misspent his years, smells compounded of smoke and horse and onions and wash water and the god knew what else; or the musty oil-and-wax smell of the homes of the wealthy, to which he had all his life aspired. Eveshka's assault on the senses set a man to thinking about *home*, whatever that was, about modest little houses and cozy firesides with bread baking.

Which was foolish, Pyetr thought, because he could not for the life of him recall any such place in his entire life, except The Doe's kitchen on holidays: that was the closest Ilya Kochevikov's son had ever come to domesticity—nipping cakes off the table and catching a cuff of mistress Katya's well-floured hand—

And here he was, sitting down to dinner, clean-shaven, smelling of soap, splendid in a fine white shirt and clean trousers, beside an uncommonly combed and curried Sasha Misurov, and—god witness—Ilya Uulamets with his hair and beard washed crackling white and not a trace of dirt under his fingernails.

Eveshka, her hair plaited with rose and blue ribbons, ladled out their supper into the waiting bowls, sat down at a tableful of waiting men and took up her spoon with a grace that made a man only hope not to spill anything on his shirt.

Every move she made was like that, every glance of her eyes, every soft, cheerful word. She prattled about the cleaning

170

and the state of the stores and sweetly chided her father for his housekeeping—

Pyetr bit the inside of his lip, hard, and thought about getting up, getting the jug, creating a little noisy levity in the evening, but the hush around the table was too deep, and Eveshka's gracious hospitality too genteel to offend.

He *wanted* something to break the spell. He avoided Eveshka's eyes and tried to find fault with her gentle voice and her laughter, which went straight for the soft spots in a man. He even reminded himself where his sword was, beside him and against the wall; and reminded himself Sasha and Uulamets both had said once, on a saner day, that they should never let her get into the house.

He wanted the boards to creak and the domovoi to manifest itself in the cellar, even for the black ill-tempered ball of fur to show up—Pyetr Ilitch Kochevikov sat there wishing as hard as he had ever wished in his life, in the hope that Sasha was doing the same thing, and in the remote, slightly foolish reckoning that a gambler's luck might be worth something—Sasha swearing that he had none of his own.

But there was no groaning of the house timbers, there was no scratching at the door.

Maybe, he thought of a sudden, it was all due to the fever Sasha swore he had had. Maybe he had never gone into a cave with a vodyanoi. Maybe the girl across the table had never died, and all the rest of it had never happened, and he had only come back to his senses this evening, still a little muddled after fever from his wound. Thoughts like that kept troubling him, complete turnabouts of reason, utterly persuasive if a man did not keep careful hold of what he *had* seen and *had* done—improbable as it was.

And two or three times during supper, when he was most tempted to distrust his memory, he took deliberate hold of his sanity and recollected that watery cave in some detail, remembered the skull and the bones and tried to keep from falling under Eveshka's spell—for spell it surely was, if there were spells at all. He told himself that. Or he clung to the belief that he believed it, which might of course mean that he was mad.

"Tell me," Eveshka said to him softly, leaning toward him, "how many people are there in Vojvoda?"

He had never counted. He reckoned, distractedly—perhaps five thousand. Ten.

Then with a sudden clutch of fear he thought about the forest, with only one tree left alive.

"I don't know," he said. "I'm not sure."

Eveshka was looking at him. Everything seemed to have stopped. The silence was unbearable and unbreakable.

"I've never been beyond this woods," Eveshka said in that silken soft voice. "My mother used to say I could imagine better than was really true. So I imagine hundreds of houses, all with carved gables and painted shutters. Is Vojvoda like that?"

"There are houses like that."

"And people coming and going all the time. . . ."

"Farms and shops," he said, trying to make it all ordinary and uninteresting. "Like any town."

"Traders used to come here," she said. "In my mother's time. My mother—"

A shadow fell on Eveshka suddenly. Pyetr started and looked over his shoulder in the conviction there was something suddenly behind him, and Sasha turned in the same breath.

But nothing was between them and the fire.

"I'm sorry," he began to say, turning about again, his heart still beating hard. But Uulamets was holding Eveshka's hand, and that shadow persisted, deeper than the ones he and Sasha cast on them both, deeper than the one in which Uulamets' hand existed, holding hers.

"Papa—" she said, her voice trembling. "Papa, hold on to me. . . ."

Pyetr held his breath, with the thought that he ought somehow to do something—lay hands on her, get from between her and the fire—and he did not know what to do—or dare to do anything. But the shadow seemed less after a moment or two.

"Papa," Eveshka whispered, staring nowhere at all, "I don't want to be dead. Please don't let me go."

"I'm not letting go," Uulamets said. And sharply: "Eveshka!"

She drew a breath and the shadow passed entirely. Her free hand fluttered toward Uulamets' sleeve. She touched it as a blind girl might, and said, "Papa? He wants me back."

"Who?"

Eveshka's breath caught. She shook her head violently and looked toward the corner.

Toward the river.

Pyetr very carefully eased his leg around the edge of the bench and began to get up, reaching for his sword.

"Don't go out there," Uulamets said.

Pyetr stood up and looked at them and at Sasha, who was getting quietly to his feet too.

"We drove him off once," Pyetr said. He wanted to believe it would work twice, that the vodyanoi truly disliked swords; and that the Thing had no power over the girl who was sitting in their midst. "You said day or night makes no difference."

"To most things!" Uulamets said. "Don't open that door."

"Master Uulamets," Sasha said very quietly, "—where's Babi?"

Uulamets did not answer for a moment. Then he said, "Good question." He carefully got up from the bench, holding Eveshka by the shoulders. "But let's think of what we don't want here, shall we? Let's all think about that—very hard."

Pyetr did, most earnestly. He thought about the River-thing going back down its hole with Babi the furball in close pursuit. He wished the sun would find the vodyanoi in the morning and shrivel it. He hated it with all his might. And felt Sasha's hand close hard on his arm.

"Wish us *safe*," Sasha said.

Then he remembered Sasha had warned him about wishes going further than one wanted, especially a wish for harm.

But in the same moment the fear just fell apart, leaving him wondering what had just happened to him, and inclined to think nothing had happened at all—

Except there was still Eveshka with them, a pale and frightened Eveshka, still holding to her father's hand.

"It's all right," Uulamets said finally. "It's all right. It's given up."

Pyetr truly wanted someone to explain matters to him. He stood there with the sword hilt like something foreign and somewhat foolish in his hand and with the constant feeling that any moment now the world would shake itself back into recognizable rules.

But he had been living that way for days.

"What are we going to do about it?" he asked.

No one paid any attention to him. Uulamets patted Eveshka on the shoulder and said to her, "Don't worry. It won't get in here." Sasha for his part looked less than reassured.

So was Pyetr. Trusting to vulnerable windows and a none-so-stout door did not seem a reasonable plan of action.

So he asked, more loudly, "What are we going to do about it?"

Evidently no one knew.

"God," he said in disgust, and slung his sword belt on, intending not to be parted from it even a step across the room hereafter—two wizards and a ghost being evidently incapable of any better defense. He took a cup from the shelf, the jug from under the table, and poured himself a modest drink— he had no intention of sleeping soundly tonight, either, or hereafter, for that matter—having no wish to wake with some nightmare laying hands on him, or coils, or whatever the case might be.

The old man had gone soft-headed over his daughter, or his entire attention was taken up with keeping his daughter from going back to bones, the god only knew. Pyetr took his cup and went over to the fireside where it was warm, sitting on Eveshka's cot while Sasha took to clearing away the dishes and the old man sat and talked to his daughter.

Snatches of their low voices came to him—Eveshka's fear of the vodyanoi, Uulamets' assurances they could deal with it—

They, Pyetr thought disgustedly—*they*. They, with his sword and his going down into dark places, which he had no intention whatsoever of doing twice.

Then Eveshka said something that made him strain his ears and stop in mid-sip. She said, "Papa, I lied: I was running away. The vodyanoi—I think he made everything go wrong.

Mama, and Kavi, and everything—I think he made her hate me . . ."

"A lie. It was the woods your mother hated. She came from the east. She stayed a season. Her folk came back and she went away, that's all. She wanted nothing of mine and nothing of this place." Here, in Pyetr's troubled glance, Uulamets hugged his daughter's head against his shoulder, pale gold against snowy white.

How old was he? Pyetr wondered.

Uulamets said to his daughter:

"Don't mourn might-have-beens. Magic can't work backwards, only forward. I taught you better than that."

"I remember." Eveshka's faint voice tugged at Pyetr's heart, made him regret doubting her and made him wish he could in fact do something—something quite practical, like proposing they all go down to the boat in the morning and set out to Kiev, where things were surely much more reasonable.

But maybe in a place where things were much more reasonable Eveshka would not even be alive.

"Pyetr," Uulamets said suddenly, and Pyetr looked up, but Uulamets only wanted him to give Eveshka her cot back. He got up, and gave a little bow and said, confidently, because she looked so frightened, "We dealt with it once. It won't get in."

Eveshka gave him a sidelong anxious glance, as if she was not certain he was not a threat himself, then sat down on her cot by the fire, turned her back and began to unfasten her belt and her boots—which Pyetr watched in somber fascination until Uulamets took him by the sleeve and drew him and Sasha over into the corner.

"We have to catch the creature," Uulamets said in a low voice. "We have to constrain it."

"How?" Pyetr asked, and drew a breath. "If you have any notion of me going back in that damned cave, old man—"

"Be still!" Uulamets gripped his arm and shook it. "Listen to me. I've no strength tonight to suffer fools."

"Listen yourself, grandfather. . . ."

"Collect your alcohol-soaked wits. That creature has a hold on her."

Pyetr had his mouth open to argue; he slid a glance toward Eveshka, whose slender shape showed, firelit through cloth—

"I want you to go outside just before dawn," Uulamets said. "Walk down to the river—taking something of hers with you. That's all you have to do."

"All I have to do." Pyetr started to suggest Uulamets could do it himself, but Uulamets said, clamping down hard on his arm,

"Failing which—I give nothing for any of our lives, do you understand me? I will not sleep tonight, but I can hold out only so long. Pay attention!" Uulamets said as he opened his mouth a third time, and the grip was all but painful. "You will go out at that hour, you will take the things I give you— you will do exactly as I tell you. Both of you."

Chasing after the vodyanoi when it was on the retreat at the knoll was one thing; stalking it on its own terms was quite another. He truly wanted to say no.

But if they lost Uulamets, he admitted to himself, he did not trust the sword that much, and, unhappily, there seemed no way for an old man, a boy, and a ghost to do much against a thing like that, either, without the sword and some fool to use it.

"Well," he said, and scratched a prickling feeling at the nape of his neck when Uulamets had told him the simple details, "lead it up to the porch. How fast is it?"

"Very," Uulamets said. "I wish I could tell you that exactly."

"You're sure it won't cross your line."

"It shouldn't," Uulamets said.

So they all went out onto the porch at the first of the dawn, himself and Sasha and Uulamets and Eveshka, Sasha with one of Uulamets' precious pots in hand and his own instructions, namely to stay step for step with him down the walk-up, then to duck down underneath immediately as they reached the bottom and stay there.

"Just stay out of my way when I come back," Pyetr said to Sasha as they reached that point. "I'll be coming fast."

He earnestly hoped so, at least, as he made the lonely walk

across the yard to the dead trees and the beginning of the path they took down to the river for water. The river, Uulamets said, was the best place to attract the thing.

Certainly, Pyetr thought.

A nocturnal creature like the vodyanoi was a little dim-sighted, Uulamets had said, where it regarded things unmagical; and therefore the small bracelet Pyetr wore about his right wrist, braided from a lock of Eveshka's hair, would shine like a lamp, Uulamets swore, so far as the vodyanoi was concerned—

Uulamets said walk slowly down to the river.

Uulamets said dip the bracelet into the water and be on his guard.

God, it was dark down there.

Sasha shivered in his hiding place, his knees going numb against the ground, while he peered out into the dark and waited.

And waited, what seemed an ungodly long time.

Pyetr would be coming fast when he came up the hill, that was the plan: attract the thing right up onto the porch, which was the highest point they could lure it; and right there, right beyond the fence and across the road, was the gap in the trees where the first rim of the sun always showed and always cast its first light on the house.

Master Uulamets had the end and the sides of the walkway up to the porch secured with a dusting of salt and sulphur; and his own post was here, with another jar of the same, when Pyetr should come racing up that walkway with the creature in pursuit. His own job was to dash out then and draw one line with the salt and sulphur to seal the trap.

That was the plan.

But he very much wished, as he sat shivering in his hiding-place, that Uulamets had set his trap a little closer to the river, and he hoped that Pyetr would not take any chances.

There was a sudden, a clearly audible splash. He heard Pyetr yell.

And nothing else.

15

✠ ✠ ✠ ✠ Pyetr collected himself on his feet, his sword still in his hand, by some presence of mind he would not have credited in himself. He could see, in the faint sky-sheen on the water, vast ripples where the thing had gone back under. He hoped to the god it had gone back—whatever had come lunging up out of the water right for his face—a horse, a snake, or something huge, dark, and wet that no rational man could ever admit seeing, involving, his shocked memory recollected, a vast array of teeth.

His legs began to shake under him. The tremor spread to his arms and his hands and he was ashamed of himself for that, but not very: it was time, he thought, to make a sensible retreat—the more so because for one very dangerous moment he had lost track of it. For that lapse he was honestly vexed with himself, and anxious, seeing the huge wallow in the clay where it might have slipped back into the river. He hoped it had.

He had been scrambling for his life at that moment. He had never seen anything so fast, never expected it to be out of the water in one move—the wallowed track went as far as the brush; and to his chagrin he realized that that brush went as far as the stand of dead willows between himself and the boat dock and the road.

That same run of brush likewise edged the trail to the house. That was both ways up, the only two routes to safety that he had, cut off if it had gotten past him onto shore, and right now he could not swear it had not.

"Pyetr!" he heard. Sasha's frightened voice, from up the hill. He was afraid to answer. He was afraid to move from

178

where he was, on his narrow strip of shore between the brush and the river, and he had no idea which direction to watch first.

"Pyetr!"

God, he thought, the boy was coming down.

"Stay where you are!" he shouted.

And saw a liquid darkness flow across that hillside trail, hip-high to a man.

It put itself between him and the house.

It lifted its head then and began to slither and heave sideways down the slope toward him.

"Sasha!" he yelled, gripping his sword, and thinking wildly of a dive for the river—but the river was where it was most powerful. "It's on the trail! Look out!"

It gathered speed, it changed its shape and size as it came, smaller and faster. He poised himself to dodge if only it reared up the way it had before, but it was not doing that: its coils rubbed along the trunks of dead trees and slithered wider again as it came.

He jumped the thing, trod a soft back and sprang for the path, but its tail whipped around and hit him with a force that knocked him back against the brush.

Its face came around toward him then, all teeth, and he hit it a blow with the sword edge, which it did not like: it reared up and turned its glistening dark head toward a crashing in the brush, a high, shouted, "Here I am!"

Pyetr's head was still ringing. He *thought* he had heard that, and he heaved himself for his feet with all the strength he had left, no wit, just a straight double-handed attack, as the vodyanoi hissed like a spilled kettle and reared up, breaking branches, screaming when he hit it, still screaming as he kept on hitting it for all he was worth.

It shrank, smaller and smaller until it was only man-sized, a withered creature dusted in pale powder, and Sasha was suddenly in the fray with a stout stick in his hands, clubbing it while it howled.

It was too tough to stab. Pyetr gave up trying and simply hit as hard and as often as he could, afraid it was going to recover and kill both of them.

"Get out of here!" he yelled at the boy.

179

Which Sasha did not; Sasha kept hitting it, too, yelling, "Keep it from the river!"

At which time Uulamets arrived and pinned it to the ground with the butt-end of his staff in the middle of its back, while the creature whined and clawed at its own now-manlike face, whimpering and rubbing its eyes.

Pyetr staggered over to a tree to catch his breath, aching from head to foot, while Sasha grabbed hold of him and asked him was he all right.

Honestly he was far from sure. He was trying only to get enough breath to stand upright, and simultaneously to watch Uulamets and the creature on the shore.

Eveshka arrived then—at which realization Pyetr got breath enough to hobble a step or two into the space between her and the prisoner, for what small protection he could be.

But it was not threatening now: it was trying to shield its face or to wipe its eyes, uncertain which. Pyetr reckoned, standing over it, that it must have met Sasha's pot of sulphur and salt nose-on—thank the god and Sasha's brave heart.

Uulamets meanwhile was threatening it with the sun, bidding it give up and swear to mend its ways, none of which made any more sense than the sight of the vodyanoi shrunk to the size and shape of a little old man.

"That thing won't keep a promise," he protested, when it did swear. "Yes," it was saying, "yes, I agree, anything, only let me go—"

"Let my daughter go!" Uulamets said.

The vodyanoi twisted onto its face and covered its naked head with its hands. It wailed, "I can't! I can't do that!"

"Hwiuur. Is that your true name?"

It bobbed its head. "Hwiuur. Yes. Give me your leave, man. The sun is coming. Give me your leave to be here—I will promise, I will never, never harm you in this place—"

"—or elsewhere!" Uulamets snapped, and fetched the creature a crack of the staff. "Free my daughter! Give me back her heart!"

"I can't, I can't, I don't hold it! Oh, it burns, man, it burns—"

Heart? Pyetr wondered, stunned by the thought. Uulamets asked with another thump of his staff:

"Who has it, then?"

"Kavi Chernevog!"

Uulamets' staff met the creature's back and held it still. Uulamets looked toward Pyetr then with a terrible anger on his face; but that look went past him and past Sasha.

"Is it true?" Uulamets demanded harshly.

Eveshka said nothing at all.

Hwiuur suddenly tried to slither for the river. "Get him!" Pyetr cried, lunging to stop the creature if he could, but Uulamets was there with his staff, and pinned it like a serpent to the ground.

Serpent it seemed to be for a moment. Pyetr watched in dismay as it lashed and writhed under the staff.

"Swear!" Uulamets ordered it. "Swear to help us!"

"I swear." It was a man again, or mostly so, wrinkled, ridge-backed and serpent-twisted, clutching the mud with thin black hands.

"Swear to come and go at my orders; swear to do what I bid you do; swear never to lie to me and never to harm me or mine."

It hissed, it writhed. Finally it said, "I swear by my name. Let me go."

Uulamets drew back his staff. Quicker than the eye could follow it, it whipped across the mud and into the water.

"That's one lost," Pyetr muttered unhappily, but Uulamets called out, "Hwiuur!"

And a vast dark head of very unpleasant aspect rose up near the shore.

"Look out!" Sasha cried, and was on his way to snatch the old man back, but Pyetr grabbed him by the arm and held him where he was.

The Thing loomed up and up and arched its sleek, dripping head over to look down at the old man.

"The sunlight hurts my eyes," it said in a deep voice like the booming of drums. "The salt was a wicked trick, man."

"Don't speak to me on that score," Uulamets said. "I want Kavi Chernevog."

Hwiuur reared back and settled deeper in the dawn-lit water, until he was on a level with Uulamets. "Ask me something I can do," it said, again like drums speaking. "Chernevog

181

is too powerful. He has what you want. You can permit me the sunlight; he can forbid. Then what will I do?"

The head sank beneath the water again, leaving an eddy and bubbles.

"Hwiuur!" Uulamets said.

It rose again, not so far as before.

"So you remember," Uulamets said. "Obey my orders. You swore by your name."

"So I did," it said, and sank below the surface again. A black back broke the surface, long, very long, as it flowed away upriver.

Pyetr took a breath and flexed his right hand on his sword hilt while Uulamets turned his back to the river.

"Back to the house," Uulamets said, and walked past them to take Eveshka's arm and bring her up the path ahead of them.

Pyetr walked along beside Sasha, reckoning to himself what Sasha had done for him, coming down that hill and well knowing what he was risking. He wanted to throw his arm around the boy the way he had with 'Mitri, the black god take him, or Andrei or Vasya, none of whom had deserved thanking for anything.

But all that affection had been so cheap, and all that camaraderie so free with gestures that should have meant something he could not find one left for Sasha Misurov. He was lately scared and battered, he was tongue-tied and frustrated, and he stripped the bracelet of Eveshka's hair off his wrist in a fury and flung it down on the path as they walked.

Dip the bracelet in the river, Uulamets had said.

Lead it to the house, Uulamets had said.

His sword hand was scored by teeth he did not like to remember. He sucked at the worst of the scratches, looked at the wound in the gray, beginning dawn, and spat, revolted by the taste of blood and river water.

"It did that," Sasha said in dismay.

"It did that," he said; and looked darkly at Uulamets ahead of him on the trail, walking behind Eveshka—who had run away from her father, it now seemed.

So, by Uulamets' own word, had the wife; and so had this Kavi Chernevog—for reasons he personally began to suspect as evidence of good character.

—

There was anger and unhappiness in the house, and Eveshka was fixing breakfast only, Sasha suspected, because she was evading her father. Pyetr had poured himself a cup of vodka. He had been limping a little on the way up, his hand was swelling, and Sasha wished master Uulamets would do something about it, but master Uulamets just sat watching Eveshka as if he was waiting for her to say something, and as if he was thinking thoughts no wizard should entertain—all too easy for Uulamets inadvertently to let something terrible fly, if he had not done it already, and Sasha had no wish to disturb his concentration if he was trying to deal with that—

But Sasha himself was angrier than he ever let himself get, considering Pyetr was hurt and Uulamets had had a great deal to do with that, whether through bad planning or callous disregard for Pyetr's life. He understood why Uulamets had not used the salt at the knoll: Uulamets had come prepared to deal with a ghost, not Hwiuur, and might not be expected, in the midst of a working that wide and that dangerous, to prepare for everything—

Though the vodyanoi should have been primarily suspect—given Uulamets had known then that Hwiuur even existed, which was by no means a certainty—or given that Hwiuur himself had not slipped around the edges of Uulamets' attention with powerful wishes of his own.

Perhaps—Sasha tried to be charitable and to control his own temper—perhaps Hwiuur had put more strain on the old man than any of them understood, or perhaps neither Uulamets nor any wizard knew enough about vodyaniye: I wish I could tell you exactly, Uulamets had said to Pyetr—which did argue for some attempt at honesty on Uulamets' part; but Sasha was not mollified. If Uulamets had known *anything* more than a stableboy knew about such creatures, he should not have sent Pyetr without protection (the creature would smell it, Uulamets had said) or given him the instructions he had given, to try to outrace the creature on a steep trail, when it was that fast and that capable out of the water—but no, Uulamets had insisted, choosing the porch for a trap, the sun will reach *here*—

If Uulamets had paid a tenth part of his attention to anything but his daughter; if he paid it now, or even said, Thank you, Pyetr Ilitch; or cared to do something about a wound that was already swelling and that, made by a creature like that, might have effects a stableboy from Vojvoda had no idea how to deal with—if Uulamets showed any least concern, Sasha thought, or even asked now what he was doing, rummaging through the herb pots and mixing up wormwood and chamomile, which were only kitchen lore and a poor second to Uulamets' knowledge—

"Excuse me," Sasha said of a sudden, as his search for a bowl took him near Uulamets. His own vehemence surprised him, but he was beyond any capability, at the moment, for Uulamets to muddle him with a look. "That thing bit Pyetr. Do you think you could possibly do something?"

Uulamets looked at him, registering a touch of surprise along with annoyance, and Sasha glared, quite ready to face an ill-wish from master Uulamets, more master of his intentions at the moment, he was sure, than Uulamets was.

Which gave anyone, wizard or no, Uulamets had once said, a moderate advantage.

Uulamets' expression showed some concentration, then, perhaps even the effort to collect himself; and he said with surprising mildness, "I'd better look at it."

That was one thing.

But when Uulamets got up and went over to Pyetr, sitting in the corner with his cup and the jug, Pyetr said, sullenly, "I poured a little vodka on it. It'll be fine."

"Fool. Let me see it."

"Keep your hands off!" Pyetr jerked away from Uulamets' touch, spilling vodka as he did so, and lurched, wincing, to one knee and to his feet.

"Pyetr," Sasha said, and blocked his escape from the corner, fully expecting Pyetr would shove past him all the same.

But Pyetr stopped and caught his breath and said, with a motion of the cup toward him, "You and I are getting out of here. We're packing up, we're taking what we've earned from this house, and we're going."

"You'll go nowhere!" Uulamets said. "Your own life may be yours to lose. But think of the boy. Think of him, when you consider going anywhere in these woods."

"I *am* thinking of him." Pyetr turned on Uulamets with such violence Sasha grabbed his arm—but Pyetr shrugged that off as if it was nothing and stood balanced on the balls of his feet. "Don't tell me about the danger in these woods! I've handled that damned creature twice now, and it's less hazard than you and your advice. You were surprised when I came back the first time, weren't you? Wear the bracelet, you said. Go down to the river, you said. You don't need a salt-pot, you said, it'll only drive it back into the river, and that's not what we want, is it? No. We just give it a little taste of what it wants. We just let it take my arm off and good riddance to the only protection the boy's got from you. He's safer with the damned snake!"

Uulamets' anger was all around them like a storm about to break. Sasha threw everything he had in the way of it, and put himself bodily between them, as somehow the cup broke and the pieces hit the floor—maybe that he had knocked it from Pyetr's hand, or that Uulamets had broken it, or that Pyetr's fingers had cracked it.

"Go ahead," Uulamets said in deadly quiet. "Take what you like. Go where you like. But the boy will stay—do you hear me, Sasha Vasilyevitch? If Pyetr goes alone, I'll guarantee his safety to the edge of this woods. But if you go with him— he'll die, by one means or another, he will die. I promise you that."

Sasha looked master Uulamets in the eye and tried to withstand him. But the least small doubt began to work in his mind and that was enough: he knew that that doubt was fatal, and that there was no chance for them.

"Nonsense," Pyetr said, and took his arm and pulled him away; but Sasha resisted and shook his head.

"I can't," he said. "I won't. He can do it, Pyetr, and I can't stop him—I'm sorry. . . ."

He was afraid; and sick at heart, because either Pyetr would leave him or he would not, and either was terrible; but he did not think Pyetr would, he truly did not believe it—and that was the worst.

"If I have to carry you—" Pyetr said.

"No," he said, looking Pyetr in the face, afraid his chin was going to tremble—because there was nothing he could do but fight Pyetr if he tried, and that was the last thing he wanted to do, in any sense. He got a breath and shook Pyetr's hand off. "But there's no sense in you staying, is there? And none in me going to Kiev. He can teach me. He needs to. I'm too strong not to know what I'm doing—I'm strong enough now to be dangerous. But I'm not strong enough to beat him. So you go. He's not lying about your being safe to leave. I know that—because he wants me to help him; and he wouldn't like what I'd do if I found out he'd lied."

He wished Pyetr would go. He wished it especially hard, because he was close to breaking into tears; and he wished Pyetr's hand would be well, even if Uulamets refused to help him.

Pyetr folded his arms and turned away and looked at the floor.

"Tell him," Pyetr said after a moment, "he'd damned well better think twice where he sends me after this, because you'll take it out of his hide someday."

"I will," Sasha said. He had never in his life intended harm to anyone: but he did, for whoever harmed Pyetr, and had no qualms and no doubt about doing it.

For a moment he realized that he was capable of wanting harm. In a heartbeat more he realized that he already wanted it; and that that wanting was a wish already sped at Uulamets—

Who was far more callous and by that degree, more powerful.

"Do as you please," Uulamets said, and added with malice: "I'd advise you try healing, boy. —It's much harder; and much more to the point right now."

Sasha looked at Pyetr. And knew—was suddenly sure—that Uulamets' warning was absolutely real; and that Uulamets was absolutely confident he would fail.

"Or do you need help, boy?"

He looked back at Uulamets.

"So you don't know everything," Uulamets said. "I'd suggest you reason with your friend. Your threat is a future one—at best; but if the day comes, boy, that you have your way, believe this for a truth—he'll be far more at risk from you then than he is now from me."

186

He did not like to hear that. Uulamets might lie. He had a feeling this was not one of those times.

But Uulamets walked over to the fireside to investigate the cooking.

"Master Uulamets—" Sasha said.

"Let it be," Pyetr said, catching his arm, and Sasha saw how Eveshka slipped away from her father, never looking at him as she gathered up bowls and spoons from the shelf.

"He'll come around," Sasha said, and looked at Pyetr. "I'll talk to him. You don't have to. Just please don't—don't fight with him."

Pyetr said nothing for a moment, his jaw set so the muscle stood out. Then he folded his arms again, tucking the injured hand under as if it hurt him, and said, with an evident effort at reason, "There'll be a way out. I'm not leaving you here."

"I wish—"

"For the god's sake don't wish. Haven't we got enough?"

It was cruel; and true. Sasha shut his mouth and stopped wanting other than what Pyetr wanted, especially about Pyetr leaving—Pyetr having very good sense when he was using his head: and having more wit than he had when it came to ways to get around people.

"We just mind our manners," Pyetr said. "You think about it. Think, that's all. I can put up with grandfather."

"You've got to get along with him."

"I can get along with him," Pyetr said, and assumed a deliberate, thin-lipped smile. "I've no difficulty with that. I've dealt with thieves before."

"Pyetr, please!"

"I've even been on good terms with them." Pyetr gave Sasha's shoulder a light rap with the back of his hand and made a quick shift of the eyes toward the fireside, reminder that Uulamets might well overhear. "So he's got us. Nothing lasts. *You* use your head, and trust me to use mine, hear me?"

Sasha nodded; and glanced to the fireside where master Uulamets was ladling out a bowl of porridge, talking the while to Eveshka, who stood staring at the floor, hands folded, not responding at all to her father.

Eveshka was not all right. Nothing seemed to be, not the

house, not Uulamets' daughter. Nothing that Uulamets had planned seemed to be turning out the way he had intended.

And Uulamets wanted them, he even wanted Pyetr, quite badly, for that matter, despite his offer to let Pyetr go—Sasha had a deep, worried notion that Uulamets had had *that* string firmly tied to his finger before he ever made the offer—that Uulamets had known Pyetr would refuse, not least because Uulamets wanted him to. There were undoubtedly wishes loose, powerful ones: five wizards, Pyetr had said, constantly pushing things back and forth among themselves; and Hwiuur's wishes and Hwiuur's cunning were not to disregard.

"Conspiracies?" Uulamets challenged them suddenly, looking in their direction.

"No, sir," Sasha said, and walked over to get his bowl and Pyetr's, to fill them, but Eveshka did that, and he stood there waiting with his hand out, looking at what looked like a live girl, with wonderful long hair that she had simply caught back with a ribbon this morning; with a smudge of soot on her hands from the pothook; and with tears in her eyes that she was trying not to spill. He felt sorry for her. He wanted to do something.

"After breakfast," Uulamets said, at his elbow, "there's packing to do—things to take to the boat. We're not finished."

"Finished," Sasha echoed, not because he did not understand that word. He was afraid he did.

"Chernevog," Uulamets said.

"You know where he is?" Sasha asked.

"I've always known where he is," Uulamets said.

16

✳ ✳ ✳ ✳ In the way of such things, the hand had not hurt until everyone began to make a fuss over it. Now it did; and Pyetr gave it surreptitious, anxious glances between trips back and forth to the boat, fearing he had no idea what—some sudden change, corruption—for the hand to turn black and rot, he had no idea what kind of venom a vodyanoi's teeth could carry. The creature had scratched him before, in the set-to at the knoll, or roots or bones had, and no one had worried then; but Sasha fretted over the wound and made a nasty-smelling concoction of chamomile and wormwood and vodka—which stung, for one thing. More, Sasha himself insisted he had no idea what he was doing, and Pyetr was unhappily constrained to believe Uulamets *could* ill-wish them at any moment.

Think of the cup that broke, Sasha had said, daubing his hand with his smelly potion. That could have been your heart, Pyetr. . . .

Gruesome notion.

. . . or he could use the vodyanoi, Sasha had said—just let it loose on us. And it's one thing to fight it when he wants us to win, but if he's helping *it* . . .

So Pyetr carried loads to the boat. A little trip across the river, Uulamets had said. Hunt down a former student. And Uulamets ordered multitudinous pots hauled out of the cellar, packed into mouldering baskets and ported downhill; after which he loaded them down with huge coils of rope and tackle and a furled sail and spar Pyetr and Sasha together had to manhandle down the eroded slope.

So the old man did know boats. One could learn from him

189

. . . all of which said to Pyetr that it was only well to keep his head down and be polite to grandfather, however bad it got.

Grandfather wanted the boat loaded, grandfather wanted this and grandfather wanted that: Uulamets and Eveshka were waiting on the porch when they came trudging back up the hill, Eveshka standing in the midst of a number of baskets—food, one guessed, the door of the house being shut, as if that was the last they had to take—food not having figured in the previous levels.

Uulamets loaded them down with baskets, five and six apiece, and they went down the hill to board, after which Uulamets plumped down on a basket on the leaf-strewn deck and announced he would tell them how to rig the sail.

The hand hurt worse since hauling the sail and the tackle down, but it seemed unlikely Uulamets would have any sympathy. Pyetr gave Uulamets a sullen look and followed Sasha forward where the mast lay on the bow in a tangle of mouldering rope.

"I don't suppose grandfather could somehow magic this up," Pyetr muttered, pulling at a rope to see where it was connected.

"He's tired," Sasha said.

"*He's* tired," Pyetr cried.

"Don't—"

"I'm not," Pyetr said under his breath, "I'm not, I won't."

"I'll crawl out there," Sasha offered, and scrambled up astride the mast, hitched himself far out over the water to cut the first rotten rope free, then worked his way back again to take the sound one, sweating and panting all the while Uulamets sat on his baskets and told them do this and do that and how they should tie the knots.

Pyetr thought about knots around Uulamets' neck, mostly, and made the knots tight, biting his lip until it bled and suspecting very strongly why the hand was aching worse and worse and what the load was on Sasha besides the weight of the rope.

He wished he *could* wish—wish Uulamets right into the river, he would, wish the venom into Uulamets' veins. Don't ill-wish, Sasha kept saying, but that never stopped Uulamets, he was sure of that the way he was sure it would get worse, and that it would go on getting worse until Uulamets got what he wanted from Sasha.

It was rig the sail then; more knots; and then haul the mast up and settle it—

"Are you all right?" Sasha asked when it thumped down and settled.

"I'm fine," Pyetr said between his teeth, while Uulamets was ordering them to take the ropes aft and to either side.

It was hitch the spar to the trailing ropes after that; haul it aloft, heave by painful heave, and secure it.

"Cast us off!" Uulamets called out to them, then, for the first time on his feet, as he headed back for the tiller.

Sasha jumped ashore to throw the ties aboard, jumped back again as the boat began sluggishly to drift free in the current. Uulamets stood at the tiller and swung it hard as far as the rail, after which the bow of the boat came slowly about until it was broadside to the current.

Then the wind which had been fitful and indecisive billowed the sail out, tilted the aged boat alarmingly, so that Pyetr grabbed Sasha and lurched for the nearest rope, with certain visions of drowning and becoming prey to the Riverthing and all its relatives.

But the boat kept turning, the sail cracked and snapped and filled again, so strongly it threatened the aged canvas.

The boat drove steadily after that, boiling up froth away from the bow, froth that went away into white bubbles on murky water. On either hand forest passed, leafless trees, gray bark peeling here and there to white bare wood, and never a touch of life.

Sasha sat on the bow beside Pyetr with his feet tucked up—he was afraid to dangle them over, however tempting it was, because he did not trust the river in any sense. Pyetr leaned against the bow rail and stared ahead of them, with now and again a glance aft, where Uulamets and his daughter stood—but one could not see their faces from here, with the sail in the way.

Maybe that was why Pyetr chose to sit here. Pyetr had this

bruised, utterly weary look—Sasha was sure his hand was hurting, but Pyetr would not admit to it. He only kept that hand tucked beneath his arm, sitting with his shoulder against the rail, staring out at the passing forest. Sasha tried to wish his pain away, tried until he quite lost track of where they were, or that it was daylight on dark water he was seeing, and not mud, roots, and shadows—

But he became aware of the water of a sudden, of a dark shape gliding just under the bow where they were sitting, a shadow beneath the surface—water scattered with yellow willow leaves.

He sprang up and away from the rail, grabbing Pyetr by the shirt—and Pyetr moved without a question, caught a rope with his left hand to steady them both.

But there were only the golden leaves, sunlit on the dark water, swirling away from their passage; and on the shore the source of those fading leaves, a willow leafed out bright gold and dying, against a haze of gray branches.

Eveshka's tree. Hwiuur's den.

No need to call out to master Uulamets to see: he could hardly fail to see. Sasha stood and watched until the wind carried them past; and when that bank was out of sight behind the sail the precarious feeling of the deck urged they sit down—but not, Sasha thought, so close to the rail or in reach of the water. He pulled at Pyetr's sleeve and drew him to sit at the foot of the mast.

Pyetr said nothing to this: he only looked back from that vantage, knees drawn up and his hand tucked against him; but when Sasha looked back there was nothing left to see but Eveshka standing by Uulamets at the tiller, the wind streaming their hair about their faces and fluttering at their clothes— as if they were gazing at something far away.

While the boat surged along with a steady, unhurried force, its sail full, no matter that the river had just bent.

Sasha settled forward again and locked his hands between his knees. The image of the tree haunted him, gold in a world of gray, the leaves on the river. . . . He did not know why that should hang in his mind more than Uulamets at the tiller or the presence of the Thing in the river—he did not know why the sight of falling leaves could be that sinister.

Gold on gray. Dying amid the dead, a last vivid color against the lifeless forest, against the dark water.

Perhaps it was Eveshka's freedom its dying signified.

He had no hesitation to accept magic and he had only small astonishment at winds that obeyed no set direction, only the understanding that it must take many wishes, one shifting to the next, to drive this boat.

But for some reason he kept seeing the gold leaves swirling in the current, and thinking that he should be wiser than he had been, because he should understand these things and he was failing, in some elementary way.

They were going farther and farther from Kiev, further from Pyetr's dreams. That was one thing. He felt guilty for that.

And afraid.

Pyetr did not like boats; he had decided that from the first time the deck tilted under him and the boat gathered speed. When the bow began to pitch and the deck tilted markedly his heart sped, and when the sail would swing and the deck would pitch over in the other direction he clung to the rail he had been leaning on and wondered at what point the boat was going to turn over.

That Uulamets stood back there with his ghostly daughter, that the wind never increased or decreased, that Eveshka's tree was shedding its leaves into the river—and that the vodyanoi swam beside or beneath the boat—what else did one expect? Wizards did what they wanted in this woods, wizards had taken him into their affairs, his hand hurt him miserably and for the first time in his life Pyetr Kochevikov felt completely helpless.

Not that drowning must be the worst that could happen, not that the vodyanoi was not waiting down there to lay its little black hands on him. None of these things was so terrible as that feeling in his stomach: he could not get the rhythm of the boat, to the extent he was likely to lean the wrong way at the wrong time and tumble right off the deck—

Naturally wizards could walk about with perfect balance and easy stomachs. They could wish not to fall off.

But he *knew* Uulamets wanted to drown him; and he was not going to stand up, no more than he was going to lean his head over that rail where the River-thing could grab it.

"Do you want something to eat?" Sasha asked him toward dark.

No. Definitely he did not.

Sasha got up and wobbled his way aft, holding on to the ropes and staggering the last distance while Pyetr watched anxiously and held on to the rail. Sasha made it all the way past the deckhouse to talk to Uulamets—about supper, one supposed.

Or about stopping. He earnestly hoped so.

Uulamets seemed to be talking to Sasha: he could not precisely see from where he was, even by ducking down. Then Sasha staggered back to the low deckhouse where they had stowed their supplies, and made the precarious trip back to Uulamets and his daughter, bringing them food and drink. Finally he came forward again, with a jug and a fistful of food, and staggered and reeled his way precariously to the bow.

Pyetr snatched at him and set him down hard on the boards.

"We'll stop before dark," Sasha said.

Thank the god, Pyetr thought.

Sasha pushed dried fruit and the jug at him.

Not even that.

No. Please god.

The boat pitched suddenly. Sasha grabbed his leg and grabbed the jug before it went sliding off the deck.

And had the temerity to grin at him. Pyetr scowled, jaw clamped, and took a tight hold on the rail. The wind had picked up, humming in the ropes, setting the very timbers of the aged boat creaking. Spray kicked up, a fine mist that slicked the rail and cooled the side of his face.

It went like that for a time, while the sun went down and the spray flew gold—until with a terrible ripping sound the sail parted, the deck pitched, and a rope snapped like twine and sang past their heads.

Pyetr grabbed Sasha, Sasha grabbed in vain at the jug, which went sliding halfway across the deck as the broken rope went on whipping about like a dying snake and the ripped sail fluttered and cracked overhead.

The boat righted itself and tossed like a drunken thing, but it still moved under its rag of a sail, gliding with fair speed toward a dark and tangled shore.

"I don't like this," Pyetr muttered under his breath, as the boat ran in. Trees were coming at them, dark and huge, shore-line branches rushing into their faces.

He flung himself down onto Sasha, knocking him flat and holding the rail with one arm as the boat shuddered over sand and branches came right over the bow, splintering and poking them with twigs.

The boat swung sideways to the shore then, floated free, and more branches splintered over their heads and all along the right side.

Then it was still, except the wild bobbing in the current, and Uulamets, astern, was shouting: "Fools! Get the ropes! Take down the sail! Hurry!"

Pyetr stumbled up to his feet, staggering in the pitch, and started untying the rope, cursing the while Sasha pulled to give him slack to get the knot free. The two of them let down the spar. Torn canvas billowed down around them while the boat scraped its whole side against the overhanging branches.

"Fine place," Pyetr said, as Uulamets shouted at them to make the boat fast to the trees. Pyetr still felt the wobble in his knees when he crossed the uneasy deck; his firm hold on a small branch of a tree solidly wed to earth came as a profound relief in one sense. He flung the mooring rope over a larger branch and tied a solid knot.

But the deep night between the trees made him glad to look toward the twilight still sheening the water, and toward human voices aft—Uulamets sharply instructing Sasha how to tie a knot, Uulamets bidding Eveshka open the stores and make supper—

Certainly, Pyetr thought, they would get no farther in the dark tonight, and with the sail lying in rags, maybe not to-morrow. He dreaded the thought of going on, he felt uneasy to be spending the night against this wooded farther shore—and he felt especially uneasy that the sail had torn and the rope had parted all at once. A handful of wizards ought to manage better than that. Or at least—

"Have we gotten there?" he asked Uulamets as he came aft, with no more idea than he had ever had exactly where they were going. The last light was fast leaving, the river reflected a dim sky, and the constant lap of water and the scrape of branches against their hull made a dismally lonely sound.

"We've gotten where we are," Uulamets muttered, and brushed past, leaving Sasha to whisper, ever so quietly,

"I think he was holding the boat together. I think he just gave out."

"*I* think we're in trouble," Pyetr said.

Eveshka set up their little stove on the stern and lit a fire in its pan with wood they had brought, though the god knew they had twigs enough lying on the deck and accessible just off it. Soon enough there were cakes baking and Eveshka even brought out a little honey to go on them—while master Uulamets lit the lamp, set it on the ledge of the deckhouse, which was really too tiny for anything but the stores they had brought and stowed there, then sat down with his book and his inkpot to write down the things he had done—

And to think, Sasha supposed: certainly Uulamets would not want to be disturbed with questions this evening.

"How far have we come?" Pyetr asked Eveshka, as they sat with her around the little stove. "Do you have any idea where we're going?"

Eveshka looked up. Her hair was plaited in two huge braids that made her face look very small and her eyes very large— eyes pale and softened, as it happened, by the little light that came up from the stove and down from the lamp. She had said hardly two words to anyone since breakfast. She had stood by Uulamets' side the day long, helping her father and suffering his anger; and now she looked very worried.

"To find Kavi," she said. Her voice left a hush like a spell on the air; any voice would seem coarse after that; and the water lapped and the branches scraped and the fire crackled and snapped.

"Where?" Pyetr insisted finally.

"My father knows where he is."

A page turned, behind them.

The silence went on a moment or two while Eveshka turned the cakes, a scrape of the spatula on the stove top. She said, "I was foolish to trust him. My father was right. I know that now."

"What are we going to do about this Kavi Chernevog?" Pyetr asked. "What's this about hearts? What did the Thing mean, this morning?"

Eveshka stopped, then turned a last cake, her eyes set on her work. She said placidly, "I was foolish. My father was absolutely right."

Sasha felt a little chill. Perhaps Pyetr did: he cradled his hand in his lap and looked at Eveshka as if he suspected what Sasha had begun to feel, that there was indeed something hollow about her.

Pyetr looked at him. Sasha said nothing, only sent him a warning look back, fearing that too many questions now might upset the peace—if there were more answers in Eveshka at all, or if she were free to speak them. The god knew what kind of hold Chernevog still had on her.

Eveshka served the cakes. They sat together in the flickering light from master Uulamets' oil lamp, ate their supper, and had a little of the vodka—the first of their jars having fetched up against the deck house unbroken: Sasha had done that much. But Uulamets took his supper over in the light, sitting cross-legged on the deck, poring over his book and paying no attention to them.

Pyetr said, "I suppose we've got to fix that sail. Did we bring any cord?"

"I don't know," Sasha said. "Eveshka?"

"Yes," Eveshka said softly, and got up and went around to the deckhouse.

"What's this about hearts?" Pyetr whispered urgently when she was out of earshot. "What was he talking about? What's wrong with her?"

"I don't know," Sasha whispered back. "I never did understand."

Pyetr looked disappointed in him—as if Pyetr expected wizardly answers from him. He could not so much as keep

197

Pyetr's hand from hurting—he knew that it was, even at the moment—and still Pyetr trusted him in life and death ways and expected him to come up with miracles.

That scared him more than the River-thing did—but maybe it was part of being a man, not to ask for help. Maybe it was part of being a man to try to do what people expected.

There was master Uulamets, for one thing, with his book that recollected everything he had ever done—while Sasha had never thought that he ought to do the same: at least he had never even imagined that he could write, until master Uulamets saw fit to teach him. But he thought now that he had not been very responsible throughout his dealings with Uulamets and the vodyanoi, wishing this and wishing that at random, simply because master Uulamets had told him he had the gift—exactly the kind of mistake master Uulamets had said most people made: but a wizard had to remember, that was all, had to figure out the connections before he made a wish, the very way he himself had used to sit and think in the quiet of the stable, sometimes for hours before he decided what he wanted about a thing.

Then Pyetr had come along, half again his age and wiser about the world than he was; and for the first time in his life having a friend, what could he do but want what Pyetr desperately needed?

But he had never until now understood how much he had lulled himself into thinking it was only himself and Pyetr and Uulamets involved in his wishes. It never had been. There was the River-thing and Eveshka and now somebody named Kavi Chernevog, and he had made so many desperate wishes lately he was on the edge of not remembering all the things he had wished earlier in his life and he was far past understanding how things fitted together. He could not even clearly *remember* the stableboy at The Cockerel, because that boy felt like someone else, someone he did not know how to be, now—

Because if he should meet Mischa now, and Mischa shoved him off a walk, he would not be afraid; he—

He could kill Mischa: he pulled back from that idea with a chill close to panic, and wished hard, *not* wanting Mischa to die, no, please, not wishing anything harmful, no matter how far away in the world, because he had been a fool. He thought—even aunt Ilenka had kept a tally with a charcoal stick, just of turnips and cabbages.

But so many things had tumbled on him one after the other he had somewhere stopped thinking how they fit together; and it was not The Cockerel's stable any more, where days were one after the other the same and where he knew everything and everyone and nobody wanted more than his supper on time.

"What's the matter?" Pyetr asked him, nudging his arm.

Sasha wiped sweat from his lip, hearing Eveshka's quiet returning step on the boards, and shook his head.

Eveshka set a basket by him. There was cord and there was an awl.

"Too dark now to do anything about it," Pyetr said, and gulped the last of his cup as Eveshka bent to pick up the little stove with its ashes. He motioned toward the bow of the boat. "Grandfather's got his book. Let's get some sleep."

It was a good idea, Sasha thought. He felt guilty: he thought he should offer to help Eveshka clean up, but he knew he should not leave Pyetr alone either, and he thought with longing of blankets and a soft spot in the canvas piled on the deck up there.

But once he had it, and once his eyes were shut, with the river lapping at the hull and the branches raking back and forth against their side, he kept thinking of things he had wanted and about aunt Ilenka and the tally board, and wondering what his added up to by now.

Pyetr for his part had no trouble getting to sleep, no matter that the dark behind his eyelids was alive with the vodyanoi's coils and murky water, and that he still felt the deck tilting under him: he knew where he was now—tied to a forest he did not want to think about, but as far as safety it looked to be the most he was going to have—and the hand hurt, but it had hurt ever since carrying the loads down to the boat, so he reckoned finally he had simply bruised it.

He was reasoning more clearly now that the boat was at rest and his stomach was less queasy. Uulamets certainly had other, more subtle ways to do away with him than pitching him off the boat, which Sasha would never believe an accident; and the boat, if they could get it to move at all, was surely not going to roll over tomorrow any more than it had today—not with three wizards preventing it. . . .

The old man got tired and the boat broke a rope and tore a sail, but it got to shore. . . .

Upon which thought Pyetr burrowed into the nest of canvas and blankets and just let go—not without knowing where his sword was, in the blankets with him; or knowing Sasha was an arm's reach away. And that there was that little bit of salt in a bit of cloth, that Sasha had given him this morning.

Keep it in your pocket, Sasha had said. —It could never hurt.

He agreed with that.

And agreed that a bed well back on the deck was better than near the rail, be it the river side or the forest side of the boat.

He slept. He woke with the sun warming the blankets uncomfortably and the impression that there had been a sound a moment ago—

Sasha was getting up. Pyetr thought about that a heartbeat or two and realized it was very late for Uulamets to be still abed, and it was very unlike the old man to let them rest.

At which point he pushed the blanket off and picked up his sword on his way to his feet.

"Master Uulamets?" Sasha said aloud, a small and lonely voice against the sound of the river and the trees.

No one answered.

"Damn," Pyetr said, with an increasingly upset stomach. He pulled his sword out of its sheath, stepped over the spar and its mass of canvas, and walked quietly toward the stern, hearing Sasha walking behind him. He worried about tangling with Sasha on the retreat: he reached back and touched Sasha's arm, warned him back as he edged around the riverward side of the deckhouse.

There was nobody aft. That left the forestward side, and

he beckoned Sasha to catch up and took the wide path around to a view of the rest of the deck.

No one there either.

"There's the storage," Sasha whispered, coming up beside him.

Pyetr took a deep breath and said, "I doubt it—"

But he had no good feeling about walking around the deck-house to make that search. He took a good grip on his sword, lifted the latch and pulled the door open—

But there was nothing inside but their stores—from which the basket of Uulamets' belongings, including the book, was missing.

"That damned old fool's gone for a walk!" Pyetr exclaimed, and Sasha came to look for himself.

"Unless the vodyanoi got him," Sasha said.

"Don't you think we'd have heard that?" Pyetr asked.

"He had to have made some noise," Sasha said, walking to the forest side, a proximity to the trees that made Pyetr nervous. "We slept through it. I don't sleep like that. . . ."

"We were tired," Pyetr said. "We wouldn't have heard thunder." He walked up beside Sasha and looked into the depths of the woods—seeing past the dead brush along the bank the green of vines and leaves. That evidence of life should have comforted him. It only looked thick and tangled through there, the kind of place an old man however crazy ought to have second thoughts about going, afoot, loaded down with, the god witness, the basket with that damned book and whatever pots he had taken.

More conjurings? he wondered.

"Old grandfather probably went off to sing at something," he muttered. "He was reading last night. He probably figured out something and decided he'd go hunt up some roots or something, what can you expect? He'll be back."

They had their breakfast on the forward deck, and Sasha kept hoping for master Uulamets to come back, he did not know why—master Uulamets not having been particularly kind to anyone; but Uulamets having gotten them here, he had no confidence anyone but Uulamets could get them back again.

But Pyetr said that they ought to see about the sail, thinking, Sasha was sure, that they should be going back downriver soon.

So they got the cord and the awl and started sewing the rip up, himself doing the pulling and the holding and Pyetr doing the punching and threading of the cord through the canvas—his hand was purpling around the wound, but he swore it was no worse than yesterday.

"I'll make a poultice for it," Sasha said. Since they had no choice but to sit and wait, it was at least a chance to help Pyetr; and Pyetr did not shrug off the offer.

They had the sail stitched by noon. "I've no idea whether it'll hold," Pyetr said; and for the first time talking about the chance of Uulamets and Eveshka not coming back: "But I think, going back, we should just go with the current, if we can. The boat ought to work with that, a lot slower, maybe, but I don't mind that."

"Me either," Sasha said, and glanced toward the forest.

"You suppose the River-thing got them?"

It was the first time Pyetr had talked about that, either, not that both of them were not virtually convinced of it by now.

"I'm not sure it ever lost her," Sasha said glumly, and thumped Pyetr on the arm. "Come on. I'll boil up something for the hand."

17

Pyetr watched while Sasha started a fire in the stove and boiled up a concoction of wormwood, chamomile, willow, and salt—the last of which Pyetr protested as willful cruelty; but Sasha insisted, saying that if vodyaniye disliked it, it might help.

It stung, of course. But the heat helped, and Pyetr sat warming himself in the sun, his hand wrapped in a hot rag which he changed from time to time, between feeding the coals in the pan a twig or two—and quite uncharitably hoped that the vodyanoi had made a meal of Uulamets *and* his book—not, he told himself, that he particularly wished harm to the old man and certainly not to Eveshka, but he saw no reason for loyalty either.

"Give him till the sun touches the trees over there," he said finally to Sasha, and nodded toward the far shore. "Then let's untie and see if we can get this boat turned around."

"Maybe he's just trying to get us to break our word."

Uncomfortable thought. Pyetr cast a look to the nearer woods and back. "We've waited all morning and half the afternoon. If he decided to go off he could at least have said to wait—and hang us if we didn't. That's one thing. But I don't think he had a choice. I don't know why he left, I don't know what he thought he was doing—but, one—" Pyetr held up his thumb. "He packed, and, two—" The first finger. "He was quiet about it. Book and staff and all. He's gone off before, but he's never taken the book. So, one, he thought he'd need it, or, two, he didn't want to leave it with us, because he wasn't coming back, or, three, Eveshka got enough of papa and stole it and ran off to her lover. . . ."

203

"If she did that, he'd have waked us," Sasha said. "He brought us all this way—"

"If he trusted us he'd wake us. Which he doesn't. We know he's on the outs with his daughter. We were talking with her last night—weren't we? And he was damned quiet about packing up, or we were sleeping sounder than usual—which he could wish. If you were asleep you couldn't tell a thing. Could you?"

"No," Sasha said.

"So? What do we owe him? The man's threatened our lives."

"Absolutely he's dangerous," Sasha said, "and he's wished this boat safe, and maybe to stay on this shore. If we try to move it—"

"You don't know that."

"I don't know he hasn't; and I certainly would, in his place. I'd wish it with everything I had."

"He could have said he was going. His wishing us asleep didn't hold up. Did it? Same with his hold on the boat."

"I'm not so sure."

"You can't always be sure!" Pyetr said. "Sometimes you just have to move. You're worried about Uulamets. I'm more worried about another night on this river. If Uulamets couldn't outwish his daughter or the vodyanoi or whoever, I beg your pardon, Sasha Vasilyevitch, but I'm not sure you can, either. So what are we going to do tonight?"

"We won't be any safer out in the middle of the river. We're a long way from the house—"

"To the black god with the house. We're bound for Kiev. Forget the old man. You don't need him."

"I do need him," Sasha said. "And if he doesn't come back, I still have to go back there."

"For what? God, you're quit of him! You don't believe his nonsense. He wants you to believe you have to rely on him. Trust *me* instead, why don't you?"

Sasha said in a muted voice, "Pyetr, I'm not sure what I'm doing. I'm not even sure what I've done. I'm scared of that. . . ."

"Because you're listening to him. Forget it! Let's get this

boat out onto the river, let's put this place behind us, that's all."

He was halfway to his feet when Sasha caught his arm.

"No!" Sasha said, and all of a sudden Pyetr doubted he was right, all of a sudden he was sitting down again, a little shaken, and Sasha was saying, "Please. Till tomorrow morning. To-morrow morning we'll go."

Pyetr looked at him suspiciously, a little angry, but Sasha refused to flinch. He had his jaw set and looked him in the eye as straight as straight.

"You're 'witching me," Pyetr said. "I don't like that. I ought to take this boat—"

But he felt extremely uneasy about doing that. He thought how Sasha had been right, sometimes.

"Stop it," he said.

"No," Sasha said, "I won't."

Sasha was upset, he was upset. He thought that he could get up, cast off the ropes and take them out anyway.

"Damn it," he said; and got up and walked over to the forest-side rail to prove the point.

But he could not even stay mad. It was enough to drive a man crazy. He looked into the forest and thought that this was a better place to be than out on the river tonight, and he knew, damn it all! where that notion was coming from.

He bowed his head, he stood there with his arms folded. He felt Sasha wishing him not to be upset, and insisted on being furious. He turned around, on Sasha's grace, he sus-pected, and said, "Boy, that's not polite."

"I'm sorry," Sasha said earnestly.

"Being sorry doesn't patch it! Don't interfere with my judg-ment! Don't *do* that to your friends!"

"I haven't got a choice," Sasha said.

"Why? Because *Uulamets* wanted us here? Because some-thing else does? What if you're wrong and it's not your wish, can you even tell?"

"If it's that much stronger than I am," Sasha said after a moment, "then you wouldn't be arguing to do what it doesn't want, either, would you?"

Sasha made a kind of sense. Pyetr hoped so. Otherwise nothing in the world was reliable.

And Sasha wanting him not to be mad was infuriatingly hard to resist.

Pyetr walked over to where he had been sitting, and slammed his hand into the side of the deckhouse, so it hurt.

That was a feeling he could rely on, at least.

Sasha came and sat down near him, contrite, Pyetr imagined: he squeezed out the water from the reheated compress and wrapped the cloth about his hand without so much as looking up.

"Pyetr, please."

"Don't talk to me," he said, because he had decided he was going to say that before he felt sorry for the boy. But he did glance up, and the boy looked so shaken it went through him the way the pain of his hand did.

At least he supposed it was his own feeling.

"Tomorrow morning," Sasha said, his voice trembling. "I don't care how mad you get, I *won't* let us have an accident."

"Who won't let us?" Pyetr retorted. "Didn't you say once, wizards are easier to affect? Maybe you don't know better. Does that thought occur to you?"

"It does," Sasha said. "And I don't want you mad at me, Pyetr, I'm sorry, I can't help that, but what do I do?" Sasha looked to be at the end of his wits, and bowed his head, his hands tangled in his hair. "Don't want to go. Be patient. Don't do things like that—"

The pain in Pyetr's hand diminished, markedly. And the boy sat there with his head in his hands, throwing everything he had into that relief, Pyetr reckoned. He felt his anger ebb and could not even make up his mind whether it was himself or Sasha deciding it.

He slumped back against the wall of the deckhouse, set his jaw and glared at Sasha in a moment that felt as though they were both irretrievably mad—and searched back to his first days in Sasha's company, trying to recover his balance.

But one never knew about those moments, either . . .

Except that Sasha had attacked the vodyanoi for his sake, with a salt pot and a stick—which he could not forget.

"You want me to remember that?"

"What?" Sasha asked, looking up, looking bewildered.

Innocent, then. But then, he did not in any sense doubt he could trust Sasha; what frightened him was the degree of trust he began to understand it took—to live with a wizard.

"Let me tell you," Pyetr said, "I don't know how far Uulamets ever pushed us—he could, I don't doubt it, and maybe he's so good neither one of us could catch him at it, but I don't think so." He soaked the rag again and squeezed it, so he had somewhere else to look besides Sasha's pale face. "Do me a favor. Don't do that again. It's not the way to get along with people."

"I don't want to do it . . . I don't want you to get killed, either!"

"Fine. Neither do I. You think there's some kind of spell on the boat. I think there's a Thing somewhere around here that got breakfast and it's coming up suppertime. What do you say to that?"

"I know how to stop it."

"Good. I'm very glad of that. Why don't we leave tonight?"

"Because it could turn us over."

"With you wishing not."

"I don't know how strong it is." Sasha bit his lip and said, "I'm not sure that's not what tore the sail."

"Are you sure about anything?"

Sasha took a little longer about that answer. "No. I'm not. But I'm afraid if we go out there—that's deep water. And we could be in it. And I can't swim."

"Neither can I," Pyetr said. "But we won't know how by tomorrow morning, either. Are we going to stay here for the rest of our lives?"

"Master Uulamets might come back."

"I'm not really looking forward to that," Pyetr said. Across the river the sun was closer to the trees, but he had lost his certainty and his enthusiasm for facing the river in the dark. "Tomorrow, then. —You're not pushing that on me, are you?"

"No." Sasha shook his head emphatically. "No, I swear I'm not."

"See how hard it is to know anything when somebody does that to you? You're liable to make me do something backward to what I'd do in good sense. Make me break my neck. Who knows? I'd really appreciate it if you didn't do that again."

Sasha looked entirely upset. "What if you're wrong? What if I know you're wrong?"

"What if you're wrong about me being wrong? You'd better be right, hadn't you, and you'd better not do it often—had you?"

"It's so easy to do," Sasha said, "and it's so hard not to—"

"I wish you had a choice," Pyetr said, sure enough of Sasha's honesty this time not to doubt himself: he felt sorry for the boy, more, he was suddenly afraid for the boy's sanity as much as his own. He reached out in a rough halfway hug, a pull at Sasha's neck. "You might be right this time. Just mind your manners."

"I'm sorry." Sasha took a swipe at his eyes, his head ducked. "I'm just scared."

"Time to be," Pyetr said, and dipped the rag in the pot again, and attended to his hand to give the boy time to dry his face. "You think you can keep whatever-it-is off tonight. Uulamets couldn't."

"We don't know that."

"Grandfather's a pretty competent wizard, by what I see. And he didn't do all that well, by what I see, either. What do we do, sprinkle salt, light a fire and hope?"

"Don't make fun, Pyetr. It's not funny."

"No, this time it certainly isn't." He wound the rag around his hand and flexed his fingers, dripping water that hissed onto the stove. "But I don't say taking the boat out in the dark is that much better, I give you that, too."

"What you have to understand—" Sasha said. "Pyetr, I honestly don't know what to do. And I can't swear to you I know it's my idea. I just have this feeling—I have this terrible feeling we won't make it home—"

"Home," Pyetr scoffed, and saw how upset the boy was, and shook his head. "I'll allow you this—I've no fondness for that old man, but I'm getting a real understanding—" Why he's crazy, was what he thought, but he said: "—that he's not as bad as he could be." Uulamets might, Pyetr thought, have done what Sasha had done. "I can forgive him."

God, he thought . . . what am I going to do with this boy?
What if he weren't as good-hearted as he is?

Or if he weren't sane as he is—or if someone crossed him,
seriously?

"If you want to go back to the house for a while," Pyetr
said calmly, "before Kiev—we can do that. Grandfather might
even turn up. He's probably wishing he was home anyway, by
now. Or wishing himself back at the boat. We'll have supper,
we'll sprinkle salt all over the deck, just in case. We probably
should have done that last night. And we'll get some sleep
and in the morning we'll untie and get out into the river."

"We hit ground on the way in. I think there's this long
ridge—"

"We put the sail up just part way—it ought to blow us
back a little. Maybe turn us around."

Sasha looked a little more cheerful then.

"Wish up a wind for the morning, if you want something
to do."

"I'll try," Sasha said, and rubbed his face with his hands.
"But you're right about the salt. He left us most of it. Maybe
he was thinking about that."

"Considerate of him," Pyetr said.

They cooked a comfortable supper on the little stove—fresh
grilled fish, right out of the river, Sasha having thought to
bring fishhooks—and they cleaned up and flung the ashes
overside, by which time the sky across the river was dimming
from its last colors and the stars were coming out.

Sasha scattered salt and sulphur all across the deck then,
one end of the boat to the other, and Pyetr forbore to suggest
he try a few incantations and some smoke as well: Sasha
would surely take it amiss, but, sincerely, if salt worked he
saw no reason to stint on the rest of Uulamets' rituals, rattles
and singing and the rest of it: it all seemed alike to him.

Sasha did take a cup of vodka and draw a circle on the
deck, which Pyetr watched, hands on hips, with some curiosity.

"So the wind won't blow a gap in it," Sasha said, "and I
don't think water's a good idea."

209

After which he scattered salt and sulphur right along that wet line, so it stuck.

Smart lad, Pyetr thought. "As a wizard," he said, "you don't do a bad job."

"I hope," Sasha said. "You've got that little bit I gave you."

Pyetr patted his pocket. "Absolutely."

Sasha looked at him as if to decide whether he was being laughed at, dusted his hands off and set the cup of salt and sulphur on the deck inside the circle. He handed Pyetr the cup with the vodka in it. "Nothing wrong with it," he said. "It's left over."

Pyetr grinned, took the cup and sipped it at his leisure.

He took a second, full one, but that was all, since he had no inclination to sleep too deeply this night. They lay looking at the stars and listening to the sounds of the boat, and planning how they would get off the shore and how they had to be sure to come to the house and the landing by daylight or risk missing it—discussing too—he could not figure out how an enterprising scoundrel had gotten to this pass—how they could get through the winter there, and how the garden could be better than it was and what they could do with the bathhouse to repair the roof.

He knew nothing about gardening or carpentry. Sasha did. Sasha was quite happy talking about turnips and beans and roof-mending, and if it eased his mind, Pyetr was willing to listen.

Only somewhere in the midst of Sasha's plans for the spring planting Pyetr's eyes began to close, and he began to drift—which he had not planned to do. He said, "I'm done. Get some sleep. I won't swear to how long I'll stay awake otherwise."

"I can stay awake."

"I'm sure. But I know I will." He did not say that he had had practice at long watches in activities he did not want to explain to Sasha. He only sat up, laid his sword across his lap and propped his elbows on his knees, settling for a long night.

Sasha started to say something else about the bathhouse. "Hush," Pyetr said. "I'm not staying awake so you can talk."

Sasha hushed. Things were quiet after that, no sound but the water, the branches and some forlorn raucous thing chirping in the brush on this warmer night. Eventually it gave up. He listened only to the river, rested comfortably, and, after some hours, as a cold breeze began to kick up off the water, he thought about it a while, then finally unstopped the jug and poured himself a quarter of a cup, just enough to warm the blood.

Absolutely no more than that.

But he found himself nodding when he had finished it, his head dropping toward his chest. He straightened and stretched his arms and his back and shifted position. He ought, he thought, to take a walk around the deck—outside the salt circle, it might be, but things were quiet and the center of the deck was no problem.

He got up as quietly as he could, because sleep was coming down on him irresistibly and he figured the vodka now for very bad judgment. He looked to the wind to clear his head and wake him up, took a walk to the middle of the deck and turned around with a start as something moved in the tail of his eye.

He saw Eveshka walking, then, near the rail, saw her hair and her gown wet and the water streaming off her sleeves as she turned and held out her hands to him.

"Sasha!" he yelled, as lethargy came tumbling down on him, in the desperate hope that Sasha was not caught in it, asleep though he was. . . .

But such salt as the wind left on the deck seemed no hindrance to her. She drifted closer, put her hands on his shoulders and looked into his eyes, soundlessly speaking to him, while he was too dazed to move; and her expression was so gentle and so concerned there seemed no threat in her. Her eyes were dark as her face was white, with moving shadow in their depths that might have been currents, or only a vision of the ropes and the rail of the boat as she put her cold arms about his neck and kissed him with the taste and the chill of river water on her lips.

It lasted a long, long while. He grew dizzy and dazed, he tried to remember what she was, but nothing he had ever felt was the same as this—profound, and dangerous, and at the same time so gentle there could never be any harm, as long as he did not move—

He drifted, then, in a dream where dangerous things moved around the both of them, but there was no harm, not so long as she was there—not so long as he looked into her eyes and not to other things.

But she drifted away then; and he was suddenly locked in one of the sweating, heart-thumping sort of dreams which usually meant he was looking for his father. He knew that somebody was going to tell him that his father was murdered, but that was long ago and he had long since gotten used to that idea. Nowadays it was not truly his father he was looking for—though he had never known precisely what or who it was. It was the searching itself that was the nightmare, a conviction that if he could not find what he was looking for, he was damned. . . .

18

✠ ✠ ✠ ✠ Sasha opened his eyes with a sudden feeling of alarm, the deck lit by dawn-glow and immediately near him, Pyetr's blanket lying there—

"Pyetr!" He scrambled up with a foreboding of what had happened the day before, of Pyetr gone from the boat—dead, perhaps. . . .

But Pyetr was lying just beyond the circle of salt, one leg bent under him, his arms in no natural posture of sleep.

Sasha reached him in two strides. He got an arm under Pyetr's head, appalled by Pyetr's deathly pallor and the feel of him—he was breathing, but he was ice cold and totally limp. Sasha let him gently down and ran back for the blankets and the jug of vodka, tucked the blankets about him and shook at him violently.

Pyetr's eyes came half-open, wandered and fluttered with a dawning concern.

"Are you all right?" Sasha asked.

Pyetr made some confused answer, tried to get his arm under him and his leg straightened from its awkward position, and came up at least as far as sitting, with a blind and frightened look on his face.

"What happened?" Sasha asked, holding to his shoulder. "Pyetr?"

Pyetr raked his hand through his hair and propped his arm against his knees. "God," he muttered. "She—"

"What 'she'?" Sasha had a dreadful premonition what 'she' Pyetr meant, and shook him hard to keep him awake. "Eveshka? Pyetr, was it Eveshka?"

Pyetr nodded, rested his head against his arm and stayed

213

that way, as if sitting up and breathing was all he had in him at the moment.

Sasha grabbed up the blankets and put them around Pyetr's shoulders. He hesitated to leave Pyetr even for a moment, considering the water and the woods on either hand and the nature of the danger, but he hurried across to the deckhouse and brought out the stove, brought wood and the firepot and with trembling, mistake-ridden efforts got a fire started in the pan, enough to warm Pyetr's immediate vicinity and make a strong cup of tea. Meanwhile he gave Pyetr a small drink of vodka, and Pyetr's hands when he touched them were still like ice.

"What did she do?" Sasha asked, steadying the cup on its way to Pyetr's mouth.

Pyetr took a sip, shook his head, and gave up the cup then to hold the quilts about him. He suddenly began to shiver, bent double and very evidently not wanting to talk about the matter.

But: "Where's master Uulamets?" Sasha persisted. "Pyetr, for the god's sake he's in trouble! Talk to me! Tell me what you know! Did she say where he was?"

"I don't know," Pyetr said, between rattling teeth. "I don't know. She's lost him—"

"Did she say that?"

Pyetr shook his head and rested it against his arm.

Sasha built the fire as high as the stove and the deck would bear, applied all his intention to Pyetr's warmth and well-being until he actually felt dizzy himself, while with another trip to the deckhouse for the honey, he made him a cup of hot, sweetened tea.

Pyetr drank it slowly, warming his hands with it, and that seemed to Sasha to have helped most of everything he had done. "I'm sorry," Pyetr said, when he had drunk it down to half. "I don't know why we're alive this morning." He felt the back of his head and grimaced. "Fell on my head, by the feel of it. I must have walked—"

"Was she alone?"

"I think so. I can't remember. I just can't remember. I'm sorry. Small help I was."

"It's not your fault. Pyetr, did she say anything?"

"She was a ghost again." Pyetr looked as if he had just realized he had not said that. "She wasn't threatening, she didn't feel—angry: she was worried. Upset. God, I don't know . . . I don't know, it's just—like she was before, lost and trying to get back and she can't. I can't say why and don't look at me like that!"

Sasha shook his head. It was hard for Pyetr to talk in terms of feeling things were so. Pyetr wanted to touch and handle things before he believed them. "I'm not," Sasha said. "I just wish I'd been awake."

"I wish I'd woke you. God, I don't know what's happening—"

Sasha grabbed Pyetr's arm and held it hard to bring him back, because Pyetr was having trouble being aware of things, and Pyetr halfway did know what was happening to him— that was the terrible part.

"Listen," Sasha said as reasonably, as steadily as he could. "I'll make more tea. Just rest. Maybe Uulamets will show up." But the thought in his heart was that Uulamets was not coming, that they were alone on this boat with the wind blowing them against the shore this morning, not a hope of getting off, for all his wishes to the contrary—and even if it turned, he doubted he could get the boat downriver—the more so if something as magical and powerful as the vodyanoi had other notions.

They had a breakfast of fish which Pyetr helped catch, but Pyetr had no stomach for them after they had cleaned and cooked them. "The smell," he said. "They smell like the water."

And several times that morning that Sasha looked Pyetr's direction he was gazing off toward the woods, just staring, lost in his thoughts or lost somewhere.

The breeze blew steadily from the west, and the boat heaved and rubbed against the broken branches. Sasha looked into the stores and had no idea what to do about feeding them, since most that they had to eat was fish and turnips and the flour was running out.

215

He made some of it into cakes; and Pyetr would eat that, and drink the honeyed tea, and a few of the berries.

But while Sasha was cleaning the stove and turning out the ashes, he glanced back and found Pyetr standing by the forest-side rail, looking out into the trees, and when he came there carefully to suggest Pyetr stay more to the middle of the boat, Pyetr said, "I don't think we'll get off this shore," in that same lost way.

"The wind will turn," Sasha said, upset because Pyetr had just echoed his own convictions. Pyetr grasped one of the ropes that held the mast and gave a twitch of his shoulders.

"I don't think so," Pyetr said, lifted the back of his right hand to his mouth and stood there looking out into the woods. "Sasha, it won't let me alone."

"Is she out there?"

"I think she is. Maybe she's found a new tree."

"You think she's killed Uulamets?"

Pyetr did not answer for a moment. Finally he shook his head.

"Is your hand hurting?" Sasha asked.

Again a hesitation, as if the question were mere distraction to his thinking. Then a shake of his head, a deliberate effort to tear his eyes away and to look at him. "I'm not afraid to go there," Pyetr said in a distant, bewildered tone. "I think that's probably very stupid. This place scares me—this boat does. In there—" A glance toward the forest an arm's length away. "In there doesn't seem safe, either, but it doesn't give me the feeling I have here, and I don't trust it."

Pyetr was asking for advice. Sasha had nothing so definite, only a sense that there was a hazard in their trying to put out again, even if the wind should shift.

But Pyetr seemed to be in touch with Eveshka, in whatever form; and Eveshka was pulling at him, not as absolutely as Eveshka could—perhaps that her power was in some fashion diminished; perhaps that it was greater—because she had not succeeded in drawing him away from the boat; but neither was he free of that pull in her absence.

More, Pyetr seemed to be reasoning quite clearly around his premonitions: his caution was persuasive; his account of Eveshka argued distress and trouble. There was a very plausible chance that Eveshka, disembodied, separated from her father, might run back to them and speak to Pyetr the way she had before—

For whatever purpose.

"You think we should go out there?" he asked Pyetr. "Be out there in the dark? That doesn't bother you?"

Pyetr sucked at the wound on his hand and after a moment shook his head. "Not as much as staying here. That's just what I think. I don't insist. I don't trust my judgment."

"I think—" Sasha said after a breath to think twice about it, "I think there's a reason the sail tore. I think there's a reason we're stuck here. —Can you talk to her? Can you get her to come here now?"

Pyetr made a face, took hold of the rope with both hands and stared into the woods a long, long moment. Then he flinched and shook his head. "Just that feeling. It's worse."

They set foot on shore—splintered limbs and gnarled roots were their bridge and their ladder to the sheer bank, likely the way Uulamets and Eveshka had left the boat, in Pyetr's reckoning, if they had left of their own free will at all.

One fear left him the moment he found secure footing off the deck; but in the moment he reached back to steady Sasha in clambering down with his belongings, he found room for another, more sensible apprehension: that Sasha might have listened to him not because he was right, but because he was older, armed, and, admittedly, experienced in things about which Sasha was naïve.

Perhaps, he thought, all his premonitions regarding the boat were nothing but fear of the water and the voyage home— perhaps he had tilted some delicate balance he should never have touched in Sasha.

He said, pulling the words out, "I'm still not sure of this. I don't know I'm right. What if whatever got Uulamets is just stronger?"

Sasha hitched the ropes of the blanket roll and the basket up on his shoulders. "Then I think we'd better find it," Sasha said. "Remember what you said about swords and magic? If it's not going to let us leave, we've got to get close to it to do anything, don't we? And the longer we wait—"

"I think I said something about fools and swords," Pyetr said under his breath, and cast a look back at the boat, thinking he might be pushing them both into a fatal, foolish mistake. "What if whatever-it-is *wants* us to do this? Have you thought of that?"

"Yes," Sasha said solemnly. "I have. But how else do we get at it?"

"God," Pyetr muttered.

But he worked his way along the crumbling rim and past the brush.

Much better feeling, then, when they were clear of the boat. Much better, when he had gotten through the first curtain of brush and in among the trees—like coming from winter's end into spring. He drew a slow breath, looked around him as Sasha was doing, at a woods where live moss was greening and springy underfoot, leaves were breaking pale from branches all around—the like of which he himself had never seen—certainly not in Vojvoda's tame little garden plots, and certainly not in the dead woods the other side.

"Where?" Sasha asked him.

He wished he could say he had no idea. But when he thought about it he did. He lifted his hand and pointed nowhere, really, that looked any different from any other way through the trees, but it was absolutely certain in his mind—

A fool following a dead girl, his old friends would shake their heads and say: Pyetr's gone quite mad.

Which was probably true, he thought—though not one of them would blink at the idea she *was* a ghost; and Sasha Misurov took it quite matter-of-factly, simply took a good grip on the ropes of his bedroll and his basket of what he called necessities, and motioned him to lead off—

Sasha having his salt pots and his herbs and fishing line and hooks and their cooking pan and such; while his own basket-pack had most of the food—and the bandages they had both thought of, Sasha because it was the kind of thing Sasha would think of, and himself because he had the glum opinion one of them was likely to need them; likewise a jug of vodka, medicinal, he and Sasha had quite solemnly agreed.

A bird started up from a limb, scolding them. A bush was in white bloom. The very sound was different, a constant whisper of wind in leaves and living branches.

"Certainly a more cheerful sort of place," Pyetr said, watching the sun dapple the bracken and the limbs as they walked—no great difficulty to find a way through, the trees generously spaced and tall, the ground rising and falling in little hillocks, the rare saplings vastly overtopped by old, wide-limbed trees. The worst going was the bracken, the old growth crunching and breaking under the new as they waded knee-deep through this pathless place; but it was over all a quick progress. "Better than the woods near the house," he looked back at Sasha to say, about to add that, over all, he had no bad feeling at all about this place.

But then cold fingers touched his neck. He spun back forward and felt a little breath of cold air hit his face.

"Pyetr?" he heard Sasha ask—Sasha was puzzled; but he had another demand on his attention at that instant, an urgent and impatient presence, carrying with it a fear he could not immediately understand. It only seemed that the contact was fading and that if he turned his head and lost touch with it now, that would be the last of it.

"It's here," he said. "Keep with me. . . ."

He had no doubt now which direction to take. He started off as quickly as he could over the rough ground, dodging around thickets and up over the shoulder of the hill. He heard Sasha behind him, trusting that Sasha would keep up, and battered through increasing brush and foliage with his arms, a course virtually in a straight line, disregarding of obstacles.

"Pyetr!" he heard, and waited a breath or two, but, he felt that breath of cold again, felt a gentle touch of icy fingers, smelled a taint of river weed.

"Pyetr!" Quite close now. Sasha was all right. They both were. He started to move again, less and less liking the feeling he had of something behind them, and feeling equally strongly that safety was in front—

Himself, Pyetr Kochevikov, who only recently believed in ghosts and vodyaniye and such, found himself fighting his way uphill in blind terror of what might be stalking them and blind trust of what was guiding them—

Knowing, absolutely, that the situation might be completely backwards of what he felt—

Sasha saying, That could have been your heart, Pyetr. . . .

He heard thunder behind him, a crack that shocked the forest, felt the increasing chill in the air and the shadowing in the sky. Sasha overtook him, held him by the arm and protested they should stop, it was coming up a rain. . . .

No, he said, brushing off Sasha's grip.

No. Not yet. *She* said not; and his feeling of where safety lay remained constant. "It's all right," he said to Sasha without looking at anything in its distracting detail, not Sasha, not the woods around them. "It's Eveshka. She's still in front of us. She's moving. . . ."

"She'll come back," Sasha said.

"I'm not sure she can," he said, and walked while a fine mist drifted down through the branches . . .

They had left the bracken. It was leaf mold underfoot now, a thick carpet glistening with rain, easier going, except the brush and the thorns. He walked, followed the wisp of a notion where he was going until his side ached and his legs were shaking with every step, jogged when the presence grew fainter, caught his breath and walked again while it was strong—until finally on the bare side of a ridge he slipped, lost his balance and skidded feet first down the slope into a rain-pocked spring.

He gasped a breath and hit the muddy ground in disgust, having landed up to the knees in water. But when he collected himself to get up he could see her reflected in the roiled surface, standing behind him.

He whirled to look, grabbing at his sword—and saw nothing but the wet leaves, the forest around him . . . and a very distraught Sasha Misurov coming sideways down the slippery face of the ridge to reach him.

Fool, he chided himself, heart pounding, and did not want to look back at that pool of water, because he had a cold, nape-prickling certainty that her reflection would still be there.

"Pyetr!" he heard Sasha calling him.

And saw her instead in his water-filled handprints in the leaf-mold, reflection after reflection, whole and part, repeated in every puddle and every water drop around him.

"God," he breathed, and slowly, unwanted and irresistible impulse, looked back at the pool.

Pyetr was sitting staring at the surface of a spring, finally, when Sasha arrived, drenched and panting, at the bottom of the slope—Pyetr was just sitting, staring as if that were far more important than the fact he had nearly lost himself in the woods—or lost *him*, more to the point.

It was certainly not Pyetr in his right mind—Pyetr scratched and soaked, flecked with bits of dead leaves with and his hands and his breeches all muddy.

"Pyetr?" he asked.

Pyetr asked, without looking at him, "Do you see her?"

"No," Sasha said, desperately regretting they had ever left the boat. He was trembling in the arms and the knees from the chase Pyetr had led him, and he wanted nothing so much now, if he did not carefully smother that thought, as to be back on the boat with Pyetr locked in the deckhouse, if that was what it took to keep him out of the rusalka's reach.

"She's the way she was," Pyetr murmured, "not—not like at the house. . . ."

"What do you mean, not like at the house?" A cold doubt bobbed to the surface with that: but Uulamets had always put it down, Uulamets had been so sure, Uulamets had always insisted—

He *felt* a wish touch him, a very strong one: he *felt* whatever Pyetr could see was well-disposed to them, and terrified of this place—

"That's enough!" he said, and picked up a branch and flung it at the surface, scattering ripples. "Pyetr!"

Pyetr dropped his face into his hands, drew a breath, and did not take offense when Sasha grabbed him by the packs he was carrying and tried to haul him away from the pool. He was not strong enough; but Pyetr made his own effort to get up, leaning on his arm—

Stopped then, looked away, distracted—

"Don't," Sasha said, hauling at him, *wishing* him not to look, because suddenly there was a wisp of white drifting in the tail of his eye. He looked fearfully toward it, saw a haziness

221

in the misting rain, as if the water was settling there a moment before it fell.

He felt reassured against his will. He saw it retreat, saw the surface of the pond ripple as a veil of droplets slowly sank into it and vanished.

Pyetr walked a few steps away and sat down as if his knees had simply gone out from under him.

"What's with Uulamets isn't her," Pyetr said, and rested his head in his hands. "Damn, it's not her, it never was, it never acted right. I should have said—"

"Is that what she told you?"

"She can't. I can't hear her. —I just know the difference."

Sasha sank down on his heels in front of him. He suddenly felt exhausted, cold, set about with too many questions.

"I'm not crazy," Pyetr insisted, starting to shiver.

"I know you're not." He reached out and grasped Pyetr's hand. It was like ice, white, flecked with bits of leaves and dirt. "Look, it's raining, it's late, we don't know where we're going. Let's stop here—put up the shelter, get a fire going, have supper."

"What were we sharing the house with?" Pyetr asked.

"I don't know," Sasha said, with a queasiness in his own stomach; he had never imagined he would feel safer spending the night with a rusalka than on their own—but in this place he did.

Keep away from Pyetr, he wished her; and felt she assented to that—

She wanted them safe.

Especially, and for special reasons—Pyetr.

Which notion far from reassured him.

They had supper—fish and turnips again, but honest fish and turnips. The trick was to keep the fire hot enough to over-power the drizzle—and not high enough to come back on a gust of wind and catch the canvas, which they had stretched from several makeshift poles and pegs to make a shelter: smoky from time to time, but the smoke meant warm air, and it was actually pleasant despite the sting it brought to the eyes. With a hot meal and a little measure of vodka afterward they were tolerably dry and comfortable—sitting on the wooded ridge, not by the pool, to be sure; and with the heat and light of the fire between them and Eveshka, Sasha had seen to that, having set up the shelter while Pyetr was gathering wood.

Not that he completely disbelieved the rusalka's good intentions. But he had marked how pale Pyetr seemed by dusk, how clearly exhausted.

And he was not much better after supper.

"How are you feeling?" Sasha asked.

"All right," Pyetr said. "I truly apologize. The stupid thing was, I knew at the time it was stupid."

"Did you know I was behind you?"

Pyetr nodded. "But I had this feeling of something else behind us. And I couldn't explain it. I don't know why I couldn't. It was altogether, irredeemably *stupid*—"

"That's how strong she is. *I* couldn't stop her. Or you." He reached out and shook at Pyetr's arm. "Be careful. I don't think, I truly don't think she's after us, or we wouldn't be sitting here right now, but that doesn't mean she won't change her mind."

"She doesn't mean us any harm," Pyetr insisted, with a conviction that did nothing to ease Sasha's misgivings; and Sasha shook at him a second time.

"Listen to you, Pyetr Ilitch. It's her. You know exactly what she's making you know. Don't start believing it. Maybe she's on our side, maybe she wants to help her father, but she's not alive, and you are, and that's what she needs. Don't *be* stupid. Don't let her close to you!"

Pyetr gave a kind of shiver, staring into the fire. "That's not easy."

"I know it's not easy. You're white as a ghost tonight. *Don't* let her touch you."

Pyetr took a drink, swallowed hard, and nodded. "I know. I know that. I'm not being stubborn about it."

"Listen, if she doesn't tell us tomorrow morning where she thinks her father is, or what's going on here, or what we're going to do about it, I think we'd do best to turn south, just start walking out of this woods—"

"I know where Uulamets is," Pyetr said, and made a motion of his hand to the general direction he had been going.

223

"She does. He's being a fool. I suppose wizards can be that the same as the rest of us. She's upset about it."

"Is she talking to you?"

Pyetr shook his head. "I just think that's where she's taking us."

"Maybe we'd still better go south," Sasha said, afraid now, wishing he had long ago listened to Pyetr when he was sure it was Pyetr's own idea. He could only see Pyetr slipping deeper and deeper, and of that he could only see one conclusion. "We can get to the house, float a log across if we have to—"

"Hwiuur," Pyetr reminded him, and Sasha's heart thumped an extra beat at that name, here, where they did not want attention.

But Pyetr had no power to wish up a thing.

"Then we just walk all the way to Kiev," Sasha said. "I'm sure there's a ferry. And too many people around for things like him to try anything. I don't think magical things like too many people around. I don't think wizards do. But I don't mind going there."

There was long silence.

"I don't think we'll get there," Pyetr said. "I don't think we've a chance."

So they were face about in their arguments. "We can try!" Sasha insisted.

And Pyetr slowly shook his head.

"What does that mean?" Sasha asked.

Pyetr did not answer.

"Pyetr, why not?"

"We won't get there."

Sasha stared at him, helpless, being far from him physically to make Pyetr do anything—and he did not *want* to wish him into it; which was immediate failure in itself.

"Feels better here," Pyetr said. "A lot better than the boat, crazy as it sounds."

"It's not crazy," Sasha said. "It *is* better. —But do you know—like you knew leaving me was stupid—that it's stupid to believe her?"

After a moment Pyetr nodded, then said, "But I just have this feeling—I think it's her, talking to me: telling me grandfather's alive—that he's in some kind of trouble; that if we don't get him back something dreadful's going to happen— something I don't understand, but I don't understand any of it anyway. Nothing new for me." He reached down for the jug and started to unstop it.

And yelled and grabbed for his sword, nearly taking the shelter down as he leapt up—

—because something was skittering along the bushes near them.

Sasha tried to get out of Pyetr's way and miss the fire at the same time; but whatever it was circled to the side behind the fire and vanished into a bush.

With a hiss.

"Babi!" Sasha exclaimed, and caught Pyetr's arm. "Don't scare him."

"Don't scare *him!*" Pyetr retorted; but a round black head had poked out of the brush and blinked at them.

It showed shiny white teeth, a huge row of them.

"Babi?" Sasha said.

It crept out into the firelight and the drizzle, a very abject and flat-to-the-ground Yard-thing.

"It can stay out there!" Pyetr said. "Throw it something to eat. We don't need it in here with us."

It crept closer, chin on ground, and folded its little manlike hands in front of its face, staring up at them.

A very diminished, very sad-looking Babi.

"Where's Uulamets?" Sasha asked of it, and it growled.

"Pleasant as always," Pyetr muttered, not about to put his sword away.

"But it *is* Babi," Sasha said. "I'm sure it is."

"One Thing probably looks a lot like another," Pyetr said. "It can keep its distance!"

It crept a little closer, flat to the ground.

"That's enough," Pyetr said; but—

"Don't hit it!" Sasha said, and grabbed up the food basket, found a turnip and tossed it.

Small black hands seized the offering, turned it. Babi sat up and gnawed at it with delicate, busy bites, darting little glances at them. Then it gulped the turnip in one gape of its mouth, scuttled into their shelter and grabbed Sasha around the ankle.

"Damn!" Pyetr exclaimed. Sasha yelped with the instant thought of those teeth and his leg. But it simply held on; and Sasha gingerly bent down and patted its head.

It grabbed his wrist, then, and held on as he stood up.

"Be careful!" Pyetr said.

"It's all right," Sasha said, trying to hold the creature in his hands. But it jumped for his chest and scrambled for his neck and ducked around behind him as Pyetr grabbed for it—after which it was still, arms locked around his neck, Pyetr in front of him with his sword lifted, and Sasha thought it a very good idea not to alarm either of them. "It's behaving itself," he said, calmly trying, pulling at one wiry arm, to persuade it to let go of his neck. "Come on, Babi. Let go."

It rose up against his ear and hissed at Pyetr.

"God," Pyetr muttered.

"It's all right," Sasha said, sat down on the log inside their shelter and carefully pulled Babi's hands loose.

Babi hissed again, bounded down onto the log and down to shelter under his knees.

Pyetr stood with his sword in hand and finally, with a scowl, ran it into its sheath and rescued the jug, which fortunately had landed unbroken.

He muttered, "I suppose it's a good sign, over all," put the sword down and sat down inside the shelter again, his hair glistening with rain and a scowl still on his face when he looked down at the creature.

Babi took tiny fistfuls of Sasha's breeches and climbed up into his lap.

"He's scared," Sasha said.

"He's scared." Pyetr made a face, unstopped the jug and drank. "What's with grandfather? That's what I'd like to know. If Ugly here ran off from it—"

Babi growled.

"Your pardon." Pyetr hoisted the jug. "Have some?"

It scampered down and snatched up Pyetr's cup, holding it up with both hands.

Pyetr poured. It drank, gulp after gulp, and held it up for more.

"I'd be careful," Sasha said.

He poured; it drank, and held up the cup again.

"Bottomless little devil," Pyetr said, and filled it again. "What's grandfather into? Do you know?"

It gulped the third cup, exhaled, and fell down in a heap where it stood.

Pyetr gave Sasha a puzzled look.

"I don't know," Sasha said.

19

Sasha slept lightly by intent, rousing himself throughout the night to keep the fire going, while Pyetr stirred only the first and second times he laid a log on and Sasha said, "It's all right, go back to sleep."

Pyetr seemed to give up caution for himself then, and tucked down and simply rested, like Babi the dvorovoi, who or which curled itself into a ball where it or he had fallen, and snored.

Babi had disappeared when the imposter showed up at the house; Babi had come back to them last night, and as signs went, that was the most heartening thing that had happened to them lately, Sasha was sure of it.

But when the rain had stopped and the morning came cold and misty, when he had stirred his aching bones to get the fire going for morning tea, he kept an anxious eye toward the pool that lay invisible in the mist.

Not, again, that he did not trust Eveshka's intentions. It was her resolve he doubted.

He started the tea, he nudged Pyetr awake, and Pyetr put a rumpled head out of his coat and his blankets and took his tea with a murmur of thank you.

Babi came and held out his hands. Sasha gave him his own cup and had his tea in their mixing bowl: if one had a well-disposed dvorovoi in a situation like this he was by no means going to offend it—Yard-things being by reputation uncouth, not so home-loving and dependable as House-things nor so wise and so dangerous as the banniks: and fierce and uncouth seemed very fine company in their situation.

So it might have his cup if it made it happy.

228

So he was thinking when he saw Pyetr gazing off downslope.

He looked that way with apprehension and saw the mist moving, swirling as if a slow disturbance were passing through it.

"Pyetr," he said.

"I'm all right," Pyetr said, and lifted his cup to the valley and the swirling mist. "Patience!" he called out with something of his old spirit. "It's cold this morning; I'd like my tea."

But Pyetr's face looked still quite pale this morning; he had his coat on, and when it came time to put the fire out and pack up, he worked with his jaw clenched and a pained, worried look on his face.

Babi dropped his cup into the basket. That was his form of helping. And when they had taken up their packs to leave, and Pyetr said matter-of-factly, with a lift of his hand, "I think it's this way," then Babi quite readily clambered up Sasha's leg and up his arm to sit on his pack.

"You're heavy!" Sasha complained. "Babi, stop it."

Whereupon Babi simply stopped weighing anything.

But he kept a tight-fisted grip on a lock of Sasha's hair, until they had worked their way down the misty slope to the soft ground around the pool.

Then Babi bounded down, growled and hissed and splashed across the pool where the mist began to swirl and move with the passage of a ghostly body: Babi followed that movement, skipping and frolicking like a puppy.

It certainly seemed to answer one question.

The mist diminished as they climbed and that clue to Eveshka's whereabouts they no longer had, but Babi told them, Babi went by his mistress through the fog and by her over the hill, when her step was too light to disturb the leaves.

But Pyetr knew by other means that Eveshka was there— knew in his heart where she was, knew in his memory how she would move, a swirl of skirts, a sheet of pale hair—

That was what he kept thinking, knowing he was a fool, knowing that his memory was making a goddess of a wisp of white, a hazy recollection of a face—

A sweet and gentle face, and a touch at his heart that made
him totally—

Stupid, he told himself. He had outgrown that mooncalf
silliness at thirteen.

But he had felt like that when he had found her by the
pool, he had dreamed of her last night, he kept remembering
the night the imposter had come to the house, how he had
known from the moment she had looked past him—that *his*
Eveshka would never have done that.

He knew it the way he had known that about a girl when
he was thirteen; and another and another till he learned that
a pretty face was no guarantee of good character.

But this one—

This one—

"Pyetr," Sasha said, catching his arm as they went, "Pyetr,
remember."

A fifteen-year-old knew better: he certainly should—but
he knew things about Eveshka, he had no idea how: he knew
the thoughts she had, he knew the anger she felt toward her
father and the longing she had that Uulamets be better than
he was and wiser than he was; he knew that the loneliness
her father had imposed on her had made her do unwise
things—

He knew that she was determined now to rescue a father
who had never been anything but grief to her.

And that he understood all too well, knew it so well it
might have been years ago, and himself searching the streets
of Vojvoda for a father he knew was in serious trouble—

Often. Only to fight with him when he had found him.
But it never diminished the fear of losing him.

Now that fear was back—over Uulamets, for the god's
sake, not even his own fear: he understood that; but it was
still real, and he knew the dance so well—

Rotten old man. Ill-tempered ingrate. Unprincipled scoundrel.

Babi was more personable.

They stopped at a stream to drink. Sasha cupped his hands
and paused, seeing Pyetr sitting on his heels only gazing into
the water.

Don't, Sasha wished Eveshka.

And to Pyetr he said: "Do you see her?"

Pyetr reached out to the face of the stream and disturbed whatever he saw. "Not now," he said, doing passably well, Sasha decided, under the circumstances.

But the farther they went in the woods the more worried Sasha became. It was no longer a question of finding master Uulamets in the first few hours; or the first day; or now, in much of the second; and with the weather continuing to threaten and with Pyetr looking paler and more distracted than yesterday, Sasha asked himself seriously how much longer they could afford this search and for that matter, how much help Uulamets was likely to be to them at the end of it—counting that master Uulamets was himself the victim of a serious and willful mistake.

In fact Sasha began to lay fantastical plots for rescuing Pyetr: the wild notion of drugging his tea, for one, and while Pyetr was in that state seeing if he could break the rusalka's hold on him.

But he might lose that fight disastrously, and leave Pyetr with no resistance at all to Eveshka's demands; or he might misjudge the dosage; or by overcoming Eveshka leave them vulnerable to Hwiuur, or, or, or . . .

Reason was not working outstandingly well, either. "Let's give this up," Sasha had said several times, and each time Pyetr had simply said no.

"Let's go to Kiev," he had said; and Pyetr maintained there was no hope of that.

"You don't even like master Uulamets," he had objected, and Pyetr had said, It's not for him I'm doing this. . . .

"Let's go back to the boat," Sasha suggested finally. "Pyetr, we're walking and walking and you're getting *sick*, Pyetr, you're not thinking right any longer, please listen to me."

Babi growled at him.

Pyetr only shook his head, slowly looked toward him and said, "She's promised me it's not far. I don't think it is. Wish harder. I'm not crazy. She doesn't want to lean on me, but she has to."

"She's doing too much of it!" Sasha cried. He knew he was not resolved in his own opinion—too much yea and nay, go back and go forward, need of Uulamets and his desire to be free of him—

In fact today he was the one who most wanted to be safe in Kiev, following the life he imagined with Pyetr for a partner, living a bit by their wits and a lot by Pyetr's extraordinary luck—which looked now to be at ebb; and seeing such things as snake-handed elephants and gold roofs—which they looked now never to see.

Sasha sat down on a fallen log and plunged his head into his hands, hurling out a fierce and angry wish that Eveshka leave Pyetr alone a while and lean on him instead.

A curious thought came to him then, nothing that he could unravel into words, rather an approach of suspicious friendliness, there was no other way to explain it. He felt warmer for the moment; and a little dizzy and a little dazed; and, sure that it was Eveshka, thought: You know what you're doing to him. You don't want to hurt him. Can't you take what you need from the forest?

No, he felt; impossible.

He objected she had done that at home. He greatly doubted that she was doing anything other than give way to her own selfish wants—and suddenly doubted all her assurances, equally with the purpose of this approach . . .

But she insisted to come closer. She *wanted* to come closer, and it was an angry presence: he was doing everything wrong; he was wasting his strength, he was endangering Pyetr himself. She *wanted* to show him better—

He felt the danger in his own self-doubt. He tried to open his mouth to warn Pyetr—and felt the temper of someone as young as he was, who ached as much as he did to be loved and was sure that everything and everyone in her whole life had conspired against her, to rob her of everything—

He understood her: for a single heartbeat he felt people had robbed him, too, and that was the mistake, that quick, that devastating a slip—because she *needed* more than he even knew what he wanted. He shoved her back and saw Pyetr suddenly slump over, putting his head in his hand—

He was doing that by fighting her, she told him. *He* was making her do it; and all she wanted was the means to stop, if he would only let go . . .

For Pyetr's sake, she said. —A heart's only in a wizard's way, Sasha. *You're* not strong enough to stop me—

He doubted he could. He could not help it.

—Except, she said, your heart would never let me hurt him. It's your weakness, but in me it could save us, it could save *him*, Sasha. Don't be a fool. Let it go—

He was not sure . . .

And felt something slip away from him, a painless loss, a little sense of something missing.

The gap where it had been closed very quickly, so that he could not much miss it—nor want back what he was not sure he even understood. Nasty trick, he thought with a certain remoteness; but on this side of matters, Eveshka's reasoning seemed sound, Pyetr was sitting up wiping the sweat from his face and doubtless wondering what had come over him, so certainly Eveshka had backed away. It even occurred to him that Eveshka had made a mistake if she hoped to get past him, because he was no less determined to protect what was his, and all she had gotten off with was worry and pain, that was what it felt like.

He wished, for a start, to *see* her, to know what she was doing; and immediately, effortlessly, saw her standing there looking worried, while Babi, a sometimes-one-thing sometimes-another that constantly shadowed her, looked up at her as much like a dog as not.

He saw Pyetr, too—how pale he was, even yet, how desperate and drained of strength.

He had none he dared spare; certainly Eveshka had very little but what held her to life; and Babi was entirely beyond his understanding—but life was all around them. Eveshka swore she could not draw from the forest, but *he* found nothing in his way when he reached for it and gave it to Pyetr— no matter that some of it passed through him to Eveshka: there was certainly sufficient.

More than sufficient—but it seemed dangerous to pour too much into a man who lacked a way out for it—excepting Eveshka. On the one hand he feared for Pyetr's state of mind and on the other he did not intend to let Eveshka grow stronger than she was.

That, he thought, would be the easiest and most natural

mistake to make; but he had no pity to lead him into it, merely the shape where pity used to fit in his thoughts—and if she tried anything sudden with him or with Pyetr, he intended no hesitation at all.

It was Eveshka who seemed afraid. Eveshka who looked at him with anxiousness and at Pyetr with concern, enmeshed in the trap a heart could be to her.

Good, he thought, and realized—it was a dizzying thought—that for the first time in his life he was truly master of the situation.

It was as if the very air had become healthier, or more plentiful—not so Pyetr realized it immediately: it only seemed to him, after a moment's profound and unreasonable weakness, that he could breathe freely again, that the exhaustion was less, that he could get up and not feel his knees wobbling. He did that, apprehensive of what might be going on with Sasha and Eveshka that could affect him that way—

But, looking at Eveshka, he met her glance and stopped—

Because there was in her eyes a kindness and a fondness for him he could not at first believe, except in the girl he had first imagined her to be. It persisted while she looked straight at him, and he felt—

God!

A moment like that had to pass. He got his breath back and looked past her, he said to Sasha matter-of-factly that he felt better, he thought that they might get moving again—

In fact he stored that stunned feeling away in his heart and took it out again once they started walking, when he had a chance to look at Eveshka, and saw her glance sidelong back at him in that same gentle way—which he tried to persuade himself was his own imagination.

God, it could throw a man off his balance. He told himself she was absolutely dangerous when she affected him that way, he told himself he owed Sasha, at least, better sense.

He kept looking at Eveshka again and again to persuade himself there was nothing different in her than there had ever been; but it was more than just the glance she gave him, it was a well-being in his bones and the change in the way she *felt* to him—so distressed for what she was and so concerned for him he found himself trying to reassure *her.*

I feel fine, he told her in his heart. I'm doing all right. . . .

"Nice day," he said cheerfully to Sasha, hoping to get his balance back. "God, I think I'm getting used to this."

Sasha said grimly, "Don't trust her too much."

Together, Pyetr thought, Sasha and Eveshka came closer to understanding him than anyone in his life; and they instinctively hated each other. He thought that—if somehow they could get everything straightened out and master Uulamets *could* get his daughter back—

He was not used to pinning his hopes on the impossible— but he could not at the moment believe in their fallibility; he felt too safe. Even when they stopped and rested, when he saw Sasha looking completely down in the mouth, he nudged him with his foot and said, "Cheer up."

Then, with the least nagging worry about Sasha's continued glumness: "—Are *you* all right?"

"Don't worry about it," Sasha said.

That was entirely enough to throw a pall on things. He had a sudden apprehension of trouble Sasha was holding back from him; and he *felt* Eveshka's growing anxiety at his back.

He asked her, if thinking was asking, and with Eveshka it seemed to be—How far? When? and What can we do, if Uulamets can't rescue himself?

But he got no answer from her.

He said to Sasha, "I'm for a little to eat, do you want any?"

Sasha agreed and took a bit of dried fish—ate it with a spiritless grimness that left Pyetr increasingly cold at heart.

Babi tugged at Pyetr's breeches leg. Pyetr passed him a bite, hardly noticing the creature, and put the back of his hand to his mouth, realizing only then that it had started to hurt again—

He ought, he thought, to tell Sasha that fact.

If Sasha were listening. Which Sasha hardly seemed to be. Probably, he thought, Sasha was trying to do something wizardly, and probably it had to do—now that his thinking was straighter—with his sudden well-being this day; and probably with his hand hurting him: he felt bruises he did not remember getting, and it seemed to him that he had been altogether foolishly cheerful all afternoon, almost as if he were drunk.

Whatever Sasha was doing seemed to tire him; and that was decidedly a reason to worry.

He reached out and touched Sasha on the knee. "You're not propping me up, are you?"

Sasha just stared at him. Sasha said, after seeming to think about it, "I've found a way to get it from somewhere else."

"From where?" Pyetr asked, afraid for that answer.

Sasha lifted a hand toward the sky, toward the trees, all about them.

Eveshka sent him warning: he felt the direction of it as clearly as he would have known the direction of her voice. He said, leaning forward and touching Sasha's knee a second time, "She's upset with that."

"I know she is. But she won't let you go and I'll kill her if she kills you, so that's the way it is. I can do that. The way I am right now I could do it. But that doesn't get either of us what we want, does it?"

Pyetr felt more and more uneasy. It was not the boy he knew, talking about killing and being killed so calmly as that: it was colder than threat. He drew his hand away, afraid to look too directly into Sasha's eyes, afraid to ask more questions—

As if Sasha was more danger to him at the moment than Eveshka was.

Then he remembered Uulamets saying:

If the day comes, boy, that you have your way, believe this for a truth—he'll be far more at risk from you than he is now from me. . . .

20

✠ ✠ ✠ ✠ The mist began to fall again by afternoon, slow, sifting rain, only enough to moisten the leaves and drip down one's neck when a tree let fall a drop. Eveshka was a sparkle of such droplets, which fell and hesitated and fell again in continuous motion.

The touch of her hand left a chill moisture on Pyetr's fingers as she came close to tug at him and make him hurry—as if, he desperately hoped, they might be close now, although he had never ceased to feel anxiety from her. He had never thought in all his life he would want to see Uulamets, but now he did, Uulamets being in his own reckoning the only help for this disaster—Eveshka and Sasha locked in silent battle and himself in the middle of it. His wits were clear enough now to know what a muddled mess they had been most of the day and to know—at least when he worked at knowing it—that they were only clear because Sasha was helping him.

Which they might not be if he shook Sasha back to good sense and rescued Sasha from the wizardly effort that was turning him short-tempered and strange to him. He had Eveshka's presence constantly flitting through his attention, recollecting to him the feeling he could have, he could still have, if only he would let go and give way to her.

He wanted to. That was the problem. Wanting her came and went like fever and chill: sometimes he was able to know quite clearly the trouble he was in (Sasha's influence, he was sure) and at others (his own weak will, perhaps: he knew his faults) he wanted what he knew damned well would kill him (but a few moments of that feeling made death seem so absolutely impossible. . . .)

He wished he had managed better than this; he certainly wished he had advised Sasha better than this—but, then, against a good handful of wizards with their minds made up he did not know what choice was even his any longer, or whether his own will weighed anything in the wizardly gale he knew was blowing.

He thought, desperately, that Sasha being the wizard he was might have an edge in figuring out things like that; and if Sasha had, then he hoped Sasha had a good reason for spending so much effort on him. In the god's name *why?* he asked himself again and again: in the god's name what good was he, an unmagical man with a sword, with no sense what he was doing, haunted by rain-sparkle and an apprehension in his heart?

He was more afraid the boy had no purpose in spending so much on him: he was afraid for Sasha's own generous nature, a boy attempting things he had no understanding of, all to save a fool from his own weaknesses.

"Tell me what to do," he begged of Sasha when they were passing through dense trees—no hindrance to Eveshka, but he and Sasha had to hand branches off one to the other and eel around the unbending brush, the limbs overhead all the while shaking water drops down on them. He felt Eveshka suddenly pulling at him with unreasoning anxiety, and it seemed to him that things had gone on entirely too long with no sight of an old man who could *not* have walked faster than they had.

"Move," Sasha said, and pushed him to make him hurry.

Which was not the advice he hoped for.

God, he thought, what's the matter with her? —Because she was moving faster and faster, feeding into him a sweating panic that had no object, only that sense of something behind them again.

Maybe it was Sasha himself, or Sasha's wizardly essence that alarmed her. Maybe to Eveshka's frightened mind he seemed that cold and dangerous. Or maybe this panic was only a weapon she had begun to use, wearing at him and through him at Sasha. . . .

Move, Sasha said, as if Sasha himself was slipping beneath

238

Eveshka's spell. If that was true, Pyetr thought, then they were both done, doomed to be bones in some thicket or other.

At some times, within blinks of his eyes, he could not even believe Eveshka existed; at others, even looking elsewhere, even distracted with some precarious slope, he felt her presence as surely as Sasha's; heard her whispering in his heart that she was not lying, that the danger was there and real as she was.

Run, she whispered in his heart, run, don't look back, Pyetr—

The rain-sparkle of her shape faded as she passed into thicker shade. The shadow seemed everywhere deeper and they were losing her ahead of them.

"Dammit," Pyetr said, fighting past a branch, with the black fur-ball darting in and out around his ankles, whining. He tried to hand the branch on to Sasha, but Sasha suddenly stopped and turned to look into the woods behind them.

Don't look back, Eveshka urged him, don't look, Pyetr, no, keep running—

He did look—saw something moving on their track, impossibly quick, stirring the brush as it came; and there was no time for argument: he grabbed Sasha by the collar and snatched him through the brush, branches raking them as Sasha flailed out and tried to get his feet under him. Pyetr did not risk letting him go, only tried to haul him upright and keep them both moving. The disturbance was following them through the brush, he heard it snapping behind them, then heard it pass virtually over their heads, sending a hail of broken twigs down on them—

Then it was gone, and Pyetr looked around him in panicked confusion, Eveshka suddenly lost from his sight and his heart, Sasha catching his arm for balance on his right hand and Babi whimpering and shivering between his feet.

"What was *that*?" Pyetr asked.

Something touched him on the shoulder.

He yelped and spun around, colliding with Sasha, grabbing him, and seeing a branch in his face, knobbly wood, a dozen twigs for fingers— Maybe, he thought as his heart started to settle, he had staggered into it without knowing he was moving . . .

But slowly the branch reached, the gray, thin twigs quivering just in front of his face as the tree blinked and scowled at him.

He caught a breath and held it, afraid Sasha was going to offend it, afraid most of all that multiplicity of bare twigs that twitched and hesitated a scant impulse removed from his eyes.

Babi trembled against his legs and hissed. The tree blinked again. He felt Sasha gather a handful of his sleeve, about to do something or simply as scared as he was, he had no idea. His heart was thumping against his ribs in helpless panic, faster and faster, until he feared it was going to burst.

Worse than Hwiuur, worse than Eveshka. Much worse. If anything, he hoped for Eveshka to come back and deal with this creature that quite evidently Sasha could not.

The twig-hand twitched and quivered its dozen fingers away from his face and past him toward Sasha, slowly then drawing them both forward as Sasha's fist clenched the tighter on his sleeve and the sleeve threatened to tear. Real twigs snapped as the Thing leaned closer.

Pyetr got a grip on Sasha's arm and pulled back, lost that grip in the inexorable pull and in desperation grabbed the Forest-thing's knobby wrist instead; but it seized *him*, then, blindingly quick, horrifically strong. It grabbed his other arm, dropping Sasha, and dragged him toward its trunk.

"Sasha!" he yelled, feeling human hands pulling at his shirt, feeling them losing their grip. He tried to kick it, hoping it would drop him, but all he hit was a yielding mass of twigs. "Sasha—get the sword! *Get the sword!*"

Sasha clawed at his waist as it dragged him upward, whether Sasha was trying simply to hold on to him or to get at the weapon. Babi yapped, then yelped suddenly like a kicked cur as Pyetr felt Sasha's hands slip from his belt and from his leg and his ankle as it carried him through the brush.

In sole possession of him then, it let go of one of his arms, the other most painfully held while it ran twiggy fingers over his body and sniffed at him. He hung there with one shoulder all but breaking, tried to kick it, but that only shot pain through his ribs and shoulder, stifling his breath. Its fingers paused then on his face, and it held him so close he could see nothing but brown eyes and two centers of deep, deep black.

"Healthy," it said in a voice that went through his bones, and took him by both arms again, relief but no reassurance. "Healthy."

"I assure you," Pyetr gasped, with what wind he had gotten in that moment, "if we've trespassed, we certainly had no intention—"

"You've brought death with you," it said.

"She's only looking for her father." He realized how ominous that sounded. He stared the creature full in the eyes with no idea what Sasha was doing, or whether he was conscious or even alive. He said quickly, on a ragged breath, "We'll most gladly leave—"

Its attention prickled through him, stranger than Eveshka's, much stranger and more thorough. One moment he was near to screaming, the next he was half fainting, his feet meeting the ground and his legs tingling with strength to hold him up, from what reserve he had no idea.

"Go," it said, relaxing its grip on him.

"Sasha—" He turned with a rush of that tingly strength through all his limbs and a sudden, desperate hope of getting the boy out of this. Sasha was there, but he only stood numbly when Pyetr took hold of him, and the same instant Pyetr thought of snatching Sasha away by force he felt a dread so thick he could hardly breathe.

"You can't," Sasha said, staring past him. "It'll let you go. It's all right. Go on."

"It isn't all right, dammit!" He looked back at the Thing in the thicket, shaking in the knees and feeling that they had no chance, if it was down to him dealing with a Forest-thing. "Listen to me. Sasha's not at fault. There's a wizard dragged us up here, he's gone off with something we don't know what, and Eveshka's only trying to stop him from killing himself. None of us want to be here. None of us want anything but to get the old man out of this woods and go home."

He felt it listening. He stood arguing with what looked, between pounding heartbeats, like no more than a brushy tree, and *tried* to believe he was sane, tried to make himself believe in leshys—which was what he was sure it was—because he had to, he could *not* let it trick him into seeing just a tree and losing touch with it while it went on killing Sasha—

It was the forest. Or part of it. It owned what had fed him and it was trying to pull away from him, trying to be something else, that was what he knew, the same way he knew that it was not trying as hard as it could because they confused it.

Why? it wondered. Why and how this fighting me?

"Because we'll never get south," he said, seizing what was nothing more than a branch, holding to it while his hand and his eyes were trying to tell him that he was being a fool, he was talking to a damned tree, Sasha was exhausted and at the end of his wits and there was no such a thing as a rusalka, there never had been. "God!" he cried, shaking at it, "you hear me, dammit!"

But he was not even sure it could hear him any longer: Sasha said there was a necessary separation between magical things and ordinary folk and maybe it no more knew he was there any longer than he could see it for what it was. Sasha was standing there helpless and still and Eveshka and Babi were invisible if, he kept thinking—if they ever had existed.

It was like a curtain being drawn, separating him out of the magical, sending him back to the sane and the ordinary world—but it was taking Sasha with it.

"For the god's sake listen to me! We never meant any harm here—" He had pleaded desperate cases with outraged landlords in Vojvoda, and it seemed no different to him. "We never wanted to be here, except this Thing—" He figured maybe it was a case of jurisdictions. "—lured her father off. She followed us all the way from the old ferry and she hasn't the strength to keep going without what she borrowed—"

The branch moved under his hand. Twigs curled around his wrist, holding him prisoner. The creature opened its eyes and stared at him.

It said, "So you were feeding her deliberately. That's very foolish."

"She wasn't trying to kill anything, not us, not anything in this forest. Neither was Sasha."

Again that cool, tingling touch, from his wrist up and down. But he stopped being afraid of a sudden. He knew he was being looked at and looked into with a thoroughness no one ever had, and it was more curious now than angry.

"I forgive you," the Thing said. "But you've still been very foolish."

"None of it was Sasha's doing—"

"There is no *fault* here. Not even hers." It swayed and pointed with one of its many limbs to a mere pool of mist among the leaves. "But she has no heart: she's taken your friend's. She has no life; she's stealing yours; and his; and mine." He felt that tingle run from his head to his feet, felt *comfortable*, and *safe*, and thought it might be a lie more dangerous than Eveshka's. "I would know if you lied to me," the Forest-thing said, and Pyetr believed absolutely that was the truth. It said, while well-being coursed through him like cool water, and its attention like a warm breeze: "Do you know what your friend has done?"

He had no idea how to answer. It said, as if he had,

"Foolish. All young. All young." It reached past him with another of its limbs and grasped Sasha's shoulder. "Wanting me to let you go. Using my woods to feed him, against *me*. Death fighting death. —What shall I do with you?"

"Help us," Sasha said, as a droplet of sweat trickled a clear path down his face. "Help us get out of your woods. Help us find her father. Help us get him free."

The Forest-thing released them both and drew back with a rustling of twigs and leaves. "My name is Wiun," it said.

"Pyetr," Pyetr said.

"Sasha," Sasha said. "—And Eveshka and Babi, if you please."

It quivered, a little rustling of its branches as they lowered. "I don't please," it said. "A dvorovoi has no place here. A rusalka has no place among living things. —But I have no choice."

The pool of mist spun upward like a milky whirlwind and spread itself wider and thinner, like tattered robes, like fine hair flying on a gale, like ghostly arms and hands and Evesh-ka's pale, frightened face.

"Rusalka!" the leshy said. "Take, take once, and not again in my woods, on peril of what life you have. Do you hear me?"

Eveshka's eyes widened; her hair and robes swirled about her, leaves flew in a whirlwind, and she *blushed*, not alone

with faint rose on her face, but pale gold in her hair, pale blue
in her tattered gown—

"Oh!" she cried, wide-eyed, and Babi yelped and sprang
from somewhere to her arms, burying its face against her.

"I will not ask your promise," Wiun said to her in that
bone-deep voice, "for the welfare of my woods or your companions: you would do anything to live. You already have. I
only advise you what you already know: a wizard who lies to
others is one thing; one who lies to himself is quite another.
Do you know why?"

Eveshka did not answer. She held Babi closer.

Wiun shifted back into the brush, or was part of it.

"—Because then all wishes go wrong," Sasha murmured
faintly, in the last whisper of the leshy's going.

Eveshka looked at Sasha, looked at Pyetr, with the mist
gathering like beads on her hair, with her eyes gone a soft blue
and a little rosy blush on her lips. "Pyetr," she said in a trem-
ulous voice.

He trembled himself, while Sasha pulled sharply at his
arm. He knew better. God, he knew better; *she* was afraid, he
only hoped he knew why; but all he could do was stare at her
until all she could do was stare back.

"Pyetr!" Sasha said, jerking at his arm.

He blinked and looked away, trying to break the spell and
get his breath back. He saw his sword lying in the brush and
went and picked it up, shaking—

Because he wanted her so much, and he knew better, and
Sasha was depending on him.

"We'll find your father," he said to Eveshka, making himself see the trees, the woods around them, and Sasha frowning
at him. "He says he can bring you back. Well—damn it, he
will!"

God, he thought, gone cold inside, he was talking about
Ilya Uulamets.

21

✶ ✶ ✶ ✶ Twilight came early in the depth of the woods, under a clouded sky, but they kept walking so long as there was the least light to see by. "How far yet?" was what Sasha had wanted to know of Eveshka when they had first set out from the leshy's grove; and Eveshka had said she was not sure of that.

"Is your father even alive?" Sasha had asked next. "Can you tell?"

Eveshka had not been sure of that either: she had confessed as much, evading his eyes, then quickly slipped away to take the lead—moving not as she had, as a wraith which had no need of paths, but with a sure woodcraft which still kept her out of their reach.

She clearly had no wish to sit at their fireside when they had stopped for the night, either; nor did she seem to need their food. No, she answered distantly when Sasha offered, after which she rose and walked away to the little spring-fed rill that gave them water.

Again, Sasha noted uneasily—water.

They had a stew of fish and the early mushrooms and fernheads that Eveshka had found and assured them were wholesome to eat. Sasha looked with new misgivings at the supper he was cooking, and again with misgivings at Pyetr gazing after Eveshka.

"I'm not so sure about these mushrooms," Sasha said.

Pyetr said, distantly, "Does she need to poison us?"

One supposed not. Sasha shrugged and dished up the stew, which thanks to Eveshka had more than dried fish and water

245

in it, and thanks to Eveshka's lack of appetite, afforded a good helping apiece for them.

"You know she's not answering questions," Sasha said.

Pyetr took his dish, took up a spoonful and blew on it—which evidently made it reasonable for him to ignore questions, too.

Sasha set out a little for Babi. Babi sniffed his and growled at it, but that was, one hoped, the heat, or a distaste for mushrooms.

Sasha took a gingerly, carefully cooled sip of his own dish and found it more than palatable, looked up again at Pyetr, who was staring off into the trees at Eveshka—wishing something on his own, Sasha feared, in a very different direction than he was wishing himself.

Maybe he should have sympathy for that—but he was vexed, more than vexed, seeing Eveshka use those soft-eyed looks on Pyetr, with what might not be, considering she had a heart to confuse her, in any sense reasoned or reasonable. In fact Sasha tried to put a stop to that, exerting himself not on her, which he suspected could demand much more strength than he wanted to spare—but on Pyetr . . . which still took more strength than he wanted to spend, fighting a natural urge that could affect even someone altogether heartless.

But considering that Eveshka could not, after all, sustain herself on the food they used—

"She's not eating," Sasha said, hoping Pyetr would think further down that line.

"Mmnn," Pyetr replied.

"She's *not alive*, Pyetr, she can't eat, she's got to get it from somewhere and it can't be the forest—"

"We'll find her father," Pyetr said, and dug into his stew.

That was the help he got from Pyetr. Sasha ate his supper, he fed the fire, glad at least that the rain had stopped.

Finally he said to Pyetr, "If we don't find her father soon, and if he can't do anything—she's not going to stay the way she is, Pyetr. You heard what the leshy said. She can't help herself."

"Shut up," Pyetr said.

Even that curt reply failed to make him angry. Perhaps it

should have, but his thinking was too clear and Pyetr's was too muddy at the moment, even to deserve it.

"She'll turn on us," Sasha reminded him, "or on her father if we do manage to find him, just as fast. I've been noticing the way she's acting—"

"There's nothing wrong with the way she's acting. She just doesn't want to be here right now."

"Don't make excuses for her. She *can't help it*, that's what the leshy was telling us. . . ."

"I know it. You don't have to tell me that."

"I do. You're not listening."

Pyetr gave him an angry look, and asked, "What's this about hearts? What's all this about hearts the leshy was saying?"

Sasha shrugged. He had no wish to go deeply into that with Pyetr tonight, or to try to explain it—knowing well enough Eveshka would seize the chance to confuse things: to confuse Pyetr, more to the point. A boy with a girl on his mind might be close to his understanding, but Sasha had no notion what to do with a man whose intentions were muddled up with a girl who was not only dead but dangerous, with feelings he had a deep fear might not be the rusalka's own idea in the first place.

How did one explain *that* possibility to Pyetr—reasonably?

"That *Thing*," Pyetr insisted, "said, 'She hasn't any heart, she's taken your friend's.' What was he talking about?"

"I don't know."

"How can somebody take somebody else's heart, for the god's sake?"

"I don't know, I don't know everything. Your supper's getting cold."

"I want to know what you did, Sasha, don't give me that! I want to know what's going on."

"I don't know, I'm telling you! I don't know everything in the world, I wasn't born knowing. I don't know what the leshy's talking about—"

A wizard who lies is one thing; a wizard who lies to himself—is another . . .

"You're not missing anything," Pyetr asked, "are you?"

"I'm fine! I'm doing quite fine. Better than I was, as happens: I kept you going, didn't I? That's *real magic*, Pyetr, not just wishing. . . ."

"So what have hearts got to do with anything? What was that creature talking about? What was the River-thing meaning, that morning, about Eveshka losing hers? —Has she taken anything from you?"

"No!" That part came through to him and joggled things like pots on a shelf, so he was afraid they would fall and break if Pyetr kept nattering at him—nattering was what aunt Ilenka would call it, aunt Ilenka would say: Shut up, Pyetr Ilitch! you're giving me a headache!

He was.

"What did you mean about getting things from the forest?" Pyetr asked. "What were you doing, that made the leshy mad? And why did it let us go? Why did it say it had no choice?"

Sasha swallowed a tasteless lump of stew and looked at Pyetr with a feeling that might have been fear if he could have reasoned it out. It came down to a sense of things dangerously out of order, with his thoughts racing in various directions trying to find an answer, whether he had made a mistake beyond what had angered the leshy, a wish that might have flown much too far. . . .

"I don't know why," he said.

"So what are you doing?"

"As little as I can! I've made mistakes by worrying about things, that's one thing I've learned, I've been worrying about stupid little might-happens, till I can't see what I'm doing just by hoping things *don't* happen, do you see what I mean?"

"You mean you're not worrying about things. We're in the middle of this forest and we can't find Uulamets and you're not worrying!"

"That's not what I mean!"

"I think you're going crazy. Stop it."

"I'm all right!"

Pyetr finished his stew with a last bite, flung the spoon into the dish and wiped a hand across his mouth, staring at him anxiously in the firelight. "That doesn't make me feel better. —If Uulamets is in this woods, wouldn't a leshy know it? If he's here, why couldn't it just save us a lot of bother and tell us?"

Sasha tried to remember, but even that much of his thinking about the leshy kept going sideways, just out of his reach.

That told him that worry might indeed be in order, if he could hold on to his misgivings long enough, but holding on to that particular memory and trying to compare it to Hwiuur was like gathering sand in a net.

"Sasha. What's going on?"

He lost it again, the thing he had just gotten the shape of in the back of his mind—

Pyetr set his plate down. The spoon clattered. That seemed equally important with everything Pyetr was asking. That was the trouble. In a situation so full of chance everything was equally important and there was no way to balance things without understanding. He was losing the threads of things he had tied together—

Pyetr got up and stepped around the little fire to grab him by the shoulder and shake him hard. "Sasha, dammit!"

He felt that. Like everything. Pyetr walked off, and he watched where Pyetr was going.

Not where he wanted. He thought he ought to stop him if he could sort it out of all the other things that were happening, from the snap of the fire to the rustle of the leaves.

Danger, he thought vaguely.

His thought took shape again.

Eveshka had color this evening. The leshy had fed her enough for days—

She was stronger than she had ever been tonight. Much stronger, brighter, more solid in the world . . .

"Pyetr," he began to say. But Pyetr was already at the streamside, Eveshka was already turning her head to look at him . . . a lifelike gesture that itself said how substantial she had become. He wished . . . and the effort cost him, so that

249

his heart raced and he was aware of the rush of blood in his veins and the rush of wind in the leaves—like the sound of water. . . .

The fire actually cast light on her tonight, picking up subtle color in her gown, and the trees along the brook touched her with shadow, making her real—a girl, no more than that, vulnerable and uncertain as she cast a glance over her shoulder.

"Pyetr," she said, turning to him with arms outstretched.

He stopped. He took a step backward when she came toward him, and she came no further, looking at him with wide, hurt eyes.

"What did you take from Sasha?" he asked harshly, which was what he had come to ask. "What was the leshy talking about?"

"I love you," she said.

He backed up another step, because somehow she had taken one he did not notice; he was aware of her eyes and aware of how the shadow bent around her cheek. "That's fine," he said, sweating, struggling to keep his thoughts together. "I'm flattered. Try answering me."

"Don't hate me." She reached toward him. He knew his danger, he knew he ought to back up and for one heartbeat he wanted to fail—wanted her to touch him and prove she was, after all, harmless, and not to be responsible for that failure—

"Stop it!" Sasha said, from somewhere behind him. A shadow crossed between them and the light. "Pyetr!"

He really regretted his rescue. What he was feeling was more powerful than wanting to live. But Eveshka drew back her hands and clenched them under her chin, her eyes full of pain.

"Get away from her," Sasha said, as if he were the boy, the absolute, heart-shaken fool, and grabbed him by the arm so hard it hurt. Probably Sasha meant it to. Not even that seemed enough. Probably Sasha was wishing him to use his wits; and that was not enough either.

"Stop it!" Sasha said harshly, not to him.

Tears brimmed in Eveshka's eyes. "I won't hurt him. I didn't. —Sasha, don't do that. . . ."

"I've no pity for you," Sasha said. "You should know that."

"I know," Eveshka whispered. "But I do. And I won't let anything happen to him."

"Then don't talk to him! Let him alone!"

"I came to *her,*" Pyetr said, Sasha having gotten that part wrong, at least. "I want to know what's going on."

"Her looking to have her own way is what's going on," Sasha said. "There's nothing else, there's never anything else in her thinking. —Leave him alone!"

Tears spilled. Eveshka looked at Sasha a long moment, and then turned her shoulder and walked away to the side of the little stream.

"Eveshka," Pyetr said, but she did not look back. Her tears *affected* him: he felt himself all but shaking, even while he knew Sasha was trying to do the right thing. He wanted her not to be in pain, wanted her not to be wrongfully accused—

Sasha turned and the firelight touched clenched muscle in his jaw, anger that Pyetr resented from the gut.

"Let her alone," he told Sasha. "She didn't do anything."

"She *wants* you to feel sorry for her. I've told her let you alone."

"You've no damn—" *Business,* was on his lips, but, dammit, that was the fool talking, even a fifteen-year-old knew that much. A fool would go after the girl, go against everything Sasha was doing to keep them apart, get himself killed so she could go after Sasha next.

Of course he would.

He *felt* her trying her spell on him, trying to draw him back. But Sasha was in the way. She seemed suddenly too real to touch his imagination: the glamor faded and she could only use what she was—which was a sixteen-year-old girl with the notion—probably it had worked even with Uulamets, pretty child that she was—that a few tears could inevitably get her what she wanted.

But he knew *that* song, line and verse: he had learned it in Vojvoda, on one notable occasion, and he was too old to play some bored girl's games. Ask anything, he thought, of a shallow girl wanting someone else to make her happy—except to give her your heart and expect good care of it.

The glamor tried to come back. Something pushed it away. Maybe it was his own intention, maybe Sasha's. He looked in Eveshka's direction and his hand hurt when he clenched it . . . it had, he remembered, since sometime during supper, when he had started fighting with Sasha, and that bothered him.

Maybe Sasha meant it to remind him, he thought, and then suffered a chill feeling of something going increasingly wrong.

"Stop it!" he said aloud, sharply; but:

"It's not me," Eveshka said, and turned, her face distraught. "Not me doing it. —Can you feel it?"

Sasha seized his arm and pulled him urgently toward the fire, while—Pyetr cast a look over his shoulder—Eveshka stood by the little stream, looking down its course into the dark.

"What's going on?" he demanded, ready to resist this sudden craziness, but not sure where the craziness lay. "What's happening?"

"Something's out there," Sasha said as they walked.

Eveshka was standing there unprotected. The feeling in his hand told him what that something likely was, which he did not immediately say because everyone in the world knew better than he did: he only thought that somebody should look to Eveshka, who was, damn it all, in particular, immediate danger.

"Get our things together," Sasha said as they reached the fire. "We're getting out of here."

"In the dark? With that? It's after *her*, is what it's after!"

"We know that. That's why we're going. Hurry."

"*Where?*" Pyetr snarled. It was too much. Nobody was making sense, people stopped in the middle of arguments to run off into the dark with a River-thing waiting out there to make supper of all of them.

But Sasha paid him no attention. So he joined Sasha, angrily snatching up their belongings, stuffing them into the baskets, in a despair beyond any fear of what might be out there. He wanted them out of this woods, he wanted, dammit!—to give up and go somewhere with Eveshka and lose himself to whatever she did, if that was what it would take to get Sasha clear of her and maybe set her free once for all of whatever power the vodyanoi had over her—

Go on, he recalled Uulamets saying, cursing their stupidity, *go running off alone. One of you will feed her. The other will be extremely sorry. . . .*

The leshy, damn its rotten heart, had sent them off with help, but no protection, no knowledge what to do or where the old man was, and now . . .

Things stalking them in the dark. Eveshka playing tricks, the god only knew if this whole alarm was not one—

"Where's Babi?" he asked, suddenly missing the Thing he had last seen bolting down fish and mushroom stew by the fireside.

"I don't know," Sasha said, tying up their bedrolls.

"Babi?"

"I thought you didn't like him."

He glared at Sasha's back. "He has reasons for his disposition. I'm coming to appreciate them." He jerked the tie on his basket tight, picked it up and slung it onto his shoulders, with a glance back—

To the vacant waterside where Eveshka had just been standing.

"She's gone!" he said, looking at Sasha—whose face, turned toward him in the firelight, was beaded with sweat.

"We won't lose her," Sasha said. "I know where she is."

"Where's she gone?" A man could grow suspicious in the doings of wizards and leshys and such, and of a sudden, seeing Sasha's face, seeing the evidence of exertion, he had the feeling that there was far more violence going on around him than an unmagical man could feel. "Sasha, dammit, what's going on? What are you doing?"

"Helping her."

He was bewildered. A host of possibilities came tumbling in, not least of them collusion between Sasha and Eveshka.

"Come on," Sasha said, shouldering his own gear.

"Where? Where's she going?"

"To find her father. As quickly as she can. She *knows*

where he is, by the *Thing* knowing where we are—and it's not far from here. She doesn't need us slowing her down.''

"Doesn't need us—" Everything that had happened since supper, even his anger and hurt, were suddenly in doubt where it came to wizards, both of whom had a piece of him, *both* of whom were surely wishing things at him. "God! What have you been doing to me?"

"Anything I can," Sasha said hoarsely, and stood up and looked him square in the face, looking older than his years in the underlighting of the fire, looking haggard, fire trails in the sweat on his temples. "I rescued *her* from you, if you have to know. You disturbed her concentration."

"What did you do? *What did you wish for, dammit!*"

"For you not to like her too much," Sasha said. "So does she. She's scared. I told her go, while she *could* go, and we're following her: I think she's finally stopped lying to us. And herself. She knows what her choices are."

They were on their way, on what track he could—god!—feel, like two lines strung between him and elsewhere, one downstream, deadly, that had to do with the pain in his hand, one moving upstream, sweetly dangerous, that had to do with the pain in his heart . . .

"How could you do something like that?" Pyetr exclaimed in outrage, dodging branches Sasha passed him, stumbling over roots and brush—remembering what mistakes of his youth Sasha's spell had raked up, nothing a man wanted a fifteen-year-old boy and a sixteen-year-old girl knowing about him . . . *especially* Sasha and Eveshka. "You don't know what I'm thinking! You can't pull things like that out of what I remember!"

"I don't have to," Sasha said. "I don't have to know what you're thinking. I just wish. That's all. Things change the way they *can* change."

"Dammit!"

"I know. I know you're mad at me. But I don't care, as long as it saves you from being stupid; I'm *sorry*, Pyetr."

"With *what!*" he said to Sasha's back, and shoved at a branch that raked him—lost in this maze of wizardry, a grown man tossed about by two children as if his own innermost feelings were nothing. "What are you sorry *with?*"

But the boy was only trying to keep him alive. The boy evidently knew what he was doing, was *allied* with Eveshka in whatever was going on—which had to revise all opinions of her.

"God," he exclaimed, "tell me who's not lying!"

"I'm not," Sasha said over his shoulder, out of the tangled dark. "You know *I'm* not, Pyetr Ilitch."

22

✣ ✣ ✣ ✣ A hard walk from day into dark and now
out onto the trail again in the mid of the
night, tired as they were—townfolk without Eveshka's wood-
craft to guide them. . . . "Dammit, can't you magic us
through?" Pyetr cried, still with that feeling of imminent danger behind them: there was a thorn-brake where Sasha had
led them, and it was *not* the way Eveshka had gotten through:
she was far too substantial, he was sure she was.

"I've got other things on my mind," Sasha said.

"We're losing her!" Pyetr protested; "We won't," Sasha
said in that maddening, lately-acquired inscrutability of his,
but all the same they had to go far around. Thickets closed
about them and forced them to backtrack too often, branches
raked their faces, snagged on their packs, and they found themselves going far aside from the course Pyetr knew was right—
because there was no way through the thorn thickets and the
brush.

Pyetr's hand was hurting, his feet had blisters, his forehead
hurt from a scratch a branch had put on it, and something
about supper was not sitting well on his stomach.

Worse, he suddenly lost touch with what he knew was
behind them and still knew where Eveshka was with unsettling certainty. Her state of mind, terrified for herself and terrified of their pursuer, muddled him and made him misstep
and miss branches, which only made him angrier and more
desperate.

"It's gone," he muttered at Sasha's back as they slogged

along, trying to find a way through this thicket, "it's gone out. —Sasha, can you still feel it back there?"

"I've lost it," Sasha said. "I don't like it."

"Don't like it! Don't like it— God, hurry us up."

"I'm doing what I can."

"Maybe it's been lying to us all along. Maybe she has."

The doubt came to him suddenly, left again. He had no idea what the source of it was—

And did.

"God, next time wish me to *know* you're wishing me to think something, do you think you can do that?"

"I'm not doing it now," Sasha said.

"How do I know that?"

"Believe me. —Stop *talking* to me!"

The boy he was talking to *had* no deep feeling of his own— or he had, but Eveshka had it instead, if Pyetr guessed anything that was going on. He was embarrassed, he had been made a fool of in his most private thoughts and he hated both of them—between moments that he wanted her with all his heart, or moments that he reckoned if the intention that drove her now truly was Sasha's, then she was likely doing everything she had done for good reasons—for Sasha's kind of reasons, Sasha being so ready to blame himself for others' fault; and Eveshka, damn her, having so much real blame for this situation.

Maybe, he thought between times, that was where she had found the strength to realize what was going on, that there was something stalking them—or found the strength to defy it before it killed them. If it was Sasha's heart in her, it must be near breaking with the guilt she really deserved—and if that guilt was somehow hurting Sasha he wanted to wring her neck—or shake sense into her, because a girl with Sasha's heart was all too likely to do something brave and foolish where that damned River-thing was concerned, endangering everything in the world he loved—

His feet skidded suddenly on a slick, leaf-covered slope; he caught himself against a sapling trunk—a branch jabbing him painfully in the eye. "Damn!" he gasped, flailed out against the brush and fought his way on downhill to keep up with Sasha.

Sasha waited for him. But Pyetr sat down when he got to the bottom, out of breath, with a stitch in his side, and Sasha slumped bonelessly down beside him.

"Rest a moment," Pyetr said, drawing deep breaths, bent over and holding a hand over his eye. He still had a sense where Eveshka was, but it seemed dimmer. "She's weaker. Farther away." Another breath. "I don't know what she thinks we are. A man can't do this all day and all night—"

He was so scared his hands were shaking. He had no idea whose fear it even was. Sasha said nothing. Sasha just leaned on his knees and breathed.

How far can an old man walk? Pyetr wondered to himself, and cradled his wounded hand, which ached the worse since his near fall on the slope up there. "God, we should have found him by now. I think we're going in circles. Wizards wishing this and wishing that, getting us damned *lost*, is what we are!"

"I don't say we're not," Sasha muttered.

Which comforted him not in the least.

Damn! the ache . . . He remembered a nightmare of a cave under willow roots, rot-smelling dark, and the lap of water—

"We'd better get moving," he said, and shoved himself to his feet, leaning against a tree trunk a moment until Sasha had gotten up. The pain dulled, perhaps because Sasha was well-wishing him, perhaps because the Thing that had caused it was busy, he had no idea.

But Eveshka's presence suddenly went dark to him. He could say that she had been in the direction he was facing, but there was nothing there now, as if he had gone stone blind to her.

"God! —She's *gone!*"

"Not far," Sasha said. "We know where she was. Come on."

He followed Sasha, half running in the direction that was his own last feeling, up the wooded slope and headlong down the other side. He took the lead, stopped his downhill plunge against a tree, bruising his shoulder, then splashed across a rill that might be the one from which they had started, for all he knew. The branch-laced sky gave him no clue. The stars were obscured in cloud or the beginning of dawn, he had no idea.

But he felt acute pain in his hand then, and a sense of direction came with it, different and colder.

Oh, god, he thought, and delayed a moment until Sasha overtook him. "The River-thing," he said between gasps for breath, and indicated the rill beside them. "It's somewhere around here—"

Sasha looked, for what good it did, and said, calmly, "Salt," as he slipped off his pack. "Salt will hold it. It's nearly dawn."

Pyetr shivered, telling himself all the while that the vodyanoi was afraid of them—he had beaten it off twice with plain steel. "But where's *she*?" he asked. His sword hand ached to the bone. His fingers could hardly feel the hilt when he closed on it. He drew, willing his fingers to stay closed, having to look at his own hand to be sure they did—while Sasha started to make a circle of salt around them in the dead leaves.

The pain eased of a sudden and the feeling began to come back to his fingers. "Sasha," he said, because the hair was rising at his nape, with an inexplicable conviction someone was looking at his back: Sasha stopping his circle-making, looking up and past him, was no reassurance at all.

Pyetr turned, slowly, holding a sword he could not feel, to that quarter of brush and trees where the circle was incomplete. Something large and winged suddenly dived at him and flapped heavily away.

"What was *that*?" he breathed, reeling back—and in the same instant felt Eveshka's presence again, so subtle that it might have been there for a heartbeat or two before he knew it, faint as a breath of air, a whisper out of the dark . . .

"Brother Raven," Sasha murmured, behind him, as the feeling of Eveshka's presence grew quite, quite certain. Pyetr looked up and saw the bird clearly—in a sky catching the first faint glow of the sun.

It dipped a wing and glided off over the ridge, opposite to Eveshka's direction.

"Follow it!" Sasha said. "It's Uulamets' creature. Eveshka's off the track—she knows it now, she's coming as fast as she can, but so is *it!* For the god's sake—*move!*"

It was not Pyetr's inclination to abandon the salt circle, but Sasha *wished* him into motion, he felt it, caught a breath and started climbing, slipping and sliding on the slick leaves with Sasha close behind him. Eveshka *was* coming toward them—Eveshka had seen the raven, called it in some fashion from downriver, Pyetr knew that in a solid, no-nonsense way that he connected with Sasha's meddling, not Eveshka's—but he did not, this time, resent Sasha shoving things on him neither of them had breath for. He reached the top of the ridge ahead of Sasha and skidded down the leafy slope on the other side, down among thick trees again. His hand *ached.* He felt an unreasoning dread here, in the dark of these trees.

Sasha arrived as the pain grew acute; from the one side Eveshka's presence was rushing at them and from the other— from the woods all around, but especially straight ahead— came a sense of cold hostility.

"Can you feel it?" Sasha asked.

Pyetr nodded, saving his breath, willing his fingers to hang on to the sword. The presence he felt ahead of them was not the vodyanoi: that one had a feeling all its own, and he had learned to trust those differences. "Woodsmoke," he said as the wind carried that to them, and reckoning no Forest-thing would build a fire, he fended brush aside with his sword and started in the direction of that apprehension.

Wings snapped: something swooped past him and brushed his face. The raven settled on a low branch by him, shadow in shadow—

A white shape had appeared in the woods ahead of them, coming toward them; and a dimmer, grayer figure beside it.

"Master Uulamets?" Sasha called out, from Pyetr's side.

"Who told you to leave the boat?" the gray one snarled as it walked, waving an arm. "Damnable fools!"

"Certainly sounds like him," Pyetr muttered.

"Papa," the white one said in Eveshka's voice, stopping and catching at Uulamets' sleeve to stop him. "Papa, don't trust him! Don't trust anything you hear from them—"

"She's lying," Sasha said, and if there were wishes flying, if there was wizardry going on, Pyetr felt nothing but *Eveshka*, coming from behind him like a hawk's strike—like a scream in the air—

She *was* there—ducked under a branch beside him and passed without a glance at either of them, walking straight toward Uulamets and the Eveshka at his side . . .

"No," it cried, lifting a hand as if to fend her off. Uulamets lifted his, as if to do the same, but Eveshka walked up to her rival and stretched out her hand. Fingers scarcely met. Then— so quickly Pyetr's eyes refused to see the change—a single white ghost drifted where both had stood.

Uulamets recoiled, cried out: "No! Damn you—"

"Damned, indeed," ghost-Eveshka said, and pointed down at her feet. "This is your *daughter*, papa, this is the daughter you called up—"

Pointing down at a muddy skull and a glistening pile of water-weed.

"God," Pyetr murmured, as Uulamets stepped back.

Eveshka said, plaintively, "I couldn't reach you, papa. You wouldn't listen—"

Uulamets turned away and leaned his arm against a tree, his head bowed.

Pyetr stood there with his sword still in his hand and a cold feeling in his stomach. He *hoped* it was his Eveshka that had survived that encounter.

Then, gathering his wits: "Babi?" he called.

Almost immediately a body pressed against his boot. It whined. The god knew it had reason.

But it turned up with this Eveshka. It always had, with the one he knew for his.

"I'm *here*," Eveshka was saying to Uulamets. "Papa?"

But Uulamets gave no sign he heard.

"Papa, can't you see me?"

Uulamets gave no answer then, either.

"Your daughter's *here*," Pyetr said, recovering his sense of balance. "Old man, she's real. She's the one who's survived. Babi's with her. Doesn't that say it's her?"

261

Uulamets pushed himself away from the tree and walked off from them.

Sasha stepped forward, made a sudden, hurt sound. Sasha's hand lifted as if to ward off some invisible attack as Pyetr looked at him in alarm—both of them frozen for a heartbeat, Sasha in the shock of whatever was happening to him, himself in doubt what to do or what to fight, until Sasha dropped that hand to his sword arm.

"She—" Sasha said, and fell on Pyetr's neck and hung on him as if all strength had just left him. "Oh—god, Pyetr—"

Pyetr cast an alarmed look at Eveshka, whose expression was quite, quite cold—and guessed by that what transaction might have passed: a bargain paid, or simply that Uulamets' daughter might have found a heart entirely too fragile a possession after all.

Please the god, Pyetr thought, that Sasha was still sane. But the boy felt something, finally; the boy could beg his pardon for getting him deeper into this place, and swear that he had never wanted to be a wizard—

"Can't help what you're born," Pyetr said, holding on to the boy, sword and all, knowing that Pyetr Kochevikov had never believed that, and that if he had, he might have died the way his father had, instead of the way he figured now he was likely to—take his pick, he could, a ghost without a heart or a Water-thing who wanted to make supper of him, neither one of which he could consistently believe in. Gambler's luck, it seemed.

Someone had to bury the remains, even if Eveshka seemed to care nothing about the matter and Uulamets stayed by his fireside and gave no sign of interest in it either. So Pyetr used his sword to loosen the dirt, and by a cloudless dawn he and Sasha piled up wet dirt and leaves such as they could, for decency's sake.

Sasha still was pale, his hands, flecked with bits of earth and wet leaf mold, were white. Wind burn was the only color in his face.

More than that, he did not look up oftener than he must,

and then with some vague shame that gnawed at Pyetr's peace of mind—such as Eveshka left him.

Pushing him and pulling him all at once, that was what it felt like to Pyetr: his would and would-not where she was concerned was so violent and muddled with anger this morning he felt half crazed himself, and he clung to the real world of mud and bone and Sasha's pale face with all the desperate attention a man could pay to anything after a night of no sleep.

"Are you all right?" he asked. "Sasha?"

Sasha nodded without looking at him, and Pyetr gnawed his lip in distress.

"Let's get the old man moving," he said. "Look, whatever we decide later, let's get everyone back to the boat, go back to the house, try this all again—"

Sasha shook his head, and did meet his eyes this time, with a bleak, exhausted look. "It won't get us out of this. We can't get there."

"Do you know that?" Pyetr asked carefully. He felt cold himself, and sick and scared. "Sasha—can you tell, are you free of her?"

Sasha stared through him a moment, and said, "None of us are free . . ."

Pyetr shook at his arm. "Sasha, damn it, don't talk like that."

Sasha gave him a strange look then—blinked and looked *at* him, laid a chilled hand on his and clenched his fingers. "I'm all right," he said, and Pyetr's confusion went away from him, Eveshka's presence suddenly so quiet he felt drawn to look and see if she was there.

Something stopped him from turning his head. Something held him looking into Sasha's face. Something told him not to be afraid.

And by everything he had been through he knew better than that.

But Sasha said to him, quietly, "Whatever else—whatever else, it's got to get me first, Pyetr. And that's not easy any more."

He felt his arm begin to shake in its awkward position. He felt the cold of the ground under his knee. "Listen," he said, fighting it out word by word, "I'm grateful, understand.

But don't do that. Don't *wish* me not to worry about you, boy! That's damned foolish, isn't it?''

Sasha blinked and his mouth made a desperate, thin grimace of a smile. His grip tightened. "Yes. —But she's not fighting me. She knows it's not good for her. It's all right a while. I can keep her away. Don't worry about it."

"Try asking out loud, like a polite boy."

The grimace broadened into something like a grin. Sasha patted Pyetr's hand, drew a deep breath and sat back on his heels.

As if it *was* Sasha, a wise, bone-weary boy carrying far too much on his shoulders. Pyetr rubbed the back of his neck and looked at him a second time, refusing to ask himself what they had just buried, or whether Uulamets' daughter had ever had a heart in her life—until she borrowed Sasha's.

And threw it back again, maybe before Uulamets broke it altogether.

Or maybe because Sasha's own unselfish kindness would not let her hold on to it . . . and that was the inevitable trap she had fallen into.

"So what are we going to do?" he asked Sasha. "Do we even know grandfather's sane?"

"I think he's sane," Sasha said, and added, with a tremor in his voice: "If any wizard is. I think after a while—after a while—"

"You're not crazy," Pyetr said. "I'm not sure about him, but I do know you, boy, and you're not going his way. If you want my ignorant advice—wish us out of here. Fast. Grandfather with us."

"When you wish, things happen that *can* happen, and not always the way you want."

"What *was* this thing we just buried, then? What was with Uulamets, fixing us breakfast and sleeping in his daughter's bed? Was that something that *can* happen? Not in Vojvoda, it can't!"

"I don't know," Sasha said in a subdued voice, and with an uncomfortable glance at the pile of dirt between them. "We know *what* it was—but I don't know for sure what raised it."

"There's at least two choices," Pyetr muttered.

"At least two," Sasha said, and looked aside as Pyetr did,

where Uulamets sat beyond a screen of branches, beside the ashes of last night's fire. "Maybe wanting something so much—"

"He didn't want *her!* He wanted a daughter who'd agree with him, say, 'Yes, papa,' and keep his house clean."

"That's certainly what he got," Sasha said, "isn't it?"

23

Eveshka was silent, withdrawn: she had surely spent a great deal of her borrowed strength to dispel the Fetch or whatever had been, as Pyetr put it, making their meals and sleeping in their company. Now she drifted as a ghost, pale, apparently aimless, among the trees that curtained the grave and Uulamets' fireside.

So it fell to him, Sasha supposed, since Pyetr and master Uulamets were not on the best of terms, to broach urgent matters with the old man.

He had washed his hands in the little spring that ran from this place, he had washed the leaves out of his hair and used Pyetr's razor to scrape the little mustache off his lip, which made him, aunt Ilenka would have said, look as if his face was dirty. It seemed respectful, at least, not to approach master Uulamets looking like a vagabond—even if master Uulamets' clothes were mud-stained and his hair and beard were stuck through with twigs and bits of leaves.

Master Uulamets had his book with him. But he was not reading it or writing in it, only holding it in his arms and staring off into the woods, as if the forest held all the answers he wanted.

Sasha bowed and cleared his throat when master Uulamets seemed not to notice him. "We've taken care of everything. Pyetr thinks we might go back to the boat and think things over. I don't think we really can, but maybe you know—"

Uulamets did not so much as look at him.

"We had no idea where you'd gone," Sasha said. "Eveshka led us. We ran into a leshy. He helped us."

266

Not a flicker of interest.

"He lent her enough strength to get here," Sasha said. "But he said she mustn't take any more from his woods. He doesn't like us being here."

Going on and on without master Uulamets' acknowledgement seemed impertinent as well as futile. He was sure that a wizard of Uulamets' skill had to know most of what had happened without a boy telling him more than the details; and he found himself more afraid of the old man than he had ever been—a fear from what origin he suddenly suspected.

She left me things, he had said to Pyetr, when Pyetr had tried ever so delicately to ask him if there was lasting harm in what Eveshka had done.

She taught me things, Sasha thought now. —I know why she did it. I still remember how clearly I could think on some things, and where I was blind . . . and I think I know why.

I knew how to be scared. That must be different than other feelings—at least when it's for yourself.

I could worry about Pyetr . . . I knew he was my friend: I wouldn't even *want* to be myself again without him, but only knowing he was important to me was enough to keep me doing right things—because they were the smart things.

Pyetr would say, Boy, don't be stupid. But he'd mean, Don't get hurt and don't hurt people—because he never was like those friends of his: he wouldn't have broken aunt Ilenka's churn on purpose, and certainly not if he knew it was her grandmother's.

He'd say he was sorry if he knew that, and he'd really mean it, because he doesn't always think through what he does: he can't wish somebody dead. But he's real smart about people, and what's right and wrong—

And if a wizard doesn't have somebody like him—and if he's put his heart away someplace and he can't feel what's right, who's going to tell him not to be a fool about what he wants?

Master Uulamets had stopped listening a long time ago, it seemed to him—even to Eveshka.

So he stood there and stood there, and finally cleared his throat again.

"Excuse me, sir. If you're thinking, I apologize and you don't have to listen, but we're going to fix lunch and if you don't have any idea what we ought to do after that, we're going to pack up and start back to the boat and see if we can get it backed out again."

Uulamets said, "Not likely."

"What is likely, sir?"

"Go away," Uulamets said.

Sasha drew a deep breath, clenched his fists and told himself master Uulamets was probably listening and taking what he said into account even if he gave no sign of it.

Eveshka hardly seemed to think so. Eveshka was angry. He felt it. He wished her not to wish anything for a while. . . . "Please," he said aloud as he walked away and left Uulamets in peace. "Pyetr and I are tired. Please. Not now."

He felt a shiver in the air—impatience, fear, anger. Always the anger. She *was* weaker, and that could only go so far—

I can't die, she insisted he know, terrified; and other thoughts that kept bobbing up in his mind—

Murder. Anger and *hurt*—half-crazed and hungry and half-killed by her father's *wanting* her to be different than she was . . . that was what had killed her. All her life she had fought just to be Eveshka, while her father was trying to wish *Eveshka* to be something else . . . and she wanted him to stop it, stop it, stop it—she *wanted* him dead—

"Shut up!" he yelled at her, and the whole woods seemed hushed, Uulamets and Pyetr both looking at him in startlement, while he stood in the middle of the clearing with his fists clenched. "Shut up, I did what you want, I killed my father and I killed my mother, and you don't know what you're talking about! I *do*, so shut up!"

And while Uulamets was looking his way in shock, while he had the old man's attention and Pyetr's, he plunged ahead with the rest of what she had set boiling in him, which he had no certainty he could ever remember in cold blood—

"You," he said, pointing at Uulamets, and *wanting* his attention as Eveshka wanted Uulamets to know what he had to say, "*you* drove your daughter away, every day you wished she was exactly what you wanted—"

"That's not so," Uulamets said. "That's not so. I gave her every opportunity . . ."

"As long as you thought she was right. What if she just wanted—"

"Was Kavi Chernevog right?" Uulamets stood up, wild-haired, wild-eyed, and turned on Eveshka. "Was it your wishes got you here, girl? Was what you wanted so wise?"

Eveshka dimmed and retreated.

"Young folk," Uulamets said, "have such potent wishes, and so damned little brains to make them doubt what they're doing—"

"Old ones," Pyetr said, from his seat on an old log, "get so damned self-centered." Uulamets rounded on him and Pyetr said, "Turn me into a toad, why don't you?" with Uulamets so furious Sasha wished with everything he had that Uulamets would not take that suggestion, but Pyetr kept right on going: "—because you haven't done so well either, grandfather, or our boat wouldn't be stuck in sand in the river, and *we* wouldn't have had to track you days through the rain and the muck in this woods to rescue you from your own damned foolishness! —And *you*—" he said, with a look at Eveshka—

The raven screamed from its perch on a limb and made a sudden dive at Pyetr's face. Pyetr flung up his arms and Sasha flung out an angry wish to drive it away, but quick as he could think it was already kiting skyward, and blood was welling up in a scratch on Pyetr's wrist.

While Babi, a suddenly very much larger and more ominous Babi, was growling and hissing and bristling about the shoulders, not at Pyetr, as seemed, but looking up after the raven.

So was Uulamets looking skyward, frowning as the raven came back to sit in the top of a tree.

Sasha said, "Remember what I told you, master Uulamets? I'll remember everything you do. And I don't need you so much as I did."

Uulamets turned, wild of eye, finger trembling as he

pointed at him. "Now *there's* a fool! Don't need me, do you? You're going to walk out of here, hike down to Kiev, you and your friend and my daughter, and make your fortune in the streets. Of course you are! —Fool! You can't get him free of her, you can't get him free of *yourself*, there's his difficulty! There's no family for a wizard, there's no friend, there's no daughter either. Take a lesson from me! I brought up a wizard-child, I let her grow the way a weed grows, *without* wishing more than her safety and her good sense, and *that*, it seems, was unfatherly neglect. When she got to a reasonable age and took to selfish wishes she didn't want me to know about, we had discussions, oh, indeed we had discussions, *boy*, about wisdom and self-restraint and consequences—lessons you apparently learned by native wit and my own offspring abjectly failed to learn from my teaching, because my daughter was far more concerned with being a weed—and, like a weed, going her own way and getting what *she* wanted, having everything I forbade her to touch! My daughter grew up a *fool*, boy, against every principle I tried to teach her—because of course I was *wishing* her to learn, and *wishing* her to use good sense—"

"*Your* good sense!" Eveshka cried, drifting into the way of things. "What about *mine?*"

"Oh, indeed! Is there a mine and thine to good sense? There's *one* good sense, daughter, and if I have it and you don't, then you'd do well to listen and do what you're told!"

"And what if you're the one who's wrong? Pyetr's right! You're not doing so well, papa! You wouldn't listen to me, you didn't want *me* back, you took that *thing* in my place and let it sleep in my bed and you treated it the way you never did treat me, because *I* wouldn't put up with your nonsense—"

"One hopes his daughter grows! One hopes his daughter learns something after all these years!"

"Everybody shut up!" Pyetr shouted, and quietly then, from his log, elbows on knees: "Does it occur to anyone that maybe something's *wanting* us to act like fools, the way something *wanted* that sail to rip, and maybe it's not having a real hard go of it, considering what it's got to work with."

It certainly made sense. "Pyetr's got a point," Sasha said before Uulamets could say anything. "We felt the River-thing out there. It's somewhere around here. And if that's what's happening, maybe we ought to trust Pyetr's sense about it—being as he's not magical, and it's harder for it to confuse him, isn't that what you told me?"

Uulamets gnawed his lip and cast a narrow glance at Pyetr.

"I'd advise," Pyetr said, "we get back to the boat, but Sasha says we'll never make it that far, so what are we going to do? Go on believing the River-thing who told us this was a good idea? Or just salt it down once for all and see if that doesn't improve our luck."

"You can't kill a magical creature," Uulamets said in a preoccupied way, and walked off to the log where he had been sitting.

"What—?" Pyetr started to say, but: "Shut up!" Uulamets hissed, and went and picked up his book from the log, sat down and started leafing through it.

"More magic," Pyetr said, and looked at Sasha. "I hope he's got a way to wish us out of this. Maybe if you and he and Eveshka got together on what you wanted—"

"You can wish a rock to fall," Uulamets snarled, turning pages. "You can wish a man to rise. But you won't wish either to fly, and you won't wish a force of nature not to exist, not if you have any sense."

"So what would happen?"

"That depends."

"On what?"

"On strength and intent. Shut up! You'd try a stone's patience."

"I want to know," Pyetr said in a low voice, looking back at Sasha, "how if you can't wish what can't happen—what we just buried back there could be walking around and calling him papa."

Eveshka vanished, just shredded like smoke and whipped away across the clearing to take shape again with her back to them.

"I don't know the answer," Sasha said under his breath.

"I didn't mean to upset her. But that thing's damned scary. How do we even know the old man's what he seems to be?"

Pyetr always had had a knack for scary questions. Sasha cast a look over at Uulamets and wished hard, that being all he could think of, to see the truth about him. All he saw was a bony, frightened old man with a book that preserved the things he had done or thought of doing, but which would tell him very little about the things he had never thought of at all.

Unless one could think like Pyetr—just throw down the walls of what was scary and what was dangerous and ask questions like that.

Why? Why not? And, Why won't it?

Actually, Sasha thought, trying to answer Pyetr's questions for himself—I don't know why we can't wish ourselves out of this.

Why not?

Why not *all* try it?

Master Uulamets thinks it's dangerous. Why? Because he's never tried it? Because none of us really can agree what we want? Why did he answer that by talking about nature?

If you wish a fire not to burn, some other force of nature has to move in a rainstorm. If you wish a stone to fly, some force of nature has to move in and lift it.

If you want a bone to live and move—nature doesn't want to do that. At least in Vojvoda it wouldn't, Pyetr's absolutely right.

But there are things that don't come to Vojvoda.

Why not?

Because ordinary people are hard to magic?

Because working with all those people that can't be magicked is like lifting a lot of rocks, all the time?

He wished Eveshka would not be angry at Pyetr, and that she would tell him what *she* knew about magic.

Maybe, he thought, his thinking *was* Eveshka answering him.

What did we bury? he wondered suddenly, and went, ignoring Pyetr's startled, "Where are you going?" to see the place where they had buried the skull.

Pyetr caught up to him as he reached the spot. And there was no mound, just a hole.

"God," Pyetr said, and hastily looked around them.

"I don't know what it was," Sasha said, "but it wasn't dead.

Size doesn't mean a thing to a vodyanoi. Shape doesn't either. We've seen that.''

"Why didn't it kill us?" Pyetr asked. "It had a hundred chances.''

"Something wants us here," Sasha said uncomfortably. "I think you're absolutely right about that.''

"*Eveshka* knew what this thing was," Pyetr said angrily. "She killed it—''

"Not killed.''

"Whatever she did to it—she's a wizard, isn't she? She has to know more than we do, doesn't she? She could have said, 'Pyetr and Sasha, don't touch that thing, it's not dead!' She might have said, 'I'm just not sure about that,' she might have said, 'Don't waste your time burying it, it'll just leave when you're not looking.' ''

A cold thought came to him. "Why didn't Babi growl at it? Babi's your friend.''

"Babi's her dog," Pyetr said in a subdued voice. "Or whatever. Babi didn't go close to it. And *grandfather*, for that matter—didn't open his mouth. He's the chief wizard around here, isn't he? So why didn't *he* tell us?''

"Master Uulamets isn't doing very well," Sasha said, feeling his stomach increasingly upset. "And I don't know why she didn't tell us. I don't know why she disappeared for a moment on the trail, or why the vodyanoi kept coming and going. I don't know why she's acting the way she is, but she's upset at her father and she's not—''

He lost whatever he had been going to say. It just dropped out of his mind.

And again something dropped out.

That scared him, and he wished he could remember what it was.

"I'm being absent-minded," he said, and lost touch with the forest around him for a moment. He wished not to, and made himself look around. "We're in trouble.''

"God," Pyetr muttered, and shook at his shoulder. "Are you all right?''

"I don't know. I don't like what's going on." He looked up at the ridge, and into the trees around them, and he took

Pyetr's arm and drew him back into the clearing where Uulamets and Eveshka were.

"Eveshka," he said, quietly, so as not to disturb her father.
"We want to talk to you."

She slipped away into the woods, pale and silent, not quite
out of sight, but not talking to them about what was not in
that small grave either.

24

✠ ✠ ✠ ✠ Nobody talked about doing anything. "Are we going back to the boat?" Pyetr asked Sasha, who at least was talking to him; and: "I don't think so," Sasha said.

The next reasonable question: "What *are* we going to do?"

"I don't know," Sasha said, managing not to look him quite in the eye.

The third: "Is everybody waiting on grandfather to make up his mind? Or is it perchance the vodyanoi we're waiting for?"

"Grandfather's thinking," Sasha said.

Pyetr muttered his succinct opinion, got into their supplies and had himself a drink, had himself two, for good measure, after which he came at least to the temporary philosophical conclusion that he was doomed, everyone was bent on a course that was assuredly going to kill them all, and if no one else wanted to take the trouble to hike back to the boat, damned if he wanted to make a pointless, exhausting trek.

At least, in a more practical vein, they could rest, eat, bandage blisters and mend rips and such against such time as it might please grandfather to think about going back to the boat and back to the house to reconsider this whole mad venture.

So Eveshka drifted in and out amongst the trees, grandfather read his book and the god knew what stalked them in the brush while the sun passed noon, afternoon, and it got on toward dark.

By then he had patched the knee of his breeches, cut a binding for a split in the side of his left boot, and had another sullen dispute with Sasha over nothing more substantial than how much water ought to be in the stew; after which he felt disgusted with himself, so he had another drink after supper. Then he sat down with his sword braced between his shoulder and his boot, using a whetstone to renew the much-abused edge, a small, steely sound—at least the hope occurred to him—to remind any Thing out there in the brushy dark beyond their fire that here was both steel and salt, and a man in no good temper.

Grandfather read even while he ate; Eveshka stayed to the edges of the firelight, evading questions; Sasha let the supper dishes lie and took to making notches in a stick he had peeled, which Pyetr took at first to be some sort of rustic pothook, if they had had a pot: certainly Sasha seemed quite purposeful about where he bored little holes and cut little lines.

"Bear?" Pyetr asked, after a while, thinking he saw a face developing. "No," Sasha said without looking at him.

A man could feel unwelcome at this rate.

He looked glumly out at Eveshka, wondering was it only him or whether the whole world was out of joint this evening—not that he wanted Eveshka's attention, the god knew, although . . .

Eveshka did at least seem to care about him.

The whetstone slipped. He nicked his finger and quickly carried it to his mouth, wincing, while he watched that shimmer of mist, and saw her watching him.

"Deep?" Sasha asked him, meaning his cut finger. He looked at it. It was in a painful spot, on the inside of his thumb—on the hand the vodyanoi had gotten, the same one the damned raven had scratched.

"No," he said, sullenly, shaking it. "What's one more?"

"Here, let me see it."

"No." He put the wound to his mouth, shook it again after, and applied a little vodka to the cut, applied a swallow to his stomach, and then a second one, casting a foul look at Uulamets.

"Old man," he began at last.

"Hush," Uulamets snapped.

"Grandfather—" Pyetr persisted, doggedly, grimly polite, but Sasha signaled him no, not to bother Uulamets.

One supposed by that, that Uulamets was making some progress. It certainly did not look that way to him.

"So what are we going to do?" Pyetr said. "The vodyanoi *lied*, grandfather, it's lied from the start. It says you have to find this Kavi—"

"Shut up, fool!"

He gave Uulamets' turned shoulder a long, cold stare, thinking of things he had done in Vojvoda he was ashamed of, considering how much more this old man deserved them. Poor old Yurishev, for one, had spitted him mostly by accident—he had no grudge for that: indeed he had never even drawn his sword against the old man, nor thought of it at the time, not being the sort who would readily think of violence against a man three and more times his age—

Until lately.

"Pyetr," Sasha said quietly, at his elbow, "don't, please don't quarrel with him. He didn't mean it. He's trying to think."

"Good," Pyetr said. "About time." He stopped the jug and set it down. "Trust the vodyanoi, why don't we? It swears on its name, doesn't it? We trek into this woods after one of his old—"

"Shut *up!*" Uulamets said, and as Pyetr looked around at him: "*It* couldn't lie. Not on its own."

There must be something magical going on, Pyetr thought: he could see the old man talking, see the sweat glistening on Uulamets' forehead, but his voice sounded distant, like listening through water.

"We're in serious difficulty," Uulamets said. "Are you listening to me? I've been trying to draw our shadow in. It's not reliable, nothing it says is reliable, but it does have very much to do with my daughter's life. We have no choice, you least of all, Pyetr Ilitch. I suppose I owe you some small debt—"

"Small!" Pyetr cried.

"—which I will pay," Uulamets snapped, "with your life so far as I can save it! But my daughter's life is ultimately all that will save any of us. You know names. Don't speak them again. Don't ask me my intentions. Do as I tell you and don't follow impulses that seem strange and dangerous to you: I cannot personally conceive how you see magical things and I don't know how else to warn you. You're both more difficult and more vulnerable a target. You *must* do what we tell you, because your own opinions are *not* reliable, do you understand me? Do you understand me, Pyetr Ilitch?"

Pyetr worked on that thought, unpalatable as it was, and looked into the old man's eyes with the suspicion, no, the sure knowledge—that the old man insisted he say yes, and that that was the feeling thick in the air. "Sasha," he said, desperately trying to resist it. "Sasha—"

Sasha said, laying a hand on his shoulder, "He's telling the truth, Pyetr."

A man had no chance. He truly had no chance. He had thought he was standing by what Sasha would want.

So he gave Sasha a reproachful look, another to Uulamets, and went back to sit at the fire, unstopped the jug and had another sip, disconsolately watching the patterns in the embers and thinking quite fondly at the moment of The Doe's hearthside and 'Mitri and the rest of his double-crossing friends. They at least were willing to applaud when he risked his neck.

"Pyetr," Sasha said, at his shoulder—sounding concerned.

Good, he thought.

"Pyetr, he's right. We haven't any choice."

He folded his arms on his knees, clamped his jaw and wished he *could* come up with a viable choice—damn it all, how could a body think with two and three wizards nattering at him?

And one of them with his feelings hurt and probably wishing hard for him not to be mad—even if he was an honest boy and knew how absolutely furious that would make him.

"God! I'm going crazy!" He thrust himself to his feet and gave a disgusted wave of his arm. "What chance have I got, with the lot of you?"

"I'm sorry. I'm *not* doing anything!"

"Good! I'm glad! Thank you!" He shoved both hands into his belt and faced back to the safe formlessness of the fire-patterns. "Grandfather's not that polite. Neither's his daughter. So we've got to go find this Chernevog—"

"Please. Don't throw names around."

"What's the matter? What's the matter with a name? I'm not magical! My wishes don't work. What is this nonsense?"

"I don't know," Sasha confessed. "I truly don't know, just—"

"It's because," Uulamets said from behind them, "when you name a name *we* hear it; and having weaknesses we want that person or we don't want: the one's a call, the other's an attack, and it's damned foolish to do either in our situation, since we don't particularly want notice, does that answer your question?"

"Well, then, why don't we call something friendly," Pyetr retorted, "like the leshy? It seems to me we could use the help."

Uulamets to his surprise actually seemed to think about that.

"It *was* friendly," Sasha said in Uulamets' silence. "It didn't like Eveshka being here, it didn't like my borrowing from the forest, but—"

"*Did* you?" Uulamets asked sharply.

"Yes, sir," Sasha said.

Uulamets fingered his beard and plucked a twig from it, and sat there looking at them, one eye cast in a band of light between their two shadows, his face a maze of old secrets.

"Clever lad," Uulamets said. "Clever boy. And a leshy helped you. A leshy *fed* a rusalka. *That's* quite remarkable."

One never knew with Uulamets what was sarcasm and what was not. Pyetr had a surly answer ready, but Uulamets went on looking at them as though they were something on his dinner plate.

"It gave us its name," Sasha said after a moment.

"Truly remarkable," Uulamets said.

"So what does it mean?" Pyetr asked.

"It means this woods wants us here."

"Oh, god! One more in the game!"

"Quite," Uulamets said. "I wouldn't swear to which side."

He picked up his book, made a little shooing gesture past that burden. "Out of my light."

"So are we going to do anything?" Pyetr asked.

"Just stay out of trouble, damn you. Why don't you go keep my daughter company?"

Pyetr opened his mouth to answer, but Sasha pulled him around by the sleeve and gave him at least that excuse to take the wiser course.

"He has *no* feeling," he said to Sasha, and waved an angry gesture in Uulamets' direction. "Is that the way you want to end up?" It was unfair, perhaps, since Sasha was born what Uulamets was, at least Sasha had had precious little choice in it. "To hell with it. He's driving me crazy. Just let me alone a while and stop *wanting* things, can't you?"

"I can't stop caring what happens—" Sasha said, and cut himself off and looked desperate.

Maybe thinking about Uulamets and his daughter, who knew?

Pyetr sighed, and folded his arms and shook his head, looking at the ground, feeling better—*damn* the boy!

He picked up the jug and stalked off with it, wanting and not wanting a drink, *wanting* it, damn it all, precisely because he suspected Sasha wanted him *not* to have it, and the whole thing was driving him mad.

So he stood at the edge of the firelight, staring off into the dark of the forest in another quarter to that where Eveshka was, just wanting *nothing* for a while, except to rest his battered brain and not to have any demands on him, not from Sasha, not from Uulamets, not from Eveshka, that damned bird, or anyone else.

He was quite out of his depth, he decided. Eveshka surely cherished no illusions about his competency; he was reasonably sure Sasha had none left; and the old man's opinion of him was never in doubt from the beginning.

Babi popped out of thin air, right at his feet, a fur-ball with solemn black eyes and a glistening wet nose.

His heart hardly even jumped, that was how numb he was becoming to things like this. He stared back at the fur-ball, which was presently about cat-sized, and it squatted, staring up him expectantly, licking its human lips and panting like a dog.

He reckoned what it wanted. He tipped the jug, it opened its mouth and caught the dollop neatly, standing with little black hands on his leg.

That, he looked at askance. But he took another sip for himself. The hand hurt, from which wound he was not even certain any longer. He made a fist and looked at it to try to tell, trying to hope it was the latest wound; but there was a coldness about the pain, like a cut on ice: it *was* the back of the hand that was hurting—and he did not like that.

He liked less the feeling he got, looking off into the woods.

So it was out there. That was no news to anyone, least of all to him, and he was in a fey and surly mood. He stood there obstinately, reminding himself he had beaten it before, thinking that maybe if he *could* get it in range he might be worth something after all; and then with a numb sort of chagrin, remembered his sword was lying against a log on the other side of the fire, which he really, immediately, *imminently* should do something about—

He drew back a step—it was like walking in thick mud. The next was harder: he had great difficulty thinking why he was going at all, except, last and most desperate thought— something was wrong and he needed Sasha's attention.

But Eveshka was insisting to tell him something, which only confused the issue. He stopped, forgetting where he was going or what he had been about to say, except Eveshka was muddling him up—

Something snarled and grabbed his leg. He yelled, spun half about to save his balance and staggered free as Babi snarled and knocked his legs out from under him, become as large as a wolf, as large as a bear as it stood over him. He yelled and tried to get out from under it, and something had his ankle, worrying it and growling as Babi trampled him and lunged that direction.

"That will be enough!" Uulamets said, and Pyetr scrambled for clear ground and looked back at the edge of the woods. The raven was shrieking, Babi had vanished into the undergrowth. "Come here!" Uulamets ordered, and something whipped away through the woods, stirring the firelit brush.

Babi popped up again at Pyetr's feet, panting, dog-sized and showing a fearful lot of teeth, just the other side of Pyetr's boots, one of which showed a single set of scrapes in the leather.

"Are you all right?" Sasha asked, shakily, behind him, and Sasha took his arm, but Pyetr was still staring Babi in the face and discovering, quite to his embarrassment, that he had saved the vodka jug and all but broken his elbow hitting the ground.

He flung it. It landed unbroken in a bush, which seemed to him the final insult. He resisted Sasha trying to pick him up, got his own feet under him and dusted himself off.

"So much for your snaky neighbor's promises," Pyetr snarled at Uulamets, who had come to stare at him, and glared at Sasha, who brought him the jug, ignoring him for a second, surlier look at Uulamets. "Won't hurt your friends, will it?"

Eveshka drifted near, her face grave and worried.

"I'm fine," he snapped, and flung out an arm to clear his path back to the fire. "I'm fine. I don't *need* the damn jug!" He stalked back to where his sword lay, at the fireside, thought of taking it in hand and going off after the vodyanoi; but he had already embarrassed himself beyond bearing, and stupidity piled onto fecklessness was no help. He sank down in disgust on the log beside his sword and picked it up, scowling as Babi came up and put his little hands on his knee.

"Thanks," he said.

Sasha came and put the jug down. "I think my wish on it must have stuck," Sasha said very quietly. "It just won't break."

"You mean I couldn't turn loose of the damn thing! Thanks! Thanks ever so much! I could have gotten killed!"

"I'm sorry. I've patched it. It's what can happen if you wish things. They can come back on you—"

Sasha looked white as Eveshka. And blaming Sasha was the last thing in his mind. He shook his head and massaged his bruised elbow. "We've got to get out of here," he said. "First thing in the morning, we've got to get *back* to the boat—"

"That solves nothing," Uulamets said from behind him.

"What do you advise?" Pyetr asked, with the sudden, uncharitable recollection exactly how Uulamets had had the vodyanoi swear. "Damn you, you said it shouldn't harm you or yours. So what am I? Not inside those bounds? You're trying to kill me, is that the game?"

"Your own attitudes gave it its exception," Uulamets said, leaning on his staff. "Think on that."

Wherewith Uulamets stamped his staff on the ground and went back to gather up his precious book.

"I'll kill him," Pyetr muttered.

"You don't learn," Uulamets said, with a sidelong look. "Go where you please. Walk to Kiev. Reason your way past the creature."

Babi patted his leg, and went over and picked up the jug, waddling back with it like a great pale gut.

Pyetr shut his eyes and rested his forehead against his hands—which hurt his elbow, but he was beyond caring.

"My daughter," Uulamets muttered at their backs, "is very much its creature. And you are hers. Remember that, too."

Pyetr said nothing to that disturbing assertion. He only looked daggers at the old man, who was back at his book.

"He means be careful," Sasha said.

"He has a damned nasty way of saying so." He took the jug from Babi, who was waiting anxiously, unstopped it and poured a big helping into Babi's waiting mouth: *Babi* had earned it.

On which thought he poured him a little more.

The jug, about half empty, seemed not particularly lighter by that. It had not, he suddenly began reckoning, gotten emptier all day.

Maybe, he thought, that was Babi's wish. Who knew?

Pyetr took to his blanket and slept, finally—Sasha saw to that, a very little wish, a very cautious little wish, for Pyetr's own good: Pyetr might catch him at it, but Pyetr was in so much misery, much of which Sasha held for his fault—as Pyetr said, what was one more at this point?

Sasha added the jug to the tally of wishes on his stick, like all the others, some not even lightly made or unconsidered—but all unsummed, until for the same reasons as Uulamets he had begun that long-postponed ciphering, spiderwise trying to patch a web that should have been orderly from the start, but which he discovered frighteningly random. Writing was beyond him, but he made marks he *wished* to remember—

While Eveshka brushed near him, angry at him, as if his attempt to understand things terrified her in some way too obscure for him.

Then he remembered that she had died at near his age.

He made a mark for that, in the line that was Eveshka.

Young for all her years since, because it seemed to him she could learn *about* things, without *learning* things, sometimes acting exactly sixteen, in his reckoning, especially about Pyetr—

No, she insisted, from across the fire.

And maybe about her father, too, he thought, making another mark. Grown folk maybe puzzled Eveshka more than they did him: working at The Cockerel had shown him a lot more about people—and she had only met a few living souls in her whole life, all of them wizards.

Until she died, Sasha thought, and maybe met others, to their regret—

She drifted closer to him, more and more upset—of which Uulamets was quite aware. He realized that without looking around. *Uulamets* was suddenly upset with his line of thought, and he recollected the jug he had so casually bespelled: his most effective spell, Father Sky! The thing had resisted accident and almost cost Pyetr's life—precisely as master Uulamets had warned him: Magic is easy for the young . . .

Nothing had stood in that spell's way—no one had ever wished that the jug break, no one had ever had a contradictory motive toward it, and the god knew he had not had a hesitation in his head when the jar had flown across the deck and he had wished it stay whole.

Magic was so damnably easy—the jug showed that: he had gotten nonchalant about such little spells, being constantly in the midst of great and dangerous magic had dispersed his lifelong cautions and made him believe he could let fly a harmless wish—

But his spell on the jug was *not* harmless. It had evidently been more powerful than the protections he had set on Pyetr himself, for reasons he could not entirely understand—unless—

Unless his spells on Pyetr had flaws—like doubts—

But that was not the thread he had started to follow. He found himself disturbed to the heart, feeling a wish happening around him, like a brush against his skin—or that insubstantial periphery he sometimes described to himself that way.

Uulamets said, from behind him, "A rusalka *is* a wish. A wish not to die. A wish for revenge. *That* describes my daughter."

"The leshy helped her," Sasha said, most carefully, and swung halfway about to look at him. "I didn't get the feeling there was anything—wrong about the leshy. The opposite, actually. It felt—"

"There used to be one near the house," Uulamets said. "It's not there anymore. Ask my daughter why."

"It's not her fault, is it? She didn't ask to drown—"

Father Sky, there was a flaw in Uulamets' story about Eveshka, Sasha thought suddenly and for no reason he understood. No matter what Uulamets had said at the first, he could never have believed his daughter a suicide: if a wizard really truly *wished* to die—

Everything we thought we knew from Eveshka—he thought, too—that was the Fetch who said it, or the vodyanoi through her. Pyetr's right: too many wizards—and too many of them lying . . .

"Don't waste your strength," Uulamets said, suddenly rising, and Eveshka fled back a little. "What did I ever tell you, girl? Remember not to forget? Don't wish without thinking? But you're nothing but a wish yourself, and you don't think and you don't remember your mistakes."

"I'm trying," Eveshka whispered. "Papa, I'm *trying*—"

"For whom?" Uulamets snapped. "Get yourself together. It's out there. —Boy, do you feel it?"

Sasha did—suddenly recognized the subtle chill in the brush out there, twisting and elusive as the snake it sometimes seemed. He wanted to move. He wanted to warn Pyetr—

"Bring it," Uulamets snapped at them. "Wish it here. Bind it here!"

Sasha shied off with a single thought for Pyetr's safety and Hwiuur lunged for an escape.

Stop! he thought, then, with Uulamets, with Eveshka, and felt it pinned, throwing wishes to this side and that like a snake under a stick. Pyetr waked with a cry of pain, that was one wish it sent: "God!" Pyetr cried, kneeling, bent over his hand, while a runaway spill of ink flowed out of the bushes and straight toward him—

Stop! Sasha ordered it; Uulamets ordered; Eveshka ordered. The front end began to rise, quickly taller than Pyetr's head, rapidly thicker as more and more of it poured out of the dark.

He had to hold onto it, *had* to hold, while it tried every way it knew to get at Pyetr, who was stumbling to his feet with his sheathed sword in his left hand, trying, Father Sky, no! —to attack it—

"Liar!" Uulamets cried. "Deceive me, will you?" It tumbled down and circled into coils like a headless snake as Pyetr staggered out of its way. "Lie to me, will you?" The raven left its branch to dive and strike at the River-thing, and Babi, untidy fur stuck all over with leaves, bristled and hissed and nipped at it.

"Let be!" Hwiuur cried, writhing. "Let be, let be!" Its hide began to smoke. Pieces of it came away in its struggles. "Stop it!" Sasha was yelling at Uulamets; even Eveshka was flinching from Uulamets' torment of it, everything was falling apart and Hwiuur was going to go at Pyetr again—throwing a quick, snaky twist of its intent about Sasha's revulsion and trying to pull him apart from Uulamets: but he kept thinking about Pyetr's safety, and it thrashed and wailed in pain: "Not my doing—not my fault. Never—"

"The truth this time!" Uulamets shouted at it, and it curled itself into a knotty, smoking ball no larger than a man.

It snuffled, "The man made me do it." Smaller and smaller. "I didn't kill her. Kept the bones, that was all, he said I could have the bones. She could have the forest, I'd have the river, that's all."

Eveshka deserted the web. Sasha felt his own hold quiver like a plucked string, felt it about to snap, cried desperately, "Hwiuur: what man? Why did he do it?"

"She knows!" Hwiuur cried, twisted in knots and grew smaller still. "He killed her, he drowned her in the river, he took away her heart and he won't let her go—he won't let anything go, not her, not me, not you if you don't stop him, and I know how! I know all the secrets she can't tell, I know what you need to know, and you burn me, you tumble down my cave, you blame me for things he did! Well, damn you all! Why should I help fools? Ask me why your plans go astray! Ask me where your daughter's *mother's* gone!"

Suddenly it flowed into the ground like ink.

"Stop it!" Uulamets cried, Babi vanished on the instant, and there ensued a frightful yowling, a disturbance running a curving line under the mouldering leaves and into the brush, where violence thrashed and spat and hissed.

Pyetr was bent over, sword and all, holding his right hand against his knees, and Sasha stumbled to reach him, dizzy as he was.

"Are you all right?"

"Of course, of course," Pyetr gasped, looking out into the woods, one arm braced against his knee. "What's one hand? I've two."

Sasha tried to help him, but his thoughts kept scattering to Babi, far out from the clearing now, to Eveshka, a distant glimmering among the trees, and Uulamets screaming at her to come back. His head ached; he could *not* stop the harm to Pyetr, that was what he kept thinking, and he had to want it more than he doubted before he could even begin to make headway against the pain.

"Thanks," Pyetr breathed, surely unaware what a terrible botch he had made of his help—or what it had felt like a moment ago, holding the creature while Uulamets tore it in shreds—until Uulamets himself had flinched, or he had, he could not even remember in the chaos of those moments which of them then had been hurting it most . . . for Eveshka's pain, for Pyetr's . . .

"Come back," Uulamets was still shouting at his daughter, or maybe Babi; and Pyetr, collapsing onto the log beside the fire, looked anxiously toward the woods.

"Chernevog," Pyetr said between breaths. "It was Chernevog the Thing meant, it had to be. Her *lover* killed her. 'He said I could have the bones . . .' —God, what kind of man is that?"

"A wizard," Sasha said from a dry throat, thinking, I couldn't let it go. It made me sick but I couldn't let it go. Even Eveshka flinched, even Uulamets, and I didn't.

25

✠ ✠ ✠ ✠ "Eveshka!" Uulamets kept yelling into the dark, wizard at wizard-daughter, who still, it seemed, did not want to explain anything to them.

But at last she came drifting back from the woods, overpowered by her father's wishes, perhaps: Pyetr had no notion. Stupid to feel sorry for her, he thought: let the vodyanoi have her and save all of us—

Because he was sore and shaken and short of sleep, and thoroughly out of sorts with shallow, silly girls who got themselves murdered by scoundrels.

But that was not the way he felt when he looked at her, and when she came trailing back looking as young as Sasha and as ill-suited to contest with scoundrels and murderers: his heart turned in him and he wanted that particular scoundrel in reach.

Still, figuring they had their hands full tonight, he was glad to see Babi come shambling after her through the brush, at least one hoped that large and shaggy thing she was not paying attention to was Babi, in his larger and less pleasant aspect. Whatever it was, it stopped at the edge of the woods—lay down there, all shoulders and jaws, gazing as watchfully as any hound in the direction the vodyanoi had gone.

"You've some questions to answer, young woman," Uulamets said, stalking along by Eveshka as she drifted near to the fire. She looked terrified. Pieces of her were coming away, the way they had from the vodyanoi when Uulamets attacked it.

"Stop it!" Pyetr said to Uulamets, not certain Eveshka's distress was Uulamets' doing, but not liking it either, damned certainly not liking it. He said that, and got up to make his

289

point, and Eveshka, who had started in that second to flee, hesitated and looked back at him with a light of hope in her eyes.

He held out his hand: it was like lifting a heavy weight, so he reckoned Sasha did not approve; but they were being too hard on the girl, even Sasha was, trying to protect him, doubtless, but she had not deserved it.

"Eveshka," he said, walked over to her and beckoned her—one could hardly take her arm—over to the side of the clearing where he did not have Uulamets and Sasha immediately to contend with. "Your papa's upset. We want to help you. That's all. You know I do, don't you?"

"You can't!" Pieces of her began to come away again. "Let me go!"

"Where? Where can you go? To that Thing? Trust your father—" God, he could not believe he was saying it: "He's not stupid. If you and he and Sasha could once get together on what you want, maybe—"

"I can't!" she cried. "I can't, you can't trust me, Pyetr, you especially can't trust me, and I don't want to hurt you—"

"Well, so you do have a heart, don't you?"

"Don't say that! Don't believe it!"

"Seems you've believed too many things. If you really want to have it back—can't you just wish?"

"No, I can't, I can't!"

"Stop that!" he said, and pieces of her that had come away hesitated like drifting gossamer and immediately reassembled themselves around the edges, to his great relief. "That's better. God, please don't do that. What's wrong with you?"

"I'm tired, Pyetr. I want to go, please make my father let me go—"

"*Where* would you go?"

She shook her head slowly, distressedly.

"Back to that cave?" he asked.

"Just—gone. Just where people don't want me to be anything! Pyetr, stop them—please stop them."

He felt that anguish like a blow—aimed at *him*, he thought; he remembered the clay cup and might have panicked as his heart began to thump against his ribs, but he looked her steadily in the eyes and said, as calmly as he could,

"Oh, come now, 'Veshka, you don't really want to go away, you certainly don't want to do me any harm—"

"You don't know me! Shut up! Shut up!"

"I'm not a bad fellow, you know. I'd certainly put myself up against Kavi Chernevog."

"Please!"

Odd feeling, to try his old beguilements with the lady's father in view; and to know the lady's safety was at stake. But he called up all his graces, smiled at her, while he earnestly wished on Kavi Chernevog all the harm he had done to her. "Nothing's beyond you. You have to really believe, don't you? Sasha tells me that's the way it works. That fellow could trick you once, but you know better, now, you're *not* as young as you were, you're not a silly girl any more—and if you don't want people wishing you things, 'Veshka, for the god's sake don't talk about running off where he can get his hands on you alone."

"Let me go!"

"You're not stupid, girl, don't act it. —Eveshka!"

He had the strongest, most icy feeling there was something else looking out at him until he spoke sharply to her: she flinched and held up insubstantial hands, less than the sudden gust of smoke that stung his eyes. "Pyetr, I'm dangerous, I don't think when I'm fading—I don't think about anything—"

"Your father believes he can bring you back."

"He can't!"

"No choice, is there? Either your papa brings you back or he can't—one way we get out of here and the other way we're all dead, because when you start to fade, you're right, you certainly won't let us alone, not here, not back at the house. Seems to me you'd do better not arguing with us, damn sure seems you'd better not go running off on your own—"

"I'll kill you!" she wailed. "I won't want to, but I will—"

"Certainly you will if you go on like that. You're a wizard. You've got the power to do and not do, don't you? Certainly more than I do."

She shut her eyes, clasped her hands before her lips and

nodded, as pieces of her came back, like threads of spider silk, and filled out her edges.

God, so precarious, and so scared—the way Sasha was scared, of himself as much as anything.

But being half-crazed himself—every innkeeper in Vojvoda would swear to that—he quirked an eyebrow, smiled at her, which he had long ago learned was his straightest way to a lady's heart, wherever kept and however perilously guarded. "Trust me, not that scoundrel." A wink and a grin. "Show them. Give me a little kiss—I've no doubt of you."

Ghostly eyes blinked, wide and apprehensive.

"Pyetr," someone else said, as she slipped icy arms around his neck and gave him the kiss he asked for, a chaste touch of cold lips, a little remembered tingling down his spine. It took nothing. But: "Eveshka!" someone said, far away, and she drew back, staring at him wide-eyed as he might for all he knew be staring at her, a little lost—

"Eveshka!" Uulamets said harshly; and "God! stop it!" Sasha cried, unlike himself—so worried-sounding that Pyetr thought that just perhaps, if Sasha Misurov was down to swearing at him, he might be in more trouble than he thought.

"I'm quite all right—"

"All right, indeed!" Uulamets snarled, and thrust his arm between them, waving Eveshka off. "There's been quite enough foolishness here—and *you*, my girl, had best take quick account of your judgment."

"I know what's best for me, papa!"

"—*and* bring your wants in line with mine for once, impossible as that may seem! A wizard who can't keep track of what she wants is absolutely helpless in this business. You've gotten better—god, you *had* no mind when you'd just died, you were only a blind intention. It's my spells have brought you back as far as you've come, it's my teaching has kept you as sane as you are, and by the god, you'll make it back the rest of the way—"

"With *what?* Papa, I died! I can't come back except through somebody else, and you had to bring Pyetr into this, *dammit*, papa!"

"It wasn't supposed to work that way."

"Wasn't supposed to work that way!"

"It wasn't," Pyetr said, made himself say—because on both sides wizardly tempers looked to be getting destructively out of hand. "Your father wanted to know what had happened to you, and you couldn't tell him. —What else he intended, the god only knows, but he did get you back. He certainly wants you alive."

"He didn't get me back, he didn't want me back, he took that *thing*—"

"It wasn't easy to see through. It fooled all of us."

"He wanted his daughter, his own way!"

Pyetr shook his head, hands tucked in his belt, and said—god, he could not believe he was saying: "He risked his neck for you—a damn lot more than my father would have done for me, I'll tell you."

Eveshka just stood there, losing and collecting little gossamer threads of herself.

"So," Pyetr said with a shrug, everyone else leaving matters to him, "so maybe you should wonder why. The god knows your father's got his faults, but he's been at his game a long time. It only makes sense to work with him, doesn't it?"

"That's what I said!" Uulamets snapped.

"Not very well, papa!"

"Shut up," Pyetr said. "Everybody. You—" he said to Eveshka. "Don't fight. Just don't fight. Not everything's important all the time. First things first. Like getting out of here. Old grievances don't help."

"They certainly don't," Uulamets said. "Think, girl! Our enemy's *wanting* us to act like fools, he wants us to forget he's in the game, he's damned powerful, and we don't gain anything by sending it one more help—which you'd assuredly be, going off on your own, daughter, don't you mistake it. When we came up here, I had some naïve hope of dealing with him reasonably, but that's clearly out of the question."

"Out of the question! Papa, you can't talk with him, you can't—can't come near—"

Eveshka seemed to lose her way in mid-word again, staring off into distances, lips still shaping some word, part and parcel of other things that seemed to be going on where it came to

Kavi Chernevog, things that collectively sent a chill down Pyetr's back.

"Seems to me," Pyetr said, looking momentarily at the ground to break the spell Eveshka's own face cast, "seems to me we've been doing a lot of odd things since we got here. As if we didn't have this—" He remembered about names in time, not so much that he believed the warning, but that he wanted no argument with Uulamets. "—As if you'd never had a reason for leaving the boat and trekking off through this woods—"

"He's right," Sasha said thickly. "Pyetr's harder to magic, isn't he? Maybe we should listen to him."

"Damn right somebody should listen to me! Does anybody remember what we're doing here? We buried a Thing that won't stay buried, the vodyanoi's trying for the rest of me, *nobody's* talking about doing anything but sit here while everything in this woods has a go at us, and I'm not sure who's to blame for the sail, but I don't think there's much chance involved with this many wizards."

"There's not likely to be," Uulamets said, looking narrowly at him. "Pyetr Ilitch, you're certainly someone's; tonight I really wonder whose."

Upon which Uulamets walked off to the fireside alone.

"What does he mean?" Pyetr asked Eveshka and Sasha, looking from one to the next. "What did he mean by that?"

"I don't know," Sasha said, while beyond the fire:

"Damn you!" Uulamets cried suddenly, jabbing his staff into the moldy ground.

Pyetr ran, sword in hand: Babi and he arrived one after the other, Uulamets still stabbing with the heel of his staff at a traveling lump of leaves. His book had fallen from the log where he had earlier been sitting to lie open on the ground, and a separate lump of leaf mold flowed over it on the retreat, escaping Uulamets' staff—after which with a curse Uulamets fell bodily on the book and covered it. Pyetr whacked one leaf ball in two as it moved, and both halves and the whole rippled off toward the brush with Babi in pursuit.

Pyetr had no urge to chase it. He grimaced in disgust, looked at his sword, fearing something noisome might have stuck to it—leaf fragments had—then reached down to help the old man up.

Uulamets gained his feet with his help and struck away his arm once he was up, hitting him twice more for good measure.

Pyetr did not hit him back, Pyetr fended him off with a lifted elbow and contained his thoughts of knocking him flat, as Eveshka and Sasha arrived to get between them.

"Is it all right?" Eveshka asked.

Meaning the book, Pyetr understood, but Uulamets gave her no answer, as courteous with family as with friends, it seemed—only sat down on the log and started turning pages in rapid succession.

Trying to find that answer, Pyetr supposed. Time was, he would gladly have chucked the book in the fire, and Uulamets after it: but not here and not now, in their precarious situation. "The River-thing was distracting us," he said, feeling his knees shaky. "We knew it had help, dammit, we were over there arguing and it was over here trying to steal the book—"

"It couldn't do that," Eveshka said, faintly. "It's protected." He felt her against his side. After a moment one could not feel the cold she brought. He thought distractedly, That's dangerous. She shouldn't do that. . . . But in their situation that presence against his side felt reassuring as Sasha's was, in a night grown altogether too lonely and too dark.

Sasha said quietly, "Sir, can it read?"

"The god knows," Uulamets muttered, still riffling pages, then looked up, and snarled, waving his hand at Pyetr, "Get away from him!"

Eveshka fled. And he knew Uulamets had absolutely good reason for his behavior, but he felt—

—lonely, after that. Even with Sasha there. That scared him. So did master Uulamets putting down his book and starting to delve into his bag, with purpose evident.

Pyetr set his hand on Sasha's shoulder. "Better get some sleep," he said, and wished Babi would come back. There was no sound out there in the woods, now, nothing like a struggle.

While Uulamets arranged little pots on the ground in front of him. "As happens," Uulamets said, "I can use the boy."

He hardly liked the sound of that.

So while Sasha squatted on his heels and helped the old man, and while Eveshka hovered silent and angry on the other side of the fire, Pyetr sank down and wrapped himself in his blanket with the fire between him and Eveshka, where he could watch what was going on.

Little pots. Coals from their fire.

"What's the matter with *this* fire?" Pyetr muttered when Sasha came to collect that item.

Sasha gave him a distressed look, and got his coals between two sticks and came to put them in the lump of moss old Uulamets was arranging, after which a great deal of smoke went up, to gust directly in Pyetr's face.

On purpose, he thought uncharitably, and glared at Uulamets, undecided between conceding his spot or stubbornly suffering the smoke.

He sat, he wiped his nose with the back of his hand, he thought—if Eveshka could hear him—that there was no reasonable connection between smoke and ghosts and Uulamets' bizarre doings, but then he thought that if there was anything to magic, and he was lately helpless to doubt it, his doubts were no help and perhaps a detriment—to Eveshka, and her welfare, which did count with him; and perhaps to their hopes of getting out of this woods, which very much did appeal to him.

So he wiped his nose, rested his hand on his chin and shut his eyes, patiently waiting and hoping that there was no danger to Sasha in the old man's magicking.

What's he doing? he asked Eveshka in his thoughts; but she sent him—if anything—only a feeling that finished upsetting his stomach.

There *might* be danger. Babi had not come back. There were River-things and Forest-things, and he had himself almost died, Sasha swore it was true, until Uulamets had brought him up from the grave. . . .

The way he proposed to do with Eveshka.

Encouraging, perhaps. He wondered if Eveshka knew that. He still resisted believing it on the one hand and *wanted* to believe it for Eveshka's sake.

Uulamets started his infernal singsong chanting, tootled

a few notes on a pipe, the sort of sound that ought at least to send shivers through dead bones, and chanted and grunted. Pyetr slitted his eyes from time to time to keep watch over the business, wanting to ask precisely what it was supposed to do, and with the burning urge to ask whether there was some chance of it helping Eveshka immediately—

But the old man never was inclined to answer a civil question and certainly breaking in now hardly invited a civil answer. Himself, he recalled the last such episode, involving the salt pot and the vodyanoi and Uulamets blasting himself unconscious on the riverbank, and quietly slipped his sword around where it was convenient, swearing to himself that if there was another such incident and if the old man's magicking harmed Sasha he was going to answer for it.

He *hated* that singing, that recalled his wits coming and going with fever, Uulamets doing things with knives—god! the smoke was giving him a headache, and he was starting to remember things—

He rubbed his eyes to clear them of the stinging, thought that it was stupid to be sitting in the smoke with his eyes hurting and his nose running, and wondered if he dared move, but—

He was going to sneeze.

He stifled it desperately. But something *happened* of a sudden, the fire at his back suddenly blasted outward in a whirlwind of stinging cinders and ash, and he saw the pages of Uulamets' book fly wild, the wind and the cinders blast back on Uulamets and Sasha, scattering burning bits of moss into their laps—he saw that while he was turning, getting to his feet, hand on his sword, to see what had happened—

To see a ghostly intruder confronting Eveshka—a thing that was at one instant a woman and at another a mouldering skeleton of a woman, with the reek of the earth about her.

"Well," it said—one *thought* it said, although from moment to moment it was only bone, and looked at them though from one blink to another there were no eyes—"well, well, my loving husband. . . . I *thought* that was your voice."

26

✠ ✠ ✠ ✠ Sasha stared at the Thing they had raised, with no idea what had gone wrong, but something had, something had gone most dreadfully, dangerously amiss, and wishes shivered in the air, cold as knife blades.

It called Uulamets husband. And with the same dreadful jaws, said, "This must be my daughter."

Eveshka looked at it in horror, and Pyetr—

"That's it," Pyetr said. "That's it, that's enough of this blundering about in the dark, let's for the god's sake do something with the little pots, put it back where it came from—"

"It's late for that," the creature said, frowning, what time it was not grinning bone, and looked at Pyetr with such attention that Sasha flung everything he had into Pyetr's safety—

Which only brought that attention in his direction, the slow, deliberate gaze of a snake. He felt that gaze, felt it crawl over his skin with sensations that disorganized his thinking.

"Draga!" Uulamets said sharply, and the raven flapped aloft and shrieked in startlement, then fluttered down like something wounded, while Eveshka stood there losing threads and streamers in a wind that reeked of something unearthed.

"Afraid?" the ghost said. "Guilty? —What did he tell you, daughter? That I'd simply deserted you? I had no choice."

"Nor sense of balance! Nor scruples!" Uulamets said, and raised his staff, waving her away. "Eveshka, trust nothing with this thief, this snake—"

"Your mother," the ghost said. "*Come* to me, Eveshka. I

298

know everything that happened—the dead do know. And there's no more pain, no more hurt. No one can do anything to you again—"

"Stay here!" Uulamets snapped, and the air went all to fire and ice, everywhere push and pull, go and come. Sasha lost his vision for a moment, his head spinning and himself without an anchor of any kind except Pyetr, except the realization that Uulamets was distracted, Pyetr was depending on him and that if he ever let go his hold on the world they would never see the sun again.

"—Your mother's a common thief," Uulamets said coldly. "When you were born she had no more interest in you than to hold you for ransom—"

"Liar!" the ghost said. "He never planned for offspring, saw *nothing* in a daughter but a threat to him—*that's* why he stole you from me, that's why I had to run for my life, that's why he guarded you all those years—"

There was too much hatred, too much pain, altogether, when of a sudden Eveshka fled to Pyetr and held to him, saying, "Everyone's lying. No one wanted *me*. . . ."

"So you took in Kavi Chernevog," the ghost said, on a cold wind. "And let him at my daughter. *Damn* your lies and your treachery. . . . He murdered my daughter, and you were *fool* enough to take that boy in, teach him what you *refused* to teach my daughter, oh, I do know, I know you never would trust any of my blood, Ilya Uulamets, least of all one that shared yours. Most especially you never wanted any other wizard's attentions to her. What *did* you have in mind for her?"

"Liar!" Uulamets cried. "Begone! Go back to your grave! Go back to the worms with your carping and your spite, she's nothing to do with your poison, Draga!"

"Licentious pig. I'll see you dead."

"Look to yourself on that day! God, what did I ever see in you?"

"I had the worst of that bargain. I had you. God, look at you, you withered stick. I don't know what I saw in you."

"There's your mother," Uulamets said, flinging up a hand, turning his shoulder to the ghost. "There's your mother, girl, god, what a baggage—"

He *wished* suddenly with such cold violence that Sasha

threw up everything, everything he had, and stood, afterward, with his heart thumping and the clearing holding only one ghost, one tattered, frightened ghost, who turned and fled.

"Eveshka!" Uulamets said, again sending out that *force*, and she paused at the forest edge, shedding little filaments of herself.

"Eveshka," Pyetr called out to her, and more pieces came away, flying out into the dark.

"What happened to my mother?" she asked, and Uulamets said,

"I've no idea."

"How did she die?"

"I'm sure I don't know. It certainly wasn't my doing."

Eveshka stared at him with eyes dark and deep and angry. "You do know."

"As happens, I don't. She left after trying to steal my book, she left you behind, which was evidently the limit of her maternal affection. She was a wizard. Of course she was. Do you think she had a heart?" He reached out his hand and the raven flapped its wings and landed heavily on his wrist before he flung it for a sturdier perch overhead. "Hers would lodge in a snake. In a toad. In a cesspool. Don't listen to her. You're not her creature, you never were and you never will be." He made a motion of his hand toward Sasha. "Put out the fire. Pack up."

"Now?" Pyetr cried. "It's dark out there! There's the god knows what crawling around in the bushes, we've walked all last night, we've slept precious little of this one—"

"You wanted something done," Uulamets snapped, and stamped his staff on the ground. "Move!"

Pyetr *felt* the shove the old man gave him, past his own pricklish shakiness of too little sleep, too many bad surprises, and too much effort yet to go. "Dammit—"

"Mind your language!" Uulamets said. "Don't curse things and don't name names and above all don't mistake your dullness to magic for immunity. I'll tell you once: yes, you're hard to attack with magic, you're slow to see, slow to feel, too dull to know what's going on around you, but once something gets its material hands on you, or once you stand this close to a wizard, you're in dire trouble, son. Distance does matter."

"Don't—" But he had just admonished Eveshka not to fight the old man. He swallowed his own bitter medicine and said, calmly, respectfully, "Can *you* make a sail rip, two and three days away?"

"You!" Uulamets said with a jut of his chin. "You damnable, arrogant, *ignorant* wretch, you with your insisting to be in the middle of things, you with your pig-headed interference, you're the open door to any malign thing that wants a distraction—sit in the smoke till you sneeze, you damned fool: go help our enemy, why don't you? It's our only hope!"

Pyetr's face burned: it was only the truth, he thought, the old man was justified in that; the old man could have spared calling him to task in front of Sasha and Eveshka both—though even that he could not complain of, since he had put them both in danger.

But it did not change the question he was asking.

"I'm still asking," he said, "is this the best thing to do? If distance makes a difference, is it smart of us to do anything but go back to the boat—"

"Why don't you teach your grandmother to suck eggs?"

"I'm saying I may be the only one in this party with his wits about him, I may be the only one with doubts about this—I'm asking can you beat this fellow? Is this the best thing to do?"

Uulamets leaned on his staff and glared at him, no less sourly, but with his brow furrowed. "Pack," he said, and his jaw looked most like a turtle's. "You think I'm hard, don't you? My daughter thinks I'm hard. But I'm telling you in words—in *words* what I want you to do. That's very polite of me, do you understand? That's very patient. *Do you understand?*"

Pyetr had a breath held for a sharp answer; but reckoning the odds, he decided that pride had occasionally to take second place to good sense, so he said, with a little bow, "Clearly," and walked back toward his blankets to start throwing their belongings together. Eveshka was in his path. He stopped, looked at her, said, "We'll get this straightened out—"

But Uulamets shouted, "Stay away from my daughter!"

So he went, remembering Eveshka's stricken face, afraid for himself and Sasha and knowing nothing was going to make sense in a place where a ball of leaves tried to make away with your belongings and the girl you were halfway in love with was standing knitting and unknitting her edges in distress over a father whose only claim to virtue was that he had not murdered her mother.

Sasha came to help him, kneeling to pick up the scattered pans.

"Where's Babi?" Pyetr said under his breath. "Can you wish him back?"

"It's—"

"—a stupid wish." A man in this company got very used to being wrong.

"Dangerous," Sasha whispered, standing up. "Pyetr, don't get near her, please don't get near her! I don't know, I'm not sure, I don't like what I've heard—"

"There's a lad." He caught hold of Sasha's shoulder, feeling solid bone and muscle, something real in this woods. "Sasha, listen to me, *she's* all right, you are, there's three of us if we work together—the god knows what her mother is."

Sasha looked at him as if he had said something very distressing, and gripped his hand hard. "Pyetr, Uulamets is right—don't believe her, don't trust her—"

"More than her father, friend, I hope you've noticed how he gets along with his last student." Pyetr snatched up their blankets, and added, since he had a stationary target: "Where in the god's name are we going?"

"I don't know."

"You know what I think? I think we're not so far from the river. I think we've come a long loop upcoast. The River-thing is no land-goer. I think upriver's where we were going, and that's the direction we've taken in this thicket, if either of us had kept track."

"It makes sense," Sasha admitted.

That was some vindication. Pyetr knelt down and tied up the blankets while Sasha packed the little items.

"Hurry up!" Uulamets shouted at them.

Pyetr muttered, "Can you kill a dvorovoi?"

"I don't know," Sasha said, and with the firelight catching his jaw, did not at the moment look at all like the stablelad from Vojvoda. "It's you and Eveshka I'm worried about. Remember what we promised each other? No ducking off without saying?"

Pyetr felt uneasy. In his heart there was already a contrary notion he had not realized until Sasha said that. "Promise me—" Pyetr almost said, Promise to stop wishing me. But he thought that might be a stupid thing to do, so he said nothing.

"Pyetr," Sasha said, "for the god's sake tell me before you do anything. At least trust me. All right?"

Pyetr nodded, and tried to explain what he felt about Eveshka, how he felt when she looked at him, how he had thought love was what people talked about when they wanted to get power over someone else, or when somebody else had power over them—and he had always sworn he would never be that crooked or that stupid. So here he was. It felt different than he had thought. There were moments when he was positively giddy—which might be a rusalka's power; and everything he had always believed might be true—

He tried to say that.

But all that came out was, "I'll try. I swear I'll at least try. . . ."

Before Uulamets shouted at them to move and Sasha scrambled to kill the fire.

27

✠ ✠ ✠ ✠ No fire. No breakfast. Once at hours like
this, Pyetr told himself, he had been lazing
about in a soft, warm bed no magician was going to chase him
out of. Now he could not remember when he had last been
thoroughly warm, his hand was hurting again, and he had
soaked his left boot, the one with the split seam, in a boggy
spot some distance back.

Uulamets, once he had decided to move, did it with dis-
concerting energy, pushing branches out of the way with his
staff and often as not carelessly letting them spring back—
while Eveshka drifted through the brush faster than flesh and
blood could move, finding the path at her father's bidding,
beckoning them to a way through and vanishing for long moments in this headlong pace they kept.

It felt wrong. Eveshka's flitting haste, her increasingly
lengthy disappearances, worried him. Faster and faster. Up
hills and down and no notion in the world where they were
going, except that it had to do with Chernevog and the old
man knowing where he was.

So what do we do with him when we catch him? Pyetr
asked himself. What do you do with a man who can make
your heart burst in your chest or wish a tree to fall on you—

"Slow down!" Pyetr said, out of breath, seeing Uulamets
get further ahead of them. Uulamets cared nothing whether
the man behind him caught a released branch in the face,
Uulamets went charging through with complete disregard for
him behind, and Pyetr found himself lagging further and further back, dodging the branches that snapped at him, trying
not to do the same thing to Sasha, who, struggling with a

considerable pack for a lad, was having trouble enough keeping up with him. "Slow down!" he asked Uulamets a second time, but if Uulamets paid him any attention at all, it was short-lived.

He swore, trying both to take care of himself and Sasha, with the gap widening in front of them, vexed that an old man with a pack of his own could get away from him—but wood-craft was making that much difference in the dark. "Eveshka!" he called out, increasingly anxious as the gap widened, hoping she might realize their plight.

But she was out of view now, and Sasha had stopped, suddenly having snagged his pack on a branch.

"Wait!" Pyetr called out to Uulamets, "Sasha's hung up!" He cast a glance over his shoulder to keep track of Uulamets while he jerked and broke the thorn branch off Sasha's pack, tearing his hand again, but Uulamets was only a fading grayness in the dark, paying him no heed.

"Come on," he said to Sasha, and tried to follow, but he could not find the way Uulamets had taken through, and the gap was getting wider: he could see the old man ahead but he could not see precisely where he stepped, and it only grew worse.

"He wants to lose us," Pyetr muttered, shoving his way through brambles. It was bad enough being behind, but with his hand hurting and no idea where the shore was, or when the River-thing might put out some slithery coil about them, he had no wish to be out of Uulamets' vicinity for a moment.

But something cold brushed against his arm, chilling right through his coat. Eveshka, he thought, had realized they had fallen behind, Eveshka had come back for them, and he looked around to speak to her—

And saw a man's pale face, a bearded, rotting face with staring eyes.

He yelled as it reached for him and the cold went right through his arm and numbed it.

"Let go of him!" Sasha cried.

It whipped away, wailing faintly through the woods: three more joined it in its flight.

"What was *that?*" Pyetr breathed, only then thinking of

his sword—but it did not seem one of those things a sword might help.

Then he thought about those ghosts—three of them. "Eveshka," he cried, and started fighting his way through the brush, desperately afraid they might threaten her more than him. "Eveshka!"

Sasha was close behind—Pyetr hoped that was who bumped into him, as all around them other ghosts came skulking in, reeking of the grave, rough and shaggy men armed with swords and knives, flitting through the brush without a care for the thorns, occupying the way ahead of them and cutting them off with a hedge of drawn and ghostly swords.

"Bandits!" Sasha said.

"Dead ones," Pyetr murmured, halted with his hand on his own sword, for what small good it might be. The ghosts moved closer on all sides, swords drawn. "Uulamets!" Pyetr yelled, as one of them popped up right in his face, grinning at him. "Sasha!"

Suddenly Eveshka was there, a bright white shape of streaming edges in the midst of the others, which dimmed and shied away like so many curs.

"Away!" Eveshka cried, flinging out her arms, and they shredded and vanished on the winds.

Like that.

Pyetr stared at her, impressed—dismayed at being rescued by a slip of a girl; and likewise to see the rage on her face— as if he and Sasha might well stand next in her intentions.

But it was to the woods and the dark that she turned that grim expression, where the breaking of brush heralded something solid coming toward them. In a moment more, Uulamets' gray shape came striding through the thicket, the black bird fluttering somewhere in the trees—one could hear the wings, beneath Uulamets' panting and cursing.

"Lag back and halloo through the woods, why don't you? Something might still be asleep! —And you, girl, don't you turn your face from me. Don't you pretend you don't hear me!"

"I don't want you here, papa, I don't want you, let me alone!"

"That's foolishness!"

"I want them out of here! Both of them! Now!"

"For fear they'll see your handiwork? They've seen your victims, girl, they've seen it plain! If that hasn't put your young man off, I don't know what I can tell him. And what will you do else, leave them to this woods?"

Eveshka began to come apart in threads again, turning her face away from them.

"Eveshka," Pyetr said, "listen to him. Look at me."

She would not. She looked out into the woods, all shrouded in blowing hair and tattered gown, her face in profile to them. "There's nothing for you to fear from them," she said. "They're trying to warn you. It's an obligation on the dead."

Whereupon she drifted off through the brush where they could not follow. Uulamets swore and began to follow her, as Pyetr jerked his sleeve free and held the brush with his back, keeping the way open for Sasha long enough to get him through, while he kept his eye on Uulamets' steps. But Uulamets, thank the god, was going slower this time.

"There's ghosts following us," Sasha muttered after a moment, at his back. "Eight or ten at least."

"Won't hurt us," Pyetr said to himself, "won't hurt us, god, I want out of this damned woods."

"Won't help," someone whispered against his ear.

"They're back," he said to Sasha, panting, planting his feet carefully on a slope the old man ahead of him took faster than he dared.

Being master of his own luck.

"Wish me to find the right way," he said to Sasha. "Damn that old man."

"Don't—"

"I'm not a wizard, I can't wish for myself, I can't even curse him—"

"Can't escape," another voice said.

"I'm doing all I can," Sasha protested. "It's not doing any good."

"It's so cold here." A third voice, up against Pyetr's ear. Instinctively he swatted at it, and chill numbed his hand.

"Don't trust her," something said at his other side.

"Don't go."

"Go back while you can. . . ."

"Thanks," Pyetr muttered, panting, overtaking Uulamets

307

with a major effort. But Uulamets only moved the faster, then, and Eveshka still went ahead of them.

"Go back," the ghosts whispered. White shapes flitted in the tail of his eye, almost having faces. "Don't go," one said. Another: "Go back while you can—"

"Eveshka!" Pyetr called out, and shuddered from a cold, reeking touch at his face. "God! Eveshka! they're back! Do something!"

Insubstantial hands touched him, tugged at his sword, one attempted his pocket. Bandits and thieves for certain.

And an old man's voice whispered, "I miss my wife. I want to go home."

Pyetr did not want to hear that one. He wanted to think that deer and rabbits and birds had fed Eveshka; and one by one, the trees—at worst, the bandits, who well deserved it; but there was that voice—

Then a young, frightened voice: "Papa, mama, where are you?"

A chance thorn branch ripped across his neck, and he clumsily fended it off, aware he was bleeding, remembering, even if he had had no grandmother to tell him tales, that there was something about ghosts and blood; and ghosts and guilt—

Not even Sasha's wishing could cure the truth or mend the past: the ghosts streamed raggedly through the brush—not threatening now, but wailing into his ears, rushing at him and circling him.

"Go back while you can," they said.

Not armed now, but altogether desperate, anguished, importunate: "Go back!" they wailed. "You're going to die!"

"Go away!" Uulamets snarled, swatted at one and hung his own sleeve in the brush. "Damn!"

So much for Uulamets' pious advice, Pyetr thought; and in the same moment Eveshka came streaming back to them in tatters, confronting the ghosts with a wild and frightened countenance.

"Leave them alone!" she cried, and the woods seemed to howl and to swarm with ghosts then. White shapes whirled around them and swept away with an ear-piercing shriek.

"God!" Pyetr said, and shuddered as a ghost came up in

his very face, but it was Eveshka, when she looked at him, Eveshka who brushed his hand with hers.

"Come on," Uulamets said, and Pyetr was willing to go anywhere that got them clear of this, but Eveshka cried, "No, papa!" and shook her head so that her hair streamed like smoke. "No, no further, no closer—we aren't strong enough! Listen to me! Don't be crazy!"

We're in deep trouble, Pyetr thought, with cold touches starting to come at him from his left, and voices starting to whisper again. He had a sudden, sinking feeling that they had finally found their stopping place, for good and all, the wizards all fighting each other and the ghosts wearing them down touch by cold touch.

"Keep going!" Uulamets said.

"No!" Eveshka cried, catching at him with insubstantial hands. "Papa, you're failing, you're all slipping deeper and I can't hold on any longer, I can't! Make a fire—quick, papa, *please!*"

"In this thicket?"

"Do what she says!" Pyetr said, it seeming to him that someone had to make up his mind and do something; and it seeming to him that it was a lot easier to keep one's wits in the light: Uulamets himself had said that once, or Sasha had. "Let's not panic, shall we? She's a ghost. And a wizard. Doesn't she know what she's talking about?"

While he was shivering, himself, and trying not to, considering Eveshka owed no one any sympathy about dying.

Uulamets jerked a sleeve free of the brush, shoved a branch aside and squatted down to open his bag of supplies, snarling, "All right, all right, then, let's get a little clear spot here, let's get some dry tinder."

Pyetr broke branches for tinder and to clear a space overhead for the fire, Sasha cleared a small spot of leaves from the ground, while ghosts howled and dived right past their hands, bitter cold.

Uulamets coaxed a tiny spark to life, bright and brighter, catching a pungent lump of moss, a little drop of fire that grew by what they added to it and blinded the eyes to everything but itself.

Then the sound of the ghosts sank away, less now than the sighing of the trees, and the cold touches stopped.

Sasha gave a little sigh, and rubbed his face for warmth before he sank down beside Pyetr, to warm his hands at the little fire. "That's better!" He was still shivering. He could not explain to himself why he had lost his wits, or why he had started believing the ghosts, or precisely why he had been able to think clearly again at the first gleam of light, except that one wanted the light, and it grew, and that one little moment had turned things around.

"Better, indeed," Uulamets muttered, and looked up beyond the fire, where the only ghost in sight was Eveshka, so dim she hardly showed at all. "If you'd kept your wits about you, and not kept us harried—"

"I don't want you here."

"Don't be contrary!" Uulamets cracked a larger stick and fed it in, while the raven fluttered to a perch somewhere nearby. "A daughter that won't use the sense she was born with—"

"A father that won't listen!"

"Stop it!" Pyetr said. "It's not helping."

The anger in the air was thick enough to breathe. One thought of angry ghosts—and tried not to.

"They—" It was another one of those slippery thoughts, the sort that kept sliding fishlike out of Sasha's grip and wriggling away, but he calmed himself and held onto it long enough to ask, "Why the bandits? Why here?"

"Hers," Uulamets said. "He's using them."

"Our enemy?" Pyetr asked.

"No, fool! —Of course our enemy! Have we friends?"

"You'll not win any."

"Don't press me."

"Mind your—"

"Pyetr!" Sasha said, and seized his arm, scared, distracted and knowing what could get at them if he or Uulamets let that take hold. "Pyetr, for the god's sake—be patient. Master Uulamets is working. You're distracting him."

"Thanks," Pyetr muttered under his breath.

"And me." Sasha squeezed his wrist, desperately afraid. "Don't fight. You said it yourself. Don't fight."

Pyetr said nothing. Firelight showed his jaw clenched, his nostrils flared.

"Don't be mad, Pyetr."

"I'm not mad."

"I've got to think. Please. Don't ask questions, don't want things from us, not now. I'm losing things—I'm scared, Pyetr, don't distract me."

Pyetr scowled and shook off his grip, looking into the fire with his arms locked around his knees.

Bandits, Sasha recollected, careful of the thought of ghosts, fearing they could gain a foothold in his wishes. Bandits. And ordinary people. Traders and travelers from long ago, maybe, when the East Road had been open and there had been no bandits in the woods—

The grandmothers said ghosts haunted the places of their deaths, and he had never known—another slippery thought— that Eveshka had haunted this side of the river, where the trees were still alive.

He's using them, master Uulamets had said, and Sasha held on to that thought, desperately reminding himself to remember and sure now they were under attack from worse than ghosts.

He saw Eveshka standing looking out into the dark as if she were guarding them, faint, gossamer figure all in tatters.

She did not speak to them now, in any sense, only kept staring outward like that. Toward what, he wondered, and wanted Babi back, desperately. He was afraid Babi was not coming back, and he was sure if they had had Babi along on this stretch, they would not have been half so afraid—and then Eveshka would not, Uulamets had said it, have distracted them so with her own panic: they might have gotten all the way—

Where? he wondered—distracted then by a slight rustle as Pyetr delved into his pack and pulled out a little packet of dried fish. Pyetr offered some to him, and he ate and passed the packet to Uulamets.

Uulamets glowered, took a piece and passed the packet back.

Of a sudden the raven swooped and landed, and looked with its one eye at the fish. Sasha surrendered the last piece in that packet and it flapped back up into the dark with its prize.

Pyetr frowned at him about that. Or about everything in general. Sasha wanted Pyetr not to be angry at him—

And remembered he had promised not to do that.

"I'm sorry," he whispered, at which Pyetr looked confused as well as mad at him. "Pyetr, I don't mean to—"

Pyetr still frowned at him, maybe thinking—Pyetr had surely been close to magic long enough to understand—that that fact was more dangerous to them than the ghosts were.

"It's all right," Pyetr whispered back, then, with a gentler expression. "It's all right, boy. Just get some sleep if you can."

He shook his head. "You," he said, at which Pyetr looked further put off. Sasha had not wanted that, not wanted above all to treat Pyetr the way Uulamets did. "I can't," he whispered, wishing Pyetr would understand him and not feel the way he so evidently did.

Which, unintended, broke his promise again with a dangerously wide magic.

"God," he said—swearing began to seem scarcely adequate for what was welling up in him, and he could not even remember aunt Ilenka's face any longer, let alone hear her admonishments. He rested his eyes a moment against his arm. "Pyetr—don't be mad. Please don't be mad at me. I'm so tired."

"Shut *up!*" Uulamets snapped at them both.

Pyetr reached out and gently squeezed Sasha's shoulder, after which Pyetr's hand suddenly fell away from him and he put the other to his forehead as if he had grown faint.

Sasha looked at master Uulamets, who scowled at him and said, "For all our good."

When he looked back Pyetr had collapsed sidelong, in sound sleep.

28

✠ ✠ ✠ ✠ Toward dawn master Uulamets began to let his head sink, drowsing by little moments. Sasha, so tired he thought he would never sleep again, reasoned placidly for a moment that it was only natural, old men did that, and Uulamets had pushed himself hard for a man of any age.

But then in his muddled thoughts he began to worry.

"Master Uulamets," he said, afraid, still.

"Let me sleep," Uulamets mumbled, so Sasha hugged himself about the ribs and tried to collect what strength and wit he had left, wondering whether he was right to think of arguing with an old man who needed rest, or whether Uulamets knew what he was doing.

The light grew, diminishing the light of the fire, and Eveshka was standing as she had stood tirelessly all night—but she was so, so faint this morning, hardly more visible than spiderweb as the light filtered through the leaves.

He thought fearfully: We've got to do something soon. We've got to help her. She's holding on, but she must be getting weaker. And crazier.

He thought that maybe he could give a little of his own strength to her, not drawing from the forest, not letting her in any wise touch Pyetr: he was not sure then that she could stop; he was not sure that even thinking about it was safe, and he wanted master Uulamets to wake, but he was afraid of bad decisions, and nothing happened.

Suddenly then he felt a little weak, felt his heart give a little skip as if it had missed a few beats. He glanced toward Eveshka in panic, forbidding her with all the strength he had.

313

"Master Uulamets," he exclaimed; and quickly shook Pyetr awake, his head spinning, with only the thought that Pyetr was helpless asleep, and that if there was reason left in her at all she would listen to Pyetr—

"She's in trouble," he said to Pyetr, and Pyetr, dazed from sudden waking, rubbed his eyes and looked out across the dying fire.

"I don't see her," Pyetr said; Sasha looked.

She was gone.

Pyetr scrambled over to Uulamets and shook him violently. "Old man, wake up! Your daughter's taken off!"

Uulamets stirred, opened his eyes muzzily.

"Eveshka's missing!" Sasha repeated. "She touched me and she got away—"

Uulamets swore and started trying to get up, but Pyetr was already gaining his feet.

"She's leaving," Pyetr said, and forced his way through the brush, rapidly no more than a grayness in the dawn.

"Pyetr!" Sasha called after him and, throwing promises to the winds, *wished* him back with all his might.

Maybe it was dread of Pyetr's anger that made him falter. He *felt* it happen, and knowing that, felt his confidence ebb away. "I can't hold on to him," he said to Uulamets, intending to follow Pyetr, but Uulamets seized him by the arm, using him for a support getting up.

"Let's not all be fools," Uulamets said.

"Bring him back!"

Uulamets was still holding his arm, and jerked him violently as he turned to go. "I said, don't be a fool, boy, use what you have."

"It's not working!"

"Then you've less hope rushing off after them, don't you? And less than that if we go chasing off one at a time. Get the packs and come on. He'll find her, surer than I can."

"I know he will!" Sasha intended to break free of Uulamets, but Uulamets opposed him, he felt it going on, and trembled with the yea and nay running through him. "Stop him!"

"I need the book, young fool! You've lost track of everything you've done, you don't know where you are, and you want to go running off without supplies and alone. That's a fine help you are to anyone. Pick these things up, or do you plan to stand here till we lose him?"

"Bring him back!" he shouted at the old man, but Uulamets was busy holding *him*, he could not break free and the longer they argued the further Pyetr could get, so he bent and grabbed his pack and Pyetr's by the ropes while Uulamets picked up his and his staff.

Uulamets led off, as quickly as Uulamets could move, ghostlike himself in the faint dawning, while he struggled with two packs, trying to remember what was in which, and trying to decide if he dared leave Pyetr's behind, because he could not get both of them through the heavy undergrowth. "Don't wait for me," he called out to Uulamets, using his shoulder to shove the limbs aside, all the while feeling cold spots thick in the air about him. "I'll catch up."

"Wish to find a way, fool!" Uulamets said to him, and left him to divide his attention between the packs, the branches raking at his face and the cold spots that chilled him to the bone.

Stop, he wished Pyetr. Wait. For the god's sake call for help or something!

His knees were weak from the theft Eveshka had already made from him and he was rapidly falling behind. He could *not* handle both baskets: he stopped, teeth chattering, ignoring the cold spots that drifted through him, and dug into Pyetr's basket—took all the food he could stuff in his own pack, took both blankets, and the damned vodka jug that he was afraid to leave loose in the world. Then he slung his pack to his shoulders and pushed on as fast as he could, shielding his face with his arms and never minding the scratches.

"Don't trust," ghostly whispers said; and it suddenly occurred to him Uulamets might not want Pyetr's safety at all if Pyetr's dying could keep Eveshka in the world.

"Save yourself," a voice whispered. "It's too late for anybody else. . . ."

He caught sight of Uulamets for a moment and made his way past a thorn thicket, in among larger trees.

The old man had stopped, in the deep shadow of the trees.

"You'll die," the voices said. "Go back, don't go any further."

Sasha struggled through the thicket to his side; and Uulamets abruptly thrust the staff out to stop him, as an earthen
edge crumbled under his foot and splashed into water deeply
shadowed by the arching trees.

Water, Sasha thought, looking up that arch. Father Sky,
she's gone to the water.

"Pyetr!" he shouted . . .

A ghost said, faintly against his ear, "Don't trust her. . . ."

Both feet this time, and the split boot had taken a flood in. If
there was water north of Kiev he had not fallen into or stepped
in, Pyetr Ilitch had no notion where it was.

But the ghosts let him alone, which might be the daylight,
he thought: he hoped so, and fought his way along the streamside with increasing surety where she was and increasing certainty she was following the stream.

He was not crazed. He knew he was in trouble, he had left
his pack and his supplies, he was less and less certain he knew
the way back to Sasha and the old man, and he was virtually
sure—in that way that wizards had of making a man know
things—that Eveshka was headed straight for Chernevog.

Alone.

After which—

After which, with Chernevog holding her hostage and with
themselves entangled in this damned forest, there was no
safety—no safety for any of them once it got down to wizardly
quarrels, on their enemy's own terms and their enemy maybe
with help of his own—the vodyanoi, for one, and the god only
knew what else.

Things were starting to go wrong for Uulamets in such
numbers Pyetr had a worse and worse feeling about the odds
in Uulamets' company, although he hoped the old man might
at least have resources left to protect himself—and Sasha, if
Sasha was standing next to him and helping him. While an
ordinary man like himself—

—seemed mostly a distraction and a perpetual cause of
arguments.

Pyetr could feel quite sorry for himself if he let himself
think about that fact, quite sorry for himself, quite angry and

quite resentful of Ilya Uulamets; but there had been altogether too much of temper and foolishness for his liking, and he did not intend to waste his time on the anger. Perpetually glum, he told himself: and no sense of humor. Maybe wizards had to be like that, but he was not, despite a most ridiculous and unmanly lump in his throat when he thought about the boy and when he slowly figured it out that that had most likely been goodbye back there, for good and all.

He had thought about going back, at first, when he had failed to draw Eveshka back; but he had thought then about his dealings with the old man, realized he was doing no one any good, and reckoned that the old man most probably could wish himself on Eveshka's track, but that in this matter Pyetr Kochevikov had his own clear sense where she was—and he could perhaps rely on a quieter and less fallible sense in Chernevog's territory.

So he had a magic of his own, of sorts, something Chernevog might not know and something he doubted even Eveshka herself could escape, if only he could keep his wits about him in this place: he had to, or lose—

—lose what he had until lately mistaken for gold and places; one was that boy back there, and one was Uulamets' long-dead daughter. Lose them he might, he thought, but not to Chernevog.

Not while he could do anything about it. Ill-prepared as he was, he had his sword, the god knew there was no lack of water to drink, and he had learned how to keep himself warm at night and fed from the forest itself, at least sufficient to keep him going.

Chernevog had wizards to worry about. Maybe the vodyanoi had told him there was a weak link in their company: namely an ordinary man; and for all Sasha and Uulamets had sworn he was hard to magic, still, maybe—wizards being a skittery lot—and considering an ill-wish by what Sasha had told him was likeliest to hit right at a weak point—

Namely Pyetr Kochevikov.

That was the way Pyetr figured it, which actually helped the lump in his throat—at least offering him the possibility that Sasha had never wanted to be angry with him, that Sasha might at this very moment be wishing him back as hard as he could—

Would he not?

Pyetr pondered that and wanted to feel it if that was the case: he truly did, even if it hurt. That was far better than thinking Sasha was still angry with him.

Absolutely no, he told himself at once, Sasha would not be angry with him, not to that extent; and he fretted at it, sorted through all the impulses in his heart, trying to find that confusion that wizard-wishing made in him; but he found himself without any ambivalence at all about his own safety—and that would be Sasha's first and strongest concern.

Maybe Eveshka's magic had taken hold of him so thoroughly Sasha simply could not get past that sense that guided him. But there were other answers, some of which scared him almost to the point of turning back and trying to find the boy.

No, he told himself, no, and no, for all the reasons that had brought him this far. He had learned about wizards, even Sasha—that a man who tried to figure out why he was doing anything could only get crazier and more and more scared.

So one reckoned the odds once, took a well-reasoned path and left the point of choice behind as quickly as possible, blinding oneself to all second thoughts, to wizard-sent ones and true ones alike.

Just keep walking, he told himself every time doubts occurred to him. If the boy's in trouble, you're no help at all going back.

There was no sign as far as Sasha could see, as thoroughly as he and master Uulamets searched the wooded streamside.

No splitting up, Uulamets insisted, foremost of instructions, and with the ghosts plaguing them continually, with the vodyanoi somewhere unaccounted for—Sasha agreed. Ignoring the touches, the whispers, the cold spots, he clambered up and along the stream bank, with ever and again an anxious eye to the water.

About the chance that Pyetr might be under that dark, sluggish stream—he did not want to think about that, he adamantly refused to think about that.

But that wish worked no more than the rest did. He kept calm, and he tried to keep his wits and his eyes sharp as he clambered with the old man along the tangle of branches along the root-choked edge, looking for any footprint, anything, be it no more than a snag of thread in a thornbush; he tried to keep his thinking straight while cold spots went through him at random, tried to know whether his thoughts were all his own or whether someone was *wishing* him to miss clues and make mistakes; and tried to reason who that someone might be.

He slipped on a root, caught his backpack on a branch that bent and all but flung him in, after which he clung, panting, to a second low-hanging limb—and staring at Uulamets with a thought: Is it you?

29

✠ ✠ ✠ ✠ No stopping to search for food, no time even to rest since afternoon, only an occasional drink from the stream he followed, for a throat gone dry with hard breathing—and the sense of Eveshka's presence grew steadily fainter: he did not know why, whether it was distance or Eveshka's own strength fading, or whether it was some other thing; but he saw the oncoming night with increasing apprehension.

" 'Veshka," he said to her, under his breath, " 'Veshka, you really don't want to leave me to this—"

He had not done as well as he might. Perhaps there never had been a real chance for any of them in the first place—

Second thoughts again. No, he said to himself, no and no.

The ghosts would come back after dark. And *she* intended to keep traveling.

" 'Veshka, dammit!"

There was only that dim, fading sense of her somewhere ahead, her magic slipping from him, leaving him with nothing but the river for direction.

No, he told himself. It was another trick; it was Eveshka or it was Chernevog trying to discourage him, no different than shape-shifting. —Just keep walking, just keep walking, follow the stream, she has a heart even if it's with Chernevog.

"Eveshka!" he shouted, his voice quite hoarse now. "It's getting dark! What are you going to do, leave me with the bandits?"

He stopped cold then, as if for a moment he could not remember what to do with his legs, or what direction he was facing.

320

Then he was able to remember faintly why he was here in this woods, but not where, or what his direction was.

" 'Veshka!"

She was all but gone now, but he thought—he *thought* that it was the direction he was facing. He walked, sucking at the back of his hand a moment, and finally thinking that that was ominous.

" 'Veshka," he called out finally, and in the darkening woods his voice seemed very small and lonely, the ache in his hand more painful, " 'Veshka, for the god's sake do something, I don't like snakes, 'Veshka, I really don't like snakes—"

He felt a decided impulse to stop and look to his left, then, and stopped with a bent branch in his hands, his foot on a massive root, and glanced with apprehension toward the tree-shaded water.

"Is it you?" he asked.

He felt it was. He felt the pull again all from his left, nothing at all ahead of him.

" 'Veshka?"

She *wanted* him to come down to the streamside.

"Can't you," he asked from a dry throat, "just sort of *show* me it's you?"

Come, was all it said. He felt after his sword, thinking of snakes, and heard her—perhaps it was not a sound at all— saying, "Pyetr, Pyetr, listen to my voice, not my wishes. Go away, go back, it's too late—oh, god, you should have stayed with my father—"

She was irresistible as curiosity. No, she said; but the pull was constantly yes, and he wanted to see her, he wanted to walk down to the edge. . . .

"Just—show me," he said, standing where he was. Stopping, he had caught a chill. His muscles began a shiver here and there, and his hands and feet were numb. "From there, 'Veshka. I can't trust you."

"Don't look at me! Go away! Please!"

Something was wrong with her. He knew that it was. He had no idea what he would see, whether there was anything to see any longer, whether, like the thing that had been with Uulamets, there were only bones and weed—

" 'Veshka, I'll help you—"

321

"No!"

"Listen to me." The shivering involved one leg entirely now and trying to spread to the other. "You're going to Chernevog. So am I. At the rate you're forgetting things you're not going to be worth much; neither's your father, neither's Sasha. But I've this—" He touched the sword at his side.

"It's hopeless!"

"Nothing's hopeless except never trying. I'm coming down there. Is that all right?"

There was no answer. The shivering became a spasm, then shivering again.

" 'Veshka?"

"I should have died. I should have died. I'm trying to die, Pyetr, if I can't do anything else right! Don't come near me!"

"You'd better get hold of yourself," he said, and worked closer to the edge, his arm resting on a limb for balance as he looked down into the reed-rimmed water.

A mist formed on the surface of the stream, faint, so very faint as it swirled up in threads and rapidly spun and spun into Eveshka's self, holding up warning hands, threads of which streamed toward him and vanished in thin air. It felt as though pieces of himself were doing the same toward her, he wanted so much to come that little bit closer.

"He'll beat you," he said, "without me. A plain fool and a sword, 'Veshka, either one's hard to magic, isn't that so?"

He wanted nothing to do with Chernevog, he wanted to be nowhere but close to her and nothing else but hers. But he clung to the branch between them as the only barrier he could rely on, and said, while the streamers from her hands began to touch him and send little jolts through his arms and down his spine, " 'Veshka, as much as you need, as much as you need, take, until you can stop—"

The streamers touching him grew more and more, the little shocks, from head to foot now, matched the flutter of his heart, faster and faster until they sped past its beats and it slowed, laboring. The touch ran all through him, the most intense sensation he had ever felt, would ever feel, a moment that, if it stopped, would never come back—

Color shimmered soft and imageless as the winter lights, growing green and flowing in curtains through his vision.

Greener still, green as spring leaves, the light flowing through him now, no pain, nothing at all—

The sun was all but gone, the ghostly cold spots whirling and diving at them, whispering malice and warnings.

"We know where he is—" one hissed against his ear. "Too late. You won't find him. . . ."

Another: "The night's coming. . . ."

"Too late, too late now—"

"Master Uulamets!" Sasha said, clambering among the roots and the low branches. He caught his balance as the jug swung at his shoulder and caught it again against a tree, as he snatched at Uulamets' sleeve. "Master Uulamets, *do* something!"

Uulamets frowned at him and gnawed his lip. "If they're together—" Uulamets' voice trailed off as he looked upstream and back again. "The vodyanoi," he said. "Damn the creature."

Sasha shivered as cold dived through him and a ghostly voice whispered,

"Too late, too late, she's found him. . . ."

He plunged his face into his hands and *wished*, absolutely, nothing more than Pyetr's safety—but even that he doubted, thinking, Aren't the dead—safe?

"God," he cried, and sank down where he was, not sure of Uulamets, not sure of himself, not sure there was any help to be had.

And by that unsureness knew absolutely that there was no help in him, that everything was gone, all hope, that Pyetr was surely dead—

He wished—

—wished with all his heart that there were hope.

And opened his eyes, saw eyes staring back at him in the shadow, eyes in a fat black ball of fur.

"Babi!" he cried, "find Pyetr!"

Babi vanished again, quick as a thought.

And Sasha dropped his head into his hands a second time, wishing, urgently wishing Babi to help Pyetr, and not sure Babi could do that—against Eveshka.

He's her dog, he remembered Pyetr saying.

And Uulamets offered nothing, wishing only, Sasha was sure, that his *daughter* survive.

Something he was lying on was poking him, that was the first thing Pyetr knew: he was lying in brush, must have fallen, he thought dimly, and remembering Eveshka, decided his most desperate hopes had come true: she *had* found strength enough to stop, was surely waiting for him to rest—thank the god he had not fallen unconscious in the water.

Time to move, he thought, and tried, his vision clearing on something alarmingly too dark to be Eveshka—

A tree, he realized, heart pounding, he was only looking at a tree.

Then it blinked at him, and the brush under him moved and carried it closer to its eyes.

"Time you waked, foolish man."

His heart thumped, once, painfully, and he thought—"Eveshka! Where's Eveshka?"

"I'm here," she said, and whisked into his view, leaning over him, anxious and beautiful.

"God," he murmured, and looked past her to the leshy that was holding him. "Wiun? Is it you?"

Solemn eyes blinked. A second tree bent close and peered at him, a leprous thing of moss and peeling bark that made him feel far less secure.

"Kill it," that one said, and Eveshka cried, "No, it's not his fault!"

"Not Wiun," Pyetr muttered, and got breath enough to cry out, as twigs moved and closed fast about his limbs, "Wiun's a friend of ours! He said we had permission!"

"Permission," a third one said in a voice like branches creaking.

"Kill him," said the leprous one. "Better dead than feeding this creature." It reached out a twiggy hand and touched him. Eveshka cried out; Pyetr flinched and tried to break free, but more and more twigs wrapped about his limbs while this terrible mossy thing poked and prodded at him and stared at him with one filmy eye. "Break his bones, I would, crack them and scatter them—"

"Let him go!" Eveshka cried. "Please let him go! It was my doing, not his."

"My forest is *dead!*" the leprous one said, canting its filmy eye at her. "And there's no touching the one responsible—is there? Give him to me!"

The twigs relaxed as others tightened, drawing him into another grip. "Now, wait," Pyetr said, heart thumping, trying to remain calm, wit being all he had left. "Wait! There's a leshy named Wiun— God! that *hurts*, dammit!"

"Gently," the other said, and a curtain of twigs folded about him from the other side, pulling while the other hung on. "Misighi, be gentle."

"Gentle with this thing!" the leprous one said, but its grip eased, even opened, and Pyetr lay there panting and wondering if there was a chance in the world of running, if Eveshka wished with everything she had. It poked him in the stomach, fingered him all over, held its twiggy fingers quivering between its mad eyes and his face. They wiggled. The great eyes blinked. "Wiun, is it? Wiun the upstart, Wiun the lunatic—"

"We don't want to hurt anything," Pyetr said, "just get back something that belongs to her from the wizard that stole it."

"From Chernevog," it said darkly. "That's what Wiun said."

"You've talked to him—"

"I am talking to him, we're always talking to him, deaf little Man, just like the woods are always talking, can't you hear it?"

One could hear nothing but the leaves. In all that stillness Pyetr tried not to move at all and shivered with the strain.

"You want Chernevog," it said. "That's very ambitious. Do you know Chernevog?"

"She does," Pyetr said, and Eveshka slipped her arms back about his neck, stroked his hair with a cold, gentle hand, kissed him on the temple.

"I know him," she said to the leshys. "And Pyetr's a great fool. Please hold him here."

"No!" he said. "No such thing!"

"Wiun also disagrees," the one said; and leprous Misighi: "I've never felt sorry for a Man . . ."

Something growled at them, far below. And hissed. Pyetr turned his head ever so slightly, trying to look at the ground and afraid to see how far it was.

"A dvorovoi," the one leshy said. "Who would think it?"

"Babi?" Pyetr asked, tentatively, and felt the leshy's grip shift.

Then he did get a look at how far down it was, and grabbed its twiggy fingers and its arm in panic.

Misighi made a thunderous sound that might be anger, held him snugly with both hands about his middle and said, face to face with him, "Health. But our gift will take you only so far. If our power sufficed in *his* woods, Chernevog would not live the hour."

"He would not," said the other. "But we have no power there. We'll carry you as far we can. We will lend you what strength we can. But it will fade quickly, I fear."

"Wiun says," said Misighi, "to take you to Chernevog."

30

There was no certainty, there was only the least frail hope in Sasha's heart, and he fought for it against the whisperings of the ghosts:

"Too late, too late," one said.

And others: "Give up. They're dead. You'll all be dead soon. . . ."

While he grew colder and colder from the ghostly touches and despair tried to take root in him.

He wished he knew what had happened to Babi; he wished he could find some sign of Pyetr and Eveshka in this thicket, but fear of what he was going to find crippled both wishes, because he kept seeing Pyetr the way he had found him by the forest pool, locked in embrace with a girl who was mostly raindrops and mist; and worse, that night on the riverside, the first time they had seen Eveshka, Pyetr lying all pale and cold in the brush—

This time—this time, beyond rescue.

Then Eveshka at least, gruesome thought, would have the strength to come back to them. He could not in conscience hate her if that was the case—and he tried to take hope from the fact that she had not; but he remembered what it was to be without a heart, and how one could know with the head that he had to care, and one could think so coldly and clearly what one had to do—

And be so angry then—so terribly angry and so much more powerful than her father was now—

She might well go straight for Chernevog, wishing them along behind her.

327

That thought was so clear and stark in his heart he felt a pang of fear it *was* true, that was exactly what she was doing—

"We're not gaining anything," Uulamets said to him, stopping, leaning against a tree, hard-breathing. "Make a fire."

"We're not giving up!"

"I said make a fire!"

"I'm keeping going," Sasha said. Master Uulamets wanted one thing, Sasha wanted the other, this time with no doubt at all, and he thought master Uulamets might strike him or wish him dead on the spot—

But after a moment Uulamets snarled, "All right, all right, young fool. Where are they?" A ghost dived through him, through the tree itself, and Uulamets winced. "Can you say? Do you have any idea? I don't."

Sasha was not about to confess to confusion. "Ahead of us."

"Do you know that?" Uulamets challenged him.

Saying yes took a lie; and lying—the thought flashed through Sasha's mind, his own recollection or Uulamets'— lying was dangerous. "They've *got* to be ahead of us—"

"Your friend could be lying dead in the brush somewhere, for all we know. We could be far past the spot—"

"He's not dead!"

"Do you *know* that?"

Sasha shivered as a ghost echoed out of the dark: "Dead—"

"I don't *know* that!" he said to Uulamets. "I don't know anything, I don't think you do, but we can't stop—"

"We *have* to stop, boy, your friend has to stop, flesh and bone have their limits—"

"So does Eveshka," he cried, "and you know what they are! The longer she goes, the more she has to take—"

"You don't have to tell *me* that, boy, I know—"

"So what are you telling me? Stop and let her have him?" He trembled with anger, struggled for breath. "I'll never forgive you if he dies, I swear, I *swear* I'll—"

Danger, he thought suddenly. Terrible danger.

"Don't be a fool," Uulamets said, grabbing him by the shoulder, and Sasha knew where that thought had just come from. Uulamets shook him, pushed him against the brush and said into his face: "It's our enemy, boy, it's the ghosts, it's *doubt*, that's what's happening to us, use your head, use your wits—" A ghost leaned close, whispering: "No use when there's no hope—" and vanished in mid-word as Uulamets diverted himself to swat at it and snarl: "Perish!"

There was a sudden quiet about them, then a concerted wailing as if the woods had gone mad, making the ears ache, making any thought impossible for a moment.

Silence then; and the whispers came back, ominously. "You shouldn't have done that. . . ."

"Perish the lot of you!" Uulamets snarled. "You were nothing when you were alive and you're less now. Get out of here! Let us alone!"

Another deafening shriek. Sasha clapped his hands over his ears, *wanting* quiet, the way he knew master Uulamets wanted it, but the sound diminished only while he was thinking about that, and rose whenever he thought about getting on their way, whenever he thought about Pyetr, about anything at all, until there was nothing to do but to endure the screaming and try to move, the two of them, as quickly as they could, while chills lanced through them like swords.

The wailing *hurt*, it ached, it occupied attention and multiplied missteps in this woods that had not so much as a deer trail, the god knew *why* no creature would come here. They had not seen the raven since they had first reached the stream they were following, Babi was gone again: they were alone in a streamside darker and darker with overhanging trees, with the white shapes of ghosts reaching at them, so real now Sasha feared it was not only thorns and branches catching at his clothing and his pack.

Then it all stopped, and in the ringing it left was a rustling and crack of brush, and a powerful, quick slither of some heavy body from the streamside.

"Master Uulamets!" Sasha said, as ripples showed beside them on the water, a little sheen in absolute black.

Branches broke above them, as something huge and dark rose straight up.

"Well," Hwiuur said, tall and black as the trees themselves, "do you finally want help?"

"Where's my daughter?" Uulamets demanded; and:

329

"Where's Pyetr?" Sasha asked, even knowing the creature would lie, *knowing* it meant them no good.

"I don't know why I should answer you. Send that wretched little creature on my track, try to chase me back to the river—"

Is *that* where Babi was? Sasha wondered, and wondered with a pang of anxiety where Babi was now, along with Pyetr and Eveshka, while Hwiuur seemed so confident and so self-pleased.

God, he thought, god, no. . . .

"You swore on your name," Uulamets said, and stamped his staff on the ground, "and you've lied—"

"Not lied," the vodyanoi said, and the voice came from lower and lower in the brush. A dank, river-smelling wind gusted at them. "I offered you my help—"

"Deceptions—"

"I *am* a snake," Hwiuur said, smoothly, gently, "and left and right aren't that important to me: everything's one thing, really, isn't it, a pretty girl—pretty, pretty bones—"

"Where is she?"

"Where? Always where and when, you folk, I swear you baffle me—as if it meant anything, to be one side or other of a place. I'm here, she's there, she might be, will be, could be, all these things, but that's not the question you should ask: you should ask where *you* are, and where you're going, and I can tell you that. You're in Chernevog's forest, and you're going the way everything here goes: his way."

"Where's Pyetr?" Sasha cried. "What's happened to Eveshka?"

"I've answered that, haven't I? Ask me another question. Or ask my help. I *would* give it."

"Damn you," Uulamets said, "you're to blame for this!"

"Tsss. I? Ask your wife."

"Ask her what?" Sasha asked, clenching sweating hands. It was none of his business, it was impertinent, but he had doubts of Uulamets, doubts of the vodyanoi's truths, doubts of everything at the moment—

Which made a wizard far less defended than an ordinary boy.

And there was no reason he knew that Hwiuur did not kill them both.

"Tsss. Ask her who taught Chernevog."

"I know who taught him," Uulamets snarled. "I know too damned well who taught him. . . ."

"Ask where he got his power."

"From my book," Uulamets said, "—the skulking thief!"

"Ask how he could read it."

"I don't need to ask."

"Ask who was sleeping with Chernevog."

"Damn you!"

"Tsss. So little gratitude. Let me help you. I *would* help you—"

The shadow rose above them, up and up above their heads.

Then Hwiuur crashed down, splintering limbs, and breaking brush in his retreat. From water's edge came a sly, soft voice: "Old fool. You're so wrong—in everything. . . ."

"Hwiuur!" Uulamets said.

But there was only a disturbance of the water, a spreading ripple, and the rustling of the leaves as the wind rose, cold-edged.

Sasha thought: Can it tell the truth?

And about what Hwiuur had said: It doesn't make sense.

"How could Chernevog beat you?" he asked Uulamets, suddenly brave enough to ask, because it seemed to him everyone was lying, or telling Hwiuur's kind of truth. "He wasn't that old. He—"

Uulamets grabbed him suddenly by the throat, hit him with the side of his staff while he was so startled he had not even his hands up to protect himself, and pinned him against the brush, a grayness of hair and beard and shoulders, a harsh breathing in the dark, a hand on his throat, not tightening, not letting him go, either.

"He was eighteen," Uulamets said, "He was a handsome, glib *boy*, as helpful as you are, until I caught him at his game."

Sasha trembled, thoughts scattering like sparrows—what Uulamets could do, what some faceless man *had* done, long ago, holding him and hitting him—

A neighbor woman saying, His father beat the boy—

"Dammit, boy, I *told* you I wanted to stop, I *told* you, you understand me, but you didn't care, you were getting your way, no matter what—I can't fight that, not without doing something our enemy can use, so I gave in to your foolishness, and keep going, and damn you! you natter and you argue and push me—"

"I didn't understand I was doing it, I didn't mean to do it—not—not except the first—"

Uulamets was going to hit him again, Uulamets was going to hit him because Uulamets was terrified of his own anger and there was so much of it. Honesty was equally frightening to him—and he was practicing it now, wanting a foolish boy to know how desperate and frightened a wizard could be.

Sasha laid his hands on Uulamets' arm, wanting Uulamets not to be afraid of him—desperately afraid that was the wrong thing to do, realizing he should have said it aloud, the way Pyetr had told him— Say, it, boy!

The raven settled, with a flutter of wings, in the thicket at Sasha's back.

"Please," Sasha said, pushing at Uulamets' hand. "I was stupid. But—" Tears threatened him. "Pyetr—"

The bird fluttered uneasily, settled its weight on Sasha's shoulder and brushed his cheek with a nervous wing. Tears spilled. Pyetr *was* dead, he was scared it was true, it was his fault, and Uulamets called him a fool.

Uulamets'·fingers slightly tightened, only slightly. "A wizard can't want too much," Uulamets said. "He can't want a kingdom, he can't want gold, he can't want things that bring him near other people; but there's one most dangerous thing he can want."

"What's that?" Sasha asked, because the old man was going to squeeze his throat shut, and the old man said, hardly louder than the wind,

"He can't want more magic than he has, he can wish himself more and more powerful. And do you know where he can get that power?"

It was hard to think past his grief, and the old man pressing him back against the branches, off his balance in every sense—most of all with Uulamets trying to get some admission from him he did not understand. "He can learn," was the only answer that came to him.

Fingers tightened again. "How did you feed my daughter?"

"I—" He panicked, unsure of what he was guilty, or what the old man suspected he had done.

"Where did you get what you gave her?"

"From the woods, from the—"

"From living things. Like the rusalka, from living things, from the inexhaustible earth—"

Is it inexhaustible? Sasha wondered, helpless, stupid curiosity, with everything tumbling through his mind, cold and distant now. He thought of the dead forest. . . .

"—or from things that *are* magical. The vodyanoi certainly would lend us his, he wants to lend us his, as he lends it to our enemy, and do you know where he gets it?"

"From the river—"

"From the river, from the earth, from his victims, but what he *is*, boy, is cold, and linked to other things like him—I don't speak of evil, boy, there's no name for what it is, except self-interested and slippery and rarely holding an ambition that has to do with men—*men* hold that kind of thought, do you understand me?"

Sasha tried to shake his head.

"You borrow from him, boy, and he'll give you all you want, he'll give you cold power, and deep power, and rivals, oh, you can't allow rivals, not on that level of power, boy, because the last thing you want is another wizard to want things *his* way—"

"I'm not against you," Sasha said faintly.

"You're lying."

"No, sir! No!"

"I taught once, and twice, and had a daughter—and what does it come to? To this! To this damned woods and a creature that for my simple asking would make me more powerful than the young *fool* who killed my daughter, than the young *fool* who fights me every step of the way—"

"I'm not fighting you, I'm sorry—"

"Let me tell you, boy, his whole *use* for my daughter was revenge on me, his whole purpose in coming to me was to take everything I had, including my free will. At least my thieving wife left me something—but look what that came to! The girl was her mother's daughter—"

"Eveshka never betrayed you. You don't believe that Thing. . . ."

"I believe in fecklessness. I believe in youthful stupidity. I believe in self-interested *treachery*, I've seen too much of it, and here we both are, boy, in the middle of this damnable woods, with you with one purpose and me with mine, crossing each other at every turn, while there's no resource our enemy doesn't have. I thought I had my daughter back, the way she was before that blackguard came, but no, I should have known the difference; *my* Eveshka went straight for another light-minded, pretty scoundrel—"

"Pyetr's not like that!"

"I'm not expecting to get my daughter back. Not *my* daughter! All I'm trying to do is stop her from joining *him*, because she will. I'm here to stop a fool who's dangerous to everything alive, because that's what he's become, that's why I wouldn't let him have my daughter and that's why I'm risking everything I've got left, damn you! I should have killed both of you at the start, I should have killed you when I knew how wrong things had gone. I more than 'don't need you,' you're *good*, you're powerful as hell, boy, and he's got both my daughter and your friend, do you understand me, do you know what you're going to do about that?"

"Kill him if I have to." Sasha had never imagined intending a thing like that, he had never thought he could, but he saw where master Uulamets was leading him and what master Uulamets was asking.

Till Uulamets shoved him back hard and said, "And *then* who'll be the power, boy, have you gotten that far in your thinking?"

"I—don't want anything but—"

My friends safe, he thought, trying to figure what else that hid; and felt Uulamets' hand relax, and close again on his shirt and pull him upright. The raven fluttered and settled on Uulamets' shoulder as Uulamets pulled him into the circle of his arm.

"Believing stops," Uulamets said, holding him so tightly for a moment his joints cracked, before he roughed his hair and let him go. "Then there's nothing. You understand: there are very few *old* wizards. And thank the god, most of the young ones lose it fast. —Make a fire, boy, do what I tell you, do absolutely what I tell you."

Sasha opened his mouth to plead their need for haste, then smothered that objection and said, bowing his head, "I'm trying not to wish, sir, but—"

Uulamets' hand came up under his chin and held him eye to eye in a little patch of starlight. "But."

"I—"

"Want *nothing* but what I want. There's another place to get magic. Do you imagine what it is? It's very dangerous."

"From another magician," Sasha said, with a little flutter of dread: he did not know whose thought that was.

Uulamets said, still holding him, "You have to stop fighting me, boy. You've got the power, I've got the experience, and it has to flow my direction: you don't want to see the harm you can do. Will you do what I want? Will you absolutely do what I want? I'm going to work a real magic in a moment. It won't be pleasant for you."

"Pyetr—"

"No promises. *No* promises. We don't even know he's alive. But that blackguard student of mine is going to kill both of us—or worse. There *is* worse—if we don't do something. Hear how quiet things are? He's thinking. We haven't much time."

"He's making the ghosts—?"

"He's feeding them. He's doing all of this. The vodyanoi is helping him; and he doesn't want us dead, that isn't half what he wants."

Sasha thought he understood. He was afraid of what he understood, and afraid of mistakes.

And helpless, by that fact.

"Go ahead," he said to Uulamets, trying not to let his terror show. "Whatever you have to do."

They went in a hail of twigs and leaves, a passing dark flurry of branches, so rapidly that Pyetr ducked his head, held on to Misighi and when some crashing impact or downward drop made him sure he was going to die—he held the tighter, Eveshka clinging as a weightless chill about his neck, told himself that leshys would never fall, and never drop him, and kept his mouth tightly shut no matter what—until of a sudden they plummeted into empty air: "God!" he cried—

But they stopped abruptly and bounced up again, continuing to bounce slightly—like his heart, he thought, swallowing the outcry he had made: Misighi had evidently caught a resilient branch to stop them. Misighi immediately stretched out the arm holding him, opened all the myriad twiggy fingers and slipped others from his grip until he dangled only from his hands, and lowered him and Eveshka rapidly down and down through empty air.

"Fare well," Misighi said, the mere creaking of branches, as its face retreated into the dark above him and shadowy limbs rushed up past them. "This is the boundary. Further than this is impossible for us."

Pyetr's feet touched ground, and it let them go, uncurling its fingers from his grip.

Then he did well to keep his shaking legs under him—instinctively tried to steady Eveshka, but his hands only met cold; and he looked up into the dark: "Thank you," he said foolishly—difficult to bow to something far above his head; and only had a shower of leaves for his trouble, the creatures passing above them like a storm through the woods.

Eveshka had his hand, always able to touch him, surer of his edges, he supposed, than he was of hers. He looked about him at a woods no worse than where they had been—and beyond, at a starlit forest of dead limbs, dead as Eveshka's own.

Closer than that, at a black ball sitting on the leaves, panting.

"Good dog," he said to it. Babi licked his lips and got up, expectantly, little hands clasping, then one finding the ground, pawlike.

"You shouldn't go," Eveshka said, and turned and put her arms about his neck, looking up into his face. "Pyetr, please, no, I'm—not—strong enough—"

Babi growled and of a sudden jumped up and grabbed his sleeve—pulled him sharply aside, for which a man could be quite resentful, except he saw Eveshka flit and stop a little removed from him, hands clasped together, pain on her face.

"I—can't," she said, "I can't not want you, and you know what that does to us. —Babi, *keep* him, watch him—"

Pyetr tugged to get his sleeve free. "Babi, stop it!" He knew what she was up to, where she was going as she started away. " 'Veshka, no!"

She paused, looked back over her shoulder, paler, much paler once she had crossed that boundary of living woods and dead. And it was not his gentle Eveshka looking back at him with that cold, resolute anger, or speaking to him in a voice so icelike still:

"I can't kill him the way I can you: there's no limit to him. But you're right: a sword might. A knife. I don't know if I can get to him, I may weaken too much. But I'll try, Pyetr—"

Something moved among the trees behind her, something walking through the starlight, among the pale, barkless trunks. " 'Veshka," he said, shaking his wrist, trying silently to urge Babi to turn loose, not wanting to make overmuch commotion and precipitate something unwanted. " 'Veshka, don't look, but there's somebody behind you—quietly, walk back here. —Babi, Babi, dammit, turn loose—"

She did turn and look, and the gray figure came walking steadily as she began to tear into threads again, streaming away into thin air.

" 'Veshka!" Pyetr said—jerked violently to tear his sleeve free: cloth ripped, but Babi held like a lump of iron, seized his wrist with his hands, strong as chain, as Eveshka dimmed and dimmed. Babi began to pull him away, but of a sudden he wanted to go toward that ominous figure, and of a sudden Babi's grip slipped, releasing him.

He caught his balance, walked across the boundary, stopped beside Eveshka all the while knowing he had made a grave mistake in his plans against Chernevog—knowing that Chernevog had wished him here all along, ahead of his companions, and a sword could do very little, when Chernevog wished not.

" 'Veshka," he said, feeling her attraction, too; and felt her attention—felt the touch of the threads that flowed from her and felt the delirious little jolts as his strength flowed out of him—to her, who was a wizard no less than Chernevog: "Take it all," he said, with what breath he could spare, hoping she would go all the way to substance then: "Quickly. Take the sword. . . ."

But she might not have heard. The theft continued the same as the flow of threads from her to Chernevog, who walked up to them, a fair-haired man younger than himself, a handsome youth with a gentle face and a smile and out-stretched hand.

The hold on him broke, Eveshka's touch stopped, sudden freedom, sudden loss: he reached, reeling in a struggle for balance, after the sword—got it from its sheath as his right leg went out from under him, and went down to his knee with the point, trembling, aimed at Chernevog's heart.

Then his arm simply would not move further, while Chernevog brushed the blade aside to close about the hand that held the blade, Chernevog a faceless shadow against the stars, holding his hand, making him look up. "You don't want to hurt me," Chernevog said, the way Sasha would wish at him, just as gently, just as subtly: nothing wicked could be that gentle, or that reassuring, and he could not move.

Then it seemed for a heart-stopping moment the touch of a snake, and he recoiled, finding his sword in his hand and Chernevog close enough; he grabbed at Chernevog's arm—

But he found himself quite, quite incapable of moving then, Chernevog laying an arm along his shoulder, taking the sword ever so gently from his fingers, saying to Eveshka, "Don't do that, 'Veshka, he's the one will suffer for it. Do you want that?"

"No," she said.

"I know what you've come for. Shall I give it back to you? I can do that. I've kept it very well. I knew you'd come, soon or late."

"No!" she cried, and Pyetr wanted with all his heart to get his hands on Chernevog's throat, but he could not, could not even though Chernevog wished him slowly to stand up and look at Eveshka.

Her face was buried in her hands, her body heaving with quiet sobs.

"She knows everything she's done," Chernevog said, beside him, and put an arm around him. "A heart is nothing I'd want. But I can make her happy. And you—what do you want? Your young friend safe?"

"All of us," he muttered, knowing it was useless.

"I'll throw in Uulamets, if he'll be reasonable, ease poor 'Veshka's mind—yours, too. There's nothing so terrible about what I want. No tsar you could find so kind as I am—"

"Go to hell!" he said, and suddenly Eveshka went pale, spinning off threads of herself, faster and faster, until the starlight shone through her, until the threads wrapped themselves about him, the shocks multiplied and he heard her sobbing, "Kavi, Kavi, no!"

"On the other hand," Chernevog said, when the sparks cleared out of his vision and he was lying numb on the ground, "you can go to hell yourself, peasant lout, much, much more easily than I."

31

✳ ✳ ✳ ✳ Uulamets chanted softly, while the smoke
went up, and ghosts swirled through their
midst—but not within the smoke. Uulamets mixed ash and
herbs into one of his small pots, then took a small flint blade
and cut his wrist with it, bleeding into the bowl. "You," he
said to Sasha.

Sasha, head spinning from the smoke, set the knife to his
arm and brought it sharply down. Blood made a steady drip
into the pot—not so painful: but his hands shook as he gave
the items back.

"Vodka couldn't hurt," Uulamets said, then, and unstopped the jug and took a drink and added that, too, which
gave Sasha a queasy feeling as much as the bloodletting.
"Don't you know?" he asked, indignant, and Uulamets:

"No." Uulamets stopped the jug, stirred the mix with a
carved bit of bone, added moss and another powder. "It can
vary." He took a twig from the fire and poked the burning end
into the pot.

It went up with a puff of fire, and Uulamets hastily danced
it from one hand to the other, tamped in more herbs, then put
the hollow bone into it and covered the bowl with his hand
while he breathed the smoke through the bone.

He passed pot and bone to Sasha. "Breathe deep," he said,
and as Sasha did that, "deeper. —Good lad."

His chest burned; his eyes blurred from tears as Uulamets
took it back, sucked in several more puffs, then suddenly
leaned forward, grasped him by the shoulder and blew smoke
into his face, saying, again, "Breathe."

He did that. He did it twice and three times, and Uulamets

340

wished him—he felt it start—let go, breathe the smoke he breathed, deeper and deeper, back and forth—

Breathe out, breathe out, breathe out, hold nothing back—

Heart and soul, boy, breathe it out—

He was not governing his own body: Uulamets kept the breath coming out of him until he was fainting, falling against the old man's hands.

Then Uulamets made him breathe in, larger and deeper breaths, until there were enough of them and often enough that Sasha could clench his hands and move his limbs and know that it was his own volition, that he was back from wherever he had been—

But not without change. Not without a feeling of intimacy that made him afraid not to look into Uulamets' eyes, and have Uulamets' look into his, but he did that; because Uulamets wanted him to.

The will went out of him, then, his hand lifted without his knowing why, and the raven landed on his wrist, its wings fanning smoke that stung his eyes. It hopped then to Uulamets' outstretched hand and then to his shoulder, not objecting to the smoke or the fire, turning its single glittering eye toward him.

Not a natural creature, very, very old, its feathers dulled, half-blind before Uulamets had wished it to his service and given it his heart, having no living thing else.

"Better him than Draga," Uulamets said, and flung it aloft, a heavy flap of wings into the night above the fire. "I wasn't totally a fool."

Sasha knew other things, when he tried to think about Pyetr's whereabouts: he *wanted* to know where Pyetr was, and instead knew too much about Draga, and women—things he had never experienced in his life; and most of all about Eveshka and Uulamets and Chernevog, so that he plunged his head into his hands and felt the whole world spinning, his innocence despicable and dangerous—

He *wanted* to know about Pyetr, it was all he wanted, it was all that was left of everything he personally wanted—and he understood now that that wish had importance to people everywhere in the land, for generations and generations of Vojvodas and Kievs as far as he could think of—knew that the wish for Pyetr's safety above all else might give everything to Chernevog, who might already have killed him.

"Head over heart," Uulamets said, laying a hand on his shoulder, shaking him gently, and Sasha wiped his eyes and nodded, trying, *god!* trying not to wish anything for a while.

"Eventually you know," Uulamets said, "you're better off without a heart. My friend up there could carry both—"

Sasha shook his head, wiped his eyes again and swallowed the lump in his throat, trying to think, simply to think what to want.

That people be free and good-minded and safe from calamities: that wizards everywhere want that above all—

"Unfortunately," Uulamets said, "we have our faults. Our hearts aren't perfect. And when we're a damned, self-centered *fool* like our enemy, we're in trouble."

We should wish for the most right things, Sasha thought.

"That's very good," Uulamets said, "but in the meanwhile our enemy has more power than we do and we're not likely to get our way just by wishing, are we?"

"So what are we going to do?"

"The power of names," Uulamets said, and jabbed a finger at his chest. "Specificity over generality. When you wish for something specific and put a *name* on that one little thing—" Uulamets measured a tiny distance with his fingers, the size of a gnat. "That will go right through a wide, vague wish, like a stone through smoke. Poof. Wishes work best on unbalanced things."

"So it's who's smarter."

"And gifted. And what resources he has. Our enemy's betting on all three. He's a fool on a grand scale—but not in the little ones."

"Didn't he wish not to get caught stealing?"

"This book—" Uulamets laid a hand on the pack that he always kept close to him. "Is like that jug of yours. Like the raven. Nothing can happen to it so long as I live. Nothing will ever break that damned jug, till the day you die. Don't *do* things like that lightly, hear me?"

"The ghosts aren't bothering us—" Sasha realized of a sudden, off the thought of having failed in his recent wishes.

"He's thinking again. Or we've overpowered them by knowing what we want. Who knows?"

"Isn't he going to know?"

"Maybe. If he's paying attention."

"But aren't—" He did not want to quarrel with master Uulamets, but he had the most overwhelming anxiety about their waiting till morning.

"What you haven't learned," Uulamets said, lifting a cautionary finger, "what you haven't learned that you absolutely must, boy, is that a wizard can do more with a clear head at a distance than he can do, muddled and exhausted, close at hand—at least where it regards an enemy well-rested, comfortable, who's had ample while to decide what he's going to do about us. What we have to do—what we have to do is find his weaknesses and deny him the specific things he wants us to do. And get close enough and wise enough to see the specific things to undo him. Back and forth, you see. Rapidly. Very like any other kind of fighting. Dawn's coming soon. I'm going to wish us both to sleep."

"If that's a mistake, if that's what he's wishing us—"

Uulamets tapped him on the forehead. "You don't *want* something to happen. Vague as smoke. Wish instead with me: that we wake up safe, unrobbed, unthreatened, and in time, in spite of him. And shut up."

Uulamets tapped his forehead a second time, he felt himself going, and had wits left only enough to grab his blanket and dispose himself safely on the ground.

He doubted their safety: he tried with all the force he had to believe everything was safe while sleep was overwhelming him . . .

And was next aware of light falling on his face and of a rustling of dead leaves, before something landed on his chest and grabbed his collar.

"God!" he gasped, eyes wide, nose-to-button nose and eye-to-moonlike eye with a black fur-ball. "Babi!"

Babi shook at him, hissing, distraught—

Babi, who had been with Pyetr—

"Master Uulamets! —Get off me, Babi, I'm trying to get up!"

"One never knows," Uulamets said. "I wished for help, and to tell the stark truth, I'd hoped for leshys. . . ."

"But I sent him to stay with Pyetr," Sasha protested, gathering the dvorovoi into his arms and staggering to his feet. Babi hugged his neck and buried his face in his collar, all of which said to him that Babi was not in fact the help Uulamets had hoped for. Babi was help to no one at the moment. "Babi wouldn't have left him—"

"It's certainly no small thing that's driven him off," Uulamets said, and immediately began gathering up his pack. "Babi! Come here!"

Babi vanished from Sasha's arms, to the dismay of both of them—simply ceased to be there, or anywhere in their vicinity. "Babi!" Sasha cried softly, casting about to find him; and from Uulamets knew only that it was a very badly used, very frightened Babi—apt to return to them at any moment, or whatever Babi considered a moment, but gone for now to a Place magical creatures could reach and no magician could.

Where is that? Sasha's wondered; and Uulamets, shrugging on his pack, said, "They know. We don't. I'm not sure we'd want to be there. Pack up and come on."

Uulamets believed Babi's appearance meant something direly wrong, that came through all too strongly, and Sasha tried to keep himself from panic as they hiked at the best pace they could manage along the overgrown bank, following the stream for a road.

One or the other of them—he was sure it was Uulamets, because he had never held such terrible ideas in his life— thought what a wizard could do to an ordinary man like Pyetr, if that wizard were vindictive: whichever of the two of them was responsible for that thought tried not to dwell on it— Sasha was sure he was trying, so maybe his own imagination had grown too wide and too terrible since he and master Uulamets had—

—had done whatever had happened last night, which left his head crammed with constantly surfacing things he had never wanted to know, understandings too fast and too terrible

even for Uulamets, who kept telling him be quiet, stop thinking at him.

Uulamets himself was upset, Uulamets tried with all his
good sense not to strike out at him or flinch from him: "Grow
up, boy!" Uulamets said to him; and Sasha tried as hard as he
could to be a man, the way he understood a man ought to be—

Which was Pyetr, so far as he had ever wanted to be anyone.

That was not by far master Uulamets' choice: Uulamets
thought Pyetr a bad man and undependable and self-indulgent.

Wrong, Sasha thought.

"Besides," he said aloud, "he's ordinary, and we're not—
you have to allow for that."

"I don't have to," Uulamets said, "and I won't."

Sasha thought something then he had no desire at all to
say to Uulamets: *You'd have been better off if you had had
somebody like Pyetr. You wouldn't have been lonely all your
life and* somebody *would have liked you.*

The old man said harshly, "And made mistakes like yours
and his, young fool." Meanwhile Uulamets was thinking, My
own are enough—because he bitterly remembered Draga and
how beautiful she had been—how for Draga, he had almost
made the mistake of calling back his heart, a long, long time
ago, where she could have gotten hold of it.

That's what Eveshka did, Sasha thought helplessly, and
tried not to: it greatly upset Uulamets, as if in all these years
he had never remembered that feeling, until he had—Uulamets' thought—a damned boy pushing at him, making him
remember too far back—

To being alone; and the fire killing his parents; and uncle
Fedya; and Uulamets' father taking him deep into the woods
when he was very small and giving him to an old woman, who
was a wizard, and crazed, and very wicked and spiteful—

It was Sasha who wanted not to remember now, things far
worse than uncle Fedya could ever think of, wishes for harm
on someone, wishes to convince someone he was a failure and
worthless, so he could wish he were dead—

"Worse than any beating, boy," Uulamets muttered as
they struggled with the undergrowth. "You should have lived
with old Malenkova. Crazy as a loon and mean as winter."

Uulamets was thinking by then of Eveshka and how he had failed with her: he had truly meant to teach her in a better, kinder way; but that had been a mistake: she had been willful as Draga.

Even so he wished, quite dangerously, that he could save her—

Because a damned boy held on to a heart that was going to ruin them both, against all advice.

"Stop it," Uulamets said, "fool!" and turned with every intent to teach a boy a lesson—

Deserved, Sasha thought: but Uulamets flinched from hitting him in the face, grabbed him instead by his collar, still aching to beat him the way his teacher had him, for his own sake, and all the world's sake, until he gained a different view of things and stopped being a shallow-minded, flittering boy—

I'm not, Sasha thought; and wondered, having had all those years dealing with Fedya Misurov, who did not think half so deeply, or deserve half so much respect: Why don't you just take it from me? You could.

That made Uulamets want to hit him for a different reason, which Uulamets himself did not understand, except it misapprehended him, and made him out a good man: Uulamets did not want people liking him, or expecting things a wizard could not in good conscience owe anybody, not his daughter, not a student, certainly not a light-witted scoundrel like Pyetr Kochevikov—

"Who's probably dead, damn you," Uulamets muttered. "You'd better make up your mind to count him gone, because he's your weakness, boy. You're going to flinch when you shouldn't, because you're too soft, you're too weak, and the one favor you can do me for the rest of this hike, *boy!*, is to watch the woods around you, look at the leaves, *think* about the leaves and nothing but the leaves, hear me? Or if your friend is alive you'll destroy every last chance we have to do anything for anybody."

"Yes, sir," Sasha said meekly, knowing what the old man in his experience was saying: no doubts, no quibbles, no holding back. He tried to think about the trees, the leaves, the sound of the wind: sometimes—Uulamets angrily pulled him back from it—about the ghosts and what their absence meant.

"Pay attention!" Uulamets said with a painful jerk at his arm. "Scatterbrain, think of *nothing*."

He understood, he apologized, he slipped with Uulamets into nothing and beyond that into nowhere, while the light dimmed, the air grew chill, and rain fell as a light patter among the leaves. "Don't wish not," master Uulamets said. "Be patient. Make no noise."

So one watched where one was walking, one admired the water drops, one thought of beads on a branch, the rim of beads on a new leaf—anything that touched eyes, touched mind, being totally *here* and wanting *nothing*, and thereby totally silent in the woods.

But there came a change in the woods. They walked through a curtain of brush into a dead region, trees so long dead their limbs were white and naked, their trunks only patched with bark.

Want nothing, Sasha thought: he had had that knack once, back home among ordinary people, for their protection. Want nothing, wish nothing away, simply watch and see and accept what came.

Tree after dead tree, a forest not only dead but long dead, their stream flowing between banks of barren earth, utterly lifeless—not so much as moss or leaves out of this tributary of the river, not so much as a lichen on a tree. Barren earth, dust, that the misting rain turned to mud—

Master Uulamets believed he knew the way, and Sasha did not question that, only wondered how he knew—and recalled long ago when the ferryboat had traveled further, and Malenkova's house, Uulamets' own teacher—

Her house was here, beside the old road, he thought, and recollected days of trade and travelers—

He shied away from that thought as Uulamets' anger warned him, because it was dangerous to think about their enemy.

Consider only the trees.

They walked farther and farther into the barren ground, amid what began to be an open, level strip along the stream, where no tree had grown, seemingly, when the forest was green: the vanished road out of the east, the route of traders in times too long ago for a boy to remember. Malenkova's old house.

Tenanted again.

One wanted to wonder—

"No," Uulamets said. "Think about the rain. Think about the sky."

"I—" Sasha began, and saw something through the gray haze of trees, distant, moving toward them, ghostly white. He wanted to know what it was.

Uulamets grabbed his arm and stopped him in his tracks, and all he knew was a muddle, as if wishes conflicted, his, Uulamets', the god knew: his wits were too scrambled to make sense of it, but his eyes saw a desperate, white-shirted man coming toward them.

It looked—Father Sky, it looked like Pyetr, *was* Pyetr—

"Wait," Uulamets said, and jerked his arm painfully the instant he saw blood on Pyetr's shirt and moved to disobey. "Scatterwits! No! Look at it!"

Uulamets *wished*, with everything both of them had, and Pyetr—

—melted, headlong, into a bear-shape shambling toward them.

"No!" Sasha cried, Uulamets wished, and it melted to a black puddle that flowed into the ground.

"That's our shape-shifter," Uulamets said, still holding Sasha's arm, wishing the thing back to whatever hole it had come from. "Know what it is and it can't work its tricks. The power of names, boy."

If it had taken Pyetr's shape, Sasha thought, trembling now it was gone, if it did that, if it was one of their enemy's creatures and not the vodyanoi's, then their enemy knew who Pyetr was. Their enemy might have wished him—

Uulamets gripped his arm, hurting him. "Save it. You're right, he does know more than we'd like. Don't think about it. Most of all don't believe what attracts you, not in this game, do you understand me now, boy? Catch me once, not twice with that trick."

I can't help it, Sasha thought. If he aimed at Pyetr, Pyetr may be with him—

With Eveshka—

Uulamets' fingers pulled at Sasha's arm as he started walking again: Uulamets was angry, angry at his own anger: smothering it, killing it with long-practiced indifference. "He's trying to shake us," Uulamets muttered, and let him go to walk beside him. "He's not going to. No tempers, boy, no resentments, what seems, isn't necessarily so, you understand me? Believe things aren't the worst, they won't be the worst, quiet your damned self-doubt, boy, you can do anything you want to do, just want it enough and don't stop till you've got it."

Pyetr, Sasha thought, and tried to unwish that—as the raven swooped low, winged past them like a shadow and went aloft again, down the road. God, no, he thought, helpless totally to *wish* no. God, master Uulamets, I'm sorry, I'm *sorry*—

"Fine help," Uulamets said, flinging his arm aloft as they walked. "—Find my daughter, that's what you're good for, you feathered thief! Go!"

"I didn't mean it," Sasha said miserably.

"Wish confusion on our enemies," Uulamets said under his breath. "And trust the bird. One of those things a magician can only do a few times in his life, don't ask me why I picked a damned crow—ask me why I didn't choose a bear, a wolf at the least."

The bird had been Uulamets' pet when he was a boy. That came through, along with a memory of the house where they were going, a ramshackle place of towers, a terrible old woman intending the raven's death—

A scared young wizard, desperately protecting the only living thing he loved—

Uulamets shut that away, like a door slamming, with the thought that their enemy's attack had already had its effect, Pyetr was their point of division, Pyetr was the unstable point—

Sasha thought—

Things change that can *change*—

32

✠ ✠ ✠ ✠ Pyetr did not remember arriving at Chernevog's house. He only recollected a screen of dead hedges and gray, dead trees, hiding a towered and rambling structure as decrepit as Uulamets' cottage; remembered walking toward it, not of his own accord, until his knees gave way under him and spilled him helplessly on his face in the dust. He was sure that that much was real.

He thought that at one point, in a room of polished wood, Chernevog had spoken to him again, saying with wizardly persuasion, "You might still redeem yourself with me—" He thought he had refused then—refused, though he was less and less sure he was right, or sane, or that he had chosen right in leaving Sasha to Uulamets.

"Come now," Chernevog had said again, or at some other time. "Isn't it foolish to fight me, when all I want is to give you everything you want? Listen to me, that's all."

"Sure," he had said, "why not?"

"But you have to believe in me," Chernevog had said, "and you're lying, aren't you? Stop pulling away from me. Do you want to live, fool?"

"Yes," he said, eventually, screamed it, because Chernevog insisted, then tucked himself up on the floor where he had fallen and held his stomach—

Or it was long ago in Vojvoda, on a dark lane with a couple of bad losers—who had robbed him besides—

One bully's like another, Pyetr thought now bitterly. Never satisfied, *never* satisfied, no matter how much you give them.

"Yes," he said when Chernevog asked, or "No," when

Chernevog insisted; "I swear!" when Chernevog half-suffo-
cated him; anything that Chernevog wanted, he agreed to,
because he had no choice if Chernevog moved his limbs,
stopped his breathing, dashed him to the ground—no choice
and no effect to his wishes, for good or ill.

At last he felt cold against his face, and heard Eveshka pleading, "Pyetr, Pyetr, get up, hurry."

He did try. Every joint hurt. "Please," she whispered,
"please, quickly, quickly, do what I tell you. He's asleep.
You've got to get out of here."

He hauled himself up by the edge of a tottering bench that
made a sound like thunder, got his knees under him and
shoved himself to his feet. Eveshka tried, with little touches
that could not touch him, to assist his balance, guiding him
through an archway of carved fishes and up a short flight of
steps.

"Where's my sword?" he asked, catching at the doorframe,
at a shelf then, for balance, within a little of knocking a pot
off it. His heart thumped as the vessel rocked and settled.
"Where's my sword? Where is he?"

"It's too dangerous, no! *I* can't get past that door. He's
protected! Just get away—"

"Where's the damn sword?" he insisted, but she *wanted*
him out the door, wanted him to get to Sasha and her father—
wanted him simply out of her way:

"Help my father!" she said. "Help where you have a
chance: you can't face him, you can't do anything against him,
you can't even get in there. Just get out of here! It's all you
can do, Pyetr!"

He saw his sword by the door, staggered that direction and
picked it up, having then to lean against the wall, his knees
shaking under him.

"Please," Eveshka said, and touched his face, tears shimmering in her eyes. "Please! You're no help to me, you only
hurt me—"

"It's a trick," he said. "Dammit, it's a trick!" He struck
out at her, passed his hand through cold: that *was* like Ev-

eshka—who recoiled from him, hands clasped in front of her mouth.

"Get out of here! Please."

The door beside him blasted open on a gust of wind and damp straight from the outside. He looked out on gray daylight, the tops of dead trees beyond a porch railing. Misting rain gusted into the room. Wind knocked something rattling, with a sound to wake the dead.

He turned his head in alarm, saw Eveshka's eyes widen, her mouth open in that instant as something blocked the wind at his back.

He whirled around face to monstrous face with the vodyanoi's head swaying snakelike above the porch rail, sleek and black and glistening with rain.

"Well, well," Hwiuur said, "come ahead, come outside. The master certainly doesn't mind. He truly doesn't. He said you'd be coming."

Pyetr moved to slam the door shut, but a rain-laden gust blew it back at him, and the vodyanoi struck through the doorway like the serpent he was, blocking it from closing as his strong, small hands seized Pyetr's ankle.

"Stop!" Eveshka was screaming. "Kavi! Kavi, no, stop it! Make it stop! It's going to kill him—"

Pyetr gave up holding on, slung the sheath off his sword and beat at the River-thing's head and body as it dragged him out into the light. His hand ached and went numb; he all but dropped the sword, sky and boards changing places as wet coils flowed over him. The sword did leave his hand. Pain ran up that arm to his ribs, where Hwiuur's weight pressed.

"Got you at last," Hwiuur said, wrapping around him.

Then the vodyanoi flinched upward and hissed: "Salt! Treachery!"

They could see the towers through the woods, a huge house that might have graced some great city, sitting instead in desolation, weathered gray as the barren trees about it.

"There," said Uulamets, out of breath.

And Sasha, with a pounding of his heart, with far too many

unwelcome memories of this place and Uulamets' own boy-hood: "Do we just walk up to it?"

"Until someone objects," Uulamets said, and struggled up the rise the land took here, up the mist-slick and muddy slope. He faltered, and Sasha without thinking steadied him, not surprised when the old man shoved him off at the top, not offended at the anger and the concentration that refused outside interventions. Quiet, that concentration wished on them both: invisibility, unexpectedness.

It encouraged Kavi Chernevog, told him reassuring things about his own power, his own cleverness—it told him Ilya Uulamets was old and failing, and that there was no reason to worry in this encounter Chernevog had long schemed to provoke. Every power hereabouts was afraid of Chernevog, even the leshys.

It was easy to believe that, it was especially easy because that was what Chernevog sent out to them, and they echoed back to him with small slight changes for his own suspicious, heartless character:

Beware of Eveshka.

She doesn't love you. Could you expect that? She never did: she only wanted power for herself.

Then a soft, insinuating doubt came from the other direction, the certainty that Pyetr was alive and with Chernevog.

Sasha faltered, felt a cold, cruel impulse to distrust Uulamets, remembering that Uulamets would spare nothing, not even Eveshka, certainly not him or Pyetr in his purposes, and rescuing Pyetr was out of the question.

Then Uulamets caught his arm and said, "Watch yourself, watch yourself, boy. That's him, too. You can't believe a thing."

But he was increasingly certain where Pyetr was, next a tree in a yard he had never, except through Uulamets' eyes, seen in his life; and he was certain that Eveshka had given way to Chernevog and accepted his gift of strength, Pyetr having no more to spare. . . .

As for Sasha Misurov, the seductive whisper came, if he would simply stand aside, if he would do that, then Chernevog would make him powerful in his own right, over all the people in the world that had ever despised him, because Chernevog did not discount him, Chernevog recognized his presence with Uulamets and knew that, but for youth, he was far more than Uulamets—

A boy who would pledge himself to Chernevog would be part of Chernevog's own household, along with Eveshka, along with Pyetr, ageless, ruling over cities and kingdoms if he desired it—

Or he could die, seeing Pyetr die before him—

"If Pyetr's there," Uulamets breathed as they walked, "Chernevog won't kill him, not while he's got you upset. *Trees*, boy!"

He was worth *nothing*, at the end, except as a hostage, a weapon on Chernevog's side, a point of leverage between Uulamets and Sasha, who were going to walk into this place—

Chernevog perhaps wanted him to know that, or Hwiuur did; or perhaps he had wit enough occasionally to know some things without a wizard to explain it to him: he no longer was sure where his thoughts came from, sitting where Hwiuur had dragged him, in the mud of the yard, at the foot of a dead tree—once Chernevog had gotten from him the little packet of salt that Sasha had given him at the start of their trek.

God, he had never once thought of it; and maybe that was the kind of luck a wizard made for himself. But to have Chernevog take it from him and throw it contemptuously into the mud—

Smiling. —God!

"Hold him," Chernevog said then to the vodyanoi; and to Pyetr: "They're still coming. The old man's tricked your young friend, quite the way he'd have used me or his own daughter, ultimately—gotten hold of him in a way your friend wouldn't choose for himself, I assure you. You *might* pull him away."

To you, Pyetr thought, and turned his face against the smooth, cold bole of the tree, expecting pain for that refusal.

"Don't you owe him to do that?" Chernevog asked.

Only stop fighting me, Chernevog kept saying, in countless ways: I have everything. I'll give you anything you want. . . .

Eveshka had tried, god, longer than flesh and bone could hold out, while Chernevog who could have killed him with a spare thought kept him alive—

"Eveshka's reconsidered," Chernevog said. "I think you understand that. Shouldn't you do the same? You could save your young friend, who has so much potential. You could amount to something. You could do so much good with your life. And you do *nothing.*"

Pyetr wept—finally, while Chernevog walked off to the house, and the exhaustion and the doubts about Chernevog and Uulamets both overwhelmed him. He hung his head and tried to get his wits about him, ignoring the soft slither of Hwiuur's coils constantly circling the tree, occasionally sliding over his legs, Hwiuur whispering in his cold, sibilant voice: "Not so glib now, are you? Not so clever after all. Such a disappointment you've proved to your friends. And to the woman."

I'm not a disappointment, Pyetr thought, remembering 'Mitri, remembering pronouncements from every father in Vojvoda. —Everyone expected me to be a failure.

"They're coming," Hwiuur said, and nudged him with his head, jaws against his cheek. "Look, look, just atop the hill."

Sasha, with Uulamets: he could make them out through the brush, under the gray and flickering sky—the both of them walking steadily toward the house, whether by their own will or not.

"You'll find out, now," Hwiuur said, resting his jaw on Pyetr's shoulder, gusting dank breath into his face.

"God!" Pyetr flinched from under that weight. "Get away from me! *Sasha, dammit, run, for the god's sake!*"

"Pyetr?" Sasha's voice came drifting across the distance, thin and frightened. He saw the boy start to run then.

Toward him.

I'm a damn jinx, Pyetr thought, cursing himself—

In a wizard-quarrel, where every player but himself could load the dice—

A gambler's son knew a crooked game when he saw it.

"He's in the house!" Pyetr yelled, and quicker than he could get it out, the vodyanoi's coils went about him, tightening. "Chernevog's in the house: get *him!*"

Sasha had stopped cold, looking at the house, Pyetr saw that as his ribs began to creak—joints cracking with his effort to keep the coils apart.

Suddenly something small, winged, and black flurried into the space between his face and Hwiuur's, driving its beak again and again at the vodyanoi's eyes.

And a heart-stopping flash of light and shock burst in the yard, with a crack of thunder.

Sasha sprawled in the mud, scrambled toward master Uulamets while burning bits of the bathhouse were still showering down around them.

While—he thought, Uulamets thought, having wished Chernevog's bolt aside—the lightnings were reshaping themselves over their heads: their hair was rising on end, skin prickled the way it had when Uulamets had realized that one was coming.

Uulamets had wanted it toward the house, but Sasha had simultaneously flinched, disagreed, feverishly compromised on something belonging to Chernevog—

Remembering his parents' voices behind a sheet of fire—

"Sasha!" he heard Pyetr screaming, then, while the lightning aimed at them again, while Uulamets a second time *wanted* the house—

Sasha wished *with* him of a sudden, scared, knowing Pyetr was in trouble.

The sky tore, the world tore, a seam of bright light. The east tower of the house went white and showered bits of burning wood.

Fire leapt up in the shattered tower and at places on the roof, fire spread on the winds of Uulamets' intention—wind rushing toward the house.

"Lightning likes tall things," Uulamets muttered, as Sasha wished a sudden, stolen skirl of wind and sparks toward the vodyanoi—wished Pyetr *free*—while more lightning was readying itself and Uulamets was trying to concentrate their attention and fight Chernevog's direction of it in less than a heartbeat.

Lightning intended them, the house, them again—struck

the mud of the yard beyond them. Sasha flung up his arms to shield himself, the shock flung him flat on his back, and when he scrambled to his knees and to his feet he could see nothing of the tree and Pyetr but that rip in the world, floating over and over through his vision, heard nothing but the roar in his ears—blind and deafened and helpless to know what had happened.

"Pyetr!" he cried, while Uulamets was damning him for a fool, Uulamets was directing his attention to the house, to Chernevog, somewhere in that direction, not dead, and not through with them. . . .

Hwiuur writhed away, lashing wildly with his coils, and Pyetr lurched upward and sprawled in the mud, shocked in every joint, scrambling away from the creature on his knees and one arm, the other collapsing under him, broken for all he knew: he only moved as fast as he could manage, half-blind, all but deafened.

Then his hand fell on something in the mud, a sodden lump tied with string, and he recognized what luck or a wizard's wish had put under him—with the vodyanoi hissing like steam off iron, thumping about and searching blindly toward him.

He clutched the packet in his fist, rolled over and sat there as it came at him, tore at the string with his teeth, and failing that, feverishly, at the leather.

It came open, as Hwiuur kept coming, as Hwiuur's cold breath hit him in the face.

He flung the salt wide, scattering it toward the River-thing.

Hwiuur screamed, reared back, Sasha *knew* what was happening: Uulamets saw it; and flinging an arm about him, Uulamets wished his sight clear, his ears to hear—

"Boy!" Uulamets said, while the light that blinded his eyes turned red, and black, and became a haze. "He's coming out, boy, Chernevog's coming out, never mind the River-thing—*pay attention!*"

Sasha blinked, wiped streaming eyes, and, looking toward

357

the house, saw a fair-haired young man arrive on the porch and walk down toward them, holding a book in his arms.

"Pyetr!" Sasha called out, wanting him with them, suddenly, obsessively, fearing to have Pyetr out of sight: the feeling the lightnings brought was growing again, and of a sudden ghosts swirled about them, cold and shrieking. The lightning was going—was aiming in Pyetr's vicinity—

It struck the tree instead, and the earth itself shook under their feet.

"Chernevog!" Uulamets shouted into the wind, wanting him, wanting his enemy's attention *and* Sasha's with unequivocal force. "Remember the teaching, *remember*, young fool, the things I told you about recklessness—"

A thin, blond-haired boy came to the river house, a sullen lad who held more power than was good for any young wizard, arrogant in his ways—

Dangerous, Sasha thought. That boy *had* been a fool, gifted as he was. . . .

Uulamets said, aloud, shouting against the wind: "I'll teach you a new lesson, boy! There *is* a way to undo the past!"

"You've lost your wits, old man!"

"It's very simple, Kavi, lad: know its effects; and cancel them!"

"Do you want the past, old man? I'll give you the past!" Memories of Chernevog's came, *Draga*, not Uulamets sitting by the hearth, with an open book: Chernevog a younger boy, no more than ten or twelve; or again, sixteen, in Draga's bed—

"Draga's lover!" Uulamets said aloud, and laughed with a sarcasm that made Sasha wince. "Father god, the woman leaves my bed, and takes to seducing pretty boys, no less! God, I should have known: you were too precocious. So it was all Draga. Did *she* set you to stealing, boy?"

The wailing of the ghosts faltered. "It wasn't," Chernevog said, "all Draga."

"Ask yourself that."

Another faltering.

"Poor boy," Uulamets said.

"Poor *boy*," Chernevog cried, and Sasha *wished* Chernevog's attention centered on them both, wished Chernevog to know what they both knew of Draga; what he knew of Uula-

mets—himself, Chernevog's successful replacement in Uulamets' household—

What they both knew of consequences and wild magic,
that from Uulamets—

The lightnings tried to gather. The air shivered with the
power, with the ghosts screaming about them.

"I killed her," Chernevog said, with his hair and theirs
standing up, the wind swirling at them. He looked like a crazy
man. "I killed her when she went too far with me, old man.
—I slept with your *wife*, don't you care about that?"

"No more than she did," Uulamets said. "She used you,
boy. She ate you alive."

The lightning was going to strike, was going to strike,
them or Chernevog. Sasha felt his hair rise, felt sparks dancing
between his fingers—

And wished it onto the bathhouse again, a course no one
was resisting, no one else expecting it. The ground shook, the
ghosts screamed.

But of a sudden Pyetr was coming through the roiling
smoke behind Chernevog: Sasha saw him, betrayed him with
that quick, repented thought—and suddenly realized Pyetr a
danger to them, diverting his attention from Uulamets, from
their own defense, while more lightning crackled in the air.

Uulamets himself *wished*, then, and of a sudden—

Fed everything into Sasha's hands, power that fed straight
through to Pyetr, caught for a heart-beat motionless and then
moving, Chernevog having caught the last lightning flash in
his eyes: Pyetr hit him while he was turning, a single blow
with a rock, in the same moment Uulamets himself fell
against Sasha, Sasha distractedly, vainly trying to hold the old
man as he slid through his arms to the ground.

Chernevog fell, Uulamets had fallen, the ghosts screamed
away into silence, and Sasha was on his knees facing Pyetr
over Uulamets and Chernevog both, still feeling Uulamets'
memories, but no longer feeling the source of them—only an
overwhelming silence where a presence had been.

"Grandfather?" Pyetr asked, in the real-world crackle and
roar of the burning house.

"I think he's dead," Sasha said, numbly, and saw Pyetr take
up the rock again to break Chernevog's skull once for all.

Maybe it was his wish that stopped Pyetr. Maybe it was Pyetr's own, that brought his hand down slowly, and had sweat glistening on his face. "What in the god's name do we do with him?"

Memory said, so strongly Sasha shivered: Wish only good.

Memory stretched out his hand, the way Uulamets had done with him: he gently touched Chernevog on the brow, wishing him a long and dreamless sleep.

"Pyetr!" Eveshka cried from the direction of the fire: Sasha could see her, on the descent from the house, clinging to the rail and hurrying, smoke-smudges on her face, her tattered blue gown. Pyetr scrambled up and stumbled, catching himself with difficulty, but Eveshka ran, ran all-out toward him and into his arms, saying, "Sasha? *Papa?*"

Memory said, so clearly Sasha felt Uulamets die all over again: *Do* it, boy; and take care of my daughter—

Memory said: To raise the dead—always costs the living.

And Sasha thought: He meant to kill Pyetr—or me. He didn't care. He didn't die for her. *I* had the way to Chernevog's back: he had to give me everything to win, that was all.

He did not know what to say to Eveshka.

Finally he did say, because he wanted it over with, and he did not want to exist behind a mask with her: "He passed me everything."

But he did not think Pyetr would understand.

"Help me get the fires out," he said, when Eveshka said nothing, nor wept, only stood there, pale and distraught. She looked him in the eyes, then, and he stood up and looked at her with too many and too confused memories.

A long, long moment like that.

"What's going on?" Pyetr said. "What's happening, dammit?"

"The fire," Sasha said to Eveshka. "Help me, *please*, Eveshka."

They found the raven dead, a sodden lump of feathers near the splintered tree, and a long, long wallow down to the streamside.

Pyetr gathered it up, smoothed its feathers, felt a genuine

sorrow for the creature that had defended him, even if it was a stupid bird; and he took it back and laid it beside Uulamets, where they were making a cairn around him, saying, defensively, "It ought to be with him."

He had mixed feelings about the gesture then, because it made Eveshka cry, and she had not, until he said that.

33

✻ ✻ ✻ ✻ They made a small fire of shingles and bits
of shattered wood, close by Chernevog's
sleeping body, to watch him as dark gathered—and close
enough to him to keep him from the chill of the wind, the
warmth from the charred timbers of the house growing less
and less as the day waned, and blowing away from them, along
with the smoke. It was a thoroughly stupid charity, Pyetr said
as much: "Let him freeze," was Pyetr's comment.

But Pyetr had not broken Chernevog's skull before, and
Pyetr might indeed say things, but being a natural man was
not obliged to mean them; and Pyetr was less willing to kill
Chernevog now that his blood had cooled than he had been
with the rock in his hand, or he would have done it. It was
either Pyetr's own reasons that stopped him, or, the god only
knew and Sasha did not at this point, it was himself or Eveshka
consistently forbidding it, all common sense and perhaps—
the point Sasha could not yet work out for himself—all responsibility to the contrary.

So they sat, Pyetr so sore he could hardly get up once he
had sat down, Eveshka exhausted and himself finding bruises
and sore spots he had no memory of getting, with no assurance
of safety. Sasha dared not even take his attention off their
prisoner for a moment, for fear of some trick on Chernevog's
part. Pyetr had no defense, except him and Eveshka; Eveshka
he was afraid to trust, counting all the years she had been at
least marginally Chernevog's, and he had no idea what to do,
except hold on, stay awake, try to rest as much as he could.

But it seemed a good idea, as Eveshka had said, to search
the house before dark, to be sure there was nothing left of

Chernevog's household—to find his heart, if they could, and keep it to be sure of him.

"If there ever was one," Pyetr muttered.

There must have been, Sasha thought, but Draga had surely gotten it long ago; and Draga was dead, likely taking it with her—which might have ended all hope for Chernevog, who knew?

Still, he did not say that, nor try to influence Eveshka's thoughts—though he waited in anguish where he had to wait during that search, watching over Chernevog, and wished very hard for their safety, especially Pyetr's, while Pyetr and Eveshka searched as much of the house as they could reach. He wished to the best of his wisdom that they would find what answers existed and that the two of them would be safe in that maze of unstable, still-smoking timbers, but his heart jumped at every crash and fall of timber from the burned wing.

They only came back, at the very edge of dark, with smoke-smelling blankets, a very substantial basket of food, a bucket of clean water from the kitchens, which had been spared the fire, Eveshka said, and a bundle of clean, dry clothing, Pyetr already having washed and changed his, and Eveshka having pulled one of Chernevog's tunics on over her gown. "At least there's this," Pyetr said, "if nothing else."

It actually seemed a great deal, on a cold and desperate night. Sasha gratefully pulled a second blanket over him for modesty as well as for warmth and began to change his clothes, which were stiff with mud in patches, and still damp in the seams.

Meanwhile, in the deepening dark, with Chernevog still sleeping the other side of the fire, Pyetr matter-of-factly put water on to boil and made tea, while he took to shaving. Eveshka warmed up the bread they had found, and offered it to them with a little honey.

"He's very well-stocked," Pyetr said. "I doubt it's wishes. Common banditry, most like." Pyetr finished his chin, between bites of bread, and the tea Eveshka had poured him, then wiped the razor on his knee, held up a finger, gulped down the bit in his mouth and reached into a pocket, as if he had only then remembered something.

He pulled out a bauble on a chain, that glanced red and

glittered gold in the firelight. He smiled, caught it in his hand again, then tossed it to Sasha.

"You shouldn't—" Sasha said.

"What's the difference—food or gold? A whole box of that stuff and not a heart to be had. Not a rat alive in there. Nor any domovoi or anything of the kind."

"They're too honest," Eveshka said, and then said forlornly: "Where's Babi gone? Have you seen him?"

Sasha shrugged uncomfortably, and tossed the bauble back to Pyetr, with the thought that Pyetr was probably very right, there was no difference and there was no reason not to take whatever they wanted—if there was any use for such things. "I don't know," he said to Eveshka. "I think he's all right. I saw him yesterday, scared out of his wits. He's probably home by now." He hoped so, fervently, and cast a look at the firelit brush around them, wondering what Babi might have met, following Pyetr, or whether Pyetr had seen it.

"I don't suppose you could wish *us* home," Pyetr said, reaching—with a wince—after the vodka jug.

"One doesn't—" Sasha began to explain, about nature and consequences, but Pyetr said:

"Or wish us the tsar's horses."

Pyetr was laughing at him. He was glad, he was very glad to see that, and told himself his anxiousness was exhaustion. "We'll get there."

"We'll get there." Pyetr motioned with the bottle toward him, offering him a cupful, but Sasha shook his head. Eveshka took a little, sipped it and shut her eyes with a weary sigh.

"Food and sleep," she said, and then drew a little breath and frowned as if some dark thought had touched her, looking down at the cup in her hands as if she could quite as easily cry.

What's wrong? Sasha wanted to know—distrusting such sudden shifts, here, in this place, with Chernevog asleep so close to them.

"It's so good," she said, aloud; but answered him, alone: I was remembering—what it felt like to need food and sleep— and being dead—

Forget, he wished her, perhaps too strongly; or perhaps nothing he could do was strong enough.

A frown had come to Pyetr's face. He took another sip of the vodka, cast a second, worried glance at Eveshka, then said, "We've got to think about getting out of here."

"It's not that easy," Sasha said.

"I know it's not that easy! What do we do with *him*, in the meanwhile? Carry him back like that? Lock him in the shed? Stand him in the garden?"

Sasha cast his own worried glance at Eveshka, who sat with her elbow on her knee, sipping her cup and certainly thinking about what Pyetr was saying.

Stand him in the garden? Ignore Chernevog's existence? Hope the spell lasts?

A frown knit Eveshka's brow, fire shimmering in her eyes: a willful, self-centered girl, Uulamets' memories said, unasked, offering the image of a sixteen-year-old slipping out of the house to meet with Chernevog; a ten-year-old sulking and stormy, insisting on her own way; a flaxen-haired, blue-eyed child, dancing down a summer road, so happy, so innocent one's heart would ache—

She's none of those things now, he thought; but she's been all of them.

A wizard. Wanting Pyetr—wanting him to love her, wanting so much—

Would he, without that? Would he forget about Kiev, and stay, without that?

God, how much of it is *me* holding him? And how much of it is me wanting her for his sake?

"What about Chernevog?" Pyetr asked again. "How long will he sleep? What do we *do* with him?"

So long as he lives, neither one of them is safe, nothing is safe, *Chernevog's* the instability. . . .

God, I'm not thinking straight; I can't sleep, I daren't sleep tonight—I haven't the surety of anything.

Can he be waking?

Sasha dropped his head against his hands, thinking that, winning, they had not, after all, won. He could not justify Chernevog surviving, wicked as he was, he could not justify a mercy that endangered others, seeing what Chernevog had done, and in his exhaustion he could not see the river house

again, nor staying with Pyetr and Eveshka, where he wanted
to be, where he wanted dangerously much to be . . .

No.

Which meant leaving Pyetr to Eveshka, alone, trusting her
to take proper care of him—when he at least had known unmagical folk, had lived with them as one of them, for the god's
sake, which Eveshka never had, and that was a terrible danger
to him, hardly less than Chernevog.

But without killing Chernevog—without sleeping enough
to have his wits about him—without the confidence to hold
Chernevog *while* he got that rest—

God, he thought, and wanted Chernevog asleep, staying
asleep—

"He's slipping," he whispered to Pyetr. Sweat was cold on
his face, in the wind out of the dark. "God, help me, I'm not
holding him—"

" 'Veshka—" Pyetr said, looking toward her in alarm.
" 'Veshka, help—"

The instability grew less, that was the only way he could
think it. Pyetr's hand stayed on his shoulder a moment.

"All right?"

"I've got him." Sasha drew a large breath, let it go slowly.
"It's all right."

Pyetr still looked worried. Sasha hit him lightly on the
knee. "Don't do that. Don't worry. It's all right."

Pyetr bit his lip. "Look. We've got him. Eveshka's all right.
Get some rest."

Sasha wiped his eyes. "I don't know what to do, I only
know I daren't take a chance."

"On what? On 'Veshka? She'll be all right. Get some sleep.
We'll both stay awake—I'm better than you are. . . .

"No."

"I can *want* to stay awake, all right?"

"Listen, we're getting out of here tomorrow. If you want
that blackguard, I'll *carry* him back."

This, while Pyetr was doing well to carry himself, and they
were too spent to patch everything. Sasha stared at him
bleakly.

"We'll make a raft or something," Pyetr said. "It's downstream."

"Don't distract me."

"Don't do that to me, dammit! Stop it!"

Sasha caught himself, dropped his head into his hands.

"I'm sorry," Pyetr said quietly. "Sasha?"

"I'm all right. I'm all right, just—don't push me."

"He's not all right," he heard Pyetr say; felt Eveshka then, wishing at him, *afraid* of him—and perhaps she spoke to Pyetr, because all at once Pyetr seized his arm and shook at him, saying harshly, "Sasha? What did he do to you? What did Uulamets do?"

He did not want to answer. He damned Eveshka's cold honesty. Or whatever made her betray him. Perhaps it was even fear for Pyetr—for all of them.

"He gave me everything he knew," Sasha said, and added, because if he was telling the truth, it did not seem safe to tell only part of it, not when it involved Pyetr and Eveshka both: "His book. His magic. Everything. Including about Draga. Including about Eveshka."

He felt Eveshka withdraw. If Pyetr's wishes had force he thought he would feel him retreating as well.

But Pyetr shook at him. "Sasha?" he asked, shook at him again, as if to make sure who he was talking to; and that hurt, that hurt beyond bearing. "Sasha, dammit!"

"I'm not changed," Sasha said desperately. "It's still me, Pyetr."

"If he wasn't dead, I'd kill him!" Pyetr slammed his hand against his knee, then looked, distraught, toward Eveshka. "God—"

"I know him," Eveshka said faintly. "You don't have to explain anything to me." She stood up, hugging her arms about herself, then looked back and frowned at them, at *him*, in particular, as if she were as unsure as Pyetr what she was dealing with.

"He's—gone," Sasha said. "I only remember things. Pieces of them. Not everything at once."

Perhaps that reassured them. He hoped so with all his heart. Pyetr put his arm around him, but he had just cheated, wanting them still to love him, and he was slipping again—

Pyetr grabbed hold of him, hugged him and held onto him,

while the very air seemed charged and unstable—fraught with power different and colder than the lightning—

"Pyetr!" Eveshka said, "Pyetr, something's out there—"

Sasha tried to use his material eyes, tried to stand up, and made it on the second attempt, while Pyetr gathered up his sword. There came a sound like wind in leaves, from all sides of them, and suddenly a smoky haze closing in about them at the farthest limits of the light.

"Leshys," Sasha whispered, and, remembering: "Uulamets wished for leshys. . . ."

Then Pyetr, to his startlement, called out like a house-holder to a neighbor, "Misighi? Is that you?"

If an ordinary man could feel anything magical, it was the good will of these creatures, so terribly reputed that the grand-mothers frightened children with the mere mention of them.

But violent, half-crazed old Misighi folded Pyetr ever so gently to his leprous heart, saying, "It *is* you, isn't it? You're alive."

After which so much strength poured into him he felt—terribly sleepy, and free of pain and free of worry.

"Let him go!" Sasha said.

But Pyetr looked down at him, at a very worried Sasha, holding, for the god's sake, his sword. He blinked, feeling sleepier and sleepier, said, "It's quite all right. They're here to help."

"Health," Misighi rumbled, touching him with gently quivering fingers. "Be safe. Leave us the wizard."

"Chernevog?" Pyetr had the presence of mind to ask, alarmed: he certainly had no notion of leaving them Sasha or Eveshka, but the dark that beckoned him seemed deeper and deeper.

"We can keep Chernevog," Misighi said. "Break his bones. . . ."

Another said: "Weave him tight, tight so he can't do harm. Make his sleep deep. This is leshys' work."

"Replant," one said.

"Regrow," a fourth.

"The forests will come back," Misighi said.

"Eveshka?" Pyetr called muzzily, feeling heavier and heavier. "Sasha?"

He thought they answered him, he thought they said they were all right. He hoped—his senses were raw and lately battered and desperate—he dared believe what he knew.

"Health," leshys whispered, leaning close with a whisper and a smell of living leaves.

"Life," one said, and another, in deep, rumbling tones: "Seeds follow fire."

After that, the whisper of leaves, a gentle rocking, eventually a sense that they were moving very fast indeed.

"Take you to the river," he dreamed old Misighi whispered to him in that sound, "send you safe home. Wiun says."

Sasha waked with a start, on sun-warmed boards, with the soft lapping of water round about, the gentle creak and heave and pitch of the boat under him; and Pyetr and Eveshka asleep beside him, walled in by sacks and baskets that were not theirs. Their hair was all snarled with leaves and twigs, their clothing was precisely as he recollected out of a dream of fire-light and burned timbers, a terrible dream, at the end of which Pyetr and Eveshka had been snatched up and taken from him in a haze of twigs.

But he could not at all account for the baskets, and here he was safe with Pyetr, and here was Eveshka, peaceful and real and alive—their clothes, the twigs, Eveshka's very self all evidence of a place so separate from this it tried, dreamlike, to fade out of memory.

But if he remembered the truth, Uulamets would be dead, Eveshka would be alive, which she clearly was, and Chernevog—

He remembered leshys. He remembered rescue, finally. He lay there in the sun reassuring himself of his friends' safety and pulling back the pieces of what was, this morning, very dim and very far, as if there had come a veil between him and that place deep in the woods—and relief from the responsibility that had been his for—it seemed—so very long—

Replant, he remembered the leshys saying. Regrow, reseed—

He had something to do, then, and something very much to wish for, since, memory persuaded him, there was a promise he had made the leshys, and there were promises they had made him in return, not in so many words, because words were not of value to them . . .

Intentions were.

Pyetr opened his eyes, looking quite as confused as he had been. Pyetr gazed at him a moment as if deciding much the same course of things, and then, rising on his arm, looked down at Eveshka, touching her face with such an expression as made Sasha feel he should look away, get up and make breakfast, do anything but intervene for a few moments.

So he got up and turned his curiosity to the baskets and the sacks, poking about in those to find all sorts of goods, the plunder, it seemed, of Chernevog's whole house loading down their deck; and most importantly, more precious than any jeweled cup, were their own packs—and Uulamets' book.

That was what brought the memories back, tumbling one over the other, but gently, as if years separated him from Uulamets and dimmed the unimportant details. It seemed sad to him now that no one had ever really known Uulamets, that not even he had, until the man was gone: saddest of all that no one acutely missed him—nor had Uulamets expected it: that was the essence of things, his own daughter as bewildered by him as his apprentices had been. . . .

But Uulamets had done as well as a wizard could, Sasha thought, and better than most: of the succession of wizards who had occupied this borderland, one teaching the next— Uulamets had been the wisest; or at least, Sasha thought, with one of those memories surfacing like flotsam—he might have made more mistakes, but never the unforgivable one; and redeemed his greatest misjudgement.

Chernevog's book turned up in a basket full of apples: Sasha's first thought was that the leshys had made a grievous, naïve mistake, that he should, without a moment's pause, pitch it overboard: but then he thought that it would surely be protected, and the god knew where it might drift, let loose in the world—down to Kiev, perhaps, among ordinary folk, or into some other wizard's hands. He wished the leshys had kept it, walled in and safe; he was thinking that when Pyetr started poking into the baskets himself and wondering if there was breakfast.

There was. There were cakes and sweets, more than their starved stomachs could deal with, so they made a fire in the stove, and sat in the noon sun and drank hot tea, the three of them, with a little breakfast . . . after which Eveshka walked about the deck, looked at their situation on the forest side and the side with the sand bar, then said they should put up the bit of a sail they had and wish the wind up strong from the east.

It made perfectly good sense, once Sasha thought about it.

Pyetr still maintained his opinion of boats—though it seemed in some situations they were very good things, and that the girl he loved knew them very well—well enough to wish them out of their predicament and to bring the tipping, tilting boat about with its bow in the right direction.

In fact, after a while of what seemed, after Uulamets' handling of the boat, quite a sedate and sensible progress, Pyetr decided he could stand up, and even walk casually to the side and hold onto the ropes that braced the mast—to look, of course, for Eveshka's benefit, as if he had only been sitting down because he wanted to.

He glanced back at Sasha, who was still seated amid their baggage, which Eveshka had insisted to shift to the center and rear—for balance, she had said, and both of them were entirely willing to oblige in that case. Sasha looked back at him with— he thought, a little concern for his position at the rail, which satisfied him: he might *look* careless of falling in, as careless and casual about the hazard as Eveshka did, which was precisely the attitude he studied—not to be outdone by a girl so sure and so cheerfully competent.

He could do that.

He could sail a boat like this quite handily, pick up the tricks of it by watching (she would think him quite clever) and sail it down to Kiev and back, certainly he could, except the little flutters in his stomach.

He thought he would patch the seams a bit first, to be sure; and mend the sail—he made his *own* luck, and that meant seeing to such things and trusting as little as possible to chance.

In fact he thought he would sail them all down to Kiev— not to go into the city: the god knew what kind of trouble two young wizards could find—but just to see the gold and the elephants, from a quite safe distance.

Then sail them safely back again, to a cottage furnished like a tsar's palace, with gold cups and fine rugs, with a flourishing garden, and a woods with all summer ahead to seed with acorns and such—he had found a bird's nest full of seeds amid the gold, and knew precisely what he was supposed to do with such a gift.

Then they would settle down for a golden fall and a white winter, and green springs and summers after that . . . having adopted the domovoi which would shift about and make the house creak quite familiarly and cozily of nights; and Babi—

That was the thing that disturbed him this afternoon— whether it was worry over the fur-ball or over the fact that he *was* worried. God, he thought, Pyetr Ilitch, after all this— the old man dying, Eveshka alive again, Sasha in his right mind this morning—to spend your worry over the little wretch—

—who can quite well take care of himself.

But Uulamets had died and the raven was dead: and it seemed to him that Babi might possibly have gone the way the bird had, not, he was quite sure, struck by the lightning, but simply because he was also Uulamets' creature.

I expect him to turn up at the house, Sasha had said at breakfast, when he had asked about Babi.

Wish him back, he had asked, why don't you? —With a look at Eveshka, who, he was sure, had at least some sort of special advantage with Babi.

I've tried, Eveshka had said, which was no comfort at all.

So wipe Babi from the image of the cottage. Maybe he *would* turn up.

Or maybe he could get a dog. A black one.

He let his hand slack on the rope, testing his balance.

Not bad at all, he thought, and looked back to see if Eveshka was watching.

He walked across the deck, past Sasha, past the deckhouse,

to the stern, to stand there quite confidently—till a swell rocked the boat and he had to grab the rail.

She smiled at him, quite kindly, considering; and went on smiling at him in a way that could make a man forget all about keeping his balance.

The Cockerel's boy was not naïve and certainly Uulamets' heir was not: the looks Pyetr and Eveshka kept giving each other meant two people quite, quite lost to reason.

It worried him; it made him wish—dangerously—for Eveshka to keep thinking sensibly, for Eveshka to know—

She did *not* want him wishing at her, she let him know that, quite angrily, hearing echoes of her father; and he:

Speak to him, Eveshka, don't wish him: your father never learned to say things in plain words. That was where he failed you: that's what I learned, that's what he was learning. *Don't* make his mistake with Pyetr.

That stopped her. He stood at the corner of the deckhouse, she stood by Pyetr at the tiller—Pyetr was steering, which was why for a little the boat had tipped and faltered, Sasha supposed, but it was steady now; and he hoped to the god Pyetr did not suspect the quarrel.

Eveshka did think about it. She went from being angry to being worried: she let him know that; and even said, earnestly, "Thank you, Sasha."

Much better, Sasha thought, feeling that she truly meant that. She wanted—

Wanted things to be right. Wanted Pyetr to be happy. Wanted that for all of them.

A generality, he thought, and stood there pretending to watch the shore, all the while thinking and thinking, deciding finally that *he* could not get between them, *he* could not tell Uulamets' daughter to mind what she was wishing.

But he had a sudden notion who could.

Babi, he said sternly to that Place where such creatures went, as he had been calling more than once today. —Babi, get back here, right now. No nonsense.

He had no answer, only what he had had before, a fey,

furtive presence, confused and lost, not sure where it belonged now.

"You!" he said aloud, walked back around the corner to the baggage, picked up the vodka jug—

And pitched it at the mast.

It stopped in mid-air.

"Babi?"

The jug waddled forward, with two moonlike eyes floating disembodied above it.

"That's much better," Sasha said, folding his arms. "I know who might well give it to you—if you asked him nicely."

A tonguetip licked invisible lips. The jug waddled past him, around the corner of the deckhouse, in search of sympathy.

ABOUT THE AUTHOR

C. J. Cherryh was born in St. Louis, Missouri, but has spent most of her life in Oklahoma. She now lives in Oklahoma City. She has a BA in Latin, an MA in Classics, plus additional language courses; she also qualified in field archeology, but never practiced. She was a professional translator in French, and has taught Latin, Greek, and Ancient History.

Her first novel, *Gate of Ivrel*, was published in 1976, and she quickly became a leading writer of both fantasy and science fiction. She received two Hugo Awards, one for her short story, *Cassandra*, and the second for her novel, *Downbelow Station*.

In her own words:

"I write full time; I travel; I try things out. I've outrun a dog pack in the hills of Thebes and seen *Columbia* lift on her first flight. I've fallen down a cave, nearly drowned, broken an arm, been kicked by horses, fended off an amorous merchant in a tent bazaar, slept on deck in the Adriatic, and driven Picadilly Circus at rush hour. I've waded in two oceans and four of the seven seas, and I want to visit the Amazon, the Serengeti, and see the volcano in Antarctica. I can read history in a potsherd, observe time in a stream-bank, and function in a gadget ancient or modern—none of which has ever cured me of losing my car keys or putting things together before I read the instructions."